White Stag

KARA BARBIERI

WEDNESDAY BOOKS
NEW YORK

To Avalon Hills Eating Disorder Treatment Center
for saving my life; and to Kayshia, Lia, Megan,
Marina, Jade, Talisa, Jordan, Sam, Eleni, Kate,
Jessie, and Courtney, my fellow ED warriors

———

This is a work of fiction. All of the characters, organizations, and events portrayed in this novel are either products of the author's imagination or are used fictitiously.

WHITE STAG. Copyright © 2018 by Kara Barbieri. All rights reserved. Printed in the United States of America. For information, address St. Martin's Press, 175 Fifth Avenue, New York, N.Y. 10010.

www.wednesdaybooks.com
www.stmartins.com

Designed by Devan Norman

The Library of Congress Cataloging-in-Publication Data is available upon request.

ISBN 978-1-250-14958-9 (hardcover)
ISBN 978-1-250-22619-8 (international, sold outside the U.S., subject to rights availability)
ISBN 978-1-250-14959-6 (ebook)

Our books may be purchased in bulk for promotional, educational, or business use. Please contact your local bookseller or the Macmillan Corporate and Premium Sales Department at 1-800-221-7945, extension 5442, or by email at MacmillanSpecialMarkets@macmillan.com.

First U.S. Edition: January 2019
First International Edition: January 2019

10 9 8 7 6 5 4 3 2 1

Author's Note

THERE IS TRUTH in fiction. That much we all know. When *White Stag* was originally conceived and written in its baby draft two years ago, I was going through a(nother) very dark time in my life. I have been, and always will be, open about my personal struggles, and those struggles come to play in *White Stag*. Writing it was a way to turn my pain into something productive that could transcend my own experiences and limitations on this earth.

Like me, Janneke suffers from a loss of agency that was not her own doing and from the failure of those who should have known better and done better (whether or not they meant well in the first place). Her journey of forgiving herself, letting go, and finding strength inside her own self and her own scars mirrors mine.

That being said, there are things in this book that you may find distressing or disturbing. Janneke's trauma and struggle regarding both her sexual assault and her attacker is a contributing part of her character arc and her healing, and there will be some descriptions or narratives you may find triggering.

Like me, Janneke also deals with an eating disorder and body dysmorphia. Our disorders manifest a bit differently, but they come from a very similar place. It is a scary, obsessive, and vulnerable place to be, especially as a young woman.

White Stag contains violence that may be considered graphic to some. So be warned that there is content in this book that may trigger you. If that does happen, I want you to know that your feelings and experiences are valid and your safety (both physically and mentally) matters more than anything else. My experience is not yours, and I would always advocate for you to do what is best for you. If that means putting the book down, then I want you to know it's okay and I understand.

I do hope that we can continue this journey together in pain, healing, and all the ups and downs that come after. I've found that sometimes we're so burdened that we think we might break, and in that moment nothing looks like it will ever be okay again. Places like the National Eating Disorder Association; the Rape, Abuse, & Incest National Network; and the National Suicide Prevention Lifeline (1-800-273-8255) are there to help.

I want to end this with a quote from *Angel* that really speaks to me as someone who has so often felt helpless: *If nothing we do matters, then all that matters is what we do.*

Who rides there so late through the night dark and drear?
The father it is, with his infant so dear;
He holdeth the boy tightly clasp'd in his arm,
He holdeth him safely, he keepeth him warm.
"My son, wherefore seek'st thou thy face thus to hide?"
"Look, father, the Erl-King is close by our side!
Dost see not the Erl-King, with crown and with train?"
"My son, 'tis the mist rising over the plain."
"Oh, come, thou dear infant! oh come thou with me!
For many a game I will play there with thee;
On my strand, lovely flowers their blossoms unfold,
My mother shall grace thee with garments of gold."
"My father, my father, and dost thou not hear
The words that the Erl-King now breathes in mine ear?"
"Be calm, dearest child, 'tis thy fancy deceives;
'Tis the sad wind that sighs through the withering leaves."
"Wilt go, then, dear infant, wilt go with me there?
My daughters shall tend thee with sisterly care;
My daughters by night their glad festival keep,
They'll dance thee, and rock thee, and sing thee to sleep."
"My father, my father, and dost thou not see,
How the Erl-King his daughters has brought here for me?"
"My darling, my darling, I see it aright,
'Tis the aged grey willows deceiving thy sight."
"I love thee, I'm charm'd by thy beauty, dear boy!
And if thou'rt unwilling, then force I'll employ."
"My father, my father, he seizes me fast,
For sorely the Erl-King has hurt me at last."
The father now gallops, with terror half wild,
He grasps in his arms the poor shuddering child;
He reaches his courtyard with toil and with dread,—
The child in his arms finds he motionless, dead.

—"DER ERLKÖNIG,"
JOHANN WOLFGANG VON GOETHE

PART ONE

THE CAPTIVE

1

MASQUERADE

THE FIRST THING I learned as a hunter was how to hide. There was a skill in disappearing in the trees like the wind and merging into the river like stones; masquerading yourself as something you weren't was what kept you alive in the end. Most humans didn't think the masquerade was as important as the kill, and most humans ended up paying for it with their lifeblood.

Here, as the only mortal in a hall of monsters, I was very glad that I was not most humans.

I kept my steps silent and my back straight as I passed beneath the white marble pillars. My eyes flickered around me every so often, counting hallways, retracing my steps, so I could escape at a moment's notice. The Erlking's palace was treacherous, full of twists and turns, stairways that led into nowhere, and places where the hallways dropped to gaping chasms. According to Soren, there were also hollow spaces in the walls where you could slink around unnoticed to the mundane and the monstrous eye, but you could hear and see all that went on in the open world. *The lair of a king,* I thought bitterly. I dared not say it out loud in case someone was near. But beside me, Soren sensed my disgust and made a sound deep in his throat. It could've been agreement.

Soren examined his king's palace with the usual contempt; his cold, calculating eyes took in everything and betrayed nothing. His lips turned down in a frown that was almost etched permanently into his face. Sometimes I forgot he was capable of other expressions. He didn't even smile when he was killing things; as far as goblins went, that was a symptom of chronic depression. He lifted his bored gaze at the gurgling, choking sound coming from his right, and it took all my willpower not to follow his line of sight. When I felt the subtle *whoosh* of power transfer from one body to the next, my fingers twitched to where I'd slung my bow, only to remember too late that it had been left at the entrance of the keep in accordance with ancient tradition.

A scream echoed off the cavernous passageways as we made our way to the great hall where everyone gathered. It sent chills down my spine with its shrillness before it was abruptly cut off. Somehow, that made me shiver even more. Ancient tradition and custom aside, nothing could stop a goblin from killing you if that was what they desired. My hand reached for my nonexistent bow again, only to be captured by cold, pale fingers.

Soren's upper lip curled, but his voice was low and steady. "The next time you reach for a weapon that isn't there might be the last time you have hands to reach with," he warned. "A move like that will invite conflict."

I yanked myself away from his grip and suppressed the urge to wipe my hand on my tunic like a child wiping away cooties. "Force of habit."

Soren shook his head slightly before continuing on, his frown deepening with each step he took.

"Don't look so excited. Someone might get the wrong idea."

He raised a fine white eyebrow at me. "I don't look excited. I'm scowling."

I bit back a sigh. "It's sarcasm."

"I've told you before, I don't understand it," he said.

"None of goblinkind understands sarcasm," I said. "In another hundred years I'm going to lose my understanding completely."

Another hundred years. It hadn't hit me yet, not until I said it out loud. *Another hundred years.* It had been a hundred years since my village was slaughtered, a hundred years as a thrall in Soren's service. *Well, ninety-nine years and eight months, anyway, but who's counting?* Despite the century passing by, I still looked the same as I had when I was forcefully brought into this cursed land. Or, at least, mostly; the scars on my chest hadn't been there a hundred years ago, and the now-hollow spot where my right breast should have been burned. The four months when I'd belonged to another were not something I liked to think about. I still woke up screaming from nightmares about it. My throat went dry and I swallowed. *Soren isn't Lydian.*

"You look tense," Soren said, breaking me out of my thoughts. I'd crossed my arms over my chest. Not good. A movement like that was a sign of weakness. It was obvious to everyone that I was the weakest being here, but showing it would do me no good.

"I'm fine," I said. "I just don't like this place."

"Hmm," Soren said, eyes flickering around the hall. "It does lack a certain touch."

"What does that even mean?" I asked.

"The entire design of the palace is trite and overdone."

I blinked. "Okay, then."

By now we'd entered the great hall where the reception was held. Every hundred years, the goblins were required to visit the Erlking and swear their fealty. Of course, their loyalty only extended to him as long as he was the most powerful—goblins weren't the type of creature to follow someone weaker than themselves.

The palace, for what it was worth, was much grander than most other parts of the goblin domain. Soren's manor was all wood, stone, and ice, permanently freezing. Nothing grew—I knew because I had tried multiple times to start a garden—but the roots never took to the Permafrost. Here, it was warm, though not warm enough that I couldn't feel the aching chill deep in my bones. The walls were made of pure white marble with intricate designs far above what a goblin was capable of creating, and streaked with yellow and red gold like open veins. It was obviously made by humans. Goblinkind were incredible predators and hunters, gifted by the Permafrost itself, but like all creatures, they had their flaws. The inability to create anything that wasn't used for destruction was one of the main reasons humankind were often stolen from their lands on raids and put to work in the Permafrost.

Soren's scowl deepened as we passed under a canopy of ice wrought to look like vines and flowers. "I feel like I need to vomit," he said.

I stopped in my tracks. "Really?" I swore, if I ended up having to clean up Soren's vomit . . .

He glanced at me, a playful light in his lilac eyes. "Sarcasm? Did I do it right?"

"No." I forced myself not to roll my eyes. "Sarcasm would be when you use irony to show your contempt."

"Irony?" He shook his head, his long white hair falling into his face.

"Saying one thing when you mean the other, dramatically."

"This is beneath me," he muttered. Then, even quieter, he said, "This place is in dire need of a redecoration."

"I'm not even entirely sure what to say to that." With those words, he flashed me a wicked grin that said little and suggested much. I turned away, actually rolling my eyes this time. For a powerful goblin lord, Soren definitely had the ability to act utterly childish. It could be almost endearing at times. This, however, was not one of those times.

In the hall, the gazes on the back of my neck were sharp as knives. I kept my head straight, trying my hardest not to pay attention to the wolfish faces of the other attendees.

From a distance they could almost be mistaken for human. They varied in size and shape and the color of their skin, hair, and eyes much like humans did. But even so, there was a sharpness to their features, a wildness, that could never be mistaken for human. The figures dressed in hunting leathers, long and lean, would only seek to torment me if I paid them any attention. As the only human in the hall, I was a curiosity. After all, what self-respecting goblin would bring a thrall to an event as important as this? That could very easily get me killed, and I wasn't planning on dying anytime soon. My hand almost twitched again, but I stopped it just in time, heeding Soren's warning.

We finally crossed the floor to where the Erlking sat. Like Soren's, the Goblin King's hair was long. But unlike Soren, whose hair was whiter than the snow, the Erlking's hair was brown. Not my brown, the color of fallen leaves, underbrush, and dark cherry wood, but murky, muddy brown. It was the color of bog mud that sucks down both humans and animals alike and it somehow managed to make his yellow-toned skin even sallower. He was the strongest of all goblins, and I hated him for it. I also feared him—I was smart enough for that— but the fear was drowned out by the blood rushing in my ears as I locked eyes with Soren's king.

Soren turned to me. "Stay here." His eyes turned hard, the glimmer of light leaving them. Whatever softness he had before drained away until what was left was the hard, cold killer he was known to be, and with it went the last shreds of warmth in his voice. "Until I tell you otherwise." Subtly, he jerked his pointer finger at the ground in a wordless warning.

I bowed my head. "Don't take too long."

"I don't plan to," he said, more to himself than to me, before approaching the Erlking's throne. He went to one knee. "My king."

I eyed Soren from underneath the curtain of my hair. His hands were clenched in fists at his sides. He must've sensed something from the Erlking, from the other goblins, *something*. Whatever it was, it wasn't good. Cautiously, I directed my gaze to the Goblin King himself, aware that if I looked at him the wrong way, I might be inviting my own death. While the behavior and treatment of thralls varied widely among goblins, I had a feeling submissiveness was required for any human in the Erlking's path.

This close, the Erlking's eyes were dark in his shriveled husk of skin and there was a tinge of sickness in the air as he breathed his raspy breaths. His eyes flickered up to meet mine and I bowed my head again. *Don't attract attention.*

Soren spat out the vows required of him in the old tongue of his kind, the words gravelly and thick. He paused every so often, like he was waiting for when he would be free to drive his hand through his king's chest, continuing on with disappointment every time.

The tension around the room grew heavier, pressing down on those gathered. Somehow, like dogs sniffing out blood, they all knew the king was weak. Beautiful she-goblins and terrifying goblin brutes were all standing there waiting until it was legal to kill him.

Beside the weakened king's throne, a white stag rested on a pile of rushes. Its eyes were closed, its breath slow. Its skin and antlers shone with youth, but the ancient power it leaked pressed heavy against my shoulders. That power was older than anything else in the world—maybe older than the world itself.

Goblins were, before all things, hunters. Born to reap and not to sow. Cursed with pain upon doing any action that did not in some way fit into the power the Permafrost gave them, the goblins fittingly had the submission of the stag as the symbol of their king's ultimate power. *Until it runs.*

I didn't want to think about what happened after that.

Soren continued to say his vows. The guttural language was like ice shards to my ears, and I shuddered. Catching myself about to fidget, I dug my fingers into my thigh. *Control yourself, Janneke,* I thought. *If they can do it, you can.*

A soft voice whispered in my ear, "Is that you, Janneka?" His breath tickled the back of my neck, and every muscle in my body immediately locked. Icy dread trickled down my spine, rooting me in place.

Don't pay attention to him. He'll go away.

"I know you can hear me, sweetling."

Yes, I could hear him, and the sound of his voice made me want to vomit. My mouth went dry.

Slowly, I turned toward Lydian. He looked the same as he had a hundred years ago. Long golden hair, slender muscles, a lazy, catlike gleam to his dark-green eyes, and skin the color of milk, unblemished and unmarred. High cheekbones, an aquiline nose, and the haughty look I'd so often seen on his nephew graced his features. Every so often those eyes would flicker, as if they had a mind of their own, almost as if he were seeing past me, past the Erlking, past everyone. Twitching eyes aside, goblin males might've been called "brutes," but Lydian's looks were anything but. That made me even sicker.

"How is your calf?" I asked, letting hostility seep into my voice, surprised I was able to keep the waver out of it.

He shifted his weight so it was equal on both legs. "It seems that civil conversation is still not your strong suit."

I ached to hurt the man before me. "And I suppose you know all about civil conversation? Where I come from, leaving someone for dead doesn't count as 'civil.'"

Lydian's face was a blank slate, but I could see the storm beginning to stir beneath the surface, and I didn't fail to notice him shifting his weight back onto his good leg. *You don't want to anger him*, a tiny voice in my head reminded me; a fearful voice that knew exactly what he could and would do. The same voice that reminded me he was so much stronger than I'd ever be, that he could hurt me with his little finger if he wanted to, if I angered him enough. I'd paid the price of that lesson in blood, and it wasn't something I'd soon forget. But another voice, strong with hatred, craved to hurt him and to see him bleed. Before the Permafrost, it never occurred to me that you could both hate and fear something at the same time, but when it came to Lydian, those were the only two emotions I was capable of. *His nephew, however . . .*

Finally, he spoke again, and the softness of his voice somehow made it even more threatening. "Well, we're not where you come from, are we?"

"Go eat your young," I spat.

Lydian's head jerked, and he shook himself. The faraway

look in his green eyes grew cloudy. "It seems you've become even more insolent and ignorant since our last *encounter*. Perhaps I should teach you a lesson."

Oh no, I've had enough of those. It'd been many years since I'd learned backing down from a fight would get me more injured than starting one. In the Permafrost, it was better to hide your fear than let it show. I infused strength in my voice. "And perhaps you'll end up with iron poisoning again, and the Permafrost will be relieved of your cancerous presence so it can continue turning like it should."

"Oh, you have no idea what happens when the serpent stops eating his tail," he hissed.

His motion was a blur barely able to be registered by the human eye. But I'd anticipated Lydian's attack from the moment I heard his familiar voice, and so when he raised his hand toward me—fingernails lengthening into claws—I was ready.

Still, he managed to brush against my cheek, almost like a caress, until thin lines of blood trickled from the cuts.

Instinct took over, and I danced backward until I could jump on what must've been a sacrificial table. I went into a crouch, my hands touching something warm and wet. Bile rose in my throat as I looked at the dead boar beneath my fingers.

Lydian howled a shrill, screechlike howl. The sound sent pain down my spine, and my arms shook; any louder and I had a feeling my ears would be bleeding. It took everything I had not to freeze from fear.

With that piercing howl the rest of the party took interest. Even the Erlking looked from where he sat on his throne, staring at me, at the fight between the prey and the hunter who sneered up at her. Soren rose, midvow, and his eyes caught mine. *Be careful*, they said. *I can't help you. If he beats you, I will bring you back to life and murder you myself for the disgrace.*

It was good to know I had someone on my side.

I swallowed, trying desperately to push down the fear rising in my throat. Fear dulled the mind and I couldn't allow it, but try as I might, little trickles spread throughout my body, inciting panic.

Without the disadvantage that came with emotions, Lydian saw his opening and lunged at me. We toppled to the ground, pain searing through my shoulder as I crashed into the hard floor.

His talons tore at my face, perilously close to my eyes, and for a terrifying moment, the wind was knocked out of me so I could do nothing to defend myself. His teeth were now fangs, snapping at my throat.

"Why can't you *listen*?" he growled. The feel of his body on mine and those too-familiar words brought back memories seeped in despair. *Don't remember. Stop remembering. He cannot take you.* "I tried to tell you! I tried to! What happens when the serpent stops eating his tail?"

I pushed his face away. Years of training with Soren came back to me as I dug my nails into his eyes. Lydian shrieked again, and blood trickled from my ears. Sound faded away until all that was left was a dull ringing, the ranting of the mad goblin before me, now only a distant echo in my head. I slammed my knee into his stomach, satisfied when the air *whooshed* out of him. Seconds later, a fist knocked into the side of my face, and I saw stars as my head cracked against the floor. For a terrifying moment, I forgot how to move, but then I jabbed my finger into the iron-poisoned wound I'd created in his leg long ago. Forgetting my fear and replacing it with cold, hard rage, I let go. Blood dripped from his eyes where I'd dug my fingernails in, and he lashed at me again. Hot wetness spread across my chest.

It was now or never. With muscles burning and fueled by hate, I pulled my legs up until they bunched under his chest and I could reach my boots. With my hands free, I dug under the straps, right as he went for the opening in my chest.

I stabbed a bent iron nail into his shoulder.

The effect was instant. Smoke billowed from his clothes, getting thicker and blacker by the second, and from it came a stomach-churning, charred-meat smell. His leathers burned away, showing blackened skin underneath. He rolled off me, shrieking in pain as he grabbed at the nail embedded in his shoulder.

I stood shakily. Blood dripped from my face, soaked my tunic, creating a wave of red on the floor. The ringing in my ears and pounding in my skull were deafening, almost bringing me back to the ground. It wasn't lost on me that we had been forced to leave our weapons at the entrance to the palace, yet nails and teeth could harm more than any weapon should have the right to. A hysterical giggle bubbled onto my lips, causing a few glances to come my way.

With a racing heart, I looked around at the monsters in the room. They all gazed at me, some with confusion on their faces, some with mild interest, and some with apparent disappointment at the outcome of the fight. But their looks didn't affect me. No, the only goblin whose eyes seemed to see through me was Soren. Something faint glowed within them, but it wasn't something I could name.

Lydian's subordinates huddled around him, making a joint effort to pull the nail out of his shoulder. With another ear-splitting howl, the nail was yanked out. The forest-colored material of his shirt flaked to the ground, exposing his now-blackened shoulder. Blood dripped from his eyes, but other than the nail, that was the only wound he took. My legs were going to collapse under my weight at any second.

He came forward. But then Soren stepped in front of me. "I think that is enough." The ice in his voice stung.

"Let me at her!" Lydian's perfect golden hair was in tangles around his face, his expression twisted in rage. "If you think I've hurt you before, it won't compare to what I will do to you now."

"You will not. She is *mine*." Soren's voice resonated across the hall. The weight of the power pouring from him *did* drop me to my knees. When Lydian began to pour out his own power, the weight of their combined strength pressed my body flat against the ground; my arms turned to sticks when I tried to hold myself up.

Lydian snarled. "I am not above killing you either, nephew. In fact, I'd rather prefer it. It would make the world right again, after all. You need to understand that, yes?"

"We don't *need* to do anything. However, I *want* to tear your still-beating heart out of your chest, so I suggest you leave before my restraint runs out." Soren cocked his head to the side. "I can count to three if it makes it easier."

Lydian's eyes burned like emerald fire, and he let out a low, guttural growl. Then he was screaming again, but the only sound my ears could register was ringing. Spittle formed at the corners of his mouth, and I scrambled backward. He looked like a madman, ranting and raving about nonsense he thought would make sense to everyone else. When I'd been his captive, he'd done the same every night; asking inane questions over and over again, and then destroying me piece by piece.

Both of them were throwing their power around so hard, black spots danced at the edges of my vision. I knew Soren and his uncle had unspeakable power—the ethereal force inside every goblin that marked their strength and could be turned into a weapon—but I'd never been in the same room when they both wielded it to its full extent. The breath was crushed from my lungs and my vision blurred, but before it faded completely I saw the two of them transforming, looking more and more like actual monsters without the inhuman, terrifying beauty that masked their true selves.

Not good. This is not good. They'll destroy the building. The ground shook, and from behind me someone groaned in pain. *How many things did they have to kill to obtain all that energy?*

But no one would stop them. It was the way of goblin life. If you were challenged, you did not back down, not unless your challenger was defeated. Like wolves, the fight for dominance was ongoing, and like wolves, the younger challenged the elder in the pack. Soren might've been the youngest lord there'd been in the history of the Permafrost, but he was strong.

As the two goblins were about to attack, three things happened simultaneously. The marble floor split open with a deafening roar, the Erlking fell from his throne, and the stag stood, shook out his fur, and ran.

2

PREDATORS

As far as bloodthirsty monsters went, the goblins at the gathering were surprisingly calm about their king collapsing onto the now-bloodied, broken floor. Or, well, ex-king, now. I didn't see who'd slashed the then-Erlking's throat, but the wickedly deep gashes gave me no doubt he was dead. The cuts in my own skin throbbed harder at the sight.

Lydian and Soren stared at each other for a minute more, their features morphing back into those of inhuman beauty, before slowly backing away from each other. Lydian snapped once, a gesture that was met by a rumbling growl from Soren, before he backed away, still clutching his smoldering shoulder. He sneered at me again and then vanished from sight.

The space where we'd fought was covered with my blood. Raw meat and other *delicacies* from the table I'd jumped on littered the floor, and I wrinkled my nose at the coppery smell. With one arm crossed against my chest to stop the gushing blood, I limped back to where the iron nail was on the floor and shoved it into my boot.

Soren gave the dead king a thoughtful stare. I stood, waiting to be recognized, hoping it'd be before I passed out from blood loss. He sometimes forgot that even though the Permafrost made it so I remained seventeen winters old despite years passing, I still was nothing but a mortal—a mortal currently bleeding out.

One hundred years. One hundred years and he can still do this to me. Despite my attempts to stay calm, I was overcome with tremors. The no-weapons rule had done nothing to save the Erlking's life in the end, and it couldn't save mine either.

Finally, Soren turned, his scorching gaze on me. His eyes, so very much like a predator's, took in my bloody body. One eyebrow was raised slightly at my bubbling laughter. "You brought iron into the heart of the Permafrost." His tone and expression implied what wasn't said. *You are clearly mad, and if not, you're well on your way.* He was right, but when had I ever been considered normal in any way?

Suddenly I didn't feel like laughing anymore. "You didn't say I couldn't."

His gaze didn't soften. "I said you could bring a keepsake."

"You didn't specify which keepsake. That's your slip, not mine."

The corner of his mouth twitched. "True. It was more mature than I expected of you." Was it the blood loss or did he actually sound *pleased*?

"Mature?"

Now a smile definitely played on his lips. A *smile*. "Mature. Crafty. Not many humans would have thought of it, but after your exposure . . ." He ran his fingers through his hair.

My legs shook. I wasn't sure how much blood I had lost, but the black spots appearing in the corners of my vision told me it was a lot. Soren's voice and the room around me went in and out of focus, and when I tried to keep my eyes on him, I found it was a bad idea. The way he looked at me chilled me even more; his normal apathetic, bored expression looked genuinely excited for once. *What were you thinking? Really?* His voice echoed inside my head. "Tell me, Janneke. If you'd been caught toting iron in the Erlking's palace, you'd be executed. And perhaps so would I. That's quite the uncalculated risk."

Frowning, I said, "I'm sure you can figure it out. Your kind is better than mine at twisted logic."

Soren bared his teeth in a wide smile at that. "Humor me."

I swallowed. "Well, as a thrall, normally I wouldn't be engaged with the others swearing fealty unless I entered into a fight. Honestly, I probably wasn't expected to be here at all. If I entered into a fight in the Permafrost—and the Erlking's palace—it would invoke the law of winter. The fight would be between me and whoever I fought to the end. The winner would remain, and the debt be settled. So, carrying iron would give me an advantage over anyone attempting to fight me, and if I lost, well, no harm would come to your estate as winter's law would be satisfied in my death."

Soren's pale eyebrows rose. "You're shaking." He said the words as if he only then realized the problem. "We'll continue this discussion later."

Finally, I thought with a relief so strong my knees shook. I tried to step forward, only to find my strength disappearing and the ground rushing up to meet me.

Pale, cold hands wrapped around my blood-soaked body, picking me up. He said his next words quietly, but with my head resting under his chin, I heard them all. "This changes everything."

Then blackness.

———✦———

WHEN MY EYES opened, I was no longer in the courtroom. Instead, the room around me was plain with sparse decoration. A chair sat across from me, but it was currently unoccupied. I lay on a fur-covered platform, the multiple pelts—wolf, tiger, snowcat, bear—strewn around my bare form doing nothing to keep me warm. It took a second to register how freezing the air was, but when I moved to cover myself with one of the wolfskins, hands pushed me down.

Tanya, Soren's healer, stared at me from the head of the platform. Her strawberry-colored hair was tied back, but a few strands were stuck to her face with blood. Both hands were also covered with blood. It always struck me how different she looked from her nephew. Her bright red hair clashed with her darker skin in a way that shouldn't have been pleasant to look at but was. With her nephew's blue-gray, nearly translucent skin, lilac eyes, and long white hair, the idea that they were related by blood would never cross anyone's mind.

She leaned back, observing me. I didn't think she was very pleased with what she saw.

I tried to will away the heat that spread through my body. I didn't make it a habit for any goblin to see me naked—healer or not. But the hurt and wooziness from blood loss had vanished, and the gashes on my skin were shiny new scars. *More to add to my ever-growing collection.* The thought moved through me like a bitter rain.

"You got yourself into quite the fight," she said. Her tone was brisk and businesslike, naturally cold. The brief displeasure that had flickered through her eyes when I first woke up was gone, and she now had a stony look to her that swallowed any type of emotion her kind could express. It was nothing like Soren's had been right before I passed out. Thinking of it made my stomach clench. It couldn't be emotion, not truly. Goblins might be able to feel rage and pain, shame and pleasure, but they held none of the deeper meaning that they held for humans. If anything, their emotions could be ignored as easily as one ignored a fly buzzing.

But the way he had looked and sounded, almost *excited,* almost as if there were something about me that had turned our relationship into more than what we currently had. I wasn't an idiot. I might've enjoyed the higher end of social fluidity that came with being a thrall, but Soren was no friend of mine. Or at least, not on my part. Sarcasm lessons aside.

"I think I got off lightly compared to my opponent," I said.

"Yes," Tanya mused, sitting on the empty chair. "Fighting Lydian with iron in the middle of the Erlking's court, you definitely got off lightly."

I held back a groan at the she-goblin's words. Why did I even try to be sarcastic? None of them would ever get it.

When I sat up, she rewarded me with a shove. I tried another approach.

"Where am I?"

"The Hunt has begun," she said. "We are required to stay in the palace until Soren gives the command to begin."

I swallowed the burning in my throat. *The Hunt.* "He hasn't gone already?"

Tanya shifted to cross her legs. "He is deciding who and what to take with him. And perhaps he'll eliminate some competitors who are taking their time as well."

I didn't have anything to say to that. I might've never experienced the Hunt in person, but I knew what was at stake. Everyone did.

"Do you think he'll win?" I asked, then bit my tongue. It wasn't like she'd say anything but yes.

She stood. "I think he has more than winning on his mind." Without looking back, she crossed the room and unlocked the door. "He wishes to see you in his apartments as soon as you're able."

Then she left.

I lay there, heart pumping fast in my chest, trying to recall everything I knew about the stag hunt. The stag was the symbol of the Erlking's power, of the fact that the Erlking was the strongest, fastest, best predator in the Permafrost. If the stag ran from the Erlking, then he wasn't the strongest anymore.

It wasn't just a hunt. The winner would be whoever had the most power as a predator; only he'd be the one to successfully reach and kill the stag. The ancient force that flowed through the very being of every goblin and marked their strength came from their kills and throughout the Hunt, you could gain more power by killing other competitors. It came with a cost, like everything did, but those with considerable power—like Soren and Lydian—dominated the goblins' martial society for a reason. The longer the Hunt, the fewer contenders, but I didn't know how long the Hunt officially lasted, only that sooner or later, the most powerful predator killed the stag and became the new Erlking. That meant that more than the stag would die, and unlike the stag, they wouldn't reincarnate as the new Erlking's symbol at the end.

If Soren died . . . what would happen to me? That wasn't something I wanted to think about.

I rose and stood at the mirror, wincing as the icy air assaulted my limbs. Despite the slowly fading ache in my chest, my body looked fine. Or, well, as fine as it could've been. Three once-deep gashes joined the mass of scar tissue decorating my chest, and the slash marks from Lydian's claws were ugly pink lines on my cheek. But I was alive. That was enough.

Next to the sleeping platform I found a pair of hunter's clothes. The good kind. The tunic was the color of the sun peering through forest leaves, and the warm wool was soft against my dark skin. Over that went a jerkin of light-brown leather, already soft and supple enough for immediate use. Next to a pair of hunting leggings, made with the same supple leather as the jerkin, were woolen wraps. Carefully, starting at the knees and working my way down, I wrapped the warm fabric around my legs, then slid on the leggings. A half cloak of wolfskin wrapped around my waist and hung down to my knees. With the boots, the ensemble was complete.

The person in the mirror was a stranger: a girl with wild,

dark hair and eyes that reflected the green of the tunic, she was in fine clothes and looked less human than I would have liked. But they made me seem fierce and brave.

I couldn't reason why I was wearing such clothes. Goblin clothes, made specifically superior by the most talented of humans to endure endless combat and hunting. I forced myself to take a few deep breaths as nausea churned in my stomach.

"You have to go now," I said to myself. "Soren doesn't like to be kept waiting."

So, with a straight back and a face wiped of emotion, I slid the door open and entered the darkened hallways of the Erl-king's palace. From holes in the ceiling, light hit gleaming crystals and shattered into rainbows. Around me the steady drips of water worked to slow my racing heart. Compared to the grandness of the courtroom, the darkened, cavernous hallway was calming. This was my element. You could hide in the dark, listen in the dark; in the dark you could see your enemies but they couldn't see you. In the harsh light of day, the sun shone on things that should never be brought to the light.

I came upon Soren's door, knocked once, and waited.

The door slid open. Soren was dressed in almost identical clothing to me, though his were tailored for a man and decorated with embroidery that indicated a higher rank. The complex, looping designs of golden thread in his dark tunic could've only been made by a skilled, human hand. A female thrall probably spent hours perfecting it, aware that her skills in embroidery were going toward the enemy's clothing.

His hair, normally loose around his shoulders, was pulled back in a series of intricate braids. His eyes were still the same cold lilac I expected, though. Those eyes looked me up and down for a long moment, before meeting my own.

"Yes," he murmured, almost to himself, "that suits you."

I bowed my head. "Thank you."

"Come in. We have much to discuss."

I followed him inside his chambers, eyeing every nook and cranny. The room was made of the same gray quartz, but there was a mahogany table and cluster of chairs, the furs on the sleeping platform looked untouched, and his favorite weapons hung on one side of the wall. Other than that, the space was much like my own. Sparse and bare, with little attempt at decoration. I had to chuckle at the irony of it.

"Something funny?" he asked.

"For someone who scoffed at the lack of decorations in the palace proper, you seem to dislike decorating yourself."

His eyes flashed quickly to the walls. "It would be a high inconvenience for everyone if I decided to carry all my things with me every time I traveled. Especially with a hunt going on."

And how did you know a hunt would happen? I left the question unsaid.

He sat at one end of the table, waving me to sit at the other.

"You're very tense," he noted.

"Is there any reason I should not be?" I shot back.

Soren steepled his fingers. "Do you not feel safe in my presence?"

I sat down roughly. "I never feel safe."

Some emotion flitted across Soren's eyes, so fast I might've missed it if I didn't know to look for it. Sadness? I couldn't tell. "I'm sorry you feel that way."

Are you? I forced my shoulders to relax, surprised at the ache in them. "What am I here for?"

Soren smiled, baring his sharp teeth. "You know what's happening, I presume?"

"As much as any human could," I said. "You're going to hunt the stag."

"And one another." The smile disappeared. "And whoever gets in our way."

"And you enjoy that?"

"Don't be coy, Janneke. You know exactly how this works, even if you like to think you don't."

I lifted my chin. "I know what you are and what you do. I know this hunt will bring death until the stag has been reborn. And I know you all will probably enjoy it much more than you will fear for your lives."

Soren raised an eyebrow. "Would you fear for your life?"

"I think fearing for my life would be a waste of time in my position."

Soren chuckled drily. "That is true, although I'd say the same of myself."

"Well, you'd be infinitely safer than me," I said, forcing myself not to be unnerved by his laughter. "You can bring hunting hounds, sworn shields, healers, anything you'd like. And very few would take it upon themselves to kill you alone. On the other hand, I'm not you, and my worth, as well as the measures in place to protect me, would be dramatically lower."

"That doesn't answer my question, however."

"Oh? How so?"

"Do you fear for your life around other goblins? Around me?" He put his elbow on the table, leaning forward with one hand.

"That wasn't your original question," I said, eyes narrowed. "I can play the word game just as well as you, Soren."

He gave another dry laugh. "Almost as well. But humor me, are you afraid?"

I was silent, chewing over the words before I spoke. Yes, goblins could rip me apart so easily, torture me until my mind unraveled. Goblins stole humans for work the Permafrost wouldn't let them do themselves. So many of the things they had—their clothing, their agriculture, their buildings—were thanks to the humans living among the monsters who possessed the skills they didn't. Humans created, goblins destroyed. It was known.

"I think I feel equal measures fear, hate, and anger toward your kind. The one that shows the most probably depends on my mood and whether or not I'm likely to have my heart ripped out by another brute in a grand hall."

"You're under my protection," Soren said with a bit of a growl.

"All of your thralls are," I retorted.

"You're not just any thrall." His words made me swallow. I was painfully aware that despite Soren treating his thralls with a considerable amount of respect, honor, and social mobility, the way he treated me surpassed all of them.

"Aren't I?"

Soren rolled his eyes. "Must we do this every time?"

"Yes."

"Janneke," he said. The softness of his voice, the way the corners of his lips were threatening to rise, caught me off guard. "You do know I regard you as a close friend, don't you?"

"I don't think you know what a friend is," I said. "I accompany you when it suits your needs."

"Most people would call that a companion. And if I'm right, that's the definition of a friend."

"In this case, companion is a polite word for concubine."

"Usually sex is required to be a concubine." A small grin flickered on his lips. "You don't think after all these years, we have something?"

I didn't say anything. I couldn't, because I knew he was right. I could deny it all I wanted, act as obstinate as a child, but there was some type of relationship between me and Soren. It was evident in the fact that I accompanied him to most places and events he was invited to, the way we spoke freely to each other, and the good-humored banter we couldn't help but throw. Perhaps "friends" wasn't the correct word to use, but we weren't enemies, and I didn't have it in me to truly hate him.

He sighed. "Fine. I protect you because you're my property. You're my property because I like you. I like you because you amuse me. Is that what you want me to say?"

The door slid open and a young man bearing a silver tray walked in, saving me from responding. His eyes were narrowed and shrewd, his cheeks a little gaunt, and his frame thinner than it should've been. I didn't recognize him as one of Soren's thralls and judging from the bronze collar around his neck, he wasn't. A slight look of disgust passed across Soren's face as the man came over. Back at his manor, thralls were only used for skills he or his household didn't have themselves, and preparing and serving food wasn't on that list. Pompous as he was, Soren hated being waited on.

When the man saw me sitting there, his eyes narrowed and he paused, before thinking better of his action and continuing toward Soren. As much as I did not want to, I understood the hatred in his gaze. Why was I sitting here, treated in a way he was not? Why did he work under someone who treated him poorly, but I didn't? I knew the treatment of thralls varied highly depending on the goblin who had captured them. From the beginning of time, humans had been stolen across the border of the Permafrost in raids, along with many other types of plunder. Those brought across the border had the status of a thrall, expected to work and do the bidding of the lord who had stolen them. They were put under that lord's protection by the laws of winter. To harm a thrall who was not your own was a grave offense, but there were no hard and fast laws in place for the treatment of a thrall by their captor. The concept wasn't new; humans had done the same to their own kind for generations as well, and I would've been lying if I said that back when I lived among humans, our village didn't have its share of thralls, all of whom varied in levels of status, safety, and treatment. Before the Permafrost, it was something I'd never thought about and I'd accepted it as the way things were.

The burning difference here, though, was that our captors weren't human.

The elder goblins especially were known to be more focused on domination, on supremacy over the thralls they had. While younger ones, like Soren, tended to view them as members of their household, the thralls were still officially captives held against their will. The dynamic among humans was slightly different, but the concept of the situation was the same.

If I was under someone else, I'd never be brave enough to sit here, seemingly without care, exchanging fire back and forth with a goblin whom I'd seen hunt down others for sport. But I'd been by Soren's side for a hundred years—though the decision hadn't been my choice in the first place—and after standing by the side of the young goblin lord for so long, I'd grown to know him, maybe better than I knew my own self.

The man set down trays of food, raw liver and heart, some type of fleshy, poisonous tubers, and an assortment of eggs in varying stages of development. I'd never consider eating any of them.

Human crops didn't grow in the Permafrost the way they did in the human world. Stalks of corn would strangle a harvester, cotton would choke those who held it, fruit would assault you from the air, and harvesting was always a risky business.

The man's gaze shifted back to me before he bowed to Soren. Soren beckoned him forward with a finger, and the man came on wobbling legs. Fear flashed in his eyes until Soren whispered something in his ear. Then he noticeably calmed and exited the room.

I couldn't help the stab of pity I felt for this man. He might've seen me as Soren's lapdog, but I understood where he came from. If I found Soren to have some . . . interesting idiosyncrasies and was occasionally baffled during the time we spent together, then others must've found him a complete enigma. It didn't help that the young lord was now ripping through the raw meat with long, clawlike fingers and tearing through the tough flesh with sharp canines.

"You should eat," he said, as I stared at the blood staining his hands. "You never eat enough."

"I'm fine."

"Are you? The last time you ate anything real was at least two weeks ago. Not to mention you look so exhausted, the bags under your eyes have bags. Have you been having nightmares again?"

I looked away, unable to meet his eyes. "I can deal with it."

"You don't have to deal with it alone."

"What are you going to do? Sing me to sleep?" I asked.

"I'll have you know, I have a beautiful voice." Soren smirked, and my unladylike snort of amusement followed.

"If you're so worried about me, I'll drink the nectar again." Nectar was the holy food of the folk—the term for all sentient humanoid beings in the Permafrost—and it bound them to the realm. It could restore health to a human as long as they stayed in the Permafrost. I'd taken the drink a long time ago and more since. Despite its sweet taste, it always left bitter memories of the intense healing I'd gone through after Lydian had finished with me.

"As you like." He put down his food. "Would you like to know why you're here?"

A chill crept down my spine. Now we were getting to the

point. I kept the emotions off my face and let myself fall behind the massive walls I'd built to protect myself. Before I was composed enough to answer, the door slid open again. The human was back, this time with a golden goblet. He set it down in front of me and then hurried out of the room without a second glance.

I glared at the cup of gleaming reddish liquid before taking a sip of the sweet nectar. "Lucky guess."

Soren shrugged. "I know you well. Which is why we need to talk."

I took another drink of the nectar and energy began to pour back into my body. "Then let's talk."

He propped his chin up with one hand. "Most humans die before they get this far," he started. "They waste away in the 'frost after their first few years. You're quite the anomaly; it makes you fascinating."

I stiffened at the warmth in his voice. Unlike other goblins, whose coldness I dreaded, it was when warmth came from Soren that he was most dangerous to me. Warmth meant he was trying to establish a connection, that he valued me enough to speak to me in such a way. Warmth was the difference between an enemy and a friend. It didn't fit with my denial and Soren knew it.

"I'm glad I please you."

"Oh, you do. And I've seen the growth in you these past months, which has led me to decide you're ready."

"Ready for what?"

"A change." His lilac eyes turned on me expectantly. "*The* change."

Understanding seeped into me like trickles of ice water. There were a few fates for humans in the Permafrost. Some ultimately died here, human until their last breath; sometimes thralls were released on their goblin captor's death; and sometimes they stayed under the new lord who replaced them, depending on the binding spell holding them to the Permafrost and the will of the late lord. And sometimes . . . sometimes those who had certain desirable skills or traits, who were able to biologically adapt to the Permafrost, those who had a close camaraderie of sorts with the lord they served, who were judged as a good addition to the species . . . they *changed*. From rituals, time spent immersed in goblin culture, and the slow biological evolution their human bodies went through, those humans became goblins eventually. Changelings.

No. I stood so fast the chair toppled over, realization hitting me like a wave. *No. No. No.* My heart raced, the emotions I'd tried so hard to rein in already spinning out of control. *No. No. He's lying.* The look the serving man gave me flashed in my mind. His eyes called me a traitor, plain and simple, but they'd seen something else as they walked past. Something I was blind to until now. I was *changing*.

"No," I said, stumbling back. "You're wrong. No." Panic set in and I looked around me, anywhere for a way out. The only door was where the man had entered, and it sat directly behind Soren. "I'm not—my body isn't—"

No. No. I stopped all pretense of trying to hide my emotions; anyone with ears could hear the terror in my voice. Sure, I could think like a goblin. Sure, I knew how to reason like them. I knew how to be serious, and I knew how to weasel my way out of situations. I was as well-versed in their courtly life and laws as a human could possibly be. But that was because I had had a hundred years to observe them. I was not *like* them. *You can digest their food, wield their weapons, feel their power* . . . The voice in my head wouldn't go away.

Sadness was not an expression Soren usually wore; it was one that terrified me now.

Friends. For someone like him, a friendship was less about emotions and more about what you could get from someone; or at least that was all I was willing to accept from him. A friend was someone who you were more likely to protect, less likely to kill, whose company you sought even if it wasn't required. A friend was someone who could technically insult you with sarcasm without you being compelled to kill them.

A friend was someone you'd gift elaborate hunting clothes, clothes that now had much more meaning than they did a while ago. From the outside looking in, it would be hard for someone to think Soren and I were not friends.

You do know I regard you as a close friend, don't you?

Soren stood, taking his time while coming toward me, as if I were some animal caught in his trap. That's what I was, too. I stood completely still as he brushed his hand across my cheek. His fingers traced over the fresh scars.

"Are you afraid of me now?" he asked.

I turned away from him, unable to speak. But it wasn't for fear of him, more for fear of myself and what I could become.

"You're still human enough to think I'm doing this to hurt you," he said softly. "But I'm not. This is *because* I care for you. Because I see your potential, your power, the force you could become. The state you're in right now—human—we've always known they were the weaker species. It's written; your kind was made from ash and elm while mine was made from blood and fire. It's not your fault the gods gave you the weaknesses you possess. Even the strongest of my kind feel the lure of emotions. We just can resist the temptation."

My breath was shaky, rasping in my throat. "I don't—I won't—" Refusing was in vain. There was nothing I could possibly do if he made up his mind. I couldn't stop my own self from evolving—if I truly was—unless I killed myself, and that option had been taken from me a long time ago. If this was what he wanted, then this was what he'd get.

But I still begged like a pathetic child. One who should've known better.

I cringed as he brushed my hair behind my ear. "I promise you'll understand soon. I vow it. We're friends, Janneke. I am doing this for you, as a friend."

I stood there. Every cell in my body ached to scream, to cry, to beg, to run and fight and argue until he reconsidered. It would *prove* to him I had a human's cowardice, at least. It would prove I wasn't like him, not every bit. But I was silent, the words I could've said drifting off into empty space.

"You'll join me on the Hunt," he said. "In place of my men-at-arms or healers. You're smart and capable. And I don't have to worry about you killing me to take my power. As I said, the transition will be easier that way."

I pulled away, touching the place where his hand had been as if it stung.

My eyes burned with held-back tears, so I was surprised

at the stillness in my voice when I finally commented, "Is that all?"

"We leave tomorrow," he said. "At dusk. You will be ready. Get some sleep."

Numb from head to toe, I nodded and began to leave the room. *You can't fight this,* a voice told me. *It was always going to come.*

"Janneke?" Soren called. *He doesn't have the right to sound so concerned. Not a soulless creature like him.*

"Yes?"

"You have no reason to be afraid."

3

A HEART FRESHLY BROKEN

THERE WAS NO shrine in the Erlking's palace. There was nowhere to mourn the dead in privacy. It was probably because goblins didn't really care much for their dead in the first place. If there'd been one, I'd have been on my knees every day from dawn until dusk, begging for forgiveness for the people who had been slaughtered, for *my* family who had died by Lydian's hand while I ran to save myself, for forsaking my father's teachings about the enemies in the Permafrost. Instead, I was rushing through the dark corridors and naturally carved halls with no idea where I was headed.

The tears were hot, building up behind my eyes. I wouldn't cry. I *couldn't* cry. The last time I'd shed a tear for myself was over a decade ago, and I *wouldn't* let the pain get ahold of me again. I couldn't afford to be weak. I owed that much to them all at least.

I turned the bent nail over and over in my hand. *As long as this doesn't burn me, I'm human.* Relief flooded through me like warm sunlight. But if Soren had his way, it wouldn't be for much longer. The relief died a short, cold death. There was some truth to what he said; I'd adapted to his kind's ways to survive against the odds. A burning part of me couldn't stand the idea of dropping dead. I wanted to live. I *had* to live.

But adapting wasn't the same as truly becoming like them. It couldn't be. I wasn't a monster. I wasn't about to *become* a monster with a mind so twisted that emotions were foreign, and bringing pain caused pleasure—all the things my father had taught me to hate since I was the height of his knee.

I hurried through the dark halls of the palace, clutching the nail in my hands, allowing it to dig into my skin, to draw blood from the heel of my palm. I wanted to feel pain; I wanted to know I could still feel pain.

Finally, when one side of the hall dropped into a large chasm and the jagged rocks made it precarious to continue, I collapsed and let myself breathe. Every cell in my body was on fire, but strangely the pain wasn't physical. I wanted to scream to drown it out, cover my ears so it would stop assaulting me. There was so much pressure inside my chest I was sure it would burst. The worst part was that I knew Soren meant well. He truly thought he was doing me a favor with all of this. Even if I didn't see it now, soon I would understand that what he was doing was a gift. It would've been easier to hate him if there was outright malice to his intentions. *Lydian and Soren are two very different creatures. One inspires absolute dread and rage, the other a mix of things I can't even figure out.*

I took a deep breath and then another, forcing my body to become calm.

I stared at the nail in my palm and remembered things I had tried to forget.

A small fishing village close enough to the forest that hunting with a bow was just as widely taught as fishing with a spear; a mother who brushed my hair each night, braiding it with care; a father who took me when he traveled into the snow, taught me the tracks of animals and the calls of birds, and told me how the world was while I sat on his knee; the smiles of my sisters when we played games together, the feeling of their arms surrounding me, pinching my cheeks and giggling at the dirt on them; and a fire that burned so I was warm all the way to the bone.

I turned the nail over, twirling it between my fingers.

"You're different than the other girls, Janneke," a broad man said.

Tears rolled down my face. "Why don't you call me Janneka?"

His beard hung braided down to his chest, making up for the lack of hair on his head. I clung to him the way children clung to their mothers, as he wiped away my tears. "Janneka is a woman's name. Janneke is masculine."

New tears replaced the ones he wiped away. I loved the way "Janneka" sounded, loved the way the J sounded like a Y, the way it bubbled on my lips like a stream. "Janneke," with its harsh J and abrupt ending, could never compare.

"I want to be a woman, not a man. Why can't I at least be a shieldmaiden?" Shieldmaidens were still considered women, even if they did fight. Not like me, the last-born daughter of a Jarl and his family, most likely the last child my mother would ever have. For that reason, I would be raised as a male heir, unable to acknowledge my womanhood.

My father only shook his head. "You'll understand someday, Janneke. I promise. For now, use the skills you've learned well. Protect those you love. Remember who you are."

I'm sorry.

I bit my lip. There was nothing I could do about it now. I had to do this hunt. I couldn't disobey a direct order from Soren.

I'm sorry I disappointed you. My six sisters were as beautiful as the moon and stars before their skin burnt and their bodies became almost unidentifiable from the fire and slaughter that rained down upon them. My mother would sing me to sleep in the language of her mother's people, tell me I was beautiful despite the hunting leathers and mud. I had her eyes, she would say, smiling down at me. All six sisters took after her, with their skin a few shades lighter, hair not quite brown and not quite red, but I was the only one who had her leaf-colored eyes. Her only flaw was sending me to chop firewood in the middle of the cold night. It was the last time I heard her voice.

My father had taught me everything I knew, everything that helped me survive in the Permafrost, everything I knew about goblins, the folk, and humans. I followed him like a shadow, absorbing every word he spoke. He would call me his pride, would revel in the fact that I was the only daughter who took after him, with dark curls and darker skin, heir in both position and physical features. He would've hated me for becoming like *them*. If he could see me, he would hate me.

But even if I were dead, I wouldn't go back to them in the worlds beyond. Those who took their life by their own hands didn't join their family in the afterlife; at best they haunted the earth, at worst they joined the dread ship *Naglafar* as undead slaves toiling forever. Either way, Soren'd placed a bind on me long ago that effectively stopped me from hurting myself. If I even thought about it, he would know. I couldn't escape in death, and if I was being completely honest with myself, I didn't want to. The urge to live, to survive, burned in me like a raging fire. Even after what Lydian had done to me, I still survived. Life might have been painful and hard and even futile, but giving up was not in my nature. I would rather survive in hopes that tomorrow would be better than take the chance away completely. But I wanted to live as a *human*, not a goblin.

There had to be another way. The Hunt would take me outside the Permafrost eventually. If I were outside the borders of the Permafrost, armed and horsed, I could escape. The bonds that kept me from escaping wouldn't mean anything once I was in the human world. They were especially strong, created with both Soren's and my own blood and spoken in the old magic language of the Permafrost. Those that tied me to Soren and the 'frost would be harder to escape from, but if I were in the human world, perhaps they would break. I doubted Soren would decide I was more important to chase after than the stag. All I had to do was join Soren on the Hunt and play along as well as I could, keep my humanity in check, and when the time came, run like Hel to my freedom. It would be difficult, but not impossible.

My lungs were on fire, and I released the breath I'd been holding. I could do this. I had to.

I don't know how long I stared at that empty chasm, but I knew it was long enough for shreds of orange light to trickle in from the skylights and for the sound of careful footsteps to come my way. Light, quiet, almost effortless. Whoever they belonged to, they were not human. After the incident with Lydian, that could spell some very nasty things for me.

Shuffling through the darkness, I gave my sight over to my touch and grabbed at the rock farthest away from the edge. Grappling for a hold on the loose, porous bits, I pulled myself up and into a crevice nearly too small, and waited. When I was in a safe enough position, I closed my eyes. Even the light shining through the skylights was too weak to get any idea what or who was coming through.

When you couldn't count on your eyes, you counted on everything else. There were at least three walkers, one with a heavy gait that he couldn't contain. Two brutes and a she-goblin, I could smell that much from here. Goblin males smelled like fire; their women, ice. Another smell played on the back of my tongue: iron poisoning. It was just a hint of the bitterness, not enough for it to be Lydian's, but definitely one of the men he'd come into contact with.

They started speaking, voices echoing down the chamber.

"You're telling me you want to ally with Elvira after the laughingstock Soren's whore made of you?" My hands curled into fists. This was the she-goblin, someone whose name I couldn't recall. She must've been Elvira's subordinate. Back during the fight with Lydian, the she-goblin's fierce eyes had looked as if they wanted to consume me.

"It was Lydian's power that brought down the Erlking in

the first place," a male argued. I knew his voice. Franz. He'd been the one to successfully pull the nail out. It smelled like he hadn't gone unscathed.

"It was the challenge, not Lydian alone. Soren could've easily been the most powerful in the room if he hadn't allowed his little pet to get in his way." The third voice was a male I didn't know.

"She's a liability, even if neither knows it. Once Soren starts the Hunt, he'll take her with him. I can see it in his eyes. He *wants* her. And that will make hunting his power easier. It's simple logic, Helka," Franz said.

Helka grunted, seemingly unconvinced. "I do what's best for my leader; Elvira wants someone who can be an asset if she loses and a strength if she wins. If Lydian wins, would we have his word that our power would remain?"

"Not untouched," Franz said. "But less taken than normal. That would only be fair. And the same would go for each other."

It's starting. It had been less than thirty-six hours since the Erlking died, and they were already making bets on the winner and the losers and who would survive with the most power intact.

"Soren's team hasn't been assembled yet. I don't even know his plans, and I take pride in my relationship with the man," the unrecognizable voice said.

"He likes his whore better than half his court. Not that he has much of that either," Helka said. "Some men have interesting tastes."

Bile rose in my throat at *those* implications. Of course

everyone thought he was bedding me. It'd probably be more scandalous if they knew he'd never laid a finger on me in that way. He'd seen me naked. With how damaged I was after Lydian, I wouldn't have survived without intense healing. Soren had been part of that. I'd spent enough time in the training yard with him to have gotten a few closer-than-needed looks at his body myself, as Soren wasn't exactly known for his modesty. But he'd never *touched* me. Not in that sense.

"Perhaps someone should take care of her—and him as well. I remember how he took down Cÿrus and the coup that followed. It was unnatural. And the girl—she's not natural either."

I racked my brain for the identity of the speaking goblin, but couldn't. Despite his status as one of the more powerful goblin lords, Soren didn't keep a very big court and found no need to. The few score of goblins in his control tended to be spread across the Permafrost as his eyes and ears. I couldn't pinpoint who this one was, but it was easy to tell he didn't like me and, from the sound of it, he wasn't so fond of Soren either. *He wants to kill him.* I froze. *He wants to kill Soren.*

I had to stop it. If Soren died, no matter his wishes, the bind spells cast upon me would revert me back to Lydian's ownership. He'd made sure of that when he threw me at Soren's feet all those years ago. Lydian might not have the end goal of turning me into a monster, but he *did* want to make me suffer in ways that still gave me nightmares. He would draw it out, keep me hanging on to life by a thread while I endured his torture endlessly. He wouldn't kill me; he had far too much pride for that and he wouldn't want to lose his toy so quickly. He wanted me to suffer.

I might've hated what Soren wanted me to become, but I'd rather join him on a hunt where I could possibly escape than take my chances with Lydian.

The footsteps started to pick up, and I dared to stretch my senses further to the inhuman. Everything had power, an energy force that flowed through it, but for goblins and other inhuman creatures, power could be used, manipulated like a weapon. For a lesser being, it laid dormant while they lived and died. A goblin's power decided everything: who ruled and who bowed, who lived and who died. It hovered over them like an aura. I was human with no power to call my own, but after a hundred years I'd begun to feel the power of others.

Another way my body has evolved. I shook the thought off.

There was the she-goblin's, Helka's, power, thick enough for me to count her as a serious threat, while Franz's was too thinned and frayed. The mystery brute plotting against Soren was strong, but nothing I hadn't taken on before.

I waited until the moment when our senses mingled, when he felt the prey reaching out to his drive with open arms. His hunger, his need to kill, his desire to do things beyond nightmares, grew bigger, as if he were a dog slobbering for meat. Before I knew it, he'd hung back and let the rest go without him. Watching. Waiting to get the drop on me.

I sprang from the crevice with the grace of a big cat and landed on the brute's back before he had any idea what was happening.

What sloppy guard. Even I, a human, could do better. I just had.

That thought jolted through me like ice, letting him get the upper hand.

"I thought I smelled you." He laughed. "Now I really get to have fun."

I was still on his shoulders and answered his statement by driving his head into the rocks. He spat and grabbed at me, forcing us both down on the ground. He had at least seventy pounds on me, and I wasn't even going to factor in the insane strength and speed he possessed. I couldn't if I tried. One thought dominated everything: Fight. Kill. Win.

Grappling with a man twice my size always put me at worse odds, but I'd learned a long time ago how to turn those odds in my favor. I let him get on top of me, pushing down the submissive fear it induced. *I am not a wolf. I am not an animal. He cannot have me. No one can have me.* Those words gave me strength as I waited, playing dead.

He was too busy trying to pull at the new clothes Soren had gifted me, salivating at whatever gruesome act he was thinking of doing next, to pay any mind to me and my actions.

I built pressure in my hips, then dug my hands as hard as I could beneath his elbows. My knees bunched together. For the first time, we saw each other evenly, crazed blue eyes staring into dark green. Then I followed through and flipped him over me, into the chasm below.

My breath pounded against my chest, the fiery feeling in my lungs turning to ash. Nothing stung or otherwise hurt, though the neckline of my tunic was as good as ruined.

I sat there, trying to quiet my heart, watching as the light from the skylights changed from orange, to red, to purple, to dusky gray. My body should've been tired, but the adrenaline pumping through me was enough to keep me going indefinitely—and I didn't know what else I could do now. Going back to my chambers wasn't an option; the man's companions could be close by. I still didn't even know his name.

The nail had rolled into a crack in the ground when I'd dropped from the crevice. I picked it up, twirling it around my fingers. *I just killed someone, and I didn't even know his name.*

I tried to make myself feel something other than the numb cloud beginning to settle over me, but found I couldn't. It wasn't the first time I'd killed to survive. Closing my eyes, I rubbed my temples to get the vision of dead men out of my head, but I only managed to make it stronger.

Killing someone would happen sooner or later on the Hunt. If I wanted to escape, I had to accept that I would take lives to save my own. Even here, in the Erlking's palace, the Hunt had begun. I couldn't be bogged down with guilt, but I wouldn't feel the joyous high goblins reveled in when they killed. It was a fine line, and so far I hadn't crossed it; the iron nail I twirled with ease told me that much. *Remember what you are, Janneke.* The cadence of my father's voice faded each day.

I stayed on the ledge by the chasm until Soren found me. He inhaled deeply, detecting the others who'd been here with me. When I looked hard, his features changed to something angular and sharp, more monster than person. But it was gone in a flash.

"Aleksey was here, wasn't he?" he asked, peering over the chasm.

"He probably still is."

"He's no use to me dead. Which brings us to why you felt the need to throw Aleksey over the side of the chasm. I could understand Franz—I never liked the annoying shit—and Helka asks for it, but—"

"Aleksey was plotting to kill you," I blurted out. Too loud. Too much emotion. I should've said it calmly or not at all.

Soren didn't spare the chasm another glance. "And you killed him? Or almost, I think he's still alive. Poor bastard broke his spine. Slow deaths are the worst, aren't they?"

I winced. I didn't think when I threw him into the chasm that he might survive. I didn't think at all, only acted. "Well, it isn't the first time."

"No, it isn't," Soren said, looking me over slowly. He must've thought I was pitiful, hunched over myself like a child. "But that's not the reason why you did it."

"Your death doesn't do me any favors."

His lips twitched, and he came to sit beside me. Only then did I notice the weapons—two daggers of different lengths strung across his back in a holster, a quiver attached to his belt, a bow across his chest, a hunting knife neatly tucked into a sheath by his boot—and the heaviness of his outfit. Hunting leathers, for sure, but also a dark cloak made of bearskin and fur-lined leather gloves. From underneath the falling hood, his white hair was braided in the style of a goblin hunter.

"Janneke," he said softly, "are you hurt?"

"No, I'm fine."

He looked like he didn't quite believe me. "Are you sure?"
I nodded.

He sighed. "Don't you trust me?"

I didn't dignify that question with an answer.

So instead, Soren moved behind me and began weaving his fingers through my hair, skillfully crafting the same braids he wore. It'd been a long time since anyone had touched my hair, and I couldn't shake the feeling of familiarity as he braided it, reminding me of another world as the sky began to brighten and my eyes began to close.

4

BEGINNINGS

THE SUN GLINTED *off the icy river—one of the only ones that ran fast through Soren's territory as far as I knew. Though the sheen of ice was bright in the daylight, I knew the water underneath was swift. Swift water bothered goblins; I'd known that even in the human world. The different lands and creatures were aware of one another, after all, despite the magical and predatory nature of those across the border.*

It'd been more than a year since Lydian's attack on me and the destruction of my village. I'd gotten used to the odd culture of the place, both uplifting and backstabbing at the same time, and understood the best ways to be useful and spend my time.

But I did not have any special skills that goblins needed. I couldn't embroider or make pottery or weave cloth. I could hunt and fight, but goblins didn't need someone to do things they already excelled at. So I wasn't surprised when Soren asked to speak with me. But I was surprised when my new job basically meant I'd be by his side at all times.

I was surrounded but not by my own kind. There were few

humans in the halls of Soren's manor, and all of them were normally busy with whatever tasks they'd been entrusted to do. In the times I wasn't by Soren's side, helping him with training or lending my voice to matters he asked my opinions on, I found myself alone with free time I didn't know what to do with. When that happened, I observed. Sometimes I escaped from everyone in order to let myself delve into the hatred and anger that burned deep inside of me, directed at myself.

Which led me to the river. The only place where none of the goblins went and the place where I could be without stares and whispers and brutal snarls.

The Permafrost could be called beautiful if I forgot what creatures dwelled here. In the sunlight, the snow glittered and the blue sky was the color of robins' eggs. The forest I'd found dead when I was first brought here was more alive than I thought, the wind whispering through the skeleton trees and hardy little animals climbing through the undergrowth to scavenge what they could. They were survivors, like me. This world had more life in it than I'd originally thought, and there was even a beauty to it that I found I could love . . . if I could forget why I was here in the first place.

"So this is where you go." I froze at the voice. I hadn't heard Soren come up behind me. Why was he looking for me? Did I forget something? My mind began to race.

"Excuse me?" I asked when I found my voice.

"You always go off when you have free time, and no one can ever figure out where. I decided to find out." The goblin lord sat beside me, and I stiffened, daring to look at him through the side of my vision.

His clothes were drenched in sweat, and the muscles in his arms were tense. He must've come from some type of chore that he preferred to do himself. I stared at the bulk of his arms, thinking how easily they could hold me down, immobilize me . . . then I snapped out of the poisonous thoughts. He'd given me no reason to fear him . . . much.

"Why here?" he asked, as he thrummed his fingers against his thigh. One of his knees started bouncing, and I caught him glancing at the river in revulsion.

"I'm able to be alone here. Goblinkind don't like the fast-moving water. You can barely keep still, even now," I said.

He looked impressed. "Not many figure that out."

"I notice a lot."

His eyes were still on me, and the curiosity in them had me squirming. "What else do you notice?"

I bit my lip. This could be some type of trap or game to cause me pain. Goblins were tricky. I looked back toward the river.

"What else do you notice?" he said again.

I closed my eyes. "You say you're ambidextrous and fight with both hands, but you favor your left, so you're most likely self-taught and biologically left-handed. You always have someone eat some of your food first; I assume because of fear of assassination. Almost every thrall claims they've never had the nectar, but almost every one of them is lying. The ones who are telling the truth ironically tend to get on better than the liars."

Soren was still looking at me; I could feel it. "Anything else?"

I opened my eyes and met his gaze, trying not to tremble. "Your castellan wants to kill you." The memory of the crimson-eyed goblin was forever burnt into my brain. Besides Lydian, he was the cruelest I'd known, and he made it a point to make sure I knew my place. But he talked like we weren't around him, like humans had no minds themselves, and therefore I'd heard him plotting.

Soren's eyebrows rose. "And how do you know this?"

"I heard him talking with another. Some courier, I think. They were speaking of a goblin who used to rule here—Cÿrus—and how he should be avenged. That you were too young and inexperienced. That you would bring this place to ruin. The castellan said he would take care of it."

Soren's jaw tightened, and I waited for his rage. He'd be angry with me, surely, for speaking ill of him—even if they weren't my words. I knew what happened to humans who mentioned bad news. Why I felt compelled to tell him in the first place, I didn't know. I prepared myself for the worst.

But he didn't hit me or even touch me. He just stood, lips pursed, and started back to the manor. "Thank you for your insight, Janneke. Be sure to be back at the manor by sundown."

I watched him go, shaken.

A few days passed after that, and nothing happened.

Then one day I noticed a new goblin stalking around the courtyard. No one knew where the old castellan had gone; he'd simply vanished. But when I went to my small room that night, on a low table beside the sleeping platform was a note in Soren's script.

There were only three words written.

"You were right."

———◆———

THE IMAGES IN my head twisted and turned, sharp claws, fire blowing up into the sky. The screams of my family and friends filled the air, and I was running, running through a burnt field full of the dead. Behind me the sound of horses' hooves was getting closer. Soon they would surround me, and then I would be a goner. As I ran, my feet were sucked down slowly into the burnt earth, until I was prone and vulnerable. The horses surrounded me, and then there was darkness.

I woke up with a shriek in my throat and my heart beating hard in my chest. The nightmare was so vivid I was surprised when I found myself swathed with furs on a sleeping platform softer than clouds. I shook my head to clear it, trying to focus on something else. When I got my bearings, a bead of panic burst in my chest, and I forced myself to quell it.

Soren was by my side, his hand on my shoulder. "You were screaming. I thought I should wake you."

I caught my breath. "It was just a nightmare."

"The same one?"

"Every time."

"Lydian won't haunt your dreams for much longer. I promise you that." He squeezed my shoulder, then winced and took his hand away before crossing the room to a drawer. I watched with curiosity as he took out a piece of cloth before ripping it into long shreds and trying to use his teeth to tie it across his palms.

I stood. "Let me help."

Soren looked wary—showing weakness of any sort, even to someone like me, went against his instincts—but he held out one of his hands and I saw the faint burns across the palm. Sighing, I began to clean the area and wrap it up. "How did you do this?"

He eyed my newly braided hair. "Apparently braiding my own hair in hunting braids doesn't go against the magic the Permafrost granted goblins, but braiding anyone else's is considered creation not linked to destruction, and so I'm going to get injured."

"You could have asked someone else," I said, changing to his other hand. "I wouldn't have minded."

"No, but I would have. I believe such intimate things must be done by those with whom it is most meaningful."

I made a disapproving noise in the back of my throat as I finished with his burns. "Try not to expose them to too much direct sunlight. You burn terribly and it'll make it worse."

Soren flexed his hand, curling each blue-tinged finger. "I swear this is a curse."

"Come on." I rolled my eyes. "The other week you were going on and on about how beautiful you looked." He did, really, look beautiful. Eerie, but beautiful. The odd blue-gray tint of his skin and lips, the white of his hair, and the pale purple of his eyes were not features found on most goblins— only a select few in the Higher North, his place of birth, ever looked like that. It was like the color had been leeched from his body; I'd seen one or two humans with a similar condition.

"I mean, I *am* beautiful," he said.

"You're insufferable, you mean."

The corners of Soren's lips threatened to turn up into a smile as he moved to lounge on a chair across the room. No, "chair" wasn't the right word. It was more like a throne. The dark wood was carved with animals, both predator and prey, and vines that twisted around them in a never-ending circle. The back had the image of Jormungard, the serpent who circled the world, eating his own tail. Soren then leaned forward on his elbow and stared.

"You know," I said, "staring at me like that is really creepy. Even for you." The serious tone I'd tried to take on was ruined when I couldn't hold in my laugh.

He frowned at that. "Does your kind normally do that?"

"Do what? Laugh? Yes. Often."

"No, I mean, does your kind normally have that really cute nose crinkle when they make certain facial expressions, especially ones of humor or anger? It looks absolutely hilarious on you. In a good way, I mean." He continued after a moment of silence, "From the look on your face, I'm guessing no. I'm also assuming you didn't know that. Don't be offended. It really is quite endearing."

"Oh, bite me," I said.

"Really?" he asked, surprised.

"I'm finding it really tempting to punch you."

"You already punch me," he said.

"I mean, without your consent."

His eyes sparkled with humor, and he let out a laugh. I twitched, my skin crawling with millions of imaginary bugs. Clenching my fists to keep myself from brushing off my arms, I waited until his amusement died down. Why did goblin laughter have to be so *shrill*?

"You know, I never noticed how vulnerable a human is when they sleep."

"You sleep," I said, voice taking on an edge. "Tell me how

vulnerable you are." I paced across the large room as my reality began to dawn on me again. If I was going to get out of this, I would need to distance myself from Soren. Pacing was a bad sign; it was what trapped, injured prey did when cornered. But that was what I was. *If I have to gnaw my own leg off to escape from the trap, so be it.* Not to mention if I didn't get some of this pent-up energy out, Soren and I truly might start going at it, and I wasn't sure that was something he would be actually mad about.

Soren's eyebrows furrowed. "You think I sleep in that bed?" he asked.

"The alternative is just as unlikely," I said, haughty.

He cocked an eyebrow. "A young lord falling asleep in the Erlking's palace is like a rabbit sleeping under the tail of a wolf. It doesn't happen."

I turned on my heel to face him. "What were you doing this whole time?"

"I already said, I was watching you. It was quite relaxing, actually."

"I'm glad *you* had a relaxing night at least, then."

He tilted his head to the side. "You know I can give you something for your nightmares, right?"

I shook my head. "I don't want to be drugged."

"You say that like I'm going to heavily sedate you, not give you something to help you sleep," he said. "If that's what you want, though. I imagine they may get worse after the incident with Aleksey."

"He was plotting against you. I did what I had to."

He nodded again. "I see. I suppose that's twice now."

"You remember?" I asked, thinking back to the castellan with bloodred eyes and suppressing a shudder.

"I remember," he said simply. But when he met my eyes, they said much more than his words.

For a second my heart froze. Gratefulness wasn't a good look for a goblin, and it wasn't one I was used to. For a goblin to openly admit to remembering a debt he owed his thrall . . . it was unheard of. But, then again, Soren had never treated me in any other way. He'd definitely treated me better than his uncle.

Lydian had been the one to take me captive after burning my village to the ground. I was great sport, the only known survivor of a goblin raid, and Lydian wanted to see how long I lasted. It was two months, maybe three, until I found a shred of power known only to me. A bent, iron nail, taken from the ashes before and forgotten by me in the haze of red I came to know. When I thrust it in his calf, he didn't think I was so amusing anymore.

But, technically, by winter law I had beaten him in a fight. He couldn't kill me, then. So, when his young nephew came, newly made a lord through the murder of his kin, I went from a plaything to a gift. An *insulting* gift.

He hadn't expected Soren to see the fight in me. But he did.

And here I was, almost a hundred years later, reaping the benefit of winning that fight long ago.

Lost in my thoughts, the jangling of bronze locks and keys and the creaking of ill-used hinges made me jump. I turned to see Soren reach for something carefully wrapped in doe-skin while being mindful of his damaged hands. At least they would heal quickly due to the magic of the Permafrost.

"I have something for you," he said, holding out the wrapped object to me.

I stared at it, unsure. A gift given in the Permafrost always had to be repaid.

Soren obviously knew what I was thinking, because he sighed and said, "Think of it as a repayment for saving my life."

Gingerly, I reached for the package and set it down on a table of black cherry. The skin was so soft beneath my touch that I wasn't surprised to see the white speckles dotting the brown. I wondered if the fawn's mother was alive to mourn it, then figured she had probably been killed too.

Inside the first fold were two leather bracers, as well as sturdy archery gloves. On the left bracer, there was a pocket too small for any knife. It didn't take me long to guess what it was for. In the second fold was a belt with a sheath; inside the sheath, an axe of wickedly sharp, goblin-forged bronze shone black as Hel. In the third fold was a bow and quiver, the arrows tipped with goblin-forged bronze, the bow whiter than snow. Dragon bone.

I swallowed. New gear and weapons fit for a goblin; so carefully wrought a human's *touch* could taint them. Weapons, hunting gear, and armor—the holy trinity of what goblins were able to create with their own hands.

"I already have supplies," I said, thinking back to the bow I'd left at the palace entrance.

Soren snorted. "Weak supplies. This is well-made. For the Hunt. You'd be wise to take them. You wouldn't want your weapons giving out mid-hunt."

I swallowed the dryness in my throat. "How long is the Hunt, anyway?"

He furrowed his brows. "I've never heard of it lasting longer than it takes for the new moon to come."

"Why?"

He shrugged, and I got a sense he didn't really care about the topic. "Most of the competition is weeded out by then, I suppose. I don't think it really matters—all that matters is winning. Still, take the weapons."

I took the items. I couldn't refuse now that I'd touched them. Even if I did refuse, I wouldn't put it past him to force them on me.

"Proper gear will help your change."

Change. Adapt. *Become like him.* Disgust curled in the pit of my stomach, but I couldn't help noticing the anticipation in my muscles. I wanted to feel the bracers against my skin. I wanted to pierce something's flesh with those arrows. I wanted, I wanted . . .

"What do you want?" Soren's hand caught mine as I stroked the bow. I didn't realize I'd been speaking aloud.

I shook my head. "Nothing."

"You know that's a lie."

I tore my hand from his grip, the skin where he touched me burning. "I can fight it," I said. "This plot you have to make me change into your species, I can fight it, I *will* fight it."

Those purple eyes looked so sad. I wished I believed they

were. "Then you'll die; a human can't survive the Hunt. It's not possible. But, I don't think you're going to die. I also think death isn't something you fear."

No. I wasn't going to die. I was going to *escape*.

He strode across the bedchamber and threw open the heavy double doors that led to the rest of the palace. "I expect you outside, fully equipped, in an hour." He paused in the middle of the doorway. "Please don't fight this, Janneka. I told you, this is because I care."

The doors swung shut, leaving me alone in the cold room.

"Janneke," I said to the icy air. "My name is Janneke."

The child who long ago wished for the feminine name was now dead.

<hr />

I WALKED OUT into the courtyard with the bracers on my arms, the axe brushing against my hips, the gloves caressing my hands, and the bow and quiver slung across my back. The bent iron nail fit snugly into the pocket of the bracers.

Chaos erupted.

Murmurs, then shouts of outrage, taunts and snarls and animal yowls assaulted my ears. I kept my back straight as I walked through the courtyard, seeing Soren in the distance. I frowned. He was talking to Elvira. Helka stood beside her, along with another she-goblin I didn't know.

A young lordling, sensing my distraction, came up to me, sneering. But as he lunged—fangs growing and features sharpening from deathly beautiful to wolfish, ugly, and cruel—I had my bow out and arrow notched. It pierced his chest without a moment's hesitation. The *whoosh* of power swept out of him, hung in the air, and hit me with its might. The intensity stung my skin, but I kept a grip on the bow, knowing I'd need it still. The power assaulted me again, trying to find a place to seep in, until it lingered on my skin like a covering of invisible dust and slowly sank into my pores with a burning agony worse than I'd ever felt before. It hurt even more realizing that since I absorbed power, I was tiptoeing the fine line between humanity and monstrosity.

I yanked the arrow out of the dead goblin and wiped the blood off with my tunic. "Would anyone else care to try?" I turned to the rest of the spectators.

The shouts quieted to whispers and the glares turned to side-eyes as I came up to Soren. He had two horses saddled and ready. I recognized his, a black stallion named Terror. But another, younger stallion with a cream-colored flank and a dark mane pawed the ground beside him. There were two other horses as well, black as Terror was, and beside them, a great snow cat. The cat was as big as the horses, its black hide rippling with muscles, its claws permanently unsheathed. Its tail twitched back and forth as it took me in, probably wondering if I was worth killing. I snarled at it, and it looked away.

I stopped in front of Soren, dipping my head in greeting. His lips twitched as he looked me over, but the scowl remained on his face. Finally, something natural. He was smiling too much for my tastes lately.

"Janneke," he said, motioning to Elvira, Helka, and the other goblin. Elvira's dark hair was pulled back into similar braids as mine, although golden strands were woven through it like vines. Her sword lay sheathed across her back, her stance easy and relaxed. The power coming off her hit me like a crashing wave. Helka smirked at me, her flaming hair loose around her shoulders, making the red in her eyes seem like embers in a fire. I narrowed my eyes at her. *I heard what you said last night. I hope you know that.* Both were near Soren's age, maybe a few centuries or a millennia older, but the third one had the look of a goblin newly grown into her power. She had on a black cloak and her raven-colored hair spilled around her like an angel's wings. Her golden eyes were eager as they latched onto me and seemed to glow against her copper skin.

"You know Elvira and Helka," Soren said. "The young one is Rekke. She's Elvira's niece."

Rekke snarled at Soren. "I am not *young*."

"Of course, you aren't," Soren said, brushing her aside. He took my hand and led me to the cream-colored horse. "I figured you needed a horse to ride. This is my last present. Name him what you will, and when you do, make sure he's bound to it."

I looked at the young stallion, and he snorted at me, pawing the ground. The look of a trapped animal, one I knew well, was on his face. I put a hand on his flank and stroked the soft hair.

"Panic you are, from this day 'til your last. Be you bound to this name and this call. Panic, running quick as thunder, fierce as lightning's flash, Panic, now you be mine." I'd never heard the words to name and bind an animal before, but they came to me as easily as if I'd always known them. A trickle of fear went down my spine. That shouldn't be possible. It couldn't be possible. But it was.

The newly named Panic nickered and nibbled my shoulder affectionately. I stroked his mane, watching as he let his hoof rest on the ground, finally at ease. The gaze of the other goblins burned into the back of my neck as I tried to calm myself.

I caught Elvira's dark gaze and forced myself to hold it. "Yes?"

She smiled a vicious and beautiful smile. "Color me surprised. I thought Soren was exaggerating about you."

"I don't exaggerate," Soren said. He clasped his hands together, his gloved fingers entwining. "Shall we ride?"

Elvira nodded and mounted her cat without a moment's hesitation. Her little niece, still glaring at Soren, and Helka mounted their steeds.

I ran my hand across Panic's flank once more before climbing into the saddle. The reins felt right in my hands, the saddle perfect against my bottom. The thrill of the Hunt started coursing through my veins. The power of the kill was still buzzing in my head. It took all my willpower to shut it down.

Soren pulled up beside me, watching as Elvira and her girls took the lead. "You know why I allied with them?" he asked.

"To stop Franz and Lydian from doing so," I said. "You must've gleaned that much from my sleep talk."

He nodded. "Elvira and Helka are skilled hunters. If they weren't, they wouldn't be able to compete."

I looked around the courtyard. Many lordlings had already

set off to hunt, but many still remained. Some of them might not even bother; the ones with lower power would find it hard to survive, much less fare well.

"Lydian hasn't left yet," I said, catching a glimpse of his entourage. "He's probably trying to find another alliance."

"Probably." Soren nudged his horse forward, and I followed. "This is the beginning of everything," he said. "For you."

I was silent, forcing down the excitement again. No, "excitement" wasn't the word. "Drive" was. A prey drive, just like every predator. I swallowed my fear. I would get out of here before he took anything else, even if I had to vow it on the ashes of everything I loved.

Panic gave a nervous whinny, and suddenly I knew my thoughts were not solely my own because our minds were now linked through a bond similar to the one I shared with Soren. I stroked his flank again. "You and I are one and the same."

Soren's lips twitched again. "Bonded animals can feel our thoughts. Does he feel your excitement? Your drive?"

No, but he feels something else. We will escape, he and I. "Yes."

Soren looked ahead to where Elvira and the others waited. "Then let's go. We have a stag to hunt."

"We do," I said. *And the sooner it leaves the Permafrost, the better.* I was about to kick Panic into a canter, but Soren laid a hand on my shoulder. Goose pimples rose on my flesh as warmth seeped into my skin.

"Watch Rekke for me," he said. "I don't trust her."

"I don't trust any of them." I gazed at the dwindling figures of the three female goblins.

He inclined his head in agreement. "Yes, but I know Elvira

and Helka. I don't know Rekke. And neither do you. So, keep your eyes sharp."

"This isn't my first hunting trip."

Soren narrowed his eyes. "It's the first one where you're not just hunting an animal. Never forget that. We're allied with them now, but that will break sooner or later, and when it does, it will be because someone has a knife in their back. I'd rather it not be you." With those words, he kicked Terror into a canter and charged forward.

Panic pawed at the ground again, shaking his mane out. I scratched his ears, letting my thoughts pour into his. Fear, anticipation, wariness, determination. Pictures formed in my head of where he'd been before, a pasture somewhere far away, where the grass was as green as emeralds.

"You're right," I said to him. *We're escaping.* His head bobbed. I took a deep breath, felt for the nail in my bracer, and followed Soren out of the courtyard.

The Hunt had begun.

5

HUNTING

W E RODE AT a breakneck speed through the Permafrost with a silver, glowing line across the ground as our trail. Beyond it, more lines connected and splayed like fine thread through the tundra, but the silver line was the one that mattered. The stag's path brilliantly lit up the ground like a trail of sunlight.

Each being had their own power and the stag was no different. Now that I'd absorbed the power of the young lordling I killed, the traces of power all around me were clearer than ever. It floated in the air like mist and gathered around every creature great and small like clouds in every color imaginable. It made the chilly silence of the Permafrost explode into life in ways that never were possible before. It also proved true Soren's statements about me changing. Humans weren't built to absorb the power of the prey they killed; that was strictly a goblin ability.

Racing through the cold, crisp air under the pale yellow sun was invigorating after being inside the palace so long.

Though the trees surrounding me were skeletal, and frost covered the dead grass and crumpled leaves, there was life everywhere, and the horses' pounding hooves could've been the beating of an ancient heart.

Joy filled me through my connection with Panic; he was relishing the feel of the forest underneath his hooves. To run, to be wild, to be *free,* was all he wanted.

But we weren't free yet. Not really.

The horse felt my doubt but shook off the thought. Thundering across the tundra, for him, was enough. Of course, having an animal as an escape accomplice wasn't the most ideal situation. I pushed down the doubt. I didn't need any more to fill my heart; I'd already gorged on it. If I thought about it too hard, I would think of the courtroom and the young lordling and the power buzzing at my fingertips. I couldn't have that. Escaping these creatures meant I couldn't let my guard down, couldn't doubt anything for a moment.

When we stopped for the day, we were still deep in the Permafrost, the icy air turning the water in our breath to frost before our eyes. The coldness filled me up as I breathed in, and it burned deep in my chest like a flickering fire.

I climbed down from Panic. He looked around, pawing at the icy ground for something to graze and settled for the patches of dry, rough weeds that dotted the earth. I dropped the rope, somehow knowing he wouldn't leave me if I did. I noticed from the corner of my eye that Soren had done the same with Terror, as did Rekke and Helka with their horses. I cast a suspicious glance at Elvira's menacing snow cat, thankful to see that at least it was tied to a tree. It was a predator after all. It might not eat Elvira or us due to their bond, but there was nothing that would keep it from eating the horses.

A gloved hand landed uninvited on my shoulder and I turned to knock it off, all of the ease I gained during the ride draining out of me. "Did you have a nice ride?" Soren asked.

"I don't think you care to hear my genuine answer."

He raised an eyebrow. "You didn't like it?"

I chewed my lip. "I was liking it a lot more when you weren't talking to me."

A growl rumbled in Soren's throat as he frowned, but before he could say something, Elvira spoke up. "Does this seem like a good place to camp for the night?"

Soren waved his hand indifferently. "It'll do." He realigned his body to address her, but his eyes were still burning into my forehead. I made it a point to turn my back to him. "We should also take turns keeping watch."

"You don't trust us?" Helka purred.

"No," Soren said flatly.

Rather than be offended, Elvira laughed. The hair rose on the back of my neck; her laugh sounded like shrill, tinkling bells, and there was an air of falseness to it even a child could pick up. She flicked her finger at me. "You, thrall, go hunt. You go with her, Rekke."

I bristled, hand touching the butt of my axe, my mouth opened with a stinging retort—how *dare* she order me around. She didn't own me. But Soren got to her first. "Don't call her that," he snapped. "You've no claim to." His unspoken words lingered in the air. *We're not doing things the way you want to.* As far as I knew, Elvira was older than Soren by a few thousand years, and with goblins, that meant a world of difference when it came to how they treated humans and thralls in general.

Younger goblins like Soren had a sense of social fluidity and understood they needed thralls in good, hale conditions to do the things they couldn't and uphold a lifestyle. Whereas older goblins simply viewed humans in their service as inferior beings. I leveled my gaze at Elvira. "I don't take orders from you." Elvira could rip me to shreds easily enough if she wanted to, but I was determined not to let her frighten me. "What do you want me to do, Soren?" Anger burned as the words left my mouth. But I caught Soren's calm lilac eyes and they told me that it wasn't worth the battle.

"Go hunting, Janneke."

I gave a brisk nod and motioned to Rekke. The young she-goblin's eyes were dull, and she glowered at her older relatives before grudgingly stalking over to her horse. My own bow was already slung over my back and everyone else wore their weapons, but Rekke's bow was attached to her saddlebags with complicated straps. It was stupid and sloppy and would probably get her killed, but I couldn't find it in me to care.

She joined my side, and I opened my senses to the other creatures in the sparse woods. Then I started to track.

I'd always been good at tracking. For my father watching his lastborn daughter fulfill the role of his firstborn son, it was one of the few things he took pride in. We'd hold competitions in the village where, during the dead of night, we would sneak through the forests to try to find and capture one another.

People would bet on which hunter they thought would get the most "kills" and who would survive the longest without being seen. To the fury of the men, I was always the winner. Becoming invisible, adapting so I was one with the environment, was always my strong suit.

I walked lightly through the underbrush, my steps barely making a sound. I could sense Rekke's presence behind me. She didn't speak, but I could feel the eagerness radiating off her in waves, and I hoped that it wasn't directed toward getting me alone.

The tips of my fingers tingled as I got close to a source of power. It was small, nothing close to the power of a predator, but it still prickled at my fingertips and flowed through my body like ice water, bringing it to life. Ever since the power of the lordling had absorbed into my skin, the goblin-like senses had become sharper. I'd never seen the prey lines on the ground as clearly as I did now, nor had I ever been able to sense the power coming off of others. Before it was an abstract concept, but now it was something tangible, as if I could feel it in my hands and manipulate it into the shape I chose. I reached for the nail in my bracer's pocket, relieved when I didn't feel the hint of a burn. I was safe. I wasn't changing, not yet.

My ears sensed the rabbit before my eyes did; and my arrow went through its eye before it could run. I picked it up, pulling the arrow out of it, and strung the dead animal across my belt. One down, countless more to go. I knew how much goblins could eat.

A deer would've been better, but I'd have more luck finding

a unicorn than a deer able to graze in these scrublands. The naked skeleton trees and the scraggily grass barely were considered life.

Rekke didn't hide her thrill at my skills. "Wow," she said. "You're amazing at that."

"For a human?" I asked, letting some of the bitterness seep into my tone. If she was mainly raised by Elvira, I wouldn't be surprised to find she viewed humans the same way.

The young goblin's eyes widened, and she shook her head. "No, I meant in general. You're really good with the bow."

I turned to look at the small she-goblin, shocked at the compliment. It'd been so easily given and wasn't shrouded in the double meanings behind most of the words her kind spoke. She really was young, then. A prick of pity stabbed at my heart. What was a girl like her doing under the supervision of Elvira? What was she doing out here on the Hunt when she barely had enough power to participate? I reached out with my senses and could vaguely grasp her power, shrouding her like purple mist, but it was brittle and easy to break. *Perhaps Elvira brought her along to kill her.*

The thought covered me like a thick, dark cloud. It wasn't unknown for goblins to kill their competitors—it was practically encouraged. Soren had killed his father to get his seat; as far as I knew his father had killed his father; the line went on and on. But the thought of this young, almost harmless girl dead because of the threat she might one day pose pressed heavy against my chest. She was a goblin. Not a girl. I couldn't think of her as one. Convincing myself she was evil would've been easier if she hadn't been looking at me with those wide eyes.

"It's an easy shot," I said, wiping off the blood from my arrow, trying not to think too hard. "You want to try the next one?"

She nodded eagerly, but when the next rabbit appeared, her aim sent the arrow flying into the tree above. I raised my eyebrows as the rabbit took off, then quickly swung my axe from where it was sheathed and threw it. It turned three times in the air before sinking itself deep into the rabbit's hide. My heart raced at the swiftness of it and the exhilaration coursing through my veins.

Rekke kicked the ground, embarrassed. "I'm . . . not a particularly good shot. I can throw knives, but they're harder to kill animals with. Besides, my throwing knives are poison, so we couldn't eat anything they killed."

That was something to tell Soren, in case an event came up where Rekke got stabby. Poisoned throwing knives. I knew for a fact Lydian poisoned his greatspear. I also knew that dying of goblin-made poison was not a good way to go.

I yanked my axe out of the rabbit and slung it onto my belt while it still dripped blood. The hot fluids covered the leathers on my thigh, but it didn't bother me.

Rekke stood with her head still bowed, looking so pitiful my heart gave a squeeze.

"Perhaps I can teach you to be a better shot, if you'll have that." The words were out of my mouth before I thought them through. She looked so human, my aching heart had to do something despite my mind screaming for it to stop. This child—no, this *she-goblin*—could not be my friend, could *never* be my friend.

She tensed, trying to judge if the offer was accepting weakness or even an insult. When she made her decision, she said, "That would be wonderful. But don't tell Elvira and Helka, please. They think I'm useless enough as it is."

"Of course. Come on, we shouldn't wander so far away. We can find more on the way back," I said, starting the trek back to the camp. The young goblin chattered the whole way, but the words went in one ear and out the other. From the bounce in her step and the way her liquid gold eyes lit up, she looked pleased that she had a friend in me. But she was a goblin. She was *not* my friend. I shouldn't be feeling anything but hatred for this creature. But the more I tried to hate the girl, the more she grew on me.

My chest ached where my breast should've been. *Remember what they are. They aren't your friends or allies. They're cold-blooded killers who want to either turn you into one of their own or kill you.* The words in my head were spoken in my father's voice—or at least the little I remembered of it.

"They can't think you completely useless," I interrupted, trying to keep my tone light. "They brought you along for the Hunt, after all."

Rekke sniffed. "That's because I'm my father's heir, not her. If I wasn't so young I'd be the ruler in my own right, but since I am she's my regent. She likes the power and wants to get rid of the competition." She fell in beside me, and we walked in silence for a while.

"Elvira could kill you herself or arrange for someone else to do it in her territory if she wants you dead."

Rekke shook her head. "My father—her brother—

preformed a bind curse on her a while back. He was older than her so he was the lord, but she killed him for his rank. Before he died, he made sure she couldn't kill me by her own hand or word. So even though she ruled the manor, she couldn't order or arrange my death. I think this is the closest thing she can get to it." She sighed. "I miss my dad. He was so nice. He taught me everything. We used to play games in the courtyard when he wasn't busy."

"My father played games with me too," I whispered. The dull ache returned to my chest. I hadn't talked about my father in so long. Much less to someone who wasn't human.

"What type?" she asked.

I had to think about it. "Well, when I was really little, he would take a piece of candy or a coin and hide it in a row of shoes. I had six sisters, so there were a bunch. I had to guess which shoe had the candy, and if I was correct, I got to keep it. When I was older, I mainly did hunting games and trained with him."

She laughed. "That's a weird game, but I like it. We had this pond, and my dad would challenge me to catch more frogs than him. Elvira had the pond filled in after she killed him. I suppose she's ordered the guards to empty my room too; she obviously isn't expecting me to come back from this."

The hurt in the young girl's voice was clear. Perhaps whatever you were, you loved your family in some way. Perhaps knowing you were being taken to your likely death was just as painful as knowing you were being taken as a thrall. I shook myself. Attempting to humanize them would only make this worse. I had to be strong enough to feel no remorse, grow no bonds, even if part of me ached to reach out to Rekke and touch her shoulder.

I was almost relieved to meet Soren and the others back at camp, throwing the two rabbit carcasses in front of them. Soren raised his eyebrows. "That's it?"

"There's not much here. It's a dead land, if you remember."

He snorted. "I remember well."

Elvira turned to Rekke. "You killed one as well, didn't you?"

"Um . . ." She fidgeted. "I . . ." Her face twisted in pain, the light that glowed in her eyes during our conversation sputtering out.

"Obviously not," Helka hissed, glaring at the girl. "Soren's whore can do better than you."

Blood pounded in my ears. *I am not a whore.* "Don't *ever* call me that," I snapped. From behind me, a growl rumbled low in Soren's throat.

"Sorry." She grinned, showing her sharp teeth. "Lydian's whore, then."

"Helka," I warned, anger burning through my limbs. Like Elvira, I was determined that Helka know I didn't fear her, and that she couldn't push me around. But if she went any further, I would explode. The thought that she knew what that brute had done to me boiled my blood.

"What? He *did* fuck you half to death, didn't he? I'm surprised you're still able to walk, let alone stand! And of course, he made lovely work of your breasts, though he must've liked one a bit too much, it seems." Her voice grew vicious.

Soren's growl turned into a snarl. Rape was a common use

of dominance in goblin culture, especially among older goblins who used it as a show of strength and power. Rage boiled in my belly.

I stepped forward. "He liked it until he got a good dose of iron poisoning in his calf—*and* shoulder now." Despite my bravado, the world was spinning beneath my feet. *Don't remember, don't remember.* Images of Lydian, his claws latched deep inside of me, flashed through my mind.

Why won't you listen? Why won't you listen?! He'd scream the words over and over until spittle ran down his chin and dripped on my face. *What's the matter with you? Don't you see it! Don't you see I'm trying to save you! Just answer my question!* Over and over as he hurt me, used me, raving like a lunatic. *What happens when the serpent stops eating his tail?*

"I'm just sore that we have to have a human slowing us down." Helka stepped forward to meet me and bent to whisper in my ear, "And I know what you did to Aleksey."

I didn't think. Redness overtook my vision, and my hand whipped across Helka's face, the *crack* of the slap echoing off the bare trees. Blood trickled down her cheek from where my nails dug into her skin. Time stopped and the only things moving were the branches of skeleton trees blowing in the wind. Then Helka lunged at me. I dodged the blow and then another, a snarl bubbling at my lips. Her axe moved quickly through the air in a blur before every strike, and I definitely didn't have time to counterattack. But I nimbly dodged every blow until I grabbed the axe's handle as she swung down, kicking her in the side of her thigh. She stumbled, and I wrenched the axe away from her, gripping it firmly in my hands. The blade was heavier than I was used to, and it gleamed wickedly in the setting sun.

But she wasn't done. She pulled her lips back in a snarl, her teeth lengthened, her brow furrowed, her nose and ears grew long, and the nails of her fingers turned to talons. "You little worm!"

I panted, already worn out by the brief struggle. It took only one look in Helka's eyes to know that she would kill me if I didn't defend myself. And I couldn't allow her to kill me. To take *my* power, however small it was. The power was *mine*. And if she thought she could take it, she was wrong. Dead wrong. I'd rip her. I'd shove her corpse in the rivers of the Crossing so she'd never rest in Valhalla. I'd destroy her until there was nothing left to destroy.

I lunged at Helka with the fury in my body becoming my strength, using her axe to block her talons as she struck out at my face and heart. I danced with her, a dance I'd done many a time with Soren in the training fields as part of my companionship to him. But no sparring session could compare to the heat pulsing through my veins, the power that coursed through me, the pure *delight* that filled me when I ripped through her. The battle frenzy filled my mind, and my vision was black with shades of red. She would pay for those comments, for triggering those memories, for things she had *no* way of understanding.

Cold, rough hands wrapped around my waist and latched onto my wrists as I tried to yank myself to freedom. "Janneke," a familiar voice said. "She's dead! It's okay, Janneke, she's dead. She's dead."

The world came to me, and I cried out, falling to my knees. Helka had more power than the lordling I'd killed, so much more, and it hurt coming in. My body fought to reject it as if it were a foreign virus, but it found its way through my pores in spite of it, burning the whole way through. I scratched at my arms, trying to wipe it off, get the pain to stop, but the thick layer of power sank in.

When it was over, I lay panting, unsure of what went on. My mind, no longer crazed and scattered by the battle frenzy, was slowly picking up the details of what had happened. The body below me was beaten into a pulp, nearly unrecognizable, and Soren's hands were still wrapped around my wrists. I found myself pressed against his chest, fighting for breath.

"It's okay," he whispered, low enough that the other two goblins wouldn't hear. "It's okay. It's okay. She's dead."

"I—I—" I couldn't find the words to speak.

"I know." His breath was warm against my hair. "I know."

I closed my eyes. Helka. Helka insulted me. I slapped her. She attacked me. I killed her.

"It's really happening," Elvira said, almost to herself.

The responding silence was deafening.

Bursts of panic erupted in my chest, despite Soren's warm embrace, and my eyes began to sting. But no, I couldn't cry or scream as my chest burned like it would split into two. I had to take it. I couldn't let them see the weakness.

It was really happening. It was *really* happening. I was a killer. A monster like the one I'd slain. The dead eyes of the she-goblin stared up at me as I forced myself to feel disgust— not for the weakened creature at my feet, but for myself. I forced the sadness onto myself, forced the anger, and forced the guilt. I found if I couldn't force the emotions, they wouldn't come.

Elvira looked down at Helka's body, then at me, shrugging. "Well, perhaps she wasn't as useful as she appeared to be."

And that was all she said about her ally's murder.

"Come on," Soren said. "Let's find somewhere to set up camp."

"We just did," Elvira said.

"Somewhere not near a dead body, I meant. Unless you want to deal with any other predator of the flesh?" Soren raised an eyebrow.

I stood and he rose with me, and I only just remembered that his arms were still wrapped around me. I flashed him a look, and it seemed like he'd forgotten as much as I had, because he let go in an instant, a rare sheepish expression on his face.

"Thank you," I said, in a low whisper. But was I thanking him for letting me go or for holding me in the first place? Somehow, I wasn't sure it was the former.

Conversation broke out again as they moved a little farther to remake camp, and I numbly followed, leaving the body of the dead goblin behind. From a little way ahead of me, Soren looked back, worry etched on his features.

Panic trailed at my feet, feeling everything I felt, interpreting it the way only he could. He feared me, like he feared any predator. I tried to stroke his flank, but he moved aside every time. "I won't hurt you," I whispered to him. "Please, I won't.

I promise." Maybe the bond could make him hear the sincerity in my voice.

When we finally set up camp, I collapsed to my knees on my bedroll. It was *so cold*. When I'd been fighting Helka, when the only thoughts I had were of killing and defending my power and the only feelings I had were of anger and bloodlust, I hadn't noticed the frost on my arms. Now with the guilt that racked my body, I shivered violently. It blasted me, and I clutched my knees to my chest. Soren looked over to me from where he sat, a hunk of the rabbit clutched in his hands. The coppery smell of raw meat hit my nose, and a wave of nausea fell over me. I turned away. *They're monsters, and I'm becoming one of them.*

The ground crunched beneath his feet as he came beside me, sitting on his own bedroll. I was shivering violently now, wishing for a blanket.

"You should stop fighting it," he said softly. "Stop fighting the transformation. It will only make things harder for you." He brushed his thumb against my cheek and wiped away tears I hadn't known I was crying.

"Stop it," I hissed. "Stop *touching* me."

"I'm trying to get you to trust me," he said, voice still uncharacteristically soft. "That's all. Isn't that how humans form bonds of trust?"

On any other day, I would've laughed. Of course. *Of course,* he was trying to do something human, but in his utter goblinness failed. Maybe I would've even admired him for it. But not today.

"I will never trust you. Never. And I'm not a fool." Yet I couldn't deny part of me felt safer by his side.

A strange expression played on his face. I couldn't place it; I'd never seen it before. But his eyebrows crumpled, his lips turned down in what was almost a scowl but wasn't. It was sadder. "I'm not a fool either," he said.

"Oh?" I asked.

"You're a terrible liar," he said. "And that's coming from a man whose species is known for being unable to lie."

"Then what, oh superior one? What am I lying about?"

He chuckled drily. "Do you really think you could run away, back to the humans, and live completely unaffected? With all the bonds tied to you? You'd either die in the attempt or be killed by humans. You've the smell of the Permafrost on you now that you can absorb power. One good hunt or fight would be all it took for your position to light up like a fire. And perhaps I'm wrong, but I doubt that you'd find fulfillment as a simple housewife. You need the Hunt as much as it needs you. Also, you *do* trust me. Not right now, perhaps, but usually."

I had nothing to say to that, so only buried myself deeper in my arms. If the power I'd absorbed could alert Permafrost creatures to my presence in the human world, then this would be trickier than I thought. Soren *was* right about one thing: I would never be a housewife.

"I can't do this right now," I said, closing my eyes.

The way he sighed made it sound as if he truly hated to see me this way, but I didn't buy it. He lay down on the bedroll beside me, and I closed my eyes. He was so close I could feel the heat coming off him. It only made me shiver harder as my body greedily tried to suck in the warmth. He jerked my bedroll so it was closer to him, then positioned me slightly so I was barely touching him. Then he reached across and draped a bearskin cloak over me.

I should've protested, but my body was crying out in relief that it was finally warm. The tremors were chased away, leaving me utterly exhausted. Soren whispered, his breath tickling my ear, "I won't ever let you hurt yourself."

My eyelids were heavy, and my body ached with the pain of the day. "You shouldn't have brought me here, then," I said softly.

He said nothing, just placed a hand on my shoulder, his thumb moving across the bare skin on the nape of my neck. For once, I didn't push it off. I didn't have the strength, and despite everything, something about the movement was calming. I fought to stay awake, even as I heard Elvira say she would take the first watch.

"Sleep, Janneke," Soren said. "It's going to be okay."

No, it's not. But my eyelids closed anyway, and I drifted off into a fitful sleep.

6

HARD TRUTHS

A SHARP JAB to my ribs woke me early in the morning. The sky was still a dark, deep blue, and the world around me was fast asleep. I was curled up close to Soren, underneath his bearskin cloak. The memories of the previous day played over in my head as I moved away from him, my body burning with embarrassment. Before me, Rekke watched us with amusement sparkling in her dark golden eyes. I groaned inwardly as the dim memory of waking up screaming again beside Soren in the early morning and shifting until I was positioned where I was replayed in my head. Something told me the young she-goblin was not going to let me live it down.

"Rekke?" I asked, rubbing the sleep from my eyes. "What is it?"

"You said you'd teach me how to shoot. I want to do it while the others are still sleeping, so they won't know I'm weak."

Damn it to Hel. I groaned internally. I'd forgotten my promise. I was mildly surprised she'd still want to train with me. After all, I did kill Helka last night. Shuddering, I studied the ground. The prey lines had become more visible since absorbing Helka's power, and the current of living beings flowing through the air was almost tangible.

A quick glance around the camp confirmed that both Soren and Elvira were still asleep. Rekke must've had the last watch. I stood and stretched my aching muscles. We'd ridden hard yesterday, and my muscles burned from the effort. The mental exhaustion inside of me from my fight with Helka didn't help. Doubt was slowly spreading through me like a poison. Now was not the time to pay attention to that. If I could sneak off with Rekke, maybe I could survey the land for when I made a run for it.

"They'll be pleased if we manage to catch breakfast," I said, keeping my voice light.

"Of course we'll manage." Rekke sniffed, obviously offended.

From where he stood, Panic nickered as I grabbed my bow. I reached out and ruffled his mane. "Stay here, boy."

Rekke raised an eyebrow at me. "Won't we cover more ground on the horses?"

"We'll scare more game," I said and started forward. "Come on, before the others wake."

Rekke paused, glancing at the sleeping goblins. "What if they're attacked?"

What if I don't give a damn? "I'm sure they'll be able to handle anything."

She grabbed her bow and followed at my heels. The cold air was sharp in my lungs as I walked through the Permafrost.

Dead leaves and branches littered the ground, forcing me to walk with care. The skeletons of trees and other plants reached high into the sky, desperately clinging to a sun that would never warm them.

If I could forget where I was, who I was with, what I was doing, it was almost as if I were back home so many years ago, hunting for my family. My heart sank in my chest; that would never happen again. Even if I managed to escape this and live in the human world, there was a nagging part of me that feared I would never belong. *And Soren, gods damn him, is right about would happen.* The idea of the goblin lord looking out for my well-being made my body burn in a way I didn't understand. Soren was better off as far away from me as possible.

I reached for the nail in my bracer, hoping for the reassurance the cold iron would bring, but snatched my hand back at the slight stinging in my fingers. When I looked, they were bright red with small burns. Nerves fluttered like a trapped moth inside my belly. *This isn't right. It can't burn me yet. I'm not like them.* Fear rooted me to the spot as the events of last night replayed in my head. Then, I'd acted *exactly* like them.

"You and Soren looked very cozy last night." Rekke's comment stopped me in my tracks.

I raised my eyebrows. "Are you implying what I think you are?'"

She gave a wicked grin. "Yes."

Gods, I was hoping I only imagined my blush. "Well, you're wrong. I'd rather eat a live rat than be with him, and I'm sure he'd say the same."

Rekke shrugged. "I doubt it. I mean, he's so passionate and

handsome and strong." Her eyes gleamed as she spoke, and I had to hide a chuckle. It looked like *she* might fancy Soren herself. Well, she could have him for the good he did me.

"Passionate?" I said. "I wouldn't use that word to describe him."

"Well, *I* would. Besides, you can tell he cares about you."

"I'm his property," I said bluntly. "Of course he cares."

Rekke sighed and shook her head. "Just keep telling yourself that."

I blinked. "Wonderful." The nagging feeling about last night was growing harder to ignore. I wasn't blind. I knew that for a goblin, Soren paid a great amount of attention to me, but that didn't change what he was. And no hunt, no gesture of presumed kindness, nothing would change that. Soren would always be a goblin. That was what mattered.

Or at least, it used to. I told the voice inside me to shut up and focused on the crisp leaves crunching under my feet and the cold air chilling my bones. I wasn't sure how close we were to the border, but from the way the trees grew densely packed together and the birdcalls up above, it was possible we were close enough for some of the life to seep over from the other side. But we could still be miles away. Once, when I'd gone out hunting with Soren, years ago, I'd tried to defy the bond that bound me to the 'frost, running for miles until he ultimately caught me. I still had the scar on my arm where our blood had mixed when he spoke the words that kept me inside the Permafrost's borders and let him know, in some telepathic way, if I was about to hurt myself.

"Considering your actions, I don't trust you not to kill yourself,"

Soren had said, a few weeks after I was put into his care. After the hunger strike and violent episodes in which the trauma of what had happened to me clouded my mind from reason, perhaps he did have a solid point. But at the time, I didn't understand why he bothered to care.

With the bond to the land of the Permafrost in effect, he let me run through the woods as they slowly gained more and more life, only for me to be jerked to a halt near the border as if I were controlled by puppet strings. I hadn't talked to him for a week afterward until the anger faded and the hatred cleared. Yet even as devious as he was, there was no doubting he protected me when he didn't need to and that he treated me better than he should've.

Perhaps he always had this sinister plan for me, from the moment Lydian threw me down at his feet. Perhaps he always knew what I'd become. Maybe some instinct deep inside him told him there was a kindred spirit in me. Maybe he found a connection or a friend. I didn't think he was toying with me; Soren might've been many things, but he wasn't needlessly sadistic. I couldn't deny that in his own sick, twisted way he cared about me, and in my own sick, twisted way I cared about him too. It was far easier when blind hatred was my only emotion.

"We'll stop here," I said. "Let me see your stance."

Rekke pulled her bow from where it rested against her back. She got into her stance, her small, pink tongue sticking out the side of her mouth as she concentrated. Despite the unpleasantness of it all, watching the young goblin lifted a weight in my chest I hadn't known was there. There was something pure and innocent about her that I hadn't seen in a long time, and a part of me couldn't help but covet it.

The girl stood with her feet pointed inward and her elbow rotated toward the bowstring, one eye completely closed. Her arm shook as she struggled to hold the string against her chest.

I sighed. She wasn't kidding when she said she was no good with a bow.

"Okay," I said. "First, keep your feet straight. Don't turn them inward toward your body. Your stance should be with feet parallel to each other or with closed hips."

Rekke scowled, but nodded and straightened her stance.

"Also, keep your elbow level, don't have it higher than the rest of your arm. Make sure it's straight or else the arrow will go flying and you'll bruise the inside of your arm." I touched her arm, lowering it until it was level with the rest of her. "Keep your bowstring taut and change the anchor point from your chest to your chin," I said, taking her hand and correcting her grip. "Make sure both eyes stay open—I know some teach you to shoot with only your dominant eye, but both eyes open increases the range of sight and strengthens the nondominant eye."

She did as I said, shaking with the effort of holding the string back.

"Now, aim for the heart of that oak tree." I pointed to a big tree a few meters away from us. "And shoot."

She did. The arrow soared through the air and hit the oak tree with a dull thud. It hadn't gotten quite in the heart, but it had been close enough.

Rekke grinned, showing sharp canines. *Hel's gates, why do*

they have to have such sharp teeth? The unease was washed away when the young she-goblin jumped in the air. "I did it!" she cheered. "All right, let's try a few more times."

WE SPENT THE hours until dawn shooting at every little thing that came in sight. Rekke was a fast learner, and each mistake I corrected was not repeated a second time. She kept getting closer and closer to her targets, until I was sure that if she handled a bow against an actual foe, they might have something to worry about. With a few years of practice, she could even be better than Soren, who while obviously skilled with the bow preferred his swords due to the problems his eyes had adjusting to light. That was if she even survived for another few years. I shook my head, not wanting such thoughts to weigh down the light feeling inside me.

As the sun started to peek over the horizon, we stopped. "We should get back before they miss us. And pick up some breakfast on the way," she said.

I nodded.

But as we walked back, I noticed Rekke's shoulders tense. She paused among the naked trees, and I stopped beside her, leaves crunching under my boots. "What is it?"

"I smell . . ." She frowned, unable to put a word to it. "I don't know, something's amiss."

I inhaled deeply; the wind had a slight coppery tinge to it, almost like meat that'd been left out in the open too long. We were standing downwind so whatever it was, it was close.

"Keep your weapon out, Rekke," I said and started forward, an arrow already notched in my bow.

Rekke crept behind me, steps silent as a mouse. The rotting smell got worse as we went forward through a twisted patch of brambles and through a grove of skeleton trees. Near the trunk of one was a pool of dried blood. I looked up and swallowed when I saw the dead body of a goblin skewered and hung on the tree.

Rekke let out a gasp before containing herself.

"The Hunt's first victims." I bent to touch the dried blood. It was brown and cracking, maybe a day or so old. Ignoring the smell of death, I took another whiff of the air to see if any goblin scent remained. A bit of the sickly, icy smell lingered in the air. Along with a sweeter smell I couldn't put a name to. "Rekke!" I barked.

"Yes?" She was shaking.

"Go back to the camp, get Soren and Elvira. The goblins who killed this one could still be around. Bring them here. I'm going to scout."

"But you could be in danger too!" the she-goblin protested.

Not many of your kind would care about that. I shook the thought from my head. "This is the Hunt; we're all in danger."

Rekke nodded and took off the opposite way. I stood silently, trying to pinpoint where the sweet smell was coming from. My gut tugged uncomfortably. It was so strange and somehow so familiar. I stalked forward, bow still aimed before me.

Only when I saw the scent's owners did I stop. A group of

human men sat around what looked like a failed attempt at a fire. *Fools. Normal fire doesn't set in the Permafrost.* My mouth fell open. There were *humans* in the *Permafrost.* While of course humans were *brought* to the Permafrost, going there of one's own volition to hunt or explore was practically suicidal. There was a reason the creatures living in the Permafrost were so deadly. I couldn't even recognize their scent as human, only something foreign. My stomach churned.

Despite their failure to light a fire, they were joking and conversing with each other, unaware of the danger of the land they were in. Stupid. The sweetness in the air burned my nose, and I held back a sneeze, not accustomed to the tickling sensation. The smell of other goblins burned my nose, but it was a good burn. This was uncomfortable. They were laughing, but not like how I'd come to know laughter. The sound roared deep from their bellies, scaring off any type of game in the area. It was unrestrained and free, unlike the held-back laughter of goblinkind, always wary that someone might hear. It was so unreal, so alien. But they were my people; I had to do something.

Focus. You need to warn them. There was a hunt going on, and I wouldn't put it past any goblin to kill them for sport. It was obvious they weren't the ones who had slain the goblin hanging from the tree. They were muscled, yes, but their steel glittered without the tarnish a goblin's blood would've made, and I wasn't about to believe that even a group of grown men could take on a single brute and survive without injury.

I found my voice. "You need to leave here."

At once, the laughter stopped. One of the men, a big one

with reddish hair, grabbed an axe from the ground; quickly, the other four followed suit. I stepped out from behind the trees, lowering my bow. *When approaching prey animals, it's necessary not to frighten them.* One of my father's early teachings came back to me. They *were* prey animals, what with the way they cast their eyes from side to side, looking for an escape, the twitchy nerves that showed even as they gripped their weapons so tight the skin of their knuckles turned white.

"Who are you?" the redheaded man asked. Then he narrowed his eyes and looked me over more carefully, taking in my clothes, my hair, all the goblin-made weaponry that adorned my body. Hot shame flooded through my veins. *Of course they don't trust me.*

"That doesn't matter," I said. "But there are three goblins very close to here. They're on a hunt. *The Hunt.* Actually, you've picked the worst time to be here. The Permafrost is crawling with goblins who are trying to kill everything worth killing. You should leave before they find you—they'll come sooner or later. If you can get out of the Permafrost before they do, you might have a chance."

Yes, running was their only chance. I'd bet ten to one even Rekke could hold her own and win against their strongest man.

"Thorsten," a yellow-haired man said, coming up beside the redheaded one. "Look at her."

"I'm looking." The redheaded man—Thorsten—scratched his beard. "Where are you from, girl? Why are you out here so deep in the 'frost? Don't you know it isn't safe?"

"I could ask the same of you," I retorted.

"The pelts from the animals here fetch a pretty price, we've heard," he said, smiling. "Of course, you have to be skilled enough to catch whatever is in this barren wasteland."

A bead of anger rose in me. What did they know of a barren wasteland? "You don't strike me as suicidal."

"Appearances can be deceiving. Why are you dressed like a goblin, for instance?" asked another man, this one with dark skin.

I bit my lip. "That doesn't matter. What matters is, you need to leave."

Thorsten narrowed his eyes at me. "You've been here for a long time, haven't you?" He shook his head, and his hand brushed against the butt of his axe. I raised my bow slightly. "That's not natural. I can smell the Permafrost on you."

Thorsten came forward, his tall and broad shape looming over me. I pointed my arrow at his chest. "Don't come closer."

Thorsten stopped where he was. "How long have you been out here?"

"Long enough," I said. A hard pit formed in my gut. These men should've been grateful I'd warned them. They should've scurried far away and saved their lives. But they were slowly approaching, their weapons drawn. "Look, I'm not your enemy."

The yellow-haired man said, "You know, one of the burnt lands near here was said to have a survivor, a long, long time ago. But after that long . . . it's not like they could be fully human anymore. At least, something must have changed for them to betray their own kind."

"I am human," I said. *Burnt lands.* That was the term for the human lands bordering the Permafrost that had been raided until nothing was left. My home was now a burnt land.

The dark-skinned man eased a hunting knife from his boots. "You don't look very human," he said, creeping forward.

I pointed the bow to him. "Tell me about this burnt land where there was a survivor. Was the village called Elvenhule?"

He nodded slowly. Movement startled me from the corner of my eyes as the other men inched even closer. The gleam of an axe caught my vision, and I snarled, ducking out of the way before it could come crashing into my skull. Red filled my mind, and I let loose an arrow, only to realize too late I was shooting at a man I'd been trying to save. *But they challenged you,* a voice said. *They want to kill you.*

The man fell to his knees, grabbing at the arrow in his gut. Not a clean shot. I could've done much better if I had really tried. It would kill him all the same.

"Where is the village—where is what was left of it?" I shouted. "Tell me!"

"Two days hard riding south and another three days southeast," Thorsten said. "But you'll never get there. It's not like any human would accept you."

The yellow-haired man nodded. "You've lost yourself. This long in the Permafrost, you must have become savage to survive. You're nothing anymore. You'll never be human again. You're confused, violent, *mixed* with everything unholy. It's sickening, but what can you expect from those creatures?"

"You're better off dead, really."

In an instant I recognized the subtle shift that came when someone gripped their weapon to go for the kill, and I loosed an arrow shaft straight into one of the men's chests.

They came forward, and I forgot they were human; gods compared to the monsters I'd lived with for so long. I forgot about my fears and my hatred. I forgot about turning into a goblin. All I knew was that a threat was in front of me. Something wanted to harm me. I would *not* let it.

The man with the knife lunged as Thorsten jumped at me from the other side. I knocked one of them back with the bow, trying to give myself room enough to grab my own axe. *Cursed long-range weapons.*

I kicked out at Thorsten's knees and he crumpled to the ground, pain clear on his face. He grabbed the edge of my cloak and pulled me down with him until we were grappling on the forest floor. I let loose another arrow as the man I'd knocked back struggled to his feet; the satisfying sound of metal sliding through flesh told me I'd hit my mark. Above me, an axe glinted in the morning sun, and I braced myself for when the steel hit my flesh.

It never did.

The yellow-haired man froze in mid-swing, shock plain on his face at the arrow sticking out from his chest. With his free hand, he scratched at the wound before falling to his knees. Behind him stood Soren, his white hair in disarray, his lilac eyes filled with a fury I'd never seen before. Faster than light, another arrow hit the dark-skinned man and passed clean through his skull. Soren took me in for a second before turning his scorching gaze to Thorsten, who untangled himself from me immediately. Power spilled from Soren's limbs, forming around him like a cloud. The strength crushed the breath from my chest as he stalked forward. As he went, he passed the yellow-haired man and, with a clawed hand, ripped out his throat.

Soren jerked his chin to the side, motioning me to move away. I did, grabbing my weapons and squeezing them to stop the shaking in my hands. *They tried to kill me. I'm one of them. I'm human! They tried to kill me. They thought I was a monster.* But I was like them. I tried to warn them.

Thorsten let out a cry of pain as Soren stepped on his broken knee. "Now, I don't normally toy with prey before I kill it," he said as the man moaned. Using his foot to turn the man over, he gave Thorsten a swift kick in the ribs. The sickening crunch was followed by a low moan. "I'm a civilized creature, after all." Another kick to the ribs. "But I feel like this situation deserves an exception." Soren pressed his boot hard on the man's hand. "Because you looked like you were interested in killing someone I'm fond of," he said, circling Thorsten before crushing his other hand under his boot. "I can't imagine why, knowing the retribution. And she was so nice to you too."

Thorsten spat red, his voice alight with pain and anger. "Someone you're fond of? Disgusting. Maybe she's not the only one messed up inside." His gaze rested on mine. "There ain't no going back to where you've been, girl! You've been corrupted. You set one foot in a town, and they'll be on you like hounds. They'll *know*! It's not natural for someone to survive as long as you! Not natural, not at all!"

Coldness spread through my bones. Soren's gaze flitted to

me. He looked like he was trying to tell me something, but I couldn't read his eyes.

Then he turned his gaze away to look at the broken man on the ground. "I protect my own," he said simply, and with a heavy step, he broke the man's neck.

The howling wind was the only noise for a few long minutes. I took a second to catch my breath before collecting the arrows I'd shot. Soren did the same. I forced myself not to look at him, not to talk to him, not to think about him. *I protect my own.* The scar on my arm from where he'd first performed a bind curse burned. *I protect my own.*

Anger rose inside me like an earthquake. I wasn't human enough. I had been away too long. This was my fate, and it was all *his* fault. If he hadn't singled me out, I would've died. I would've been happy dying and returning to my family in the afterlife. Even if he'd decided to kill me the day Lydian threw me at his feet, like he should've, then I'd be happier. I'd be with my family, feasting eternally. There'd be no more coldness, no more pain, no more bitterness and rage and shame threatening to overflow every single day. Instead, I was here, stuck, becoming a monster.

This was all *his* fault.

"Are you all right, Janneke?" he asked. "We need to get back to the others."

I gritted my teeth. "No," I said. "No, I am *not* all right. I will *never* be all right."

Soren raised an eyebrow, confusion clouding his features. Did he expect me to thank him?

"You should've killed me," I said, as the anger bubbled up

to my lips. "You should've killed me when Lydian threw me at your feet. But you didn't. Was I some experiment for you? Someone who survived when no one else did? Did you want to see how far you could push me? How far you could make me go until I snapped? Everything you've done, you say you want to help, but all you want is to fuel some twisted type of amusement your kind love so much. He's right. You're sick. Protecting me, keeping me from killing myself, as you say, for what? Because I amuse you? You're disgusting. You—you—you—" I stopped, the intense emotions jumbling the words to garbled mush.

Soren was quiet. "You're wrong," he said. "I've never once delighted in seeing your pain. I've never once thought of hurting you."

"Liar!" I spat.

"I can't lie." He stepped forward. "All I've done, I've done because I care for you."

I took a step back, then another, and then another. "Don't get any closer to me." My voice shook. "You ruined me. You *ruined* me. I will never be the same again." It hurt now, knowing this. I was surprised my body was still whole; the aching was so strong I was sure I'd split in half. The mangled spot where my right breast should've been began to sting, and every other scar on my body burned with the pain of knowing how far I'd gone.

"Come back with me, Janneke." Soren's voice was soft, almost pleading. "Come back with me, you'll feel better soon."

I took another step backward. "No. Never."

"Janneke." He came forward with his hand outstretched.

"Come on, Janneke. You don't feel well. You're shaking. Let me help you, let me talk to you. Trust me, please. I can *help*."

I shook my head. "No." *He can't make the hurting stop.* He couldn't. Not when I was splitting apart.

"If you go, I can't protect you from the others."

"That's exactly what I want," I snapped, and turned, racing away into the tundra.

7

BIRTH

I RAN UNTIL the breath burned inside my lungs. The world whipped around me in streams of gray and blue and white. My eyes stung with the tears I was fighting to hold back.

I needed to leave. I needed to get out of here. *I'm a monster. I'm a monster.* The words echoed again and again in my head. If it wasn't natural for me to have lived this long, then what if something was wrong with me—what if I had been unnatural before I even lived in the Permafrost?

My father always called me his little thinker. As a child, I could worm my way out of any situation with whatever means necessary. He would take me to the market because I could haggle down prices and barter better than anyone he knew. If I fought against the other men, I could use their words against them to make them look a fool. I noticed more than others. Being shrewd and resourceful helped me win the hunting games alongside the men, and those skills served me well in the Permafrost. Sometimes the other men would be angry, but my father would only laugh and exclaim that I didn't take after him just in looks, but in brains too.

Just because you're clever doesn't mean something is wrong *with you*, I thought as I stopped to catch my breath. Even now, I could feel the pull of the bond between Soren and me slowly bringing me back to the Permafrost. My skin itched, knowing that we were bound by blood; even if I scrubbed myself all the way down to the bone, I would never get rid of that tainted feeling.

I turned and punched a skeleton tree. My hand cracked against the bark, and a shower of snow fell off the branches. I hit it again and again until my knuckles and the tree were smeared with blood. They stung like mad, but it gave me a release sweeter than honey.

I sank to my knees, my head in my hands. Wandering alone in the Permafrost was death—even without the hundreds of goblins currently out for blood. If I managed to stay alive by myself, it would be out of dumb luck, one thing I put zero stock in. And I couldn't cross the boundary without Soren crossing first; even if he *did,* he would feel me. I still wasn't goblin enough for the spell he put on me to break by its own accord. I was goblin enough for humans to notice, though. A small part of me withered and died. I'd nursed the hope of escaping, of being *free* back in some human town far, far away. But if these men could tell I was goblin-like, others would too. Thorsten was right; they'd be on me like hounds.

So, I was a monster, like them. There was a nagging inside of me that argued that Soren had *saved* me. That it was the humans—the ones who were supposed to be good—who tried to kill me. I remembered the fury blazing in Soren's eyes as he attacked the men. That was because they were hurting *me,* not a piece of property that he owned. He reached out his hand because he was worried about *me.* And could I deny that even when running away, part of me worried about him with Elvira, about what might happen if the vicious she-goblin fought him? Could any part of me deny that I couldn't picture Rekke as anything other than being sweet and innocent as any child despite her heritage? I couldn't. Just like I couldn't deny that despite the war going on in my head and the urge to cross the border back into the world of humans, I couldn't see my life there anymore.

Running now, miles away from the Permafrost and with the Hunt in full swing, would kill me. Standing, I balled my hands into fists and forced myself to breathe evenly. As much as it killed me, I had only one rational choice of action. I sighed and started back, hoping I could catch up before they got too far.

WHEN I GOT back to the campsite, I was mildly surprised to see Soren and the other two goblins still there, talking among themselves. They hadn't left me alone in the Permafrost after all.

As I stepped through the bracken, Soren caught my eye. He raised an eyebrow but said nothing.

Rekke beamed when she saw me. "See? I *told* you she probably got lost following that lead. You should be more careful, Janneke. What if they'd actually been here still?"

"Yes," Elvira said. "She should be more careful. Soren wouldn't want to lose his protégé."

Soren shot a warning glance at Elvira. "Well, considering we found another body with its guts smeared across the forest floor, and the scent trail *and* power trail died after that, I'd say she's fine."

You don't need to cover for me. Both of you know where I was. I don't care if Rekke knows. I don't care if that brings shame upon you. I kept my mouth shut, though. I might start screaming if I did otherwise.

Panic pawed at the ground when he saw me, his eagerness spilling through my limbs. I grabbed his bridle roughly, pulling his head down. "Not long ago you thought of escaping," I muttered.

If he understood me, he didn't show it, only jerking his head back. I mounted him and waited for Soren to take the lead. Surprisingly, he stayed back, allowing Elvira and Rekke to go forward. Shock was plain on Rekke's face; I figured this was the first time she had the honor of riding before a goblin such as Soren. Elvira hid her thoughts better, but I could still see through to the surprise underneath her icy mask. Obviously, she hadn't expected Soren to give up the lead any time soon.

I kicked Panic into a canter and started after them, not bothering to let Soren catch up with me. I didn't want to hear whatever he had to say. I wasn't ready—close, but not quite. His eyes burned on the back of my neck, never leaving my body as our horses ran the twisted route the silver prey line took. The silver line turned sharply away from the border of the Permafrost, plunging deep into the west of the territory.

I'd never been to the lands west of the Erlking's domain, so when warm air hit my skin, at first I thought it was my imagination. The hot air hung heavy with humidity like a hazy summer day. The grasses and trees surrounding our path were burnt black by lightning strikes and charred with ash. The scent of burning lingered in the air.

Soon the air weighed heavy in my lungs as the smothering heat covered me. Panic's laboring breath grew heavier with each stride, until I was forced to let him go at a slower pace.

"We're in the Fire Bog." I jumped as Soren spoke from beside me.

I grunted something unintelligible, unwilling to start an actual conversation.

As usual, Soren's abysmal social skills didn't manage to pick up the message. "You came back. I knew you would."

"I don't want to talk about it."

"I need to tell you something," he said, nudging his steed closer to me.

I recoiled. "I don't want to talk to you, or hear you gloat about being right, or listen to you try to explain how this is all for my benefit, or *anything*. If you try, I swear I'll take my axe to you, you lilac-eyed bastard." I spat the words out venomously, the anger and hate, for Soren, for myself, for the accusing thoughts in my head, for everything, begging to be let out. "I don't care that you saved my life! It doesn't make you any better. You're a monster, you all are."

Soren growled low in his throat. "What exactly is a monster to you, Janneke? You hunt down a doe, and she believes you're a monster with her dying breath. A dog kills a rabbit and a mountain lion kills the dog. Which is the monster there?" He jerked his head to where Rekke rode. "Is she a monster because she's on the Hunt, or is Elvira, because she's trying to kill her? Or are the monsters the ones who tried to slay you for attempting to save their lives? What *exactly* is a monster?"

A shadow of doubt flickered across my face, but I said nothing, instead looking away from him.

"My point is we're all monsters to someone or something by some definition. It's the context of the situation that matters." His eyes rested on mine as the gnawing feeling from before grew in the pit of my stomach. There was a beat of silence before he continued. "You know I'm right. I can see your jaw clenching. You always do that when you don't want to admit you're wrong."

I breathed out hard and slowly unclenched my jaw. "Do not."

"Do too." A challenging look sparkled in his eyes.

"Not."

"Too."

"I do *not.*" I felt my lips beginning to twitch into a smile and set my jaw hard, adamant that I would not prove him right.

"You're literally doing it *right now,*" he cried out, causing Elvira and Rekke to look at us strangely.

"You're making it really hard to continue being angry," I said, shaking my head.

"I'm irresistible." He said the words so seriously that I couldn't help but give an unladylike snort of laughter.

"Insufferable, more like." I rolled my eyes.

"I actually resent that." A smirk played on Soren's lips. "You know what they say about those who protest too much . . ."

I was saved from responding when we met up with Elvira and Rekke. Elvira's snow cat was pawing the ground, leaving dark furrows in the earth. A harsh smell churned in the air; I crinkled my nose. Rekke was giving me a knowing grin from where she sat on her horse and all-but-mouthing, *I told you so.*

"What is it?" I turned away from her, feeling my face heat up.

Elvira turned her tense body toward me. "Something is off. Can you smell the air?"

"I smell it," I said. The strong sulfur-like stench was hard to ignore now. My eyes were stinging and watering while Panic flattened his ears and snorted. "Do you know what it is?"

Elvira shook her head and anxiety flashed across her face. "No."

There was a muffled thump as Soren dropped to the ground and put his ear against the mud. He listened, then let out an agonizing hiss, jerking back from the ground.

"Go!" he yelled, as he climbed onto his horse and kicked it forward.

"What is it?" I asked.

An odd sucking sound emitted from the ground below us as sulfurous clouds blotted out my vision. Panic whinnied in alarm as I urged him toward Soren and Elvira's distancing figures. Rekke raced next to me, her small, lithe body crouched forward on her stallion. She urged him ahead with a hushed voice, but I could hear her panic breaking free. The sucking sound grew louder and louder, catching up to us, and I looked back in horror to see the ground collapsing behind us and dropping away into a never-ending abyss.

Yellow gas spewed from bubbles in the bog mud, emitting a toxic odor that had me swaying in my saddle. I gripped the reins harder, wrapping them around one of my hands. "Go, Panic! Go!"

Panic charged ahead, leaving Rekke in the dust. The tremors from the sinking ground boomed like thunder, and the rising mist burned my skin like acid. I screamed as the skin on my arms burned and blistered, as my vision turned black and I swayed in my saddle. Soren looked behind him, eyes wide as they locked onto mine.

My arm throbbed, the bright red skin burning, swelling, as bulbous blisters spread across its length. I gritted my teeth in pain as they burst and sickly yellow pus spilled down my arm. The air around me was filled with yellow, choking gas, and the sucking sound was getting louder, approaching us with blinding speed.

I spurred Panic onward, shouting encouragement. The pounding of his hooves was loud as crackling lightning, crashing like thunder while he raced against the crumbling ground. His breath wheezed in my ear as he pushed himself forward. Soon we were neck and neck with Elvira and her giant snow cat. Soren raced ahead of us, Terror heaving with each and every breath.

From beside me Elvira's snow cat snapped at Panic, and the horse bucked up in fright. I held on, grateful my arm was wrapped in the reins, and urged Panic to move again as he re-gained his footing.

"Control your animal!" I shouted to Elvira, barely able to hear my own voice above the sound of the sinking ground.

Elvira snarled at me, baring her teeth. Then she rammed her cat into the legs of my horse. Panic stumbled, fighting hard to keep his instincts under control. His thoughts echoed in my ears: This cat would kill him. This cat would eat him. It was a predator and he was its prey. The horse's wild heartbeat raced as he realized death was not just behind him, but around him too.

The glint of metal caught my eye as a short sword swung toward me. Almost automatically, I had my axe out and caught the edge of the blade against the wood. The maddening gleam in Elvira's eyes grew brighter as she hissed and brought her sword down again. I veered Panic away, getting dangerously close to the sucking mud.

She's trying to kill me. Despite the thought, I was strangely calm. So what if she was? This was the Hunt. I heaved my axe into the air and swerved closer to her snow cat, bringing the blade down on her animal's haunches. It shrieked in pain as it stumbled and gave me the opening I needed. Urging Panic forward, I rode ahead into the mist.

BY THE TIME we had escaped the Fire Bog, the agonizing blisters on my arm were dripping pus, the reddened skin flaking off to expose soft, sensitive flesh underneath. I clenched my jaw as even the slightest brush of air sent a wave of pain so terrible it was as if I'd stuck my arm in an inferno. Behind me,

Elvira's glare burned a hole in the back of my neck, and her snow cat growled in pain.

The silver trail of the stag was gone, but if I closed my eyes, I could hear the animal's heartbeat thrumming in my ears. Somewhere deep in my core, power resonated; the prey line *had* to be close. Darkness was falling swiftly, though, and we needed to set up camp and do something about our injuries. The stag could wait. It had to.

Soren stopped by a small half-frozen stream. The water was running at a slow enough pace that it wouldn't bother the goblins. I shifted in the saddle and lowered myself to the ground, cringing as sharp pain shot up my arms. The magic of the Permafrost would heal the goblins by the end of the night, but as I was still a human, the painful burns would heal naturally or not at all.

Doubt formed a pit in my stomach. I could barely manage the pain while riding. Even now, my flesh burned like it was melting off the bone. When the time came to shoot an arrow or wield my axe, I would barely be able to stand it.

I needed to survive. I *had to* survive.

Even if I survived the Hunt, even if I escaped, I had nowhere to go. The scene from this morning played through my head again as my heart crashed in my chest. The humans didn't accept me; I tried to run and I failed. I couldn't even convince other humans that I was on their side.

There's something wrong with you. You're not natural. I cringed. *You don't want to die.* The thought was like a punch knocking the breath out of me. No. I didn't want to die. There was a gnawing feeling in the pit of my stomach growing ever stronger. I didn't want to die—I wanted to *live*. To run, be free, feel the wind in my hair, the exhilaration of the Hunt, and the adrenaline coursing through my veins. Maybe I didn't know exactly *why* I wanted to live or *what* my place in this world would be, but I knew I *needed* to live as much as the trees needed sun and the earth needed rain.

But I don't want to be goblin. And if I didn't become goblin— if I didn't accept the cruel ways of this world—then death would be lurking around every corner. Unless I found a way in between.

The resolve that was as strong as steel right before the Hunt—that I would escape and forbid myself from growing close to my enemies, *becoming* them—was cracking. If I let down my guard, the memory of Soren's hand stroking my shoulder and the warmth of his body lulled me into relaxation. The memories of conversations we'd had made my chest fill with laughter. If I tried to reason with myself, all I could think of was the instinct that kept me alive when the men attacked— if death *truly* was something I'd prefer to living in the Permafrost, then I would've taken it when it was offered to me. Soren's words about monsters bounced around in my head, stinging like hornets because I knew they were true. Despite what I grew up believing, despite what my father taught me, despite the rigid rules by which I had been raised, telling me anything so unnatural was wrong.

Frustration brewed inside me like a storm. I couldn't understand. I needed to be alone. I needed to think.

Unaware of the war going on inside me, Soren and Elvira were debating whether to go for a swim.

"The water should help wash off the effects of the smoke," Soren said. "Better to get it out of our clothes too."

Elvira's lip curled. "I'd rather not get wet."

"Scared of a little water? It's barely even running," Soren taunted.

"Scared?" she scoffed. "I'd rather not be naked in a river while others are out there hungry for our blood. We also leave trails, you know. Stopping would be foolish."

"No," Soren said. "What would be *foolish* is trying to cross the Fire Bog after we ran through it. What would be *foolish* is letting the smoke and debris from it stay on our body and possibly harm us more. The Permafrost heals, but only just."

"*I* think it's a good idea," Rekke butted in, and immediately began stripping off her clothes. Without a moment's hesitation, she jumped into the lazy river. "Come on! Don't be so scared!"

Soren smirked at Elvira as the older she-goblin grumbled under her breath.

The sight of Soren as he undressed created heat that spread through my body and lingered like a hard ball in the pit of my belly. "I'm going a bit downstream," I said, forcing my voice to be steady.

"Awww," Rekke said. "Janneke's shy!"

Elvira snorted as she leaned against the riverbank, her bare, perfect breasts breaking the surface of the water. Envy choked away any retort I had. I might have hated the she-goblin and her beauty might've been an illusion, but it was a *damn good* illusion.

I caught a flash of Soren's pale, naked body out of the corner of my eye. His chest was hard with muscle and scar tissue. I forbade myself from looking any lower. "Janneke can bathe wherever she wants to." Was it me or did he sound amused?

Fighting off embarrassment, I stalked downstream. If Elvira was right and some goblin was going to slaughter them, at least I'd know by the blood in the water. It was blissfully cool against my burning skin, turning the pain in my arms from agonizing to tolerable. I dove down, relishing the sharp coldness. Before everything, when I was still normal, I used to swim all the time on the fishing docks that were a half hour's ride from my village. But now, I was among creatures who couldn't stand the idea of running water, and setting the village record for breath-holding was the least of my concerns when we could literally be killed any time.

I dove into a deep patch of the river, darkness surrounding me with walls of stone as the current rushed to pull me under. I could live among these people and try to make whatever bonds I had blossom. I could let Soren grow closer to me than he already was, become a true friend to Rekke, hunt the stag, and revel in my own power. Or I could run away. If I ran and managed to live among humans again, then I might have to forsake hunting forever. I would never feel the forest beneath my feet or hear my heart roaring in my ears during a successful hunt. I would never feel the reassuring weight of a taut bowstring or the smooth sides of an axe. If I was goblin enough for men to notice, I might secrete power without realizing it. Any Permafrost creature might be able to find me. Any goblin surely would; my power would mark up the town I settled in like a flare. I didn't have the desire to be anything but a huntress, a shieldmaiden, but other than death, in the human world my only option would be to leave life as a huntress behind.

I had lied to myself over and over and over again. Maybe it was time to stop trying to convince myself of things I knew weren't true. Maybe it was time to start living for me, accepting the feelings I felt, and unshackle the burden of my past.

By now, my lungs were crying out for air, and I burst onto the surface of the water, gasping. As I cleared the water from my eyes, I found myself almost nose-to-nose with Soren, who was sitting on the riverbank.

Before I could control myself, I shrieked. "What the Hel do you think you're doing?" *Gods be damned. Can I ever be alone?* At least he was clothed. The thought of his naked body sent shivers down my spine in an unfamiliar, but oddly pleasant way. I was not used to that reaction and wanted to squash it.

He looked unabashed. "Waiting for you to emerge. You can hold your breath for a long time."

"How long were you crouching there?" I asked, flustered.

"At least a minute, maybe two," Soren said.

"And you didn't think, 'Gee, maybe crouching like this by the riverbank is going to scare the life out of Janneke!'?"

"You're alive, aren't you?" he said. "So, where did you learn to hold your breath for so long?"

At the moment, I was gasping, but it had more to do with Soren attempting to frighten me than the dive. "I used to dive . . . before."

"You must've been very good at it," he said.

"Yes I—" I froze. Maybe *he* wasn't naked, but *I* was. Humiliation burned through me, and I sank back down until the water came up to my collarbone.

Soren eyed me like I was being ridiculous. I guess from his perspective, perhaps I was. Considering he and the others had stripped down in front of each other with no hesitation, I doubted nudity bothered goblinkind as much as it bothered me.

"Do your arms hurt?" he asked.

I brought them out of the water, careful to keep my chest from being seen. It was stupid, I knew. He'd already seen the mass of scar tissue, the bits of skin that snagged and curled grotesquely where Lydian had dug in his fingernails and sunk his teeth and burned with a white-hot brand, but I couldn't bear the idea of showing them to the world again.

"Yes, they hurt," I said, glaring at the blisters and burned flesh. From the sight of Soren's smooth, pale skin, he must have already healed. That had to be the single good thing about being a goblin: As long as they weren't near a swift-moving source of water and were inside the boundaries of the Permafrost, the spirit of the landscape healed them.

"May I see?" he asked.

"Why?"

He tilted his head to the side. "You don't trust me?"

"Must I answer that, again?" I asked, then sighed. "Fine." He took one injured arm in his hand and brought it close to his lips. I jerked back. "What are you doing?"

Soren let out an irritated hiss. "Just wait." Then, he twisted my arm to the lightly colored underside and brought his lips to the vein in my elbow. As he pressed his teeth to the skin with the slightest of pressure, his humanlike features melted away. His eyes grew slanted and his face became gaunt, the tips of pointed ears peaked out of the cascade of white hair, and the length of his canines grew until they pierced through my arm. I shivered as a chill went through me from my neck all the way to my belly. When he pulled away, the burns on my arm had gone.

I stared at my now-healed arm. No scars—nothing remained as a reminder of the Fire Bog. The light-brown skin was as smooth as it had been this morning. While I marveled, he took my other arm and did the same.

When he was done, he sat back and admired his handiwork and looked utterly satisfied with himself.

"I didn't know you could do that," I said.

"We're all full of surprises," he replied. "You don't know everything about me."

"You don't know everything about me either."

He chuckled. "I bet I know more than you think."

I rolled my eyes. "While this conversation is lovely, some of us need to get out of the water and change. Go back to the others."

"Is that an order?" he asked, his voice almost teasing.

I glowered at him in response. "Go."

He stood, brushing the frost-covered dirt off his leggings, and turned away, heading toward a stunted tree in the distance. "Meet me by the lightning-struck tree after you're dressed. We need to talk."

Muttering some choice words under my breath, I slid out of the water and wrung my hair dry, then quickly dressed. The warm woolen wraps felt good against my legs, and the thick furs lining my tunic took the chill from my body. My hair, which I'd taken out of its braids, was plastered against my face and neck, dripping water down the length of my back. I tied it up in a high ponytail, hoping it would keep the worst of the water away.

Dread rose slowly as I glanced to where Soren went. In a crowd of goblins in the Erlking's hall, or in his manor's archery range shooting at corpses, it was easy to be around him. But as soon as the others disappeared, everything changed. Maybe it was the infuriating way he'd tilt his head like a child acting at innocence, maybe it was how what he said needled me into long conversations where we shot words at each other like arrows. I was good at snark and being witty. I was not good at *talking*.

So I gathered myself, composed my features into an emotionless mask, and joined Soren by the stunted tree.

He lounged among the roots as if they were his own personal throne. The ancient tree was blackened by lightning, and its skeleton arms reached up toward the sky. The sun-bleached white roots covered the ground around us, growing over each other and twining together like a mass of snakes. I sat a few feet away from him and waited.

He turned so his body was facing mine. The animalistic features of his face had returned to their natural, eerie, too-perfect-to-be-human look. "Do you think something is wrong with you, Janneke?"

I almost choked, the mask I'd composed shattering into a million shards. "Is this some kind of sick joke?" Of course something was *wrong* with me. I was sitting here next to the world's most deadly predator, hunting a sacred stag in the middle of the Permafrost, after one hundred years of servitude that should've left me dead. I was the *epitome* of wrongness.

"I'm serious," Soren said, and from the glint in his eyes, I believed him.

"Yes."

"Even before you were brought to the Permafrost?"

I thought about it. Growing up, I watched my sisters get married and have babies, one by one, while I ran wild in the woods and learned to use a bow and axe like they were extensions of myself. When the young men of the village erected courtship poles outside the huts of the girls they admired every midsummer, I ran out to see if one would have my name carved into the side, until one year my father took me aside and told me that would never happen. When stories were told by a brilliant fire in the middle of the long winters, I was forced to sit far at the edge away from the others as if somehow my very presence was tainted. For the longest time, I thought it was just because of the role I played in my family—the seventh daughter raised to be a son in the absence of male offspring. But maybe it was more.

"Yes," I finally said.

"Do you know how old I am?"

"Is there a point to this?"

"Just answer the question." He sighed in frustration.

"Relatively young, for a goblin in your position," I said. "Not yet a millennium."

"Seven-hundred and sixty-eight." He paused, his eyebrows furrowing. "I think. It gets a little fuzzy after a while."

"And?" Impatience crept into my voice. The sun had almost sunk beyond the horizon, letting the sky bleed crimson red. Soon the temperature would drop, and I didn't want to be without my bedroll and bearskin cloak when it did. I would've frozen to death last night if it weren't for them. *And for Soren.* I banished that thought from my head before it could take root and grow.

"One hundred and eighteen years ago, before I succeeded my father as lord, I was on a hunting mission near the edge of the Permafrost. It was just me, enjoying myself before I had to go back to court and deal with the numerous assassination attempts being thrown my way by various relatives. I was after a snow cat, the biggest thing you ever saw, and I wandered a bit too close to the border between realms."

Something about his voice made the hair on the nape of my neck rise, but I forced the unease down and nodded. "Go on."

"There was a woman near there with a man, her husband, or so I assume. She was pregnant, though I'd say she easily had two months left at the least. I'm not sure what they were doing so close to the border either. I probably could've killed them and added to my hunt. I debated it, but before I could decide anything, she started screaming something awful. The man was trying very hard to keep calm, but I could smell the fear on him." He paused, waiting to see how I took that.

My mind felt strangely numb. "And what happened?"

"To spare you the gory details, she collapsed on the border

and gave birth. The current between the realms probably didn't help the birth; but even so, soon enough a child slid out from between her legs—a girl. It wasn't crying or, I suppose, breathing, and its body was turning blue." He leaned forward to rest his elbows on his knees and waited a minute, his eyes catching mine as the purple reflected the fire in the sky. "They placed the child on the ground so they could hold each other and mourn the dead girl . . . but as the girl touched the earth, she started to scream louder than I would've thought possible."

Beads of blood trickled down my skin, and I released my arm from the grip I hadn't known I was holding. My heart was hammering in my chest, thrumming away like a bat trying to escape a trap, millions of thoughts rushing in my head, all too fast for me to understand them. The numbness that was spreading through my body covered me like a blanket, shielding me from the conclusion that was right in front of me.

"Three years later, I found myself at the same spot," Soren continued after a moment. His voice was quiet, as if he thought any loud sounds would scare me away. "And I saw her again, the girl. I'm not sure how I knew it was her, but I did. I'd gotten into a fight with some young lordling my father had sent to kill me and was dragging his body across the border so he would be denied a peaceful afterlife. She was standing there, looking more inquisitive than a toddler had the right to. In all honesty, she looked older. Her limbs were leaner, her eyes possessed a certain type of cunning. She came up to the dead body and examined the wounds, then looked up at my bloody sword and *touched* the metal, giggling as her hand was smeared with blood. That's when I knew this human child had the Permafrost in her blood, and the human world would never satisfy her. Not for long, anyway."

I closed my eyes. "Please don't continue. Please don't."

A soft sigh passed through his lips. "I waited until it was dark, and in my impulsiveness, I tracked her back to her hut. I wasn't sure what I was planning to do once I had her—again, it was impulse, almost instinct I acted on—but I lifted her from where she lay and was about to leave when the father woke. I could've killed him, but if I did, I probably would've ended up slaughtering the whole village and I felt like it wasn't worth the effort, so I listened to him plead. He begged for the child's life, and though I said I had no intention of killing her, he begged still. We made a deal. I would wait until she became an adult, let her live among the people of her birth, and then I would come and I would take her home."

I covered my ears, screaming. "Stop! Just stop! Don't say anymore! *Stop!*" My body shook violently, and I dug my nails into my cheeks until they drew blood.

There was the rustle of boots against the ground, and his strong hands wrapped around my wrists, restraining them so they could cause no harm.

"Janneke." His eyes searched my face, and I turned away, squeezing my own shut. *No. No. No. He's lying. He's lying. No. That never happened. He's lying. He's lying. Father wouldn't— Mother—no. No.* The world spun until I couldn't tell which way was up or down. The sky collapsed inward, crushing everything I knew to be true. The world fell apart in front of me, and I had no way to stop it, only the feeling of grim certainty as my life turned to ashes and scattered in the breeze.

"Janneke," he said again, his voice almost a whisper, "it's all right. You're right where you're supposed to be."

8

RAPPROCHEMENT

THE WIND BLOWING through the trees was the only sound I heard while I digested what Soren had told me. Every cell in my body ached to reject it and prove it wasn't true, but I knew he wasn't lying. The revelation had me shivering.

My mind whirled with the memories of the past; bits of stories that at first had no meaning now held all the answers in the world. The way the other villagers looked at me, the scornful whispers as I streaked by them with a bow in my arms, reveling in the feeling of solitude in the freezing forest, the ambitious drive that pushed me to be faster, stronger, smarter, *better* than all the others, the things my father told me when I was no higher than his knee about the Permafrost and the despicable creatures who lived there. Was it his ultimate goal to poison my mind against my eventual home? Somehow, I thought it was. It *all* made sense except for one thing that sank in my stomach like a large stone.

"You didn't . . ." I could scarcely get the words out, ". . . have anything to do with the raid on my village, did you?" I fought the dread threatening to swallow me as I waited for his answer.

Soren's eyes shone brightly with concern.

"No," he said, and my heart lifted in relief. "During the time of Lydian's raid, I was busy finalizing my lordship."

I nodded. It was no secret that younger goblins usurped and killed their sires when they became strong enough to rule in their place. If there were goblins loyal to their old lord, they were dealt with just like the castellan was all those years ago. For a young goblin, the path to power was always stained with blood.

"When I came to the village, it was already in ruins," he continued. "You can imagine my surprise when Lydian threw you in front of my feet."

I looked away as Soren searched my face. I didn't want him to see the fear there.

"I don't know all of what he did to you, Janneke, and I'm not going to force you to tell me before you're ready to," he said softly. "But I know some of it, and I know I will never let him touch you again. What's more is I know you won't either."

I took a deep breath, pulling my arms around myself. The temperature had dropped to freezing, the sun all the way below the horizon. In the dark, moonless sky, the trees stretched up like fingers trying to steal the stars. It was so quiet, so still, nothing but the sound of the breath in our lungs.

"So why didn't you tell me? Why was I like any other thrall? Why for the past one hundred years was I in servitude— *enslaved* by you?" I asked, the question burning inside of me.

"In all that time you could've said something! Why didn't you?"

Soren shook his head. "That wasn't part of the original plan. But the original plan was foiled when Lydian captured you. You know some of the laws of winter, about fighting and gift-giving. Another one is that a gift can only be used according to its nature, unless the gift fundamentally changes. In the spirit of the Permafrost, Lydian gave you to me as a thrall, thinking I would kill you. Obviously, that backfired. I thought I could make your nature change and keep everything to myself. If things had worked out the way I planned, then I would have tried to go down the path of a changeling anyway." He sighed. "And . . . I was scared. I told myself I'd say something when you were healed, but then I didn't. I kept promising myself 'next year' but the longer I said nothing, the harder it was to tell you the truth. I wanted to win your trust, and I was afraid the truth would break it."

I swallowed, hoping to dislodge the lump forming in my throat. "A hundred years and you couldn't take ten minutes of bravery?"

Soren looked down at his feet, something similar to shame and a hint of humility in his body language. "I know that while I never thought of you as truly enslaved or treated you like that, my lack of communication, my fear of telling you the truth, left you afraid and imprisoned, like you were trapped in Hel. Lydian might have captured you and the law of winter might've imprisoned you, but I—I did nothing to change it. I continued it. That was wrong, and I know none of this can make up for the past, but I am so sorry."

He was right. Nothing he said could make up for the years passed by, but at the same time a fissure in my soul mended and knitted back together like yarn. It was a crack I'd never realized was there, but as the weight lifted off my chest I breathed my first truly unburdened breath in a long, long time.

The wind howled around us. I swore the roots we sat on were coming to life. The Permafrost was full of the sounds of night: hooting owls, the calls of wolves, and the far-off cries of fighting goblins. My mind wandered back to the camp where Rekke and Elvira were. I wouldn't put it past Elvira to be plotting another way to kill me. After I injured her snow cat, she looked mad enough to disembowel me right there and then.

I looked down at my hands. The tawny-colored palms were full of calluses and old scars. Hard muscle shaped my arms and shoulders, rippling down my sides. Was this the body of a human or a goblin? Did these hands, which could bear the razor-sharp bowstring of a Permafrost bow without bleeding, belong among other humans who would never understand them? Somehow, I didn't think it mattered anymore.

Pain burst deep in my chest at the thought of my family: my mother, my father, and my sisters. They must've known my fate as I grew wilder by the day.

In the deepest, darkest part of my memory, my parents whispered about me by firelight and a dream of a frozen land reappeared over and over while an inhuman voice called for me.

"What are you thinking, Janneke?" Soren asked, appearing alarmed at my long silence. "What are you feeling?"

Nothing. Not horror or anger or sadness. Numbness, yes, so thick and strong it was almost painful, blocking out any type of thought, emotion, or reaction. Just a blank stare wondering if this had always been my fate and the feeling that yes, yes it probably had been.

"I don't know," I said. "I really don't."

Born on the border of the Permafrost with the coldness of the land in my blood, it made *sense*.

Soren reached out and brushed a lock of my hair back into place. The brush of his fingertips against my cheek sent a jolt of electricity down my spine, but for once it wasn't one of fear. *He thinks it's how you build trust.* I had to give him credit for trying.

"You've earned my trust," I said. "You don't need to keep trying."

"Maybe I just like touching you." The smirk was back.

"I think you're ill. You've been smiling way too much." I was only half teasing. I truly had never seen Soren smile or smirk so much in the entire hundred years I'd spent with him.

He immediately trained his features back into his signature scowl. Conversation lulled into silence for a few moments.

"Will I really turn into a goblin?" I asked.

"Your blood is laced with the same type of power as mine, so you have the blood of one, so to speak," he said. Then after a moment, he added, "But you have the heart and mind of a human. You clutch to the heart as if it's your lifeline, but you need to be one with your blood if you want to continue to survive, otherwise you'll go mad."

I took a deep breath. Continue to survive. The chanting

of the flickering flames inside me grew stronger. *Survive. Survive. Survive.*

"Then what was the point of this, of you taking me on the Hunt? Did you lie?"

"I wanted you to accept your blood and"—he paused, sharp canines biting his lower lip—"I went about it the wrong way. I should've told you the truth from the beginning, but I didn't know how. The longer I kept putting it off, the harder it was for me to tell you. I was afraid. I'm sorry."

I stilled. I didn't think Soren would ever apologize for anything. I didn't think he understood the *concept* of an apology, and here he was, apologizing for the second time in under five minutes. Maybe he *was* ill.

"What will you do now?" he asked.

"Do I have a choice?"

"Always," he promised.

"I've had illusions of choices, Soren. Not real ones."

Soren dropped his gaze again, like the guilt was holding him down. "You're right, again. I apologize; that wasn't fair of me to say. For true, this time. You will always have a choice. Every option and every path. If I break faith with thee, may the sky fall upon me, may the sea drown me, and may the earth rise up and swallow me. Until I die, so long will I keep my oath."

The air crackled as Soren finished the words of the ritual oath. "We're on even ground now, then," I said, the ghost of a smile on my lips. "So, what now?"

"As far as I see it, you could leave. Releasing you from the bind I've made would be hard. It might even kill you, which was why I thought it would be better to dissolve it over time as you embraced your nature. Assuming you survived, you could go back to the human world. You'd have to travel far away from the Permafrost, somewhere where the burnt lands are no more than just legends. With the power built up inside of you, you probably wouldn't be able to hunt again. It would attract others. But you could have a chance at a normal human life. Fall in love, raise a family, the things you wouldn't have had even back in your own village. Or . . . you could stay here . . ."

"And become a goblin, or as good as," I finished.

"There aren't many like you, Janneke. Human-hearted and goblin-blooded. I don't know which choice would make you happy and which wouldn't. I know that you'll go mad if you're torn between the worlds."

The stillness in my heart frightened me; there should've been turbulence. There should've been pain crashing down like spiked ice and despair rushing through me like sucking mud. There should've been hate and fear and rage. But instead, there was the quiet calmness of a land after surviving a strong storm.

I could leave. I could leave the Permafrost and go back to wherever I had been before here; find Elvenhule, see the remains of what was left of my family. I could find some other village, far, far away from the Permafrost, and assimilate back into human culture. Fall in love, raise a family. I could lock all the memories of the Permafrost in a corner of my mind and never let them out again.

But the heartbeat of the Permafrost was like thunder underneath my feet, and the prey lines were clear as the morning's sun. Insects began their symphony, and I could recognize each of their individual songs and hear the direwolves singing their serenade to the moonless sky. The cold air on my shoulders was a mother's caress, and the darkness in my eyes a warm, thick blanket.

This place could become my home if I let it, if I accepted the beauty, however cruel, that it possessed. If I left, I would never hunt again, much less in the near-magical way I was doing now in *the* Hunt, and I'd forget the whispers of the trees and the language of the living. If I stayed, there was a chance my humanity would slip away. It was such a thin line: happiness and comfort, spirit and safety.

"I don't know what I'll do," I said finally. "I need to think."

Soren glanced up at the dark, moonless sky. "You'll need to decide soon."

"It's more than a decision . . . I don't want to be—"

"A monster?" Soren cut me off. "Remember what I said before? We're all monsters, Janneke, in some way. Every creature is prey of something . . . or someone. That doesn't mean we're evil. Besides, I always thought that a being was only a monster when they became blinded to the outcome of their actions." He let out a small smile. "I don't think you're the type of person to forget that everything comes with a price."

"I never took you for a philosopher," I said.

His lips twitched. "I won't lie and say my kind are never monstrous. Just that we're only as monstrous as your kind are."

A chilly breeze blew against my still-wet hair, and I shuddered. "We should probably get back."

Soren nodded. "Your teeth are beginning to chatter. Besides, we don't want Elvira to think someone picked us off now, do we?"

"We've been lucky." A fight with Helka and a few humans, a race against collapsing ground, a few dead bodies—those were nothing against a full-scale fight between us and any other armed group out for our power and the stag.

But as we headed deeper and deeper into the stag's territory and farther away from the edge of the worlds, it wouldn't be long before we ran into *someone*. Not to mention sooner or later our alliance with Rekke and Elvira would break for good. There could only be one winner of this hunt.

We trudged through the darkened landscape with Soren in the lead. His eyes were stronger than mine by far, picking up little anomalies in the blackness that I couldn't see. I was silent as I chewed over my question, wondering if it was worth asking. Then I spoke.

"When are we going to double-cross Elvira and Rekke?"

Soren turned to me, and through the darkness his purple eyes glittered. "Do you think so little of me that you believe I'd betray our most honorable allies?"

I snorted. "Does that question need an answer?"

"Can you just humor me?" he groaned. "I'm trying to be sarcastic."

"That's not sarcasm."

"I can tell." The words came out in a quiet growl.

"Why do you do that?" I asked.

He frowned. "Growl? It's . . . a way to express how I'm feeling, I guess? Different tones mean different things. I was frustrated. So, I growled."

"Like a cat," I said.

"A cat?"

"Every meow means something different," I explained. "Every growl means something different. Like a cat."

Soren tipped his head to the side, looking *very much* like a confused cat. "A cat," he repeated, frowning. "I'm much more regal than a cat."

"You're as arrogant as one."

"I will pretend I didn't hear that," he said. "Also, cats aren't arrogant. They just know who's in charge. Besides, if I'm a cat, you're a dog." He smiled at the look on my face. "You'd be one of those scruffy little mutts. A hybrid of some sort, I think. You would look cute. I would even let you on the furniture. As long as you didn't shed. I hate shedding."

I blinked. There was no responding to that. Soren chuckled to himself, as we continued back toward camp. Right here and now, he definitely didn't seem like a monster. He had given me a choice. He'd given me the opportunity for my freedom. The idea was almost as painful to absorb as another goblin's power, but it was slowly sinking in. The sleeping forms of Rekke and Elvira materialized before us. I glared at the older she-goblin. Now *there* was someone I could do without.

"You don't like them?" Soren asked.

"Rekke is fine. She reminds me almost of a human. It's Elvira who bothers me," I said. "Not just because she wants to kill me either."

"You threaten her," Soren said, shrugging.

"How can *I* threaten *her*? She's more than a millennium older than me, and I don't even want to guess how many times more powerful. Then again, considering that she took Rekke on the Hunt in order to kill her, perhaps she has an inferiority complex."

He shook his head, sighing. "Rekke shouldn't be on this hunt."

"I thought you didn't trust her."

"I didn't. I thought her innocence was an act. It isn't." He scowled. "She's young. Younger than you are, even. She should still be learning with a tutor and playing games with goblins her own age." His eyes grew dark. "I've done many things and I don't regret most of them, but I can't abide those who snatch little birds from their nests and break their wings before they're even ready to fly."

My hands clenched into fists.

Soren's gaze was thoughtful. "Are you afraid?"

"No," I said. "I'm not afraid. I'm angry."

The conversation ceased as we reached the camp. Both women were fast asleep on their bedrolls, the giant snow cat resting its leopard-like spotted body against his master's. When his chest rose and fell with each breath, the wound on his flank glistened red. Rekke was curled in a tight ball, little whimpers escaping from her lips every so often. My heart hurt watching her.

"We can't do anything about it," Soren said from beside me, but reproach glittered in his eyes.

I unrolled my bedroll, placing it as far from Elvira and Rekke as I could. I wasn't going to tempt fate with the elder goblin. Panic trotted over to me, his sleepy brown eyes blinking lazily. Attached to his saddle were my bow and sheath, as well as my axe. I unhooked them, placing them where I could easily reach them in case of an emergency or assassination attempt. The horse nickered and pawed at the dry, dusty ground. I shook my head at him.

"Sorry, Panic. No grass." He flattened his ears, so I added, "I don't have anything to eat either. We'll be hungry together."

I lay on my bedroll, trying to get comfortable when the whoosh of air suggested someone was lying down beside me. My shoulders tightened. Soren was so close I could feel the warmth radiating off his skin. Like before, my body greedily sucked it up. His breath was even in his lungs like a gentle nighttime rhythm among the silent darkness.

"Give me some space," I grumbled.

Soren rolled over so he was facing me. "You know, you could eat if you wanted to."

"I don't like raw meat," I said. "It doesn't matter if I can digest it. It's gross."

"Suit yourself." *You'll cave sooner or later,* his eyes said.

I scowled and tried to get comfortable on the bedroll. The bearskin was on the other side of Soren, and if I got closer to him, I was sure I'd end up in a position like the night before. The last thing I needed was Rekke commenting on my *relationship* with Soren. "Go to sleep," Soren said softly.

My eyes closed, and I willed my body to relax, releasing muscles I hadn't known were stiff. The hard riding, the humans' attack, the sinking ground, and the revelation all were echoing in my head like the pulse of a beating drum. Icy wind blew through the trees, and I shivered, only to be covered with the thick bearskin. When I turned around to shoot Soren a glare, he lay still, feigning sleep.

"I don't need you to take care of me," I said. The barrier between us was dwindling faster than ever. I had to at least try to keep some defenses up, even if they felt futile.

Still, I wrapped the bearskin around myself and burrowed my head under its softness. The precious warmth was a godsend in this freezing place.

"Janneke," Soren whispered in the darkness.

"Yes?"

"Promise me that whatever you do, whatever you decide, you won't hurt yourself. I don't think I could live knowing you've done something like that." He rested his gaze on me, and I found myself trapped in his light eyes.

"You would get over it. After all, I'm a human."

"Is that what you think?" he asked. "Or is that just your excuse?"

I was silent.

He reached out and brushed my cheek with his thumb. I shivered, but not from fear. There was something burning deep inside of me that was beginning to make itself noticed. Something about his soft words and caresses, the strange mingle of fury and concern drew me close. Yes, the walls were crumbling and the defenses were dying, replaced by soft thoughts that told me to let him in and a burning want that desired something I didn't even understand.

An owl hooted somewhere in the distance, calling to its mate. Soren was still watching me with softness in his gaze.

The burning traveled down to my navel and stayed there. "Promise me," he whispered.

My eyelids were drooping. I was too tired to argue. Too tired to do much more than curl into a semi-comfortable position and sleep. "Fine," I said. "I promise."

For the second time, I fell asleep wrapped in his warm embrace.

AROUND ME THE forest was dark. The lush, full leaves rustled with every step I took, hiding the world around me. I ran with my bow across my back, an axe in my hand. Screaming. They were in this forest somewhere—my mother, my father, my sisters. They were here. I couldn't doubt it. I couldn't let myself believe otherwise. The smell of smoke stung my nose as I jumped over log after fallen log.

"Go get some firewood," Ma had said. "Avette needs the lodge to be warmer if her baby is going to grow strong."

My beautiful sister with her long brown hair that took on a reddish tint in the sun held her baby boy to her breast. The winter was harsher than usual, and if her milk dried up, that would be the end of him.

Those memories burned through my mind like the smoke that stung my nose and throat. One thought repeated over and over: I should've stayed. I should've stayed. I should've stayed.

I was a coward, diving into the underground river the moment I heard the battle cries. I was a coward who'd rather save her own life than die with her family. I was a coward because I knew exactly how to survive and I didn't try to bring anyone with me.

Now, alone on the bitter, broken field that used to be the vil-

lage, plumes of vile purple smoke plumed high into the air. Bile rose in my throat at the charred smell of human remains, and as I walked throughout the burnt village, I couldn't help but see bodies I recognized. Women frozen in expressions of sheer terror and pain, men dead with their weapons in their hands, their bodies covering their loved ones, children who lay with their skulls crushed in. Some still had flesh on their bodies, and the carrion crows overhead circled while they waited for their feast. Some were only scorched bone. I tripped over the growing pile of bones, hands splaying out on the head of an infant. There was just enough skin and flesh left to make out beautiful red-brown hair and dark eyes. Avette's sweet baby boy. I scrambled back, screaming, as something sharp pierced my hand. I wrapped my fingers around a bent iron nail; the only thing to survive the carnage untouched.

*The bodies around me fluttered away like ashes in the wind, until the barren field was empty. Standing before me was a white-furred stag—*the* stag—*its hooves raking across the once-fertile ground.*

A deep, burning rage came from the pit of my stomach and rooted me to the earth. "It's dead!" I screamed. "It's dead. Everything is dead, and it's not growing back! And it's your fault. You let this happen!"

The stag snorted and threw his head back, his antlers catching the beams of the sun like crystals. The light broke across the ruined ground in a pattern of rainbows.

"Don't you understand, you stupid animal?" I screamed. "This isn't supposed to be a beautiful place! It's a place where people died! It's the place that changed everything."

The stag came forward until his warm breath tickled my face.

I stared at him coldly. "What do you want from me? I can't do anything for you."

The animal looked up at me with wise dark eyes and blinked slowly, ashes catching on his white lashes. He pawed at the ground once more, and the land beneath him turned white as snow. The sweet smell of spring filled the air, and flashes of the village as it'd once been caught my eye before disappearing like the wind. He pressed his nose into my shoulder, and the ancient power flowing within him crashed down on me like an avalanche. The smells of spring and growth mixed with winter and blood; the dead and the living twining together, trees that reached up to the sky and roots that sank deep into the earth. The land slid from beneath my feet as I found myself staring at a massive ash tree. The stag backed away from me and bounded into the distance as I watched him go.

PART TWO

THE HUNTRESS

9

PANIC

THE DREAM FROM last night still haunted me as we trudged along the trail of the stag. The parched air of the Fire Bog soon turned into the cool, sharp air of the mountains. Ice glittered in the sunlight, hanging off trees, growing on rocks, and even shooting up straight from the ground. The only sound was the wind whistling between the mountain passes. No one said it out loud, but we all had the same thing in mind. With the stag's trail so thick before us, it would only be a matter of time before we ran into another hunting party. One that was *alive*.

My mouth tasted like ash. The dream was so real; almost as if my family was trying to remind me who I was and warn me about what I would become. But the stag's appearance only made Soren's words the other night replay over and over in my head. Shame ate at my insides as I remembered waking up with my head pressed against Soren's chest. Even after the terrifying dream, his presence lulled me into a sense of safety. *And that can't happen. I can't get attached. I've spent too long fighting to accept it now.* But I hadn't left when given the chance either.

I closed my eyes, allowing Panic to steer me. The horse was smart enough not to get caught in a trap.

"You shouldn't think about it so much." My shoulders tensed at the sound of Soren's voice.

"How do you always know what I'm thinking about?"

His lips quirked. "You get this look on your face whenever you're worrying over something. It's almost too hard not to notice. Also, because I know how you work. You really need to loosen up."

"Loosen up?" Acid dripped from my tone. "I *am* loosened up."

All he did was raise an eyebrow.

"Shut up."

"I didn't say anything."

I rolled my eyes. "Look, I just don't want to talk to you right now."

Soren shook his head, his long, unbound white hair rippling like a wave. "It's a tough thing to realize, isn't it? I don't envy you."

"I haven't realized *anything.*" I wish I believed those words as strongly as I said them. But roots had begun to dig deep into this world, into Soren, and I wasn't sure that severing them was worth the pain. I peered at Soren again. His hair was whiter than the pristine snow coating the ground, brushing skin so pale it was almost translucent with a blue-gray tinge, and even his thick hunting furs did nothing to hide the strong build of his body. His long, delicate fingers clutched at his horse's reins, easily navigating the treacherous mountain path. There was a sharpness in his purple eyes as he gazed up into the sky. That body shielded me from the cold, those hands kept me from hurting myself, those eyes burned with fury at the sight of me in danger. Something strange stirred in my chest, and I turned away.

"You know what the best thing about being a goblin is?" Soren asked. When I didn't respond, he continued. "Not being able to create due to the power the Permafrost gives us isn't the only restriction. You can't lie either. You'll hear it, like a ringing in your ears."

"How is that a good thing?" I asked, thankful there was at least a change of topic.

"It's not just others," he said. "You can't lie to yourself either."

"I'm *not* lying to myself about anything."

He gave me a soft, sad look. "Liar."

I turned my body away from him. Hunger gnawed my insides, and I thought back to the last time I'd had any real food and wished that I'd eaten some of the rabbit when I had had the chance. In the Erlking's palace I had drunk a goblet of nectar, but that wouldn't keep me going forever, and the effects were wearing off rapidly after the race through the Fire Bog. I needed real food and I needed it soon. Permafrost or not, I needed to eat like every other being. I eyed the saddlebag on Soren's horse. It was soaked red with blood from the fox they'd caught earlier. The goblins ripped into the animal raw and were carrying the still-edible remains.

"You can have it if you want." Soren followed my gaze. "You'll have to eat something sooner or later."

"I'd rather eat toadstools," I retorted.

Soren gave me a look. "Suit yourself."

From ahead, Elvira halted her snow cat and whipped around. "Be quiet. We're in enemy territory, I can smell them, and with all the bantering you two are doing, they can probably do *more* than smell us. Honestly, Soren, I expected this type of amateur thing from *her,* but you're just a disappointment."

My muscles clenched as I tasted the air. Yes, she was right. Definitely goblin stench, but from whom, I couldn't tell. Goblins didn't make prey lines, but even so, I cast my eyes to the ground, hoping to find something that could help us. Instead, there was the same mess of green and blue that blended into the icy pathways and the harsh whiteness of the sun glinting off the mountain rocks.

Soren gave an easy smile. "We can handle anything."

Elvira huffed. "Maybe. For now Rekke can ride by you and Janneke by me."

Rekke's eyes widened and a blush crept up her cheeks. To make it worse, Soren winked at the young goblin. *Dear gods above, I can't take this.*

"Don't encourage her," I said, underneath a cough.

Soren gave me a wicked smile. "I am sure I don't know what you mean."

I nudged Panic forward toward Elvira and her snow cat. The young stallion whinnied nervously at the sight of the animal's sharp fangs. I ran a hand through his mane. I hadn't forgotten they tried to kill us either. The snow cat bared his teeth at us, and Panic struggled to keep his footing. *I won't let him hurt you.* Even the telepathic link couldn't calm the horse's frantic nerves.

"He doesn't like you," Elvira said with a toss of her raven-black hair.

"I wonder why," I said drily.

"You do?" She narrowed her brow in confusion.

I sighed. She was even worse than Soren. One hundred years later, it was surprising I could even joke at all at this point. "You're going to be the death of me."

"Yes." She nodded. "I am."

It wasn't what she said that froze my blood, it was *how* she said it. So simple and emotionless. She could've been ordering lunch.

I wasn't about to let her see me shake. I gripped Panic's reins hard and narrowed my eyes. "I have to warn you, I'm notoriously hard to kill."

"I've heard." She snorted. "Lydian proved that when he tore into you."

Heat flashed across my body, lingering on the scar tissue of my chest. It was almost as if his crazed rambling carried on the wind. *Why won't you listen to me? Don't you know what's coming? Don't you get it? What's so special about you? I wish I could kill you.* Invisible ants crawled across my skin as I was brought back to when he'd forced himself on me night after night.

Elvira grinned, knowing she'd hit a nerve.

I shook the pain from my mind before it could take root. "He will also never walk or use his left arm the same way again."

"You even being in the presence of someone like me and Soren is an insult," she spat.

"Soren doesn't think so," I said, narrowing my eyes at her.

"Soren should've killed you the moment your filthy hand grabbed his robes. Instead, he treats you like a pet. Tell me, do you sleep at the foot of his bed or do you curl around his naked body?" She glared back to where he rode with her niece, the two of them engaged in a conversation that looked a lot less dire than ours. Rekke was practically glowing with happiness, and Soren's small grin was enough to show that even he couldn't resist the young goblin's enthusiasm. Elvira curled her lip as she watched them.

My eyes widened, finally realizing what Soren meant when he said I "threatened" Elvira. It wasn't about power or skill. No, this was personal. From the way she ate him up with her eyes and the almost palpable hostility rising from her, there was no mistaking it.

"Why do you want to know? So you can wish it were you? That *is* why you hate me, isn't it? You're in love with Soren." The entire thought was completely disgusting.

"I don't have to explain myself to the likes of you," she hissed.

"Jealous?" I taunted. "You know as well as I do that Soren would never lower himself to someone like you."

Her eyes widened, anger burning in them, but her objection fell away as the mountain pathways opened before us. The sheer walls dropped from every side, glittering from the cold tundra sun. The paths widened and spiraled high above us like icy vines crisscrossing the sky. I bit my lip, the hair on the back of my neck rising at the exposure. We were sitting ducks if anything went wrong. Whatever Elvira thought about Soren and myself, she wasn't lying when she predicted company was coming.

There were so many places to hide and jump from, and all around were loose bits of rock that gave way under the slightest pressure. The paths were slicked with ice; one wrong move would send us plummeting down into the chasm below.

A high-pitched whistle broke the eerie silence and echoed across the canyon, bouncing off the walls until it surrounded us from all sides. Almost immediately I had my bow in hand, an arrow notched. The whistle came again, so high that blood dripped from my ears and the ice hanging above us shattered, coming down in shards like rain.

"Get ready," I said through gritted teeth to Elvira, throwing a glance behind me to make sure Soren was prepared. He was.

Arrows rained down from the sky.

I kicked Panic into a hard gallop, running him across the sheer edges of the icy pathways. My vision blurred at the stream of arrows streaking toward us. There were so many the air was thick with them and I was forced to dodge as I rode. Even so, multiple arrows nicked my skin. I quieted my heart and urged Panic onward down the slippery slope despite the hesitation that filled his every limb.

The pathway twisted into two forks, and I took the one leading to higher ground. Soren, right on my tail, nodded toward me and took the other. I unhooked one foot from its stirrup and propped it against the saddle, paying no mind to the vicious rocking back and forth or the shower of rock and ice above me. My eyes scanned the horizon, and a flash of bronze caught my gaze. I shot.

A goblin fell out of the sky, tumbling down to the path I raced on. His power slammed into my body, but the stinging as it sank into my skin was nothing compared to the adrenaline pumping through my veins. Below, Rekke had her twin daggers out, hugging her body tight to the saddle as she slashed at the two goblins who came up beside her, her moves as graceful as a dance. I brought another arrow into my bow, shooting one of the goblins attacking her and watching with satisfaction as he fell.

Another goblin burst from his crevice, a battle cry on his lips. Panic swerved to avoid the blows, and I dug my heel into his side, turning him before he toppled over the mountainside. The goblin raced after us, his speed turning his body into a blur.

"Too cowardly to come out and fight face-to-face?" I taunted, my lips pulled back to bare my teeth. "Is an ambush all you can do? How long did you lay in wait for someone to stumble across your path?"

I didn't wait for an answer, instead freeing my feet and letting go of Panic's reins. I hooked my bow and quiver across my shoulders and slid down the saddle until I was level with the goblin, taking a swing with my axe. His eyes were black in his gaunt, hollow face, and his features were sharp and wolf-like. Gone was any unearthly beauty he may have possessed—this was the face of a killer. He howled in pain as I hit his side and fear spread through me like cold water as the goblin sprang onto Panic's back and grappled with me for the reins.

"Who's a coward?" he snarled.

Panic's sides heaved, and he slammed his body against the cliff face. *Good boy,* I thought. *Get him off your back.*

The goblin swung at me with a blade that I barely had time to deflect. He pressed down on me, using his weight against mine. The ground beneath Panic's feet came closer and closer to my head.

Wincing in pain as my shoulders brushed against the rocks, I grabbed Panic's cinch and braced myself. The goblin let go, and my legs hit the path with searing pain as Panic dragged me along with him. Grunting with effort, I hooked my legs into the cinch and began to inch my way back up to the saddle.

My axe fell somewhere down the cliffside, and though my bow and arrows were firmly attached to my back, there was no way to reach them. With gritted teeth, I fumbled with the straps on my bracer and pulled out the bent, iron nail.

Before the nail had merely stung. Now it blazed with a type of pain I didn't know existed. Blood trickled in my mouth as I bit down hard on my cheek to keep from screaming. But if it was this bad for me—someone who wasn't even a full goblin—it would be Hel for my attacker. With the last of my strength, I swung upward and plunged the nail into his throat. His eyes grew wide and his long-nailed fingers clutched at his throat, scratching until rivulets of blood ran down his collarbone. The skin grew black and putrefied, flaking off to expose the muscles and veins underneath. I kicked him off Panic, watching as he fell a thousand feet below. I curled my lips at the smell of burning flesh as I shoved the nail back into the bracer. Dark-red marks covered my fingertips.

Adrenaline kicked my senses into overdrive, and the power I absorbed reached out wildly to touch the other fighters. Below me, Rekke finished off her last attacker, but one of her hands was draped across her bloody belly, holding in her insides. The young goblin's laughter would never brighten the forest again. Hatred burned away the pain in my body. She was young, so young. She shouldn't even have been on the Hunt, and now she would die before ever growing into her own.

I glared as Elvira hacked away at the last of her pursuers with her sword and dagger, not even sparing a glance at her dying niece. She'd gotten what she wanted. At the very bottom of the trails Soren streaked by on Terror, the dead littered around him like fallen leaves. His face, body, and hair were streaked blood red, and the static of power that pounded through him stole the breath from my lungs. The hard muscles in his arms and shoulders rippled with strength. For once, the sight of a blood-covered goblin didn't terrify me. With an arrow pulled back toward my chin, I shot again and again, helping him fell his foes.

A horse screamed, and I broke out of my daze a moment too late. A dagger was stuck in Panic's eye. He skidded through the ice and fell, only to rise and fall again. Blood gushed from his wound, and he shrieked as the life drained out of him. I jumped off the horse, my own eye so full of pain I barely stopped myself from ripping it out. I skidded across the rocks, the hard fall and momentum bruising and battering my body. My insides turned to fire as the animal connected to my mind died. With my body screaming, I pushed myself upright to find Elvira a few levels below me with an arrow aimed right at my heart.

I gripped the cliff face and pulled myself up, staggering at the weight of my own body. From off in the distance someone shouted my name, and phantom aches told me to lie down and give in to the cold numbness spreading through me. A single thought broke through the cold.

I will not die. I will not die here in the ice. I will not die here by that woman's blade. I will not die. I will not die unless I take her with me.

I jumped off the side of the ledge, free-falling down and down and down. The wind whipped my face, stealing tears from my eyes. My body was boneless, weightless, melting as I fell through the air onto the wide-eyed goblin below me. *Bet you've never seen that before.*

The impact knocked the breath from my lungs, and I gasped for air. But I had my hands in Elvira's hair, my legs wrapped around her torso, screeching like a madwoman. The cat reared and fell as Elvira's sword stuck through its belly in the confusion.

We wrestled on the ground, her lengthening nails tearing chunks of skin out of my shoulders, ripping at my clothes. I reached up, digging my fingers into her eye sockets until they were warm with her blood. Rolling over and over, weapons forgotten, I slammed against the dwindling ground. Above me, Elvira's sightless eyes blazed with fury, and blood streaked down her once-beautiful face.

"You're supposed to die!" she shrieked. "It can't be this hard to kill such a pathetic thing!" I grabbed a chunk of rock and bashed her in the head, fighting to get her fingers away from my chest. Once they sunk in, all she had to do was rip my heart out.

"I told you I was hard to kill!" The taste of her blood in my mouth sent me into a frenzy, and I slammed both hands over her ears.

Momentarily deaf, she let go, and I scrambled back away from the edge of the cliff. My bow and quiver pressed into my back, mocking me.

Elvira lunged and grabbed at my shoulders with her clawed hands, leaving bloody grooves in my skin. She slammed me against the back of the cliff as ice shards fell around us. I brought my knee down on her crotch, and she yowled like a dog, but didn't let go. Blood plastered my face, blinded my eyes, and covered the ledge in a slippery pool.

A sharp stone cut into my back, wetness seeping through the once-fine tunic. Elvira and I rolled until I was facing open air.

"You're not so pretty now." She smiled in a bloody, freak-ish grin.

"Take a look at yourself." I spat blood in her face. In the split second it took for her to regain her bearings, my legs were already wrapped tightly around her torso, and my fingers dug deep into the roots of her hair.

"If I'm going to die," I snarled, "then you'll die with me." Then I let myself fall back into the abyss.

10

MONSTERS

Y MUSCLES BURNED like molten lava. A slow, agonizing pain spread throughout my body and left me fighting for breath. I gasped, greedily sucking in the cool air. The blue sky was a small speck far above me.

Vines and cobwebs wrapped neatly around my body, restraining and suspending me in midair. Every time I struggled to break free, the vines tightened around my body like a constrictor. Elvira's broken body lay below me, a snarl across her dead lips. The twinges of power forcing their way through my skin were already fading.

On instinct, I lashed out at the vines, kicking and tearing. Elvira's power fueled my tired, injured body, giving it the adrenaline I needed. But no matter how much I struggled, the vines held me tight, and I swayed, helplessly vulnerable in their grip.

Images of the battle on the mountain flashed behind my eyes. The memory of Panic's dying shriek broke my heart into pieces. He'd been a good horse, and all it got him was a dagger in the eye. Rekke was gone too; someone who despite my best efforts had managed to worm her way to a place close to my heart, someone who could've become a friend if I'd let her. She shouldn't have been on the Hunt in the first place, and now she was dead because of the crumpled body below me. Every cell in me ached to pummel it to a pulp until it was unrecognizable. It was as if the feeling of Elvira's blood between my fingers would make up for the lives she'd cut short. The small satisfaction that her gambit to kill Rekke and secure her position had ended in her demise did nothing to quell the rage and sadness inside of me.

Once more, I twisted in the vines, lashing out with bound legs, and once more I failed to get free. The small speck of blue sky was now an indigo blanket. I closed my eyes, praying to whatever deity would listen that Soren got out all right and that the blood streaking his body was not his own.

The hair on the back of my neck rose as footsteps echoed through the dark caverns. I thrashed wildly. If I got a glimpse of what this place looked like, I might know what type of creature called it their home—and more important, if they wanted to eat me.

The high walls of the cavern glistened with crimson liquid too thin to be blood, dripping down onto moss the color of moonlight. Bones and feathers littered the floor, and among them sat a humanoid skeleton. I swallowed the fear threatening to rise. Escape was my goal and fear only got in the way. I brought one vine-covered arm up to my mouth and gnawed at the bitter-tasting plant.

The echoing footsteps stopped. "You won't get out that way." Someone giggled.

"Where are you?" The voice came from behind me, but there was only darkness.

"You should be more polite," she said. "It's not fun when everyone doesn't get along."

"Show yourself!" I snarled. Whoever, *whatever* these creatures were, they needed to know they wouldn't cow me no matter how vulnerable I was, swinging from the vines.

"Poor girl." This voice was obviously male, and his words stung like dripping acid. "So much to lose, so little understood."

"Odin's ravens! Who are you people?" The voices echoed all around me, the words repeating themselves over and over like a chant. I whipped my head around the cavern, but besides the feathers and old bones, the only moving thing was the sluggish liquid dripping off the stone.

"That's not very nice," the female said. This time I pinpointed her voice to a crevice above me. The creature's large dark eyes twinkled with amusement, cracks formed along her eggshell-white skin, and a shock of brilliant green hair hung in her face. *Oh no. Gods above, not this.*

The male clucked his tongue and stepped into a patch of the shining moss. He stood there as I hung from the vines, boredom in his reddish gaze. His ebony skin was also cracked in places, and a tail swept beside his legs, the tip twitching back and forth. The bare skin of his chest flaked away at his ribcage until the bloody bones and muscles underneath were exposed.

I swallowed my rising dread. Svartelves. It had to be

svartelves. The good news was that they probably weren't going to cut me up and eat me; the bad news was that they were notorious for driving people insane. Somehow, that made becoming an hors d'oeuvre a lot more appealing.

"Tibra is right. You should be nice," the male said, leaning against a jagged stone. The red liquid dripped onto his bare chest and spread out like roots to his shoulders and fingertips, to his neck and breast, and down to his stomach before sinking into his body and disappearing. He circled around me, and I caught a glimpse of his hollow back. With his eyes on me, I felt very, very naked. "You could've ended up like her"—he flicked his tail toward Elvira's broken body—"but we decided to catch you."

"She didn't die from the fall; I killed her."

He raised his eyebrows slightly. "Oh? Well, perhaps you could explain the broken neck, then? Or the spine?" He curled his upper lip as he nudged the body with his foot. "Of course, a fall couldn't have gouged her eyes out, now could it? I guess we can share the credit, if you wish. You already possess her power, anyhow."

From behind me, the girl giggled again. "Can we keep her, Donnar? *Can we?*" With the way she widened her eyes at Donnar and clasped her hands together, Tibra looked like she was begging for a pet. I swore inwardly.

Donnar did another circle around me, his tail flicking back and forth with contempt. Almost like Soren's growls, it had a language of its own. "She smells like goblin," he said as he stuck his face in mine. "A strange odor for a human."

"And you smell like svartelf, and that's a strange odor for

anyone," I countered. "Now if you would be kind enough to let me *go.*"

Donnar laughed. "Go where?"

"Home," I snapped.

"And where is that?" Like Tibra, his eyes sparkled in delight at this new game. Like Tibra, he was also very lucky I was restrained right now.

"Stop playing with me. I'll give you whatever you want, but just let me go home!" There was a sinking feeling in the pit of my stomach. *And where is that?* If I tried to picture home, the image became blurry, unfocused. I shook off the image. I *knew* where my home was.

Donnar shook his head, tutting as if I were a naughty child. "You didn't answer my question, though. Where is your home? Your village has burnt to the ground, your blood relatives have all perished, humankind see you as a blood traitor. Yet here, no matter what changes you make, you will always be human first and goblin second, and your morals will be compromised by the way society has run for thousands upon thousands of years. Not to mention, why leave and search for your heart when it beats right in front of you?"

A chill went down my spine. "How do you know so much about me?"

He smiled, showing yellowed fangs. "It is my job to know. I wait and I watch and I see your fates play out in the blood-water that flows down the mountain. There are those who seek me for this knowledge, but the more I give, the more they come away with their minds broken. But you already experienced that—even if you did not know it at the time."

"Strangely enough," I snapped, "I don't know what you're talking about now either! Stop playing mind games with me. Let me leave!"

"Why?" he asked again, his tail sweeping across the floor as he knelt beside me. "You have nowhere to go. And what world would accept a creature warring against herself?"

"I'm not warring against myself," I said. My stomach churned at the thought that this creature knew of my every struggle and was laying it out before my eyes. The pit in my belly grew as his words goaded me like a cattle prod.

Donnar clucked his tongue again and drew a line down my jaw with his dark fingers. I shivered as claws protruded from his knuckles. When he brought his hand away, he left a warm, wet mark behind. Then with a flick of his wrist, he slashed the vines apart.

My head cracked against the ground, and I groaned at the multiple stinging cuts and bruises. It was hard to think through the thick haze of pain; my injuries screamed, demanding my attention. The blurry, sleek rainbows of the bloodwater and the shining moss doubled before my eyes, and the world slipped further and further away with every throb of my head.

Wildly and half-blind, I groped the bone-littered ground for my bow and quiver, praying they had survived the fall. If these creatures wouldn't let me out willingly, then I'd force them to. Gods damn the pain in my body, I'd had worse and survived. "Looking for this?" Donnar balanced the bow on his fingertip, twirling it like a baton.

I lurched forward, stumbling to the ground on deadened

feet. "Give me that." I scrambled to get up, only to realize my arms had gone numb.

Tibra flitted to stand beside him. "Aw, you hear that, she's like a baby. *Please* can we keep her?"

"What did you do to me?" I panted, curled on my side. Icy coldness was spreading like liquid through my insides. It burned, it froze, and I wanted it out. I dug into the underside of my arms but nothing stopped the pain. Tears glistened in the corners of my eyes as the world spun around me. The coldness crushed the breath out of my chest. My mouth opened, but only a strangled cry came out. My senses turned upside down as I failed to push myself up and crawl away.

Claws clacked against the stone as Donnar came to stand beside me. He squatted down, clutching my chin. The claws on his knuckles brushed against my cheek, glistening with something dark and wet. "You're so afraid," he said, smiling. Rows upon rows of sharp, pointed teeth stared at me. "I'm not doing anything to you, dear child. Your body is finally catching up to your mind. Didn't the young lord tell you that agonizing over your decision would drive you mad? It breaks you from the inside out. You survived the fall because like all things that end up here, you seek knowledge. Knowing has the power to kill." He glanced at the bones scattered across the cave floor. "I don't envy you."

No. No. Let me leave. I don't want to die. I don't want to die! Each breath was a struggle, each conscious second ticking by a battle, but no matter how hard I fought, the darkness that crowded my vision pulled me deeper and deeper into its grasp.

Donnar smiled sadly at me. "I guess that is the nice thing about being undecided. You can choose between the blood of battle and the blood of birth, of good war and bad peace, of which arms you wish to push away and which arms you wish to hold you close. It's a beautiful thing. A maddening thing."

My eyelids drooped. His riddles turned my brain to mush and the cold darkness surrounding me whispered invitations in my ear.

"Make your choice wisely, little one." I closed my eyes as Donnar's dry lips pressed against my forehead.

⸻

THE SVARTELVES' DARK CAVERN was gone. Bones of be-ings, both animal and human, immortal and mortal, littered the floor. I stepped carefully, waiting for my injuries to scream in pain, but they never did. No body lay on the ground, twisted with a broken neck and spine, face bloodied from my nails. My bow and quiver were pressed against my back in their familiar embrace.

I continued down the cavern, ducking under stones that pointed down from the ceiling, jumping over those that surged upward from the ground. Far ahead of me, the manic cackle of a goblin echoed off the cavern walls. I picked up my pace, careful not to make any noise as I followed the sound. The high-pitched shriek of a human child mingled with the manic laughter, and I broke into a run through the passageways.

I sprinted around the corner only to come to a stumbling halt as the scene unfolded in front of me. The small child raced around the rocks while the goblin guarded her like a sentry, fondness in his eyes, as she tried to climb the wall of the cavern. A rock came loose, and she shrieked as she fell, but the goblin's arms were waiting to catch her. He said something to her in a language I didn't know, but I picked up the worry in his tone. The girl crossed her arms, pouting, but relented to his demand. He set her down again, and they raced through the shadows.

Their silhouettes danced around me, laughing and hooting with glee. In between the flashes of their bodies, their features merged and changed at random. Sometimes the girl had blue eyes, sometimes brown. Sometimes the goblin's hair was cropped short, sometimes it was down to his back. Both silhouettes stopped their dance and came to a halt in front of me. Their features changed so fast that they were both everyone and no one. Only one thing remained the same: One was goblin and the other was a human child.

The two forms melted away, and I stood alone in the darkness. "Donnar! Where are you? What are you doing to me?"

The only answer was the steady dripping of bloodwater. My fingers curled around my bow, tucking it under my arm as the passages twisted and turned. There had to be a way out or at least a skylight. "Donnar?"

In the distance a voice was chiding someone, but every time they spoke, the sound changed. An old woman, a young man, a toddler barely able to form words, all saying the same thing.

"You wouldn't have to suffer if you just gave in."

"Who's there?" I called, rounding a corner so fast I nearly smacked into stone.

"I would suffer more if I just *gave in*." This voice was spitting and spiteful, fueled with fire and fury. Underneath the fury was passion kindled by the flames. "You act like this is an easy choice for me."

"That's only because you think about it too much." The voices might've been strangers, but the conversation was eerily like the one I'd had with Soren hours ago, and a small ball of nerves was hardening in my gut. "If you don't tell the truth . . ."

"I can't!" the other voice shouted, its words echoing across the walls, surrounding me.

Bones and scales crunched under my feet as I wove through the small passages. The walls shone like oil spots, a dark rainbow against the shining moss. A human skeleton was on its knees with hands outreached. I shuddered as I passed by. It looked like it was begging for mercy.

"Don't complain then if you don't feel right. It's your own fault."

I kept an arrow notched, but there was no one to shoot at. The voices came from everywhere and nowhere, carried by the cold tunnel winds.

"You know the thing they say about goblins, right?" the voice asked. "We can't lie to ourselves."

A growl shut out the voices and resonated deep within my bones. I clutched my bow, keeping the arrow aimed at wherever the sound appeared next. There was a lump in my throat, and it was growing bigger by the minute. Unsteady hands shook the bow, making it impossible to aim.

A shadow stood before me, long, lean, and goblin-like. Faceless and nameless, it was a stranger, but I couldn't shake the growing feeling that I *knew* it. It came forward toward me as if it could hear the sound of my heart racing. My blood froze as I aimed at the creature, the arrow shaking against the bowstring. Cornered, trapped, and with nowhere to hide, sweat dripped down my face and my eyes darted around wildly.

The shadow reached out to my cheek with long, delicate fingers dripping with darkness and blood. I closed my eyes at the faint feeling of a hand brushing against my cheek.

"Maybe," the voice agreed with the first. "But I can try."

With a hiss, the shadow-creature vanished, spluttering out in short, staccato bursts.

I stood there too stunned to move as the fear dwindled until all that was left was the hard lump in my throat. *These are just mind games.* Svartelves were known for playing with people's minds, driving them mad with their tricks and visions.

You seek knowledge. The phantom voice spoke in my head, and I shivered at the intrusion, my body going cold all the way to the core. *Choose wisely.* The sound of a child at play floated from behind me, and the shadows swirled and merged together until they covered the dark passages of the cavern and exploded into light.

I stood, staring into the distance. The harsh light burned, and I held a hand up to shield my vision. It was brighter than fire, brighter than the sun glinting off the snow, and the light called to me. The soft, motherly voice spoke my name as I drew closer, and wind whirled around me as I stepped into the light.

There was no more darkness, no more dripping of red water onto stones, no more shadows flitting around, or voices muttering cryptic warnings. The field of wheat shimmered in the wind like an ocean of amber, and the smell of warmth and springtime brought long-buried memories back from the dead.

And the sun, oh the sun. It hung in the sky unmuted, sending rays of warmth down onto me. I tilted back my head, soaking up every last drop.

"I knew you'd never change."

My arrow was ready to go before I even turned, but the man in front of me smiled as he waited until I was over my shock. I stared, unable to believe my eyes. Crow's feet webbed around the man's brown eyes, and his shaggy hair was the color of night and was wound in curls so much like my own. His bushy beard was a few shades darker than the rest of him. Like me, his dark, tawny skin blended in with the amber field.

Unable to take my eyes off the man before me, I drank in his features. Whoever this was, whatever this was, it was in the form of my father. The man who raised me, trusted me, and made me his heir. The man I failed. I choked back my tears.

"When you were born," he said, "it was the happiest day of my life. Not just that you survived, but that I finally had a child who was like me, and who was an heir. It was such a little thing, but out of all my children, it was you who was closest to my heart."

"Father," I whispered. "Is it really you?"

The man smiled at me. "You've been so brave. My beautiful child, my lastborn."

Weapons forgotten on the ground, I raced into his arms.

This was my father. My *father*. Whether he was an illusion or flesh and blood, I didn't fight his embrace. The scent of wood musk and smoke came off him just like it had when he was alive. I breathed deeply, hoping the scent would still linger with me when he disappeared.

A hand touched my face. "I knew you'd never change. You always loved the sunlight on your face."

I looked up at him, afraid to see disappointment in his eyes. I *had* changed. He must know that. He'd lived for seventeen years with the burden that his child would be as good as goblin-born one day. He knew *everything*.

"There's sun in the Permafrost, but not like this. It's not warm. I missed the human sun," I said. "I missed you too."

There was a long, quiet moment. My father rested a hand on my shoulder, squeezing it lightly, before he spoke again. "There is a way to return." His breath tickled my ear. "If you would have it."

My heart leapt in my throat. "What? How? What can I do?"

He smiled, the crow's feet by his eyes crinkling. "I knew you would want to return." He let go and dug his hand in the satchel hanging on his waist. Resting in his palm was a tiny iron knife.

I took a step back. "What . . . what are you doing?"

"Don't you want to be with us? With your *family*? After a hundred years among *them*, don't you miss us?" I flinched at the coldness in his words.

It took me a minute to find my voice. "Of course I miss you! I think about you every day!"

He thrust the knife toward me, and I stepped back. "Did you? Or were you too busy becoming part goblin to notice?"

The warmth drained from my body. "You can't speak," I said. "When were you going to tell me I was born on the border of the worlds? When were you going to let me know a goblin would take me away once I turned eighteen?"

My father spat, "I would've expected you to weasel your way out of it like you did with everything else."

"You *lied* to me," I shouted. "Maybe not by words themselves, but by omission! You knew what would happen to me and fed poison in my ear!"

He narrowed his eyes. "And all that poison still couldn't stop you from becoming a goblin's lapdog. But you have a chance to redeem yourself now."

My fingers curled into fists. "I am not Soren's lapdog. I am my own person and I make my own choices, and I *don't* need redemption from *you*."

His face turned dark at my words, and he gestured wildly around him. "You're corrupted, then. Don't you remember? Don't you remember walking in the ashes? This is what he did! All of it! This is what he and his kind do!"

"And are we any better?" The burning inside of my reached its peak. "We raid and steal and capture! Why is it okay for us and not for them?"

"They're *monsters*, Janneke. You should know that by now, after all they've done."

One by one, the dead appeared beside him. My six beautiful sisters with their faces marred and bodies scarred, my mother who bled from a wound in her breast, three children with crushed-in skulls, a man almost ripped in half, a woman whose scalp hung from her head. They stood there in silence, but the anger in their eyes spoke for them.

I stared back at them calmly, meeting each and every one of their gazes. They could blame me for their deaths and call me a traitor for surviving under Soren. They could replay the horrors they'd gone through over and over until every image was engraved in my brain. They could remind me of Lydian pounding away inside my body, tearing chunks of flesh out of my breast until it was so full of infection it had to be removed.

They could do all those things, but they could not make me feel ashamed.

It's a wonderful thing. Donnar's voice rode on the wind. *Being able to choose. It's a wonderful thing to know and not have that knowledge destroy you. It's a terrible burden to bear alone. I don't envy you, child.*

I lifted my chin and straightened my shoulders, staring my father directly in the eye. "It wasn't Soren's fault the village was raided. It wasn't Soren's fault that I am who I am. And it's not my fault either. If you really were my father, you wouldn't try to guilt me into admitting it."

The man before me laughed bitterly. "You think this is an illusion? I *am* your father. You *are* my daughter." His laughter died, and a tear slid down his face. "You were my pride and joy, my little shadow, my Janneke. You can still be that. You can be here, with me and your sisters and mother and those who love you for eternity. You could escape from those *monsters,* who poison your mind day and night. Who make you believe they care."

My gaze was steely, but inside, my heart was breaking. This was my family, whom I'd mourned and missed and prayed for each night. Yet when I looked at them all, their faces were full of contempt, of pent-up anger and jealousy and mistrust. *If you really were my father, you wouldn't try to guilt me into admitting it.* This man twisted in rage *wasn't* the father who raised me. The hate he spoke, which he tried to instill in me so many years ago, that was real and true and powerful, but it was something I could understand because I knew now how much it was mixed with his fear for me. But even at my father's worst, he would never ask me to take my own life. My family would never blame me for their fate. These things before me . . . whatever they were, they weren't them.

Promise me you'll never hurt yourself. I couldn't bear it if you were hurt. It was as if he were right next to me, whispering in my ear. *Did I do something wrong? I thought touch was how humans established bonds of trust?* That infuriating smirk that he saved just for me. *Is it normal for your kind to do that? Does your kind normally have that really cute nose crinkle when they make certain facial expressions, especially ones of humor or anger?* Maddening, self-centered, arrogant, vain, passionate, protective, concerned, playful, teasing: all the things Soren was. And maybe he was a monster too. But if he was, then so was I.

My father turned the small knife over and over in his hand, the iron barely tainting his flesh. Even with the antler bone grip, just holding it would be agony. I bit my lip, the scars across my body burning.

"Why won't you let me die?" I asked the she-goblin hovering

over me. In the dark room it was hard to tell if her hair was natu-
rally red or if it was just my blood. There was so much blood.

The she-goblin huffed. "If it were up to me, I would. But it
isn't up to me. I'm just following orders." She plunged another
needle deep into my arm until I was silent.

The man that replaced her had white hair that hung just past
his hips. His eyes burned into me from a chair across the room as I
feigned sleep. If I woke, something terrible would follow. I knew it
in my bones. But I was past the point of death; the infection in my
body was no more and the deadly fever had broken.

"I know you're not asleep," the man said. "I want you to know
you're safe here. I protect my own."

My father continued, "It will be over quickly. And then
you'll be free. You'll never be a monster."

I looked past him at the sun spilling across the wheat,
turning it to waves of amber. When I spoke, it was almost as
if it were the voice of a stranger. "And what exactly is a monster, Father?"

My father took me into his embrace. "A monster," he whispered in my ear, "is anything that is not us."

He released me, then cradled the blade in his hands and
offered it to me hilt-first. Taking a deep breath, I gripped the
bone and waited for the pain. The ironwork didn't even sting—
or if it did, it was nothing compared to the agony inside me.

I admired the designs carved into the blade and the way
the hilt was shaped like a ram's horn. It was a shame that something this beautiful could be so tainted. "There are monsters
in this world."

My father sounded pleased. "Go on. Make the right choice."

"I loved you all so much," I whispered. Then, before fear stilled my hand, I shoved the knife between my father's ribs, through his sternum, and into his heart. "But you are not my father."

He gasped, eyes widened with shock as he fell to his knees. Blood spurted from around the knife. He scratched at his chest with his hands until he ripped the blade out, but all that did was quicken the spill of blood. He screamed one word over and over.

His body shuddered and convulsed. His eyes rolled back into his head as his mouth stayed open with a silent accusation. His body shimmered, morphing until it no longer looked like my father but like a faint echo of myself, before dissipating in the wind. Tears dripped from my cheeks. "Yes, I am a monster." *I pity the fool who can't remember that.* "But so is everyone else."

With those words, the world exploded into whiteness. As my vision faded, I swore it took the shape of the stag.

11

TO FEEL

WHEN MY EYES opened again, I was back on the cold ground of the black ice caverns. Vines lay in a pile around me, and I coughed as dust and cobwebs stirred up in the air.

My mind reeled. The bruising from the fight on the mountainside and subsequent fall was now an ugly yellow instead of hideous purple, and pale scabs had begun to cover where my wounds were. My brow furrowed at the sight. The wounds looked a few days old instead of a few hours.

I glanced at my hands, half expecting them to be coated with my father's blood, but there wasn't even the burn of iron on my fingertips. Bile rose in my throat. It'd all been so real.

"I do not envy you, child." Donnar approached from the darkness, his tail swishing up the dust.

"What . . . what happened?" I coughed. The dust and cobwebs stirring in the air didn't help my already parched throat.

"You simply made your choice," he said. "And though

winter law dictates I be impartial in the wars to come, I must say I believe you chose well."

My bow and quiver lay against one of the rocks. I scooped them up, the familiarity of the bow against my back easing my anxiety.

"Was it real then? All of it?"

Donnar frowned. "When faced with a choice between what has been and what will be, either option is as real as the other. You chose your future over your past, though the decision took quite some time." I blinked in confusion. It couldn't have been an hour since Donnar kissed my forehead. Donnar smiled at me sympathetically. "A few days, dear, nothing drastic."

A few days could be a lifetime on the Hunt. I shivered. Soren could be dead; he could think *I* was dead. He saw me fall down the cavern with Elvira, I was certain of that. All that time I was in my limbo, he was alone and ally-less, if not dead. *Soren is strong.* I tried to convince myself. *He can survive without help.*

"He's down here," Donnar interrupted my thoughts. "Your goblin. I can tell. He smells like another who came before; they must've been related."

I frowned. "What do you mean?"

Donnar shrugged. "It was a long, long time ago. Some seek more knowledge than they can bear. They usually do not last long. I wouldn't concern yourself with such things. Either way, you will find who you are looking for down here."

He began to turn away, but as he did, something he said stuck out. "What do you mean, 'the wars to come'?"

Donnar met my eyes. "For thousands upon thousands of years, you have sat beside your throne, firmly rooted into the earth. After thousands upon thousands of years, the roots are devoured and torn away. A thousand wars have been fought for you, thousands of deaths offered to you. Each time you have been ripped from the earth, and each time you regrow stronger than before. One day your roots will spread across the worlds, and when they do, they will be all that is there to anchor it in place. As I said, I do not envy you."

"I was hoping for something a little less cryptic," I said, my voice quivering at Donnar's warning. Gooseflesh rose on my arms, and I rubbed it away.

"I must go now, child," the svartelf said. "Don't linger in this place; it is not for your kind."

"Wait!" I called. "You must be able to tell me *something else*."

The svartelf's soulless eyes stared into mine. "By the new moon's time, all will come undone. Now *go*." The words came with a powerful wind, blinding me and pushing me to the ground. When I stood, the svartelf was gone.

I muttered some choice words under my breath. Frustration bloomed inside of me, bursting like an ugly sore. Of course the svartelf wasn't going to give me a straight answer. Still, for all the dire warnings mixed in with riddles and nonsense words, I had the unshakable feeling that everything that had happened to me in the dreamland limbo was real. And the warning he gave me before he disappeared—if it was one at all—chilled me to the bone.

I stood and started through the cavern. I'd made my

choice, and now it was time to live with it. The passages around the svartelves' caverns wound and twisted deeper into the earth until there was only me and the dark silence, not even the trickle of water or the crunching of bones underneath my feet. The sides of the caves glittered with iridescent stones, enthralling in their beauty. In some places bits of the regular wall had been worn away with what looked like a miner's chisel. But none of the stones were missing. Perhaps a miner had come down here years ago to take the jewels and ended up losing his sanity. Perhaps his corpse was still down here.

Perhaps the corpse of Soren's relative was down here somewhere, undisturbed and unseen. I would have to ask Soren after if he knew of any family member who perished in these caverns—that was, if there was an "after."

Donnar was right about one thing: A war was coming. On one side there was me, and on the other, Lydian. My blood was hot with the desire for revenge, and I pictured myself standing over him, the axe hanging over my head gone forever. One thing was certain: Lydian and Soren were the ones who split the marble floor. If one of them became the Erlking, the other would not be allowed to live. If Lydian survived, Soren was done for and I was as good as damned for eternity. Even after the Hunt ended, even if we all survived unscathed, I would never be safe until Lydian was dead.

I curled my fingers into fists to stop my hands from shaking. *He has no power over me.* He didn't. He didn't, and I had to believe it with every ounce of faith, even if his mere name made me quiver with fear. If I remembered those nights with the pain and the blood and the soft, crooning voice, I would be lost. The spiral walls of the underground pressed heavily against me, until the breath was crushed from my lungs. No wonder people went mad in places like this; even without the svartelves, being alone in the dark, utter silence with just your thoughts was deadly. I stopped to gasp for breath, leaning against the slick stones. Each breath of air I sucked in cleared away the darkness in my mind. I focused on the coolness across my tongue and nothing else, until the shiver of my body came to a halt and the panic seeped out of my skin.

Finally, the passageways opened into a wider tunnel, and the tension in my body eased. Up above, bits of light shone through the cracks of stone. They were dark purple now, casting a haze of violet inside the tunnels. I'd have more luck falling off a cliff to my death than finding Soren now. The air below turned icy and the shivering returned.

I found a small alcove carved into the side of the stone; the hole was just big enough for me to squeeze in if I curled into a ball. Wintry blasts chilled me to the bone, and I hugged my knees to keep in what little heat I had. Eyelids drooping, I wished for a bearskin cloak and a warm body beside it. Exhaustion overtook me, and I fell into a deep sleep.

I WOKE WITH the morning lights shining from the stones. Their iridescence glittered in the daylight, swirling with greens, blues, and purples. Above me, pieces of a blue sky and the cold sun broke through the cracks in the stone. My body ached in places I didn't think could ache, and a dark, troubled feeling had settled in the pit of my stomach. Pushing it away, I got up, checked that all my equipment was in place, and continued on my journey.

The route I picked took a sharp decline. Doubt gnawed in my belly, churning like acid inside me. I wanted to go *up* to the surface, not down to gods knew where. Before I could turn back, a familiar voice stopped my heart.

"You should really stop this self-denial horseshit." Using some dark magic, Tibra managed to sound harsh *and* bubbly at the same time.

"I'm not in denial," Soren snapped. A joy so fierce it was frightening filled me as his growl rumbled throughout the caverns, and I could barely stop myself from hurtling down the cavern. Last night, alone in the cold, I had wished for the now-familiar warmth and protection his body provided. It hadn't dawned on me until now how much I missed *him*.

"Does it frighten you?" Tibra asked. "She's very pretty. Does that frighten you? You could hurt her. Do other goblins act this way when this happens? I've never known. Is it just you? Are you different?"

"*I won't ever hurt her.* Which is much more than I could say for *you*." Soren growled a low warning.

"You can already feel the effects of the potions wearing off, can't you? You knew you couldn't make them yourself; it was quite risky bringing her along. Unless you *wanted* something to happen."

Soren snapped at Tibra. "Yes, you've found out my master plan. Take Janneke with me on a ceremonial competition involving hunting one another to the death and hope romance blossoms between us so we can take each other in the throes of passion. You are *such* a good detective; you should get a medal."

I stumbled down from where I stood above them, legs half-numb with shock. The goblin and the svartelf stared at me, caught totally unawares by my fall. So many words bubbled on my lips, but the ones that came out were: "Did you just use sarcasm?"

Tibra's egg-like eyes widened, and she scampered away, throwing one last sentence over her shoulder. "My way would've been funner! But I guess you're stuck now!"

"More fun," Soren growled. "It's more fun, you heathen."

My insides crackled with a static current as I stared up at him from my spot on the ground. "Grammar *and* sarcasm? You're hitting a lot of firsts today." The buzzing inside my head was akin to being drunk. Unable to process what he had said, unable to process how my body reacted to those words, I picked myself up from the floor and straightened my tunic.

Relief passed through Soren's lilac eyes and changed to fear as he put two and two together. "How . . . how much of that did you hear?"

"I never would've guessed your master plan if I'd lived a thousand years," I said.

Soren glanced around wildly for something to save him, his pale skin glowing faintly pink. My lips twitched, and the fire inside me grew stronger. After all the times Soren needled and teased me, it was amusing to see him squirm.

"You know I'd never do anything to hurt you," Soren began. "I—I—" For once he was at a loss for words.

"You just want to take me in the throes of passion," I dead-panned.

Soren blushed harder, the tips of his ears turning pink. "I was being sarcastic."

I rolled my tense shoulders. The muscles ached when they loosened. The fire in them was nothing compared to the one in my chest, though, and I found the courage to speak my mind. "Then what *do* you want to do to me?"

He looked away, scowling. "I don't want to *do* anything to you."

"What do you want, then?" I asked. The voices in the cavern were no mystery now, but instead of fear, my stomach churned with anticipation.

Soren walked down the slope, skirting around a pool of black liquid too thick to be water. I followed, always one pace behind him as per custom. He inclined his head to the side and waited until we were walking side by side and something warm bloomed inside of me.

After a long moment he broke the silence. "You know, goblins don't feel *nothing*. We're not emotionless. *I'm* not emotionless."

"It's hard to tell when you always look like you're suffering from intense boredom."

Soren's lips quirked. "We feel in extremes. Either complete apathy or complete obsession with whatever emotion takes us over. It makes us effective killers, but it's also a weakness when it works against us."

I was quiet for a long second. The drunk feeling was evaporating and the idea that Soren might actually *want* me in a physical sense, maybe something even more, was slowly seeping into my head. Strangely, I couldn't seem to feel afraid, just hot in a way I'd never been before.

"Go on."

"There's a reason we don't utilize certain feelings often. Rage, hatred, they're wonderful when you're on a hunt. Anything softer is a liability. We're predators. We can't afford to put anything else first; we can't afford to think about anything other than our survival," he said, his voice rough with frustration.

"You're saying that I make you vulnerable. You're saying you care for me." When the words crossed my lips, the last fragments of my wall shattered. I'd seen him torture and butcher his enemies like pigs and the way he paid no attention to things he considered beneath him. I'd seen his unstoppable rage when someone threatened to hurt something he loved and the hidden compassionate side that offered me the warmth of his cloak and body. But never had he admitted he was vulnerable. In that second when fear flashed in his eyes, he was as human as me.

Soren watched me. "Are you afraid?"

"I don't know." Yes, there was something like fear inside of me, but it wasn't the type I was used to. I wasn't afraid for my life and didn't sense any danger. There was only fluttering in my stomach that grew faster with each passing breath. It wasn't *fear*; it was something more.

"I see you," he began. "I see you and I feel like I need you. I want you with me. I want you by me. I don't want you to cringe away. I want you to come close. But then I get angry because I *shouldn't* want that. I *can't* want that. That's what my mind says. It's a liability and it makes me weak as a predator. It makes me vulnerable. I hate it. And yet I don't want to stop feeling it." At first, he was spitting the words with a furious tone, but then his voice became softer. "And I don't want to force you into something that will make you unhappy. And if that means that I release you from your bind and you go back to the human world and find a man of your own, then I'll do it. Your happiness means more to me than anything in the world."

"I understand what you mean now, Soren," I said softly. "About monsters."

His lilac eyes latched onto me, smoldering with feeling. "What happened to you down here?"

"I realized where I belong," I said. I knew I'd never be able to speak of exactly what happened with my father to anyone, no more than anyone else could speak after death. "And I realized you were right. We're all monsters in some way. But the only ones who are dangerous are the ones who don't realize it. And—" I paused, my voice dying.

"And?" he encouraged.

"I know you won't hurt me."

His gaze softened as he looked down at me. "No, I won't." He reached out and brushed a loose strand of hair behind my ear. For once, I didn't recoil from his touch. I knew what I was now; I knew what I wanted.

"I'm staying," I said. "I know where I belong now. And I know what I need to do."

Silence hung heavy after I spoke, as if Soren knew exactly what I meant. A small smile graced his features, but his eyes turned grave at my words. As if we'd made a silent agreement, understanding passed through his eyes and he nodded.

It was silent for a few moments more before I spoke again. "Did you think I was dead when I fell?"

He shook his head. "Not for a moment. I would know if you died. The bond. I went searching for you after I buried Rekke."

My heart gave a painful tug. "Normally you don't bury the dead on a hunt. We left Helka out to rot."

"Yes," Soren said. "Well, Helka knew what she was getting into. Rekke was a child and shouldn't have been involved in the first place. The only satisfaction is that Elvira didn't survive. Her entire clan will fall into ruin because she killed off her only heir. Rekke deserves to go to the afterlife, and she wouldn't if no one buried her."

It eased the heartache a little to know that Rekke would have her revenge in death, and she would be reunited with her father, but it didn't replace the memory of the young girl with light twinkling in her golden eyes.

"How long did you search?"

"A few days, I think. I ran into that svartelf who led me around in circles. Have you ever met one? Nasty little creatures." He curled his lip in disgust.

I held back laughter. "I did, actually. And I'd never thought I'd say this, but I'm glad I spent a hundred years with *you* and not them. I'd be talking in circles."

"Even though I lied for all those years?" Soren asked.

"When it comes to thralldom, I think I was quite lucky," I said.

Soren closed his eyes for a brief moment and took a deep breath before opening them again. "Janneke, I don't know how to say this. I'm not very good with heartfelt dialogue," he said softly. "But I want you. I want you to be mine. Not, like, in ownership, not like a thrall. But like . . . like how people are when they're close. When they *feel* something. When . . ." His eyes closed in frustration.

Something came over me, and I took his hand, clasping it tight. "I know what you're trying to say."

Be his. The words clung to me. It would be all too easy for him to *make* me his, but a hundred years had passed without that fear ever creeping up inside me. *Be his.* That strange, terrified feeling came back. I swallowed to try to calm the butterflies in my belly as they fluttered and spread heat down my navel. During the battle at the mountainside when he raced and fought with unbound hair and sharply defined muscles, he'd been more handsome than terrifying.

Be his. Soren was arrogant, infuriating in the way he turned his head and his permanent scowls. He was surly and childish and argumentative and never knew when he was defeated. And I liked that; I liked knowing I could break through that surliness to the rare smiles he showed, I liked that I could throw him off when he thought too highly of himself, and when we exchanged words like others exchanged arrows, I found I *enjoyed* it. Whatever his faults, no one could deny that he was passionate and strong and that he cared about me. I knew if I told him no that would be the end of it. He would let me leave. My choices were my own and my wants and desires were on equal ground with his.

Be his. The thought scared me. The thought *petrified* me. But not in the way it should've. Not in the way a human should feel about having the love of an apex predator, a goblin, a cruel merciless monster. No, it scared me because for once I was walking out onto thin ice. *But maybe he's worth the risk.*

"Janneke," he said softly, "are you afraid?"

"No," I said. "Not of you."

He turned sharply until he was facing me, blocking my path. He reached out and stroked my hair. Our braids were long gone, our perfect hunting clothes near ruins, but none of it mattered. "You were never afraid of me," he said, his thumb stroking the side of my cheek. So gentle, so soft; I'd never imagined a goblin's touch could be so soft.

I leaned into his hand, ignoring the human instincts that screamed at me to stop. Even now, knowing what I felt, knowing what I *wanted,* my body responded like it always did. A rabbit didn't easily trust a wolf, after all. But I wasn't a rabbit, not entirely. Not anymore.

"Are you all right?" he asked.

I nodded. "I'm fine, it's just . . . memories."

His thumb skimmed my bottom lip. When he spoke, his voice was husky. "I'm not going to hurt you."

"I know," I said, though it did nothing to stop my racing pulse. "I know."

"Tell me to stop," he whispered, "and I will. I promise."

"I trust you." The words were barely louder than a breath.

One of his hands cupped my cheek. The other roamed against my skin until it reached the small of my back. My eyes closed and my lips parted as his brushed against mine. Softly at first, so soft I melted into him, my body burning with a desire as new as it was fierce. My hands tangled in his silky hair.

He made a sound in the back of his throat, almost like a purr. Shifting, his hips pressed hard against mine, and he brought his lips down to the column of my neck, the underside of my throat. My breath was heavy, and by the time his lips were back on mine, the tips of his sharp teeth gently brushing my bottom lip, I was breathless.

My hand roamed under his tunic, feeling his muscles and the sharp contours of his body. I let my fingers trail along his spine, feeling the ridges of his bones underneath his skin. My fingers splayed on his ribcage, tracing the hard muscle.

His kisses became rougher as part of the control he was desperately trying to hold on to slipped. I wasn't the only one vulnerable anymore. As he brought his hand down to my hip, endorphins dulled the prick of his nails. A small bit of blood trickled down my side.

"I'm sorry," he whispered. "I'm sorry."

"It's okay."

And it was.

In that moment in the darkness, I was more alive than I had ever been before. With my breath pounding in my lungs, my heart racing in my chest, and the mix of fear and want and adrenaline that shot through my veins like a drug, I was not afraid. For this small moment, he wasn't either.

Then the booming of raucous laughter broke us apart, and Soren spun, immediately stepping in front of me with his arms out on either side. His nails grew out into claws and with a vicious snarl, his teeth became fangs. When I caught sight of our threat, all the warmth drained from my body.

Lydian stood before us, and from what I could sense, he had more men down the pathway. He leered at us, his teeth sticking out in a sneer. "And what do we have here?" he asked, his tone playful and mocking. "Don't you know it's dangerous to lose your focus in the dark?" He eyed me. "Don't you know it's dangerous to be kissing monsters?"

Oh, I know all too well. But you have no power over me. Not anymore. Not ever again. In an instant, my bow was out and an arrow was notched. Soren's stance changed ever so slightly, giving me the room to shoot and fight. *We are a team. Let him see that now.*

"Nothing to say?" Lydian's voice became as soft as a smothering pillow. "If I knew you liked it, I might not have given you up. But no. Who can argue with destiny, right?"

Soren's snarl came with a surge of power and shook the cavern walls.

I lifted my chin and stared at Lydian. "You have no power over me."

He scoffed. "We'll see about that. I have more power than all of you. I *know*." The goblins in the shadows came forward, their eyes gleaming, weapons shining in the darkness.

The cavern trembled like it was preparing for the bloodbath about to come. Soren let his power loose in a surge that nearly knocked me off my feet. Like any physical being, it had a form. The light was so bright I had to shield my eyes, and the weight of it pressed hard against my chest.

Stones rained from above as the ceiling twisted and turned, the stones coming to life.

Soren glanced up. "Janneke." His voice was low. "When I say run, go back the way we came as fast as you can."

"I'm not leaving you," I whispered back. "Not after that."

"Trust me." A hint of amusement colored his voice. "I'll be right behind you."

Lydian advanced with his men as Soren and I slowly repositioned ourselves so we faced the opening behind us. An echoing roar grew louder and louder until it turned into a sharp whine. I followed Soren's gaze above us. Two dark red eyes peered down from where the coiled stone of the ceiling used to be and a creature yawned, its wicked red maw showing sharp, poison-coated fangs. It tensed its two front legs, red scales glistening as its claws stroked the stone.

I'd been told stories of this creature while sitting around campfires, all the hunters trying to frighten one another, but never in my darkest nightmares had I seen one. My feet stuck to the ground in fear, and Soren gave me a push.

"Janneke, run!"

I turned and sprinted, Soren fast on my heels, as the lindworm lunged and attacked.

12

DRAGON KILLERS

THE BLOOD RUSHED in my ears as the sound of my footsteps bounced off the black ice. Soren was one pace behind me, checking back over his shoulder to make sure the lindworm wasn't preoccupied with its now-running prey.

The immense power from the lindworm, one of the most viscious types of dragons, squeezed the air from my lungs until every breath was a gasp. Soren's power, the Erlking's, they had nothing on this creature. This was the type of power, a crimson wave that lingered in the peripherals of my vision, that could level cities, kingdoms. This was the power of a predator unrestrained by any earthly or personal ties.

So why were we running?

"Wouldn't killing this thing give us a significant boost?" I shouted, following Soren's sharp left turn into a narrow tunnel through which the lindworm wouldn't fit.

He paused, catching his breath. "Are you mad, Janneke?"

"Think of the power that thing has," I said. "We're just going to run?"

"Yes," he said, grabbing my arm and pulling me down the pathway. "We're going to run and hope that Lydian and his retinue are enough of a feast that we're not followed."

For the first time, there was a tremble in his voice.

"Are you *afraid* of it?" I asked, incredulous. I didn't think Soren could be afraid of anything.

"You aren't?" he said. "My nursemaid told me bedtime stories about those things before I started walking. You'd have to be an idiot not to be."

Soren had a *nursemaid*?

We hurried through the passageway, the walls constricting. My lungs heaved in my chest as the walls closed in. They were so close together, if they collapsed, we'd be buried under a mountain of rubble. I forced myself to breath normally. *Calm down. You're not going to smother to death.*

"Your kind has an odd idea of what constitutes a bedtime story." Soren shoved me through an opening in the tight passage, and I tumbled to the ground, landing in a mess of feathers, moss, and bones. The iridescent crystals from before formed piles high to the ceiling, and stalagmites shot up from the ground.

Soren slid down after me, stopping before he fell facefirst onto the rough earth. But as soon as he got his bearings, his eyes widened at something in the corner of the large cave.

Along the floor, littered with the leftovers of prey, among the swirling feathers, were giant eggs. They were a rich golden color swirled with soft cream, and sleeping soundly beside them was another lindworm.

Its massive body curled around itself, the blue sheen of its scales glittering against the lights from above. Five wickedly sharp claws lay at the end of its massive front legs, and sharp fangs slid out over its lips. Even its snoring shook the walls until pebbles rolled to the ground.

Soren swore softly, eyes scanning the area for another way out. His hands trembled until he clenched them into fists, fighting for control. The nervous, panicked look on his face, his darting eyes, and the way he stood frozen on the spot were all alien to me.

"Let's climb back up the way we came," I offered, looking at the hole we dropped from. Smooth stone surrounded it, but both of us were strong enough to give each other a leg up, and if it came to it, we'd find another way. Otherwise, we were lindworm food.

Soren cast one more glance at the sleeping lindworm, then up at the hole. The tips of his ears sharpened as he cast out his power and heard beyond the normal limits. Then he jumped back, pulling me with him, and unsheathed his double swords.

"Hey! What are you—" I stopped midsentence as Lydian and four other brutes tumbled from the hole. His once-blond hair was plastered to the side of his face with blood, and more blood seeped from a large gash on his shoulder. A dark stain covered one of his men's trousers and another stain bled through a tear in another's jerkin. The other two goblins looked dazed, but they weren't bleeding. Yet.

From above there was an eardrum-shattering roar as the

pursuing lindworm clawed at the opening, and the melodic snores of its sleeping companion before us came to a stop.

"Are you an *idiot*?" Soren snarled, slowly backing away from the waking monster.

"Idiot?" Lydian spat. "I wasn't the one who found the nest in the first place."

"Yes! But you were the one who *followed me into it*." Soren's teeth clenched as the lumbering dragon stood and stretched, then gazed down at us with beetle-black eyes.

From above, the earth shifted and moved in spirals as stones rained from the top of the cavern. Cold dread formed a hard pit in my stomach as the second lindworm descended on us, its fangs dripping yellow venom from its maw.

"So," one of Lydian's men said in a rather cheery voice. He looked younger than the seasoned men surrounding Lydian and his dark hair was cropped short around his ears, showing tattoos that spiraled around his neck and scalp. "Who wants to slay a dragon?"

Lydian hissed, "This is not the time to be *funny*, Seppo."

The goblin, Seppo, just smiled. "Nonsense, it's *always* time to be funny." He unhooked a feather staff from a holster on his back, shaking the decorative metal shaft until three wickedly sharp prongs slid out from the top.

"You keep strange company, dearest uncle," Soren said, almost to himself.

"I could say the same of you, beloved nephew," Lydian said.

Then the lindworms attacked.

I rolled out of the way, back into an open area where my

bow might be of more use. *Odin's ravens, how am I supposed to kill these things?* To think I'd wanted to *hunt* them.

The red one lashed out at Lydian, its jaws dripping with venom. Lydian swung his greatspear, once, twice, backing the creature away from him. His eyes narrowed, and I shuddered as his body changed, adapting from inhumanly beautiful to a monstrous predator. As his proportions lengthened, I swallowed down my terror. The last time he was like this did not end well for me.

One of Lydian's men—the one who had blood all down his leg—stood with Lydian, swords out, trying to goad the monster into a corner. But the lindworm was smarter and whipped its tail around, smashing the goblin against the stone wall. The goblin fell to the ground, twitched once, and then lay motionless.

Another earthshattering roar filled the chamber as the blue one raged at me. *The blue one is female.* I skidded far away from her nest. *The red is her mate.* The blue one would be more dangerous then. The first rule of a hunter was to never get in between a mother and her children.

My arrow, still notched and ready, shot forward at the blue lindworm, but it broke into pieces upon contact with her scaly armor. Instinctively I reached down for my holster, only to remember that my axe was somewhere on the mountainside, far away from here.

"It's no use." Seppo materialized beside me. "You need something stronger to pierce through the scales."

I grunted. "Thank you for the information. Now if you'll

kindly excuse me," I said, lunging forward. The blue dragon was after Soren, who agilely jumped like a hunting cat between the rocks that burst from the ground. We shared a glance and understanding flashed through his eyes. The lindworm's scales would stop any blade, but they didn't adorn the dragon's belly, throat, or forehead. All we needed to do was take advantage of the weak spots.

My blood roared in my ears. My arrows really were useless, but there had to be *something* I could do. From the corner of my eye, the red dragon was ripping into the body of one of Lydian's goblins, tearing hungrily into the meat. Bile rose in my throat at the screams of the dying male. Evil or not, I couldn't help but pity the goblin as he was eaten alive.

Soren was still hopping across the rocks, the blue lindworm swerving back and forth as she tried to get to him. The lindworm's snake-like body rose, then crashed down again on the floor with every grab. One claw snagged at his tunic and Soren brought his sword down, cutting the claw clean off and taking part of his tunic with it. Blood dripped steadily from his side. The claw rested on the floor across from me, where the dragon, now enraged, was shrieking loud enough to wake the dead.

I had an idea. It was absurd and probably more than a little foolish, but each swipe of her claws and each gnash of her teeth were closer and closer to where Soren was before. Blood dripped from a gash in his side, soaking his tunic. If he kept this up by himself, then the dragon would catch him. I had no choice. I took a deep breath, hooked my bow and quiver across my back, and sprinted toward the lindworm.

I dropped to the ground and skidded underneath the dragon's belly as she rose for another swipe. Frantically, I grabbed her missing claw. One second too late and she would smash me to bits. As the dragon crashed back down I stabbed her underbelly. There was a screech of rage and the weight of the dragon pressed down against my body, forcing me onto my back. The monster rose to crush me.

She didn't get the chance.

Seppo was there, his feather staff cutting thick slices into the dragon's underbelly. He sighed in relief, then grinned at me. "Told ya you needed something sharper." The lindworm roared and ripped herself from Seppo's blades, stumbling away to regain her bearings.

I gripped the claw in my hand. "Come on!"

The dragon turned, her fangs dripping with venom, saliva pooling at her lips. Her eyes burned with the fury of a thousand Hels, the hate in them almost palpable. Soren stood atop an ice-and-rock ledge, looking down at me with horror in his eyes as she charged forward.

Seppo eyed the dragon's oncoming fangs. He cupped his hands out before me. "Give me your foot, I'll boost you up."

"Onto what?"

"Her back, of course," he said, as if it were completely obvious. It struck me that Soren might not be the oddest goblin in the Permafrost. The lindworm coiled as she prepared to strike. Her claws made furrows in the stone, five on one side, four on another.

"Are you insane?" I hissed.

"Yes," Seppo said. "Unless you have a better idea?"

I scowled but put my foot into Seppo's cupped hands, and braced myself for the dragon's strike. It would be close, so close. Seppo was with Lydian, and Lydian wouldn't stop until he killed me. For all I knew, he would plunge me directly into the lindworm's mouth.

"Also," Seppo said, "before I forget anything, here." He thrust something sharp into my hand, just as the gaping jaws of the lindworm came for us. With his leverage, I sprang up into the air and onto the monster, stepping on her elongated snout and running across the flat of her head toward her neck.

The dragon swung her head around to throw me off. I tumbled to her spine as she curled beneath me, shaking with monstrous force. Compared to this, the battle on the cliffside was child's play. The sharp spines of the lindworm threatened to skewer me if I fell on them wrong, but I wrapped my arm around one and hung on.

Balling my hands into fists, I yelped when a blade cut into my palm. Seppo had placed a stiletto knife in my hand. The blade was small and slender, but the dark metal had a wicked gleam to it. I hoped to the gods it wasn't poisoned.

With blood dripping from my hand, I clutched one of the dragon's spines as it reared up to claw at Soren. He jumped to a higher ledge as a claw pierced his calf and pulled him back down. Somewhere else the red dragon screeched with fury, and another goblin screamed as it was ripped apart. A dark, dark part of me prayed that it was Lydian.

Soren lay still, the wind knocked out of him. "Get up!" I screamed. "Go!" He pulled himself to his feet, blood flowing from a deep puncture in his calf. His eyes widened at the sight of me on the dragon's back.

"Don't just ogle like an idiot!" I screamed. "Go!"

The dragon reared to strike, and I tumbled down her back. Before I hit the ground, I wrapped my arm against one of her spines and caught myself. Her neck was far away but the soft flesh between her eyes sparkled with silvery skin. *I can do this.*

Seppo danced back and forth around the lindworm, weaving in and out of her legs, darting underneath her for quick stabs to her belly, then skipping back to avoid being caught in her claws. Blood ran down from a cut on his forehead, and sweat glistened on his face. The dragon managed to back him against the far side of the cave, away from her mate, her eggs, and the other goblins. He narrowed his eyes as the monster descended for the kill.

That was my opening. I pulled myself forward using the dragon's spine and raced up her back, gripping her with the balls of my feet until I was on her neck, staring into her eyes. The lindworm's dark eyes bore into mine with rage, then fear, then sadness.

Her feelings washed over me. We were intruders, bent on destroying her family and home. Soon her babies would be without a mother to warm them; she would never see them grow to her size. We'd come here, foolish beings set on ruining her life. We had no right to punish her for protecting herself and her family.

They were not the monsters. We were.

We all are monsters to something, somehow, someway. "I'm

sorry," I whispered and drove the blade between the lindworm's eyes.

Dark blood spurted between my hands as the giant body of the dragon crashed to the floor for the last time. Soren jumped out of the way as the body hit the cliff face, shaking the iridescent stones from the ceiling.

The dark power I sensed before from the male dragon rose as the power inside his mate vanished, and he screeched in agony, but she was still. Her power swirled around her before hitting me with the force of a stampede.

I'd absorbed power before. It wove its way into my body like a foreign virus, seeping in through my pores and flowing into my mouth, hitting me over and over until it broke through the barrier that was my skin. I remembered in crisp detail the stinging of Aleksey, the burn of the young lordling, and the absolute agony of Helka's power as it forced its way inside me.

The power of the lindworm stole the breath from my mouth and tunneled through my throat until I choked, gasping for air. It hit my body again and again, pummeling it until little by little it sank in. My cells were on fire and each muscle was screaming with agony, but no matter how hard I tried, I couldn't even twitch a finger.

I lay on the floor with my mouth open in a breathless scream. The dark power wrapped around my throat and pulled at my limbs until I was sure my body would rip into pieces. My blood was fire; it was ice and lightning and steel. Blood ran down from my eyes and nose, dripped from my ears as the power fought its way inside of me, each push more agonizing than the last.

My body might've been paralyzed, but the fight still raged on. Three goblins still stood: Seppo, Lydian, and Soren. They were panting hard, their features turning more and more animal-like by the second as they drew on their power. Except for Seppo, who other than his slightly pointed ears, remained the same.

The red dragon roared in rage as the last of his mate's power left her body. His red eyes burned with rage, and then he tipped his head back and sang a low, mournful note. While he was distracted, Lydian lunged. But not at the lindworm.

Soren caught Lydian's greatspear between his two swords, twisting to throw the weapon off course and move out of harm's way. Seppo's eyes widened as he watched the two of them duel. Lydian snarled while a fierce growl bubbled from low in Soren's throat.

"I don't know if you realized," he said darkly, "but there's still another dragon!"

Lydian laughed. It was a cold, tinny sound, like a spoon banging on the inside of a metal pot. "You think that matters to me? We're all doomed anyway, my beloved nephew."

Soren narrowed his eyes. "I will kill you."

Seppo raced forward only for Lydian to knock him back with one hand. "Stay out of this, Seppo. Don't taint your future; don't get in the way of fate."

"You think it's your fate to kill me?" Soren ducked another swipe of the spear, his blades sending it the opposite direction.

"It's my fate to stop you from ruining everything!" he shrieked. "If I have to kill a thousand young goblin girls and burn a thousand villages to the ground and kill a thousand competitors to grow my power, then I *will* if it means the future is secure!"

The blue dragon's power still held my muscles captive, sinking into my skin with agonizing slowness. My body burned with the desire to fight, to stand back-to-back with Soren and finish the blond monster in front of me once and for all. There was something about his words that sent a chill down my spine. The goal of every goblin in the Hunt was to be the Erl-king, but there was something different in the tone Lydian took. Sheer desperation clung to his words as he spat them out, wild-eyed.

The flash of his blade caught my eye; the greatspear's point gleamed a wicked green with Lydian's poison of choice. I didn't know what it was, only that it was agonizing and slow—the type of death he preferred to give his enemies.

Soren sidestepped another blow, his movements as graceful as any dancer, though much deadlier. His swords slashed, his body spun, his muscles quivered with effort.

The red dragon stopped howling and turned his gaze on me, then on the lifeless body of his mate at my feet. The grief burned away from his eyes, and he charged with his fangs ready to rip into my flesh. I fought to move, to run, but my body was still held captive by the blue lindworm's power. *This is it.* Separate from all the pain was a twinge of disappointment. This wasn't the way I wanted to die, not when I'd just chosen to live.

Lydian and Soren were moving too fast for a human to see. The dragon opened his mouth, his gaping maw dripping with the blood of the goblins he'd already killed. Soon it'd be dripping with mine.

I closed my eyes, waiting for the pain, but it never came. The smell of copper and the tang of metal wafted around my head, and someone grunted as they held up a weight too heavy to bear. I opened my eyes to see Soren, his sword stuck through the lindworm's mouth, one of the monster's fangs embedded deep into his arm.

"No," he growled, his body shifting back to his regular form. "She is *mine*." He pulled his sword from the roof of the dragon's mouth and thrust the dead body aside.

"Janneka," he said, voice cracking as he used my real name. "Janneka, can you move?"

The grip of the blue power was releasing me little by little. "I think so."

One of his arms went around my body, and he picked me up as easily as a mother would a babe. "Your arm," I said, touching the oozing wound. "It's—"

"Never mind it," he said. "Just never mind it."

Lydian stood by, grinning from ear to pointed ear. "It's a pity," he said, taking slow steps toward us. "I was mistaken to believe you'd last longer than this. Though I suppose it's only a pity for you two. I am saddened—I could've had great use for you, dear nephew. But I guess fate likes to fool all of us." He shook his head. "It would be a kindness to kill you both now. Don't you think that would be kind of me?"

Soren bared his teeth. "Go ahead and try." But his breath was already sour with sickness, and his arm was green where the fang had punctured it.

If we die, we die fighting. We die together. The blade Seppo had given me shook in my hand. Overhead, the stone dome surrounding us crackled like thunder. There had to be millions more layers of stone and ice lying above it.

A sharp, eerie whistle echoed through the dome, growing louder as it bounced off the rocks. Cracks grew like searching fingers across a section of stone and a mass of boulders fell down to us below. I squeezed my eyes shut as they came crashing to the ground.

When I opened my eyes again, blinking away the grit, a massive barrier of fallen rock blocked Lydian's way. Through the cracks, his face was reddened with rage.

"Seppo! You little bastard!" he screamed. "Where are you?"

The dark-haired goblin was gone. "I don't know, where are you?" His voice came from somewhere, laughing. Lydian answered with a snarl. Unlike most goblins, Seppo's laugh wasn't a cackle but came from deep in his belly. "I'd leave if I were you, my lord. You're standing on the wrong side of the barrier. When those beautiful eggs begin to freeze—which they will shortly—the babies will come out early to devour as much as they can before they die. You really wouldn't want your reign to end before it began, would you?"

Lydian snarled one last time, and then he ran, feet pounding against the earth. Pushing his way out of the mix of stone, Seppo gave Soren and me a bow. "Seppo Satunpoika," he said. "At your service."

13

DEAREST WISH

SOREN STRAIGHTENED UP, grasping his wounded arm in one hand. The power from the red lindworm was absorbing into his body much faster than the blue had into mine. Every so often he hissed in pain, but his eyes were clear and he moved without effort.

"Satunpoika? Your mother is Satu?" Soren asked.

Seppo nodded. "Yes, she is."

Satu. Satu. I'd heard the name before. I was always brought along to Soren's council meetings as a cupbearer, though my real job was to listen and look for anything that would be of use to us. One night when one of the goblins had too much to drink, he complained about a rejected marriage proposal. Soren had laughed in his face and asked what he expected from Satu; she was the fiercest she-goblin in the realm, after all, and she wasn't about to give that up for some brute seeking her claim.

"You're not a goblin," Soren accused. "Not a human either."

"No," Seppo said, "I'm both."

Both? He wasn't like me. Somehow, I could tell that.

He sighed. "You see, when a female and a male love each other *very* much—and one of them masters the self-control needed to not ravage their sexual partner—sometimes that results in something known as a *baby*."

"A halfling," Soren snorted with contempt. "Figures Satu would have such an unconventional son."

Seppo raised his eyebrows. "My mother is an unconventional woman."

I looked closer at the halfling. He had sharp eyes and a long nose, ears tapered to tips, but his build was lean and lanky, more like a human's, and when he smiled, he bore no fangs. In all my years in the Permafrost, I'd never seen anyone like him.

"Unconventional" was the word Soren used, but I had a feeling he was trying to be polite to our savior. I had a feeling the word he wanted to use was "taboo."

Seppo's sapphire eyes latched onto me. "Close your mouth. You'll swallow a bug. Besides, I'd like to think this is nothing new to you at all, sweetheart. Considering . . ." He motioned between me and Soren with his little finger.

A choked sound came from Soren, whose hand was still clutching his arm. The puncture wound went deep into his nerves and muscles. His face didn't betray an ounce of pain, but his eyes grew wide at Seppo's words. "Let's talk about my choice of sexual partner another time, shall we?" he grunted. "I don't know if it escaped your notice, but the damn lindworm bit me and the venom usually is fatal."

This time the choked noise came from *me*. Soren's arm was

a nasty shade of yellow and green. Lindworm venom wasn't *usually* fatal; it was *always* fatal. It hit me with the force of a tempest, and the pain from the fight turned into a much deeper, less physical pain. It could've been me clutching my arm, dying slowly. It should've been me. The newfound feelings inside of me that had taken root during my time with the svartelves churned into a mixture of rage and pain. I could only stare at Soren, who turned paler by the second.

He looked down at me. His eyes were soft. "I'll be all right," he said. "I have to be."

"I thought goblins couldn't lie to themselves," I said.

"Well," Seppo pointed out, "he's lying to you. You're not the one with a built-in lie detector, sweetheart. He has a couple hours at least, maybe a day or two. The power he absorbed should keep the venom from killing him for a while. We might be able to figure something out."

"We?" I asked. "Who is we?"

Seppo blinked, taken aback by the hostility in my tone. "Well, you, Soren, and I. I had an idea. Besides, it's not like I'm going to run after Lydian while he licks his wounds. I *did* just save your lives."

I bristled. Even if he *was* sincere, he abandoned Lydian the moment he judged him weak. Who was to say he wouldn't do the same to us? "How do you know there's a way to cure him? Lindworm venom is fatal; there's no antivenom."

Seppo rolled his eyes. "If there was only one solution to every problem, the world would be insanely dull, don't you think, sweetheart?"

I gritted my teeth. "Do *not* call me sweetheart."

"I know you don't like me, and I understand it," Seppo continued as if I hadn't spoken. "But I would ask you to trust me, if you can."

"How could you understand?" I took a step forward, the stiletto in my hand out and ready to strike. "You've worked for that—that *monster*—and suddenly decide to betray him? Is this a trick? Do you think we're stupid enough to fall for it? I *know* the games he likes to play, or has he forgotten that? He's half-mad, after all."

The rage and hatred inside me threatened to spill like poison from my mouth. Soren was dying. Lydian was up to something. This halfling was shoving himself into our business when he had no place there at all. The feelings of security and peace that had calmed me like a drug when I kissed Soren in the cavern had disappeared without a trace. I'd *lost* it. I'd lost what I loved. Again.

Soren's hand brushed against my shoulder, rubbing my arms in a soothing circular motion. "Calm down, Janneke."

I turned on Soren. "Calm down? How in Hel can I do that? You're going to die! You're going to die and leave me here, and we both know what happens if you die! We both know!"

I couldn't do it. I wouldn't. I would never be Lydian's again. I would never feel that man's touch on my skin. The fear built up in me, and I sucked in my breaths quicker and quicker until I was hyperventilating. I stumbled forward, and Soren caught me in his arms.

"I'll never let him touch you," he whispered.

"And I had just decided I wanted to live too."

"And you will." His breath tickled my ear.

Soren didn't let me go as he addressed Seppo. "Satu is still alive, isn't she? Why isn't she on the Hunt? Why were you with Lydian and not her?"

"Well," Seppo said, kicking at a bone, "I never really intended to win. It just sounded fun. So, she gave me permission and here I am. As to why I was with Lydian, well . . ." He paused. "We both know the reason for that."

Soren grunted. "There doesn't seem like there's a reason for it anymore."

I detached myself from Soren, breathing deeply to draw out the shame spreading through my body. I shouldn't lose control like that; it would never serve me well. I straightened my bow on my shoulder, put the stiletto in the now-empty sheath on my hip, and let my face fall into a mask.

"What do you both mean?" I asked. I certainly didn't know the reason Seppo joined Lydian or why it mattered to Soren now. For Odin's sake, I didn't know why *anyone* would want to join up with Lydian.

"Do you remember when the stag ran?" Soren asked. "What happened right before it?"

"Yes, you both were throwing power around like mad, and the floor split and—" I stopped, having answered my own question. "Lydian's and your power were the strongest in the room that day. When you both released it, the stag recognized it and ran. Lydian and you are the two most likely candidates to be the next Erlking."

Soren nodded. "Yes, exactly. You don't know how many alliances I shot down before we went off." He shook his head. "Sometimes my fellow goblins are little more than vultures."

"Why, though? Why didn't you tell me?"

He sighed. "Do you think, at the time, you would have hated me any less?"

He had me there. Even now, picturing him on the Erlking's throne, the most powerful predator in the Permafrost, I couldn't help the disgust that threatened to curl my upper lip. But the idea of Lydian was worse.

Seppo looked behind him at the massive rock wall. Something shuddered, and the ground beneath us shook. "We have to keep moving. I wasn't lying about the eggs. There should be another way out of here. I mean, the male got in from somewhere, didn't he?"

I looked up toward the ceiling. Yes, I could see it. It was a treacherous climb with sharp points and jagged edges, black ice and loose rock, but there was a hole up top big enough for the creature to get through.

The others followed my gaze. "Let's go," Soren said. He let go of his wounded arm, the dark green of the puncture mark now spreading up the length of his arm. I forced back the fear. *We'll find a way.*

I followed him, casting a glare at Seppo as he came beside me. "Why did you betray Lydian?" I asked. "Or did you really?"

He eyed me calmly. "You really dislike me, don't you?"

"Give me a reason to like you," I said.

Seppo started ticking off fingers. "Well, one, I saved you from becoming lindworm chow. Two, I saved you and Soren from Lydian. Three, I think I have an idea about how to heal Soren. And last, but definitely not least, four, I know what Lydian is planning."

We'd reached the rock-and-ice wall. From where I stood, looking up at the daunting climb, the hole seemed miles away. But without a word, Soren boosted himself up against the crags, his body searching for any hold it could get. I found a foothold and started the ascent myself, forcing my gaze upward, never down at the ground, as I slowly went higher. Soren hissed as a piece of ice broke apart in his hand, leaving him hanging on by his bad arm. In one smooth motion, he swung his body until his back was against the wall, his feet on precarious ledges.

Before I could do anything to help him, he tensed the muscles in his legs and sprang up, managing to grab a higher hold that jutted outward. The muscles in his arms were quivering, a sight I'd never seen before. But despite the pain he *had* to be in, not a single sound escaped from his lips.

My fingers curled against the ice as I pulled myself farther and farther up. The temptation to look down gnawed at my insides, but if I did, I was positive I would freeze on spot. The muscles in my arms screamed as I pulled myself from handhold to handhold, jagged piece of ice after jagged piece of ice. When I finally got through the hole, which Soren had already climbed through, my body crumpled to the ground with exhaustion. I lay on the smooth stone, muscles still shaking with effort.

Seppo came up last. For a moment we just lay there, fighting for breath. I wrinkled my nose at the smell of putrid flesh. Soren's arm was getting worse.

Even though my body screamed at me to rest, I stood and straightened my weapons. "You said you knew a way to heal Soren," I said to Seppo.

"I did," he agreed.

"Well, then let's hear it," I snapped, glancing back to where Soren lay, clutching his arm. Fear fluttered in my throat. *He can't die. He can't.*

"You know you'd make a lot more friends if you weren't so tense," Seppo said.

"I'm not here to make friends," I said. "Do you know how to heal Soren or don't you?"

Seppo rubbed the back of his neck. "When she was younger, my mother spent a lot of time down here. She befriended the folk who lived here and mapped out every passage and which creature lived inside it. She even had a nickname."

"Fairy Tail," Soren rasped. "Because she followed the folk more than she did goblinkind."

"She taught me about the passageways. About how if you whistle high enough, you can cause rocks to cave in, about where each creature resides, what it does, what you can get from it. Svartelves give knowledge about yourself, if you can survive the twisted way they show it; others grant pleasure, riches, wishes." His gaze narrowed. "There's a nøkken down near here, and I think if we play him right, he can give us something."

Soren nodded gravely, standing with slow, heavy movements. I hoped it wasn't the venom, but instead his body aching from the climb. My own muscles were still spasming in pain, but I forced myself to keep standing. I would go on until I dropped.

"Nøkkens grant wishes, if you give them something in return," Seppo said. "Something personal, usually. It doesn't matter if there is no known cure for lindworm venom. A nøkken can make it if you desire it."

"They also like to trap their victims down underwater until they die," I said. The mothers of my village told their children the story before we could even walk. *Don't wander too close to the water's edge. The nøkken will take you down to his realm.*

"That won't happen," Seppo said, his voice sure. "We can outsmart them. *You* can outsmart them."

We'd started moving again, following Seppo down the darkened tunnels. Every nerve in my body urged me to kill this man. I didn't trust him. I'd made that clear, and whatever Soren thought of him, I would continue to be wary. He'd been Lydian's man.

"Why *me*?" I asked.

"Can't you hear it?" That was Soren, his voice stronger now than before. "The rushing sound? Wherever that creature is living, the current's too strong for any goblin to stand it. It'll have to be you."

I closed my eyes, straining my ears. Yes, he was right. The violent, thunderous sound of rushing water was close by, like a hundred horses stampeding past. It wasn't a current any goblin could survive in; it would suck all their power away the minute they hit the water.

"Seppo, can you give me a moment with Soren alone?"

He nodded and stepped away, back the way we came.

Soren eyed me. "You really don't trust him, do you?"

"Do you?"

"No. But I'd also rather not die, and I know he's telling the truth. Even if he *is* only half goblin, I can still tell if he lies, just like every other goblin. If we let him leave, we risk Lydian knowing what we're up to. If we keep him close, at best he can tell us what Lydian is planning; at worst, we have a hostage."

I nodded. Soren's words didn't help me relax, but they made sense. "He told me Lydian is planning something, and I don't think it's something good."

Soren snorted. "When does Lydian ever plan something good? No, but I heard him too. He's definitely up to something. I figured that out the moment he said he could *use* me. But if we kill Seppo, we might never know what's going on."

I sighed. "We have to do this, don't we?"

Soren nodded, his hair falling in front of his eyes. "I know you can do it. Whatever the nøkken asks of you, I know you have it in you. You're strong and brave, you can do anything you wish."

A giggle spurted from my lips. *Strong? Brave?* I didn't feel like either of those things. But Soren thought them, and brutal honesty was his specialty.

"Let's go then," I said.

"Seppo," Soren called back. "Come on."

Footsteps sounded until Seppo popped up again. As we walked, the rushing sound grew closer until the salty tinge of water was in the air. Back in Elvenhule we would go down to the docksides to swim, and the smell of the ocean was always my favorite. In the dark cavern, my heart twisted with homesickness as once again I smelled the sea. I pictured the water rushing, sloshing, roaring like the force of nature it was. I had been a good diver when I was young; I could still hold my breath for a long time. Surely, I could do this. I could, I *would* save Soren, just like he'd saved me.

"It's my fault you're poisoned, you know," I whispered, hoping Seppo wouldn't hear.

"No," he said plainly. "It isn't. I could've let you die, saved myself. My instincts would have agreed with that course of action. But I wasn't listening to my instincts, I was listening to something else."

"Your heart?" I raised an eyebrow.

He smirked. "You should know by now I'm a heartless monster."

From behind us, Seppo was pretending to heave. "Ugh. If I wanted to see a blossoming relationship, I'd have stuck to my mother."

Heat crawled up my neck.

"Seppo," Soren said, "I hardly ever agree with my uncle, so take this as the special occasion that it is. You talk too much. And you're beginning to annoy me."

Seppo's eyes widened at the dangerous tone Soren's voice had taken, and he nodded vigorously. Then, because the man couldn't seem to help being obnoxious, he pantomimed zipping his lips and throwing away the key.

"If I don't kill him because he's working for Lydian, I'm going to kill him because he's a pain in the ass," I muttered under my breath.

Soren's lips twitched into the ghost of a smile. Then he

stopped sharply, good arm out to block us from going farther. I peered over his shoulder, and my eyes widened in awe.

The salty water fell from a waterfall overhead, the current swift as it spiraled down and down into a whirlpool. The water was as black as night, moving at a pace that could sweep even the strongest swimmer away. I was a good swimmer, but *this*?

It doesn't matter. You need to save Soren. And this is how you'll do it. I swallowed. I could do this. *I hope.*

"Do you know where the lair would be?" Soren asked.

"There's got to be an underwater cove somewhere," Seppo said.

I unhooked the bow and quiver from my back, but kept the stiletto at my side, just in case. Then I narrowed my eyes at Seppo. "You better be right; if you're not, I'll kill you."

"I am right," he said. "I know I am."

Discreetly, I turned and whispered in Soren's ear, "If it came to it, you could take him, right?"

He snorted with contempt. "A half goblin? I'd have to be an inch from death not to take him."

I stepped forward onto the cold, slippery rock.

"I'll be back soon," I said, and dove in.

The coldness of the water shocked me, and I barely had a chance to recover before the rapid current swept me forward. I took a breath, forcing as much air into my lungs as I could, and dove deep. Despite the salt in the water, I opened my eyes to watch the dark currents spiral down. With a powerful kick, I pushed my body into one of the faster currents, riding it down to the bottom. My eyes blurred at the speed, and behind my ears the pressure built up until I was sure my brain would explode. There had to be an entrance somewhere.

The steady burning in my chest reminded me of my everdwindling supply of oxygen, but I'd held my breath for seven minutes in my prime. Even now, with my body begging for air, I was sure I could go for at least five.

I spotted the hole and propelled myself to it. The current pulled at me again, its ever-seeking fingers grasping at my clothes. I should've taken them off, never mind the embarrassment, but there was nothing I could do about it now.

I fought as the current tried to pull me back into the vortex, dragging myself from rocky outcrop to rocky outcrop. My muscles burned with exhaustion, my lungs burst into flames. Fighting a flow this strong was using up all my extra air. As my head grew light, I made a final thrust into the hole.

Inside the small hole, the water was calmer, lapping back and forth in gentle waves. My muscles relaxed as the calm water became clear, and as black spots edged my vision, the tunnel shot upward, then to the right, and my head burst from the water into the sweet, cold air. I sucked up as much as I could, gasping until I caught my breath. Then I pulled myself forward, up onto the stones where the water lapped gently.

A few feet before me the loose stones changed into hard ground. Above me, the ceiling glittered with crystals in an array of blues and purples and reds. I followed the stone, hearing the sound of a violin playing ever-so-sweetly.

I paused, listening in shock. Music wasn't really a thing in the Permafrost. I was sure some goblins enjoyed it, but they would be quiet about it. It was not something anyone would dare partake in by choice—or at least that was the illusion. I was beginning to learn not everything was so black and white. Back before I was taken, I'd loved music. My father would strum his guitar, and I'd sing the beautiful songs my mother taught me about fair maidens and dazzling heroes. That was a long time ago though, and I didn't know the words anymore. It didn't matter; it wasn't like they were true.

The hypnotic sound wrapped around me in a warm embrace, inviting me forward to stay forever and listen to the sweetness. The chords changed, managing to be sweet and melancholy and somber all at once. They seized my heart and brought it a-flight. The crystals twinkled with the music, and the world danced around me, blissful and beautiful.

I stopped suddenly, hand on my stiletto, and drew a quick slice across the tip of my finger. As the blood welled in the cut, the spell broke. The music was still beautiful, there was no doubt about that, but it no longer enthralled me. The crystals disappeared into dark stone formations colored red as blood.

The nøkken loved a fisherman's daughter who lived by his lake. The fisherman was poor and bad at his trade until the nøkken made an offer. Never would the fisherman want for anything, if he gave him his daughter when she turned eighteen. When the woman was brought down to the lake to meet her husband, she cringed at his scales and webbed fingers. Thrusting a knife in her chest, she cried she'd never love a monster as she died. The blood poured into the water, and the nøkken in his sorrow let the flowers in the lake turn red. He played his song every night, one of love and loss and

mourning, in hopes that one day another would come down to the
water and be with him forever.

I shuddered, casting my gaze across the cave. In the shadows was the figure of a man, and in the corners, lying in beds of flowers with seaweed in their hair, were the bodies of women who had come down to the water. All of them were perfectly preserved, even though time should've turned them to dust.

The figure moved, and I gripped my blade, ready to strike. But as the nøkken came out from the shadows, I found myself lowering my weapon. His clothes, once beautiful and elaborate, were ripped to shreds, his long coat tattered and frayed. He watched me silently, gazing with sad eyes the color of pond scum. His skin was mottled green and black. He brought his violin to his side as he came forward, slowly, carefully, as if the slightest movement would scare me away.

"You have heard my song?" he asked, his voice low and mournful, with a slight pinch of hope mixed in.

"It's beautiful," I admitted. "But not why I came." I had to word the next part carefully, as not to offend this powerful creature with sadness in his eyes. "I come to ask for a favor, and in return, I will give one to you."

The nøkken sighed, and lines of sadness creased his face as he looked back at the bodies of his loves, then at me. "You've felt sadness too," he whispered. "Ours would not be a happy love."

I doubted many of his loves were happy, but I wasn't about to say so.

"I need your help," I said. "Something only you can do."

His eyebrows rose. "Pray tell, but if I can do it, there will be a price. There always is a price. I keep my word, but you must keep yours. She did not, but I always did." He caressed the flowerlike stones surrounding us. "They've turned to stone, it was so long ago, but my heart, it aches as if it were just this morn."

"I'll keep my word," I said, swallowing at the thought of what this creature might want me to do. "But you need to help me."

"What do you wish for?" he asked.

"My . . . someone I care about, deeply, has been poisoned by lindworm venom. He doesn't have long left. I need an antidote; I need to save him." The desperation in my voice was palpable. Just a few decades ago I'd have been glad to see Soren burn. Out of pettiness if nothing else. Now I was begging deadly magical strangers for help to keep him alive. What a change.

The nøkken nodded. "He is not human, like you, is he? If he was, he'd be dead already."

I bit my lip. "He is goblin."

The hint of a sad, sad smile played on the nøkken's lips. "Then I suppose I am not the only one with unlucky loves. I will help you for a price."

"What is it?" I braced myself; whatever it was, I could do it.

"You have such sadness in your eyes, child," he mused. "Sing me a song to play in the caverns. Maybe it will give me luck."

I blinked, taken aback. A song? He wanted me to sing a song?

"I—I can't do that," I stuttered. "I'm not, I don't have any material or ideas or—"

The nøkken chuckled softly. "Oh, I think you do. That is my price, a song from your heart. That or your love dies and maybe you can stay here with me."

14

NEEDLESS/WANTLESS

I SEETHED WITH rage. Sing him *a song*? Anything remotely songlike was ripped from my lips the moment my village turned to ash. No lullaby, hunting tune, or ballad survived the destruction. Sing him a *song*. He might as well have asked me to lasso a star.

Maybe I could try to reason with him. *Or maybe you'll be stuck for centuries and Soren will die.*

"I don't know any songs," I said again, more forcefully this time. "So, I can't sing something for you. Is there anything *else*?"

The nøkken laughed a cruel, bitter laugh. "You've no songs? You have plenty. All there in your head. Do you think the pain you feel is meant to be stuck inside of you, never released? No. That's why the Aesir and Vanir granted us music and the wonderfulness of words. You have a song, sweet child, but if you can't find it, there's nothing I can do. Your boy will die, and letting you go . . . I don't think I like that idea."

My fingers tightened around the stiletto. "Okay," I said. "Okay. Just give me a minute to think."

"A minute, an hour, a millennium," he mused, "it's all the same to me."

I shivered at his tone. I'd been around insane beings enough to know their danger. Whether it was the lost lovers and endless solitude of the nøkken or whatever sickness in the head plagued Lydian, I needed to be really careful. One wrong move . . .

A sliver of fear found its way to my heart. *I could've been like this if I were a normal human. If I'd survived this long, if Lydian's torture had gotten to me, I could've been exactly like this.* I shook the thought away, focusing back on the issue at hand.

A song. I didn't even know whether I had a decent voice, much less if there was a song somewhere deep in my heart. *Get your head straight, Janneke. If you don't do this, Soren dies.* I'd lived through the raid of my family, the torture from Lydian, the endless battles of the Hunt, I could sing a fucking song.

"All right." I breathed in deeply. "Give me a moment. I just need some inspiration."

The nøkken bared his rows of sharp teeth in a smile. I shuddered; the multiple rows pressed down one behind another like sharks'. I pitied the dead women on the ground who were forced to kiss that mouth.

"I can help with that." He held out a hand. His skin was warm and slimy, like the mud and mossy mixture of a swamp, but his grip was strong. He bent down, sharp teeth still out, and pricked my hand. I jerked back as a small trail of blood dripped from the heel of my palm.

"What did you do?"

"I have given you inspiration."

The blood had already stopped flowing, but a sharp wave of vertigo hit and I stumbled forward. Up and down, left and right mixed together until the world twisted around like a kaleidoscope.

Are you dead? I knew that voice. That voice made me shudder, scream, and cry. It'd taken everything away from me. *You're not supposed to die yet. I need to know first! I need to know!* I blinked rapidly, haunted by the images flashing across my eyes. *Dragged by a horse. Tormented every night. Are you dead yet, little girl? Are you dead? No? Good. Don't worry, it'll all be over soon.*

Pain blossomed inside my breast, powerful enough for me to double over, clutching my stomach. The breath escaped my lungs in quick spurts as fear and pain and memories I'd long tried to forget spun a weave inside my head.

> *"Are you dead?*
> *Little girl*
> *Why don't you close your eyes?*
> *Are you dead?*
> *Little girl*
> *Tonight*
>
> *Are you dead?*
> *Little girl*

Are you an angel in flight?
Or are you lost in your body?
Lost in the world?"

It was a thick blanket smothering me: Helka's power, the young lordling's, Elvira's and the lindworm's, Panic's death and Rekke's, it threatened to choke the life out of me and leave me lifeless on the floor.

"It slowly takes and captivates
And wraps around our skin
The curtains that we hide behind
Cradle us in our sin
The night is dark
The world is cruel
And the stars are all on fire
But that little girl
That little girl
Her one and only desire"

My throat was on fire. The words had always been there. A bloody hand grabbing a new lord's cloak, darkness lining my vision and the hope that it would never lift, coldness inside my chest when I passed by the betrayed looks from the dead who considered me a blood traitor in my dreams; all I longed to forget now bubbling to the surface.

"Are you dead?
Little girl

Wear your heart on your sleeve
Are you dead?
Little girl
You're not supposed to grieve

Are you dead?
Little girl
Why does your skin feel so numb?
Little girl
Little girl
What have you done?"

The river water was cold against the agony of my burns, and the lies and secrets swirled around, battering my body. Hunger gnawed inside me, so fierce I couldn't ignore it. But the hunger was for more than food; it was for blood and pain, desire and revenge.

"The world it shatters like raining glass
Veils eyes, thoughts, and minds
Our daily bread is all we ask
But it is too much to find
Your heart is weak
My breath is stone
And we weave a web of lies
Are you dead?
Little girl
You're not supposed to cry."

Strength poured from my once-quivering voice as I straightened to look the nøkken in the eye. His glee-filled gaze at the
pain coming from my lips made my stomach churn in disgust.
His shrewd, calculating nature made me naked before him.

But he wouldn't have me. No one would. Not unless I
wanted it. No hands would roam where I forbade them, no lips
or teeth would press against my flesh unless it was my wish. I
was my own. The dregs of pain and fear I'd long buried bubbled to the surface, but I stood strong against their blows.

> *"Are you dead?*
> *Little girl*
> *Have they ravaged your skin?*
> *Are you dead?*
> *Little girl*
> *Have the demons come in?*
> *Are you dead?*
> *Little girl*
> *Like a lamb in the field?*
> *Little girl*
> *Oh little girl*
> *Your soul won't be healed."*

I was alive and breathing and fighting with every step I
took. The mocking voice asking me over and over inside my
head why my heart still went on was nothing more than the
blood rushing in my ears. My voice rose with anger as I spat
out the words in revulsion.

"Are you lost?
Little girl
Are you scared?
Little girl
Are you weak?
Little girl
Are you angry?
Little girl
Are you sad?
Little girl
Are you numb?
Little girl
Are you there?
Little girl
Are you there?
Little girl
Are you there?
Little girl?"

My father's blood drenched my hands as a million pairs of eyes judged me, the daughter who chose the future over her past. But the shame that washed over me was nothing compared to the rage burning me up. *We are all monsters even if we choose not to believe it.* And the worst type were those who didn't understand that. I was *not* a blood traitor for surviving and thriving. I was *not* damaged or broken or twisted beyond repair. No dead, mocking voices could tell me otherwise.

> *"We fall on our knees for you, sweet little child*
> *We would die and appease for your sweet darling smile*
> *But we don't have a need for you*
> *We don't have a part*
> *So go out in the wild*
> *Let the wolves eat your heart."*

I breathed out, the anger gone from my voice, and once more I whispered.

> *"Are you dead?*
> *Little girl*
> *Are you dead?*
> *Little girl*
> *Are you dead?*
> *Little girl*
> *Why are your eyes still open?"*

I shuddered at the last words but kept my gaze on the creature before me. "There is your song. Now give me what I need to heal Soren."

The nøkken slowly nodded; I could almost see the thoughts stirring inside his head. "You do have a story, don't you?" A slow smile spread across his face. "I can feel it like your own heart beating."

I scowled. The remains of my past still whirred through my adrenaline-addled brain. I pushed them far away, locking them back in the place they belonged. *The past is the past.* I was alive. My eyes would always be open, watching every creature's every move. I would withstand whatever life threw at me. I was as sure of it as I was the breath in my body.

"I want what we bargained for," I demanded.

The creature smiled sadly. "And you will get it."

The calculating look in his eyes made my shoulders itch with discomfort. "All right, then," I said. "Let's have it."

The nøkken ambled his way across the cave like there wasn't a goblin a hundred feet above him dying of lindworm venom. He paused by the stone flowers and spoke to them as if they were people. One of his scaly hands brushed against the water lily–adorned hair of a dead girl.

I don't have time for this. "Excuse me, I'm kind of on a deadline."

He looked over at me, a clear film covering his eyes like a snake. "Patience, sweet child."

I clenched my fists and reminded myself this was the only way to save Soren, and if that meant dealing with a senile nøkken, then I could do it. At least my throbbing palm was sealing up.

But then the strength the song gave me seeped away until the fire in my body turned to cold ashes. Voices came, scowling, snarling, taunting, all mocking every flaw, every vulnerability.

A thin sheet of sweat broke out across my body as my heart picked up speed. Regret tugged sharply at my gut as I pictured my father's last moments with me, but deep inside I knew there was nothing I would've done differently, given another chance.

Lydian's words came out of my father's mouth. *Worthless.*

Needless. Wantless. A lucky human left to die. They were more painful than any poison.

Someone cleared their throat, and I stared up at the nøkken. He had a vial in his hand, full of some odd purple salve. "Spread this directly on the wound," he said. "And he should be fine within the hour."

I took the vial with trembling hands, remembering those first long nights in Soren's manor when Tanya worked tirelessly to save my broken, beaten body. The look of myself in the mirror, realizing the extent of what Lydian had done to me. The massive scar tissue, the ugly blotch where my right breast used to be. The lines along my spine and stomach and ribs, the deep grooves on my face as stark white scar tissue stood out against dark skin. I'd never thought I was pretty, but I'd never believed I was ugly either. Not until then.

"Although, I wonder," the nøkken said, "are you fine?"

"I'm fine," I said. "I just need to get out of here." My fingers curled tightly around the vial. "Thank you."

The cave beckoned for me to let the creature soak away my sorrow and turn it into red stone in the shape of flowers. I forced myself to take one step, then another, focusing on the cold water lapping steadily against my bare feet. I stuffed the vial in the pocket on my bracer, now grateful I hadn't taken off all my clothes before diving in.

It was relatively calm at first. The coldness of the water shocked away any lingering memories. I swam down the cavern, back to the dark, black water that waited for me, swirling in a merciless trap.

The second I hit the blackness, the force of the whirlpool

nearly blew me back into the cavern. I grasped a jagged rock, pulling myself into the stream. Water beat my body without pity, throwing me around like a ragdoll. I grasped another rock, then another, pulling myself up as the whirlpool greedily sucked me down.

My head broke through the surface, and I gasped as air filled my burning lungs. The water wasn't ready to relinquish its hold and tugged me back down under the waves.

In the blackness, a green hand glowed. Its long fingers wrapped around my ankle, nails digging into the skin. The nøkken's eyes burned with an eerie green fire as he dragged me under. I thrashed in the churning waves, panic beating in chest.

He gave me his word. But he never said he'd let me go once I got the cure. I reached for the stiletto on my belt and with difficulty pulled it free. Then I swiped at the nøkken's fingers. He let go, letting blood flow from where his nails had dug into my ankle. Light flashed behind my eyes, and the pain, loss, and regret spilled back out from where I'd buried it. *Worthless, needless, wantless. Whip marks on bare flesh, glares from ghosts, rejection, death. The taste of raw meat in my mouth. The arrows through dead bodies, countless dead bodies.* It was too much. Just too much. If my chest burst open and spilled my insides into the water, I wouldn't be surprised. The pressure and pain threatened to tear at the seams inside me.

I sank, my lips parting, eyes closing. A force hit me like a boulder, shoving me into the rocky wall of the abyss. Fingers pried the stiletto from my hand, and I couldn't even try to stop it; the horrifying visions of blood and flesh and death played like a wheel spinning endlessly. The same force wrapped its arms around my waist, under my armpits, and jerked heavily once, twice, then again until the cold air blasted me from all directions.

Gasping for breath, a pair of pale hands pulled me up out of the water. Soren's concerned eyes latched onto mine, and in the darkness they raged with fever. The wound on his arm was turning black, the skin open and ugly. Without a second to waste, I ripped open the pocket of my bracer, pulled out the vial, and rubbed the contents into the deepest part of his wounds. Then I collapsed, the visions dancing before my eyes, taking over.

SOMETIME LATER, I woke up screaming, trapped in a pair of arms. *Lydian. Lydian. He's come to kill me.* The vicious goblin was right before my eyes, his once-pretty body now animalistic and bending over to take what he thought was his. But the voice that spoke wasn't Lydian's. It calmed my racing heart, but only just.

"Shh," he said. "You're going to be all right. It's going to pass. I've got you."

The sweet darkness returned and took away the pain with it. A scream disturbed the peace, and I was on a field of bodies, those of my family, those of my friends, the bones of children piled high at my feet. *Your fault,* the skeletons said. *Your fault. You could've warned us. You could've helped us hide. But you saved yourself. Your worthless, worthless self.* The disfigured body of a young boy sat up, staring around with one good eye, the other half of his face ripped into bloody shreds. His auburn hair spilled down in ringlets, darkened by blood. The boy's eye found me, and he tilted his head. *Auntie,* he said, *why didn't you save me?*

I clawed at my face and eyes if only to make it stop. But strong hands held me in place. The arms still pressed me firmly against a body that was hard and warm and almost shield-like as it enclosed me in its embrace.

"It's not real," he said. "None of it is real." I shook. It was right in front of me! All of it! The piles of bones and the ghosts, the skeletons and the demons towering over me. I couldn't be the only one who saw it.

I'm sorry, I wanted to say to my sister's son. *I'm sorry. I'm so sorry! I would change everything if I could!* But no words came out of my dry, dusty mouth.

The boy frowned and said, *How come I get half a face and you get a whole one? It's not fair.* The heartbroken look in his single blue eye tore my body into pieces, and I madly clawed at my own skin.

I'll make it up. I'll make it up. I'll make it up!

Even though the strong hands were restraining now, their grip didn't hurt. The warm body curling around me calmed me with its rapid heartbeat. The breath that'd rushed from my lungs was steadying.

"There," he said. "It's almost over. It's almost out of your system." A hand ran through my hair, the sharp nails pricking my scalp. The sensation lit every nerve in my body in a mix of anxiety and euphoria.

Then I was by Soren's side as countless ghosts trudged by,

their burnt bodies and dead eyes glaring at me accusingly, and their mockery leaving their skeletal mouths as the sound of clinking bones. *Who are you, thrall, to follow behind him and keep his company? Who are you to reject your homeland and the teachings of your family?* Targets became dead humans whose stares haunted me. With what little emotion they had left, they glared, they judged. *You're a blood traitor,* they said. *You should die with us, not lower yourself to their standards. You're nothing but a whore. A pet. A lamb in wolfskin pretending to howl at the moon.*

My howl isn't pretend anymore. The thought floated into my head. *Neither are my claws.*

WHEN I WOKE for real, it didn't surprise me that I was wrapped in Soren's arms. His muscular body pressed against mine, curling protectively around me. The wounds on my ankle from the nøkken had faded, but the lingering smell of brine made acid churn in my stomach.

Soren's hands were firmly wrapped around my wrists. I noticed red beneath my fingernails. I shifted slightly, my head pressing against Soren's chest. Where his heart should've been, there was a deep indent. In my nightmares there'd been rapid thumping, but it could've been the waterfall. Did goblins have normal heartbeats? I didn't know.

"Janneke." His hard face relaxed in relief. "It's over now. It's over."

I breathed in his scent of woodsmoke and pine needles. "You know," I murmured, letting the scent overwhelm me, "you were wrong."

"What could I possibly be wrong about?" I didn't see the smile, but I knew it was there, just like I knew there'd be a twinkling light in his eyes.

"You're not a heartless monster," I said. "You're a monster with a heart."

He laughed.

"Are you all right?" I asked. The sickening smell of dying flesh was gone, though the copper tang of blood was still in the air. With a little bit of maneuvering, my eyes rested on a long, newly formed pink scar on his arm.

"I'm fine," he said. "You had me worried for a while." He started to disentangle himself from me, leaving a cold space where his body had been. My body ached with the desire to reach for him, to keep him close.

"What happened to me?"

The answer came from behind me. "Nøkkens draw blood to increase the emotional anguish in their victims. Anything that hurts them or makes them feel regret, sorrow, anger, comes out in waves. They feed off those as much as they feed off the love of humans. I should've warned you before you dove. I didn't think the deal would go sour so fast. I apologize."

Seppo stood a little away from us. The swirls of tattoos around his ears and cheeks glowed dark sapphire in the little light.

"You saved my life," I said. "You went into the water when you knew it would hurt you, maybe kill you."

Seppo shrugged. "It's nothing."

"It is something," Soren argued. "Thank you."

The tips of Seppo's ears reddened. "Well, if both of you

died, then I'd have no one to tell Lydian's plans to. And then I'd be stuck going against him alone and then probably would die in a horrifying or painful way. Probably both. So, this is a better outcome."

I stiffened. Seppo had mentioned Lydian's plan in his list of reasons not to hate him. I grumbled as it dawned on me that now he had another reason—he'd saved my life *twice*. Being in another's debt was not something I enjoyed. "All goblins make plans on the Hunt. What makes Lydian any different?"

Seppo looked over his shoulder, back at the churning water. He shuddered and faced us. "All goblins have plans during the Hunt, true. But I don't think any of them have plans anything like his."

Soren raised his eyebrows. "And what are they?"

Seppo gulped, and fear glistened in his dark blue eyes. "He wants to kill the stag."

"Every goblin wants to kill the stag." Irritation colored Soren's voice. "I doubt Lydian is different."

"No," Seppo said. "You don't understand. He wants to *kill* it for *good* so he can be Erlking for eternity."

15

LYDIAN'S GAMBIT

THE SILENCE WAS deafening, then Soren stood and paced. He reminded me of an animal trapped in a cage waiting for the correct moment to escape and rip out its captor's throat. Pacing was not a sign of weakness for him.

"That's impossible," I said, trying not to choke on my fear.

"That's what I thought too," Seppo said. He looked over his shoulder, back toward the nøkken's lair. The swirling water was green. "We need to get out of these caverns. I don't think the nøkken is very happy. Which isn't a surprise since they're eternally depressed creatures. But still."

"That's what we've been trying to do," Soren grunted. "It's a maze down here, though, and I'd rather not run into any more dragons." Fear tinged his voice. I almost laughed. I spent a hundred years thinking nothing frightened this man, but I was wrong.

"Well," Seppo said, "you two haven't been scouting this place for days."

For days? There was no way two groups of goblins had been able to linger in the mountains without detecting one another. The ambushers on the cliffsides must've detected Lydian's group at some point, unless . . . my stomach turned sour. *I'll kill a thousand little goblin girls if I have to.* Lydian's crazed words now made much more sense.

"You were the ambushers." I turned on Seppo. "It's your fault we're in this mess in the first place!"

Lydian was behind it all along. The mountainside ambush, my subsequent fall, and Rekke's death were all *his* fault. The golden-eyed goblin girl should've lived. It wasn't like she would've won. She barely had any power, but Lydian gutted her anyway.

"How many of you are out here?" I narrowed my eyes, voice hard.

Seppo put his hands up in a submissive motion. "Look, I'm not with them anymore. Promise." He pulled out the stiletto he'd given me earlier. "Here, I took this to fight the nøkken. Take it back."

I snatched the weapon back, though unease still turned in my stomach. "You were the ones responsible for the ambush, for Rekke's death."

"That's how it is, Janneke." There was sadness underneath Soren's calm tone.

"I thought you were on my side with this! We both knew she wasn't going to win." I turned and punched a rock wall, pain shot up my arm, and I clenched my wrist. "Go fuck the crows!"

Seppo glanced at Soren. "Is she usually this . . ." He searched for the right word.

"Finish that sentence, Satunpoika, and I will shove that feather staff up your ass," I spat.

"Yes," Soren answered.

I scowled. "So, you were the ones who attacked us. Have you been stalking us the whole time?"

Seppo shook his head. "No, we were on the mountain for another reason." A drop of sweat fell from his forehead as he hushed his anxious tone. "And it's got to do with what I need to tell you."

I crossed my arms. "But there are more of you."

"More of *them*, yes," Seppo said. "Lydian has about twenty-five, or well, I guess twenty-one men at his disposal. We have three."

"There is no 'we,'" I growled.

Soren stepped in between us. "All right, all right. I can't believe I'm the one saying this, but both of you just calm down. We need to get out of here, and we need to know what Lydian is planning. If he's planning anything." He shot a glance at Seppo. "I know when you lie to me."

Seppo rolled his eyes. "I'm all about cordiality."

Soren raised an eyebrow at me.

I gave Seppo a withering look. "I won't shove your feather staff up your ass."

"I appreciate that."

"Come on." Soren sighed. "We shouldn't stay here. The water is riling us up." He headed for an opening in the chasm, one that glittered with blue light. "The darker the ice, the lower we are. I know that."

I followed, boosting myself up into the crack and squeezing in after Soren. Seppo was right on my tail, and for a long time we climbed up the dark, cold slit in silence. The sides soon opened up, and bright light dazzled me.

The last ledge was within my reach, but when I stretched, the rock underneath my feet gave away. Before I could fall, Seppo dove ahead, catching me with his broad shoulders. "That's three times now," he said.

"Are we counting?"

"Yes."

I snorted with contempt, and with muscles burning, I flopped down onto the solid ground of a cliffside cave. Still wet from my swim, I was chilled to the bone from the arctic air. I rubbed my arms but nothing worked.

Soren watched from where he sat, frowned, then came over and set me in his lap. One of his hands gently brushed back and forth over my shoulders.

Heat rose from my body. It was so *human*. When I turned my questioning gaze to him, he smirked. "You're cold. I'm not. We lost all our supplies."

Seppo eyed us with a mixture of disgust and curiosity. Glaring, I mouthed *feather staff*, and whatever he was about to say died on his lips. Instead, he shook himself and said, "So, now that we're all above ground and nice and cozy, let's talk about Lydian."

"I can still push you off the cliff, you know."

Seppo's eyes narrowed.

"So, Lydian. What *does* my dear uncle have in store?" Soren's voice was dark with fury. For all I knew about him, very little was about his relationship with his uncle. They hated each other as plain as day, but otherwise Lydian's name was never spoken in the manor.

I sat up, leaning slightly against Soren's shoulders. Whatever happened, his scent of woodsmoke and pine needles calmed my restless heart. *Lydian can't hurt you. You're so strong now.*

Soren purred. "You being close." One of his hands wrapped around my waist. His fingers splayed and stroked the bare skin underneath my tunic, and I shivered in delight. "I like it. A little too much, I think, for this conversation."

"Sorry." I began to straighten and move off him.

"No, stay where you are. We can hear about the plotting of my horrific uncle and have our skin touch at the same time. I can multitask."

I almost laughed. If someone told me a year ago this would happen, I'd say they were absurd. But now, it was almost as if I were the absurd one. But the happiness would die a quick death if Lydian came anywhere near the throne, so I straightened despite Soren's protest and leaned back against the dank cave wall.

"Lydian," I said. "What's his game plan? How come you know it?"

Seppo twisted his fingers around the fringes of his tunic. "Satu was originally invited to go along with him, but she declined. He's been chasing her for years, and she figured even the dumbest goblin could figure out she meant no if she sent the son of her human lover. I agreed to go, mainly because when he's not a raving lunatic, Lydian's kinda fun to mess with."

Soren and I looked at each other. Part of me was horrified for Satu and what she dealt with; the other part was awed that Seppo enjoyed messing with someone whose very name made me quake in fear.

"Anyway," Seppo continued, "he wasn't very happy I was sent instead, but I reminded him that his invitation said he was looking forward to seeing Satu's clan at the Hunt and I *was* Satu's clan. He had no choice but to accept me."

"I'm surprised he didn't kill you," Soren said. "He's done more for less."

"Well," Seppo deadpanned, "he really wants to sleep with my mother, and sending my head back on a platter would probably kill any blossoming desire he's sure she's hiding."

I cringed. "Okay, less talk about Lydian wanting to sleep with your mom, more talk about the plan." If I heard one more word of this, I was going to throw up—preferably on Seppo.

"Well, I was taught acting ignorant was a better way of getting information than being the bruiser for the tough guy, so I played that angle. Lydian and a few other men were planning to reach the mountain top and call Skadi while the rest of us waited in ambush. I managed to tag along without them knowing."

I grumbled something under my breath. I had to hand it to him—he had guts to spy on not just Lydian, but Skadi, an actual goddess and giantess.

Seppo glanced around the cave. "So he called her and asked for an exchange; he would provide a favor for her if she did one for him. Lydian asked if there was any way the stag could be killed for good. He started rambling about destruction and betrayals and how something terrible would happen unless he could stop it. Something about a snake eating its own tail or whatever. It really wasn't very coherent."

Soren's eyebrows furrowed into a deep frown. "Lydian is clearly mad. So why would Skadi *tell* him anything?"

Seppo shrugged. "I'm not sure the exact reason. She might have thought he meant to prevent whatever terrible thing he said would happen. But I do know that something was preying on her pack of wolves and she couldn't defeat it, and she was anguished over it. When the Aesir killed her father and she fell out with Njord, she went back to the mountains and the wolves became her family. She said if Lydian killed the creature, then she would give him the information he sought. He came back with the severed head of the monster, and she gave him information."

"Which was?"

Seppo swallowed, eyes shooting around. "I'm not sure. By the time he got the information, the others found out where I was. I only just managed to convince them I got lost. I'm pretty sure I still have a dislocated rib."

Soren's eyes narrowed. "So, we know what he's doing, but we don't know *how* he's going to do it? That's helpful."

I scowled. "We're back to square one." The moon was a sliver in the night sky. Donnar's warning came back to me. *By new moon it will all be undone.* Soren said there was never a hunt that lasted past the new moon. That could have something to do with Lydian, or perhaps it was another way we could stop him. No matter *how* he was planning to kill the stag for good, there was no denying that if he did, he'd upset the balance of the world.

Back when Lydian and Soren almost fought in the Erl-king's hall, their power almost brought the mansion down. The stag was all that stood in the way. Just as goblins absorbed the power of the creatures they defeated, the stag absorbed the power of the strong and released it to the weak, keeping some type of balance in effect. It detected when the foundation the world sat on became feeble and ensured that new blood would make it strong again. Like winter after a long summer, it let the old die and made way for the new. If the stag died forever, the power pledged to the new Erlking would be his, unregulated, forever.

The whole idea was mad. It was insane. *Lydian* was insane.

Soren and I shared a mind. "The bastard," he said. "We need to stop him. But for that, we need to figure out what he's doing."

"Seppo?" I asked. "Why are you doing this?"

The halfling shrugged. "It seemed like the right thing to do."

I stared at him in shock.

"I know that's hard to believe," he said. "But it's true. It's not right. And it shouldn't happen. And we need to stop him from whatever he's doing."

Wordlessly, Soren and I stood. He slung his swords in their holsters, checked that his knife was still in his boot, and slung his quiver and bow across his chest. I adjusted the stiletto on my hip and the bracers on my arms. Deep inside the leather, the nail was burning.

"You need to dispose of that soon," Soren said, looking at the bracer. Could he smell the burning? I could. "I know why you have it, but it's not worth it now. You don't need iron to gauge how human you are. You're as human as you want to be."

My gaze hardened. "I need to keep it. I just need to." I couldn't take the time to explain to him the tugging in my gut that told me the nail had yet to fulfill its purpose. Maybe it was just in my head. Maybe I couldn't get rid of it because it was the last thing with ties to my old life. Either way, I couldn't let it go.

We gathered outside the cave, the harsh wind whipping us with ice and dust. My hair streamed in the wind until I tucked it under my hood. In his free time while dying from lindworm venom, Soren had rebraided his hair, and it hung loosely to his waist. I scowled. It shone like snow. Mine still smelled of brine and pond scum.

He caught me glaring and smirked. "You're cute when you're jealous."

"Go eat your young."

Seppo snickered. "Any young of his are coming from you."

I made a scene of looking down the sheer cliffs to the blackened, icy forest below. "Do you have a death wish? Because I *will* push you off the mountain."

The snickering stopped at once. "I believe you."

Soren rolled his eyes. "You two, seriously? It's like a dog bickering with a much tinier dog, and the tinier dog is winning." He shielded his face from the sun, looking high for a path to lead us out.

"Your analogy skills need work." Mountains spread as far

as the eye could see; some were just dots on the horizon and others were huge behemoths in our path. The pathway Soren chose soon faded into the rocky randomness of the wilderness. We'd have to climb and lug our way out of the mountain range. It could take days, maybe weeks. We had no food, no water, worn-out clothing, and the weapons on our backs. By the time we got to the ground, Lydian might've already won. *He wants to use Soren, but he doesn't need him.* Soren met my eyes and offered me a small smile, and his gaze burned with the warmth I was coming to know.

I narrowed my eyes at the ground, hoping to see the silver line the stag left behind. There was nothing. Just ice and dust and snow.

"We're never going to get out of here in time." I finally spoke the words everyone was afraid to say aloud. "We'll die out here, if not from hypothermia, then starvation or dehydration." The artic wind howled as if it was agreeing with me. The tips of my eyelashes were dusted with frost, and despite the leather gloves on my hands, I barely felt my fingers.

"We need horses or something to ride," Soren said. "That's the only way."

I looked at Seppo. "I don't suppose you have three horses up your sleeve, do you?"

He shook his head. "Afraid not."

The howling of wolves echoed in the crystal-cold air. I pulled my half cloak around me. From the corner of my eye, I saw Seppo shiver. If I weren't freezing myself, I could almost pity him. Out of the three of us, Soren was the only one whose body was made for this weather. But even a full-blooded goblin born and raised in the Higher North would freeze eventually.

"Well, then," Soren said, his breath turning to frost. "We'd best keep going. We're not going to achieve anything by standing here."

"We're not going to get anywhere fast, but better to move, I guess." Doubt wasn't the only thing gnawing my hollow stomach. I was sure Soren could hear the growling. The effects of the nectar were now almost gone, and every muscle in my body screamed with fatigue.

Hopelessly lost in the mountain range, banged and beaten from our time in the caverns, I wouldn't be surprised if an animal tried to pick us off. We were sitting ducks for any goblins in the range too. Every once in a while we came across a frozen body, and each time it reminded me that the longer we were out here, the more likely we would be killed. There was no fast escape and no place to hide if an attack came.

The mournful howls of wolves filled the nighttime air with song. It was almost as if we spoke the same language. Their song was of loss and grief, pain and fear, tiredness and the ache for revenge.

Skadi. They killed your family too. The Aesir thought they were better because they were gods and you a giant and they sought to tame you with a man you could never love. But you went and took your revenge. You rule these wilds. You rule all of us. When I was a child, I prayed to her almost constantly, hoping she could help me discover my destiny. Going to the Permafrost stopped that. I'd never been closer to the gods or farther away.

The wolves sung so mournfully, as if they were still griev-
ing their lost brothers and sisters. An uneasy thought struck
me. "Seppo, are you *sure* Lydian killed whatever was preying
on the wolves?"

"Well," Seppo said, "considering that he brought back the
head of a troll, I would hope so."

"You *hope* so. There could be a potentially dangerous monster lurking in the Permafrost that even an ascended giantess
can't kill?"

He worried at his lip. "Well, when you put it *that* way . . ."

Something inside me broke, and I started to giggle. It was
quiet at first, then grew louder and louder until my sides were
heaving in pain from laughter. I doubled over, hitting my knee
with my fist. Tears were in my eyes.

Seppo eyed me like I'd gone mad. "Why is she laughing?"

Soren's eyebrows furrowed. "I . . . don't know. Do you
think she's still sick?"

"You—" I choked down another wave of laughter.
"We've— Since we went to the Erlking's palace, I was almost
killed by Lydian for the second time, got into a fight inside
the palace, threw a man over a ledge, killed a goblin at point-
blank range, pounded Helka's corpse into pulp, almost burned
my arms off in the Fire Bog, fought and fell off a gods-forsaken
mountain, had a shitty dream quest with a svartelf, kissed you,
killed a fucking *dragon*, held my breath for six minutes inside
a whirlpool in order to sing a song to a senile nøkken who almost drowned me so I could save your life, found out Lydian
might end up destroying the world, and *now* we might be facing a mystery monster if the thrice-damned wolves don't get

us first!" I started coughing. I couldn't remember the last time I'd laughed this hard. "How in Hel's gate am I still *standing*?"

Soren frowned, then slowly smiled. The points of his canines gleamed in the cold sun. "Because you're the tiny dog."

"The tiny dog?" I asked as the last waves of laughter left my body.

"I said Seppo and you fought like a dog and a tinier dog, and the tinier dog was winning. You're the tiny dog. You're the most vulnerable of us, but it doesn't stop you. You could break your arm in three different places, have an eye gouged out and an arrow through your back, and you'd *still* keep fighting. You're the tiny dog."

Seppo snorted. "Tiny dog, not-so-tiny teeth."

The chorus of wolves began again as the sun was sinking in the sky. My body was strangely light, as if all the laughter was weight I'd carried on my shoulders. But the threat of death out here was looming as the sky turned to crimson. Even if Lydian *did* kill the monster preying on the wolves, the wolves themselves . . . I froze in place and Seppo smacked into me.

"Ouch!" He held his nose. "What's the big idea?"

"The wolves," I said. "Skadi's wolves."

"What about them?"

"We can ride them," I said. "It's possible. The Valkyries did it. They can get us out of here." Like lightning, another idea struck me. "If the monster Lydian killed isn't the one who preyed on her wolf pack, we could strike a bargain. She could tell us what she told Lydian and lend us wolves to ride in exchange for us killing the monster."

"Unless she kills us for being associated with Lydian in the first place," Seppo said. When I glared, he clarified. "I'm associated with Lydian because I was his ally, you are because you're my allies."

Soren gave us a withering look. "Skadi is fair. Even if Seppo is with us, we might be able to strike a deal. If it means figuring out what Lydian is planning, then I would rather fight what's out there than go in blind. We handled the lindworms; we can handle this. Besides, those wolves are ungodly fast."

I looked up at the snowy peak before us. The rocks poked through the snow as the slope got less and less prominent. Soon, we'd be at the top. I sucked in a breath of air, knowing the elevation was taking a toll on my lungs more than on the others'. We had to find a way. This idea, it *had* to work.

"We'll summon her," I said, my breath turning to ice in the air before me. "We'll summon the Mother of Wolves."

16

MOTHER OF WOLVES

EFORE WE SUMMONED the Mother of Wolves, we had to lug ourselves another twenty meters up the mountain. For once, I took the lead as the blinding wind whipped my hair against my face.

"You should've let me braid it," Soren said after my hair got in his face for the ninth time.

"In what downtime did you ask to braid my hair?" I tried to stick it back underneath my hood but strands kept escaping, and I finally gave up.

"Well, I tried while you were unconscious after your swim, but you hit me. Hard. I have a bruise."

"I told him not to do it," Seppo said. "I told him that trying to braid the hair of a person undergoing a chemical psychotic spell wasn't a good idea. Did he listen? No."

I smirked. "Where did I bruise him?"

"Nowhere important." Soren was trying hard to keep his voice light. A little *too* hard.

"Oh, it's important all right," Seppo said. I tuned out as

the two men began to bicker over what happened when I was unconscious. I was a little disappointed that I missed my own show.

I spat out a strand of hair. *Maybe I should cut it if I live after this.*

If I lived after this and stopped Lydian from carrying out whatever scheme he had up his sleeve. If I lived through seeking the help of a giantess god and whatever task she would request from me. Gods above, if someone told me a few years ago I'd be in this situation, I would've laughed. And maybe hit them.

I walked to the flat bed of rocks and dusty snow that was the peak of the mountains. The crisp air stung my ears and eyes, freezing the moisture inside my nose. The temperature dropped rapidly as I made my way to the center of the peak. Soren and Seppo lingered back near the edge. I turned toward them, eyebrows raised.

"Problem?"

"I'd rather not be in blasting range of the goddess I might've unintentionally scorned a few days ago," Seppo deadpanned.

"Soren?"

He looked away. "Skadi doesn't like me very much."

"Why?"

There was a slight rosy tint to his pale face. "I would rather not specify."

I sighed. I probably didn't want to know anyway. "Fine, I'll do it."

I forced myself to sit on the freezing stones. Crossing my legs, I brought out the stiletto Seppo'd given me when we fought the dragons. It was an old weapon. The bronze twisted in the shape of a snake eating its own tail on the hilt, and the blade was the green of a serpent with a line of silver-blue in the middle. Someone had blessed this weapon; the power in it said that much.

For now, all that mattered was the sacrifice. I bared my right arm and let the sharp edge of the stiletto run across the underside. A thick band of blood rose to the surface, and I angled my arm so the blood would drip onto the ground.

I closed my eyes and chanted, "Wake, Skadi, Mother of the Mountain. Wake, Skadi, Mother of Wolves. Wake, Skadi, the Huntress, the Avenger, the Mother of the Wilderness. I call to thee. Wake, Skadi!"

The wind picked up around me, swirling and piercing through my thick clothes with its freezing chill. The sound grew louder and louder, until the force of the wind became the howling of wolves. I opened my eyes as the goddess materialized from ice and snow, the wind becoming the pure-white strands of her hair.

She stood seven feet tall, her cold gray eyes narrowed as she gazed down at me. Despite her regal looks, a bow was slung across her back and an axe against her hip. Her silver hair whipped around her like dozens of ribbons in the wind. She swept her gaze beyond me, to Soren, then Seppo. Her eyes darkened as she narrowed her brows.

"You," she said. Her voice shook the mountains, the raw power seeping out of her forcing my words from my mouth to the pit of my belly. "You *dare* show your face here again, mongrel? You dare come back while your tribesmen leave a debt unpaid and my wolves still die?"

I stood, swallowing. At least now we knew whatever was killing the wolves was still out there. "I summoned you, my lady." I wasn't exactly sure how to address a goddess, but I didn't think adding honorifics would hurt. "It was I who summoned you, who woke you from your sleep. It is I who begs for your aid."

The goddess turned her cold, hard gaze to me. Her eyes softened. "You, child. I've not heard your voice in a long time."

I cast my eyes to the ground. "The will to pray was lost from my own human weakness."

She made a sound in the back of her throat. "Not so weak, from where you stand now. I feel the power of the lindworm in you, the power of goblins, and the Permafrost beating in your heart. You have done well. But that does not explain why *he* is in my sight." She hissed the last word, rage in her eyes. "He and his cur asked for my wisdom and *tricked* me. Now my family lays dying, and I can hear their mournful yelps from sunrise to sunset."

Seppo fell to his knees, head bent so low it brushed against the earth. "Honorable Skadi, from the bottom of my heart, I apologize. I truly believed the man who deceived you had killed the creature that terrorized your family. I no longer align myself with this deceitful man and come in peace. Out of respect for your dead brethren, I will pay you any favor you wish so long as it doesn't hurt the ones I love."

I snorted. Seppo made a good speech when he wanted to, that was for sure.

"As you should be," Skadi said. "But I hear the honor in your words, and I accept your proposal. I will think of a fitting favor for my brethren, and the blood will be washed from your hands.

"But you"—she pointed a finger at Soren—"didn't I tell you to never come back here? Not while you had another person in your—" She paused, looked closer at me, then smiled pleasantly. "Ah, I see our quarrel has come to an end, then."

A strangled sound came from my throat as I turned to Soren, eyes wide. He avoided my gaze and gave a small shrug. *Oh, we're definitely discussing whatever this was about if we live past this.*

"Girl!" she snarled, and I snapped back to attention. "You want something, so ask. The mountains are no place for a human, even one like you, and they aren't as forgiving as the ground below."

I heard the warning laced so gracefully in those words. I raised my chin to look her as closely in the eye as I could. There was something about her, the set of her shoulders, the tilt of her head, that made me want to cower in fear. This woman was a wolf in human form, a regal predator taking the time to deal with the rabbits at her feet.

"We need to stop Lydian," I said. "The goblin who disgraced you before, who asked for your knowledge about the stag."

She nodded. "And?"

"And we need to know what he's planning. Without the information, it will be impossible to know how to stop him. He wishes to kill the stag for good. And—and—" I got to my knees. I didn't make a habit of it, but groveling wasn't the worst way to deal with an angry deity and renowned giantess. "We humbly ask for the companionship of your wolves, if any of them will have us. We have need of their ferocity and agility and their great speed. We will keep their company no longer than our need lasts. We humbly ask this, and in exchange, whatever it is you wish, we will do."

The wind picked up around me, and, if possible, the temperature dropped even lower. I forced myself not to stick my hands underneath my arms, but the cold brought spasms to my muscles. I couldn't feel my fingertips, and I dared not look underneath the gloves, but I stayed on the ground with my hands spread out before me. In the most vulnerable position I could think of, head bent, neck exposed, hands out with open palms.

"You ask me to betray the confidence of another who asked for a favor. This would leave a smirch on my honor, child."

"The honor of the man whose information you gave was smirched when he tricked you into giving with nothing in return, and he lied about the reason he wanted your information," I said softly. "He offered you a favor and left it unpaid. We would be willing to take this favor—to actually kill what is preying on your pack—if we can learn how Lydian means to kill the stag and complete his plans. We will do whatever it takes to be deemed worthy by you and your wolves."

The silence dragged on until I dared to look up. Skadi gazed down at me, her features brooding. She motioned for me to rise and I did. "You speak well, child," she said, a fond look in her eyes.

"Thank you, my lady."

"You're right about the favor," she continued. "They must

be paid in full, and though I normally wouldn't betray the knowledge I'd given another, perhaps I was too foolish as to the consequences of my actions and too blind to see the truth." She sighed. "We may make a deal. I will summon my wolves and they will take their pick, then they will take you to the spot where their brethren were slain. You will defeat this monster, so it can die its second death and leave us in peace. Then I will give you the information I gave to Lydian, and the wolves who've chosen you will help you forward."

Second death? What creature dies a second death? There was a cold feeling in the pit of my stomach, and it was only growing colder. "I accept this deal."

The giantess raised her arms, and once again the wind spiraled, howling as it did. Out of the blinding snow came a pair of yellow eyes, then another, until we were surrounded by the eyes of stalking wolves.

I stood and backed up to where Soren and Seppo were, each giving the other uneasy glances. They were as out of their element as I was. I closed my eyes and reached out with my mind, trying to feel the ribbons of power these animals possessed. *Come to me.*

Hot breath blew against my face, and I opened my eyes to stare at the muzzle of a smoky, dark-gray wolf. He inclined his head, his yellow eyes flickering to mine, and I knew he had accepted me.

It took longer for the silver wolf to approach Soren, but when she did, she curled her bushy tail around his legs. The dark-gray wolf by me huffed, like something about that amused him.

Finally, a younger wolf, the color of cedar trees, trotted up to Seppo and put his nose in the young halfling's ear. Seppo jumped from the cold nose, inviting a lick from the young wolf. "Hi," he said, trying to dry his ear. "Nice to meet you too."

"Go forth," Skadi said, as the countless eyes began to disappear. Her form wavered too, but I shouted out into the wind. We still had no clue what we were up against, but she had to know something.

"Why do you need us to kill this creature? Why does a being of your power prove no strength against it?" I asked.

The giantess looked sadly down at me, like she was counting the lives she'd already lost. "The cold can't kill the dead."

The wind blew through her, and she shattered like ice.

Soren came over to me, his wolf pressed close against him. He looked down at her, awkwardly trying to shove her away. "Hey, ever heard of personal space?" The wolf blinked and Soren grumbled.

"What?" I asked.

"She told me her name was Lykka, and I should be honored that she deems me worthy of her presence." He frowned at the idea.

I choked back a laugh. "Sounds like a perfect match to me." Soren made a face.

The smoky wolf pressed his nose into my palm. *I am Breki. You are?* The deep voice inside my mind startled me, until I figured that was probably how these animals communicated.

"Janneke."

You have come far, Janneke? And much farther to go still, yes?

"I suppose," I said, frowning.

Breki huffed and sat by me, looking expectantly at the younger, brown wolf. Seppo's wolf was kneading the ground with his paws, his rump up in a playful position. Breki growled lowly, and the brown wolf straightened.

"He says his name is Hreppir," Seppo said. "And that he's really excited, and he hopes we succeed in our goal because he doesn't want to eat me."

I bit my lip to hold in my chuckle, the skin harsh and chapped from the cold.

"May I, um . . . ?" I motioned toward Breki's back. The large wolf nodded to me and bent so I could climb onto him. It was awkward, nothing like sitting on a horse. My body fell between his shoulder blades, in the dip of his neck, before I managed to sit straight, but he never once complained.

He waited for Soren and Seppo to climb on their own wolves and then he ran.

I gripped his dark fur and buried my face in his shoulder as the mountain air stung my face. The tundra and rocks whipped past me at a frightening speed and my stomach tensed, then rose as my body became weightless. This was as close as I'd ever be to flying, Breki's smooth leaps creating an almost undetected rhythm underneath my body.

We could've run for hours or minutes or days; time melted away as our bodies flew across the snow. When he slowed to a trot, my heart sank in disappointment. How wonderful it was to *run* like that.

Seppo and Hreppir and Soren and Lykka flanked me as the wolves began to pick their way across the rocks. The smell of rot and carrion wafted through the air. The bitterness of death tasted rancid on my tongue. Bones littered the mountainside, the skeletons of animals both huge and small. Pools of frozen blood, turned black from the cold, surrounded half-decomposed bodies. Not just of wolves, but of giant mammoths, of lindworms, of the predators of the mountains. The place was eerily absent of the maggots and flies that usually flocked to the dead.

"I don't like this," Soren said, his hand reaching back to check if his swords were still there. "I don't like this at all. What does this?"

Something the giantess had said struck me. "She said we needed to deal it a second death. It's already dead, whatever it is, and we need to kill it again."

"Draugr." For once, Seppo's voice was grim. "It's a draugr."

"I thought you didn't know what it was?" Soren said.

"I was never close to it," he said. "But Hreppir confirms it's a draugr. The stench of death is everywhere."

I shuddered, gripping Breki's warm fur. The creatures of nightmares, undead shapeshifters who were strong enough to move mountains, cruel enough to dine on the bones and flesh of the living, dangerous enough that the mere presence of one could drive you mad—*that* was what we were facing.

"Well, then." I tried to keep my voice from shaking, with little success. "Let's kill this thing."

Sliding off from Breki, I came close to Soren, whose eyes flickered anxiously around him. "Scared of draugrs too?" I teased.

"My mother was killed by one."

I kicked myself internally. *Way to be an ass, Janneke.*

Like always, it was as if he read my mind. "It's not your fault. You didn't know."

I gripped his hand. "We can do this," I said. "We have to."

"Well, the other option is being ripped to shreds by wolves." He tried to sound lighthearted and didn't quite succeed. "So yes, we have to." His hand squeezed mine, and I took reassurance in the pulse that beat there.

"So, does anyone have an idea how to kill this thing?" I asked.

Soren pursed his lips. "Decapitation and dismemberment is one way, I think. The only one possible at this rate."

Seppo swallowed, his Adam's apple bobbing. "This will be fun."

Soren paced, his hands folded behind his back. Before he paced like a trapped wolf, but now he was a strategist, a battle commander, thinking of every way we could possibly take this creature down.

I turned toward the three wolves, who had seated themselves away from the opening in a semicircle. "You three don't have to fight with us if you don't want to. I know how many of your kind were killed."

Breki stood, stretching to his full height. He was more like a horse than a wolf, honestly. Even Hreppir, who was the smallest by far, dwarfed the size of a pony. The three wolves came forward, and three voices spoke in unison inside my head.

We fight with you to avenge our brethren.

Soren paused in his pacing, staring at the wolves. Seppo jumped in surprise. "Odin's ravens, I'm never going to get used to that. Magical wolves or not, it's *weird*." Lykka huffed, turning her back on him. Hreppir just whined and poked Seppo in the ear with his nose again.

"I think you hurt his feelings," I said.

"Sorry, Hreppir." Seppo ruffled the wolf between the ears. "It *is* weird, though."

The three wolves trotted forward until they stood beside us. Soren came to a halt. "We need to draw it out of its den; we can't fight it in an enclosed space. Remember the lindworms? This will be bigger and deadlier. We're burning our own funeral pyres if we go in there."

I stared ahead, past the boneyard to the mouth of a large cave. It was so close. Could the draugr smell us already? "We need to lure it out, then."

"How?" Seppo asked.

Lykka and Breki looked at each other, some type of knowledge flashing between them. Then they turned to Hreppir. The younger wolf jumped up from where he'd been sniffing a flesh-covered bone. *Who? Me?*

Breki huffed. *Of course, you. You're the least threat, pup. Besides, you can act well.*

It's an honor, really, Lykka chimed in. *You have the ability we do not.*

"You can do it, Hreppir," I said. "I know you can."

The young wolf thrust out his chest.

Go, Hreppir. We will be right behind you.

Hreppir started forward, faking a limp. A high-pitched whine came from his parted lips, and he shook, dragging his back foot uselessly against the ground.

All was silent until the ground shook. The smell of rot and things long dead grew stronger at every beat. I curled my nose in disgust, though it did nothing to help the smell. I took four arrows in my hand and nocked one into place, holding the other three in my spare fingers. It'd been the first trick my father'd taught me. I may have forsaken him in the family's eyes, but I'd never forget what he taught me. From beside me, Soren's swords clinked sharply together as he drew them out, and Seppo's feather staff whistled from the hollowed spot where the blades were kept.

My eyes burned as raspy, labored breathing came from the cave. It was the sound of someone whose lungs had filled with water; the last heaves of a suffocating man. The draugr was large, larger than Skadi, his body made of half-decaying flesh and exposed bone. Where his eyes had been, there were now only sightless gray masses of skin, and I gagged at the rotten smell that came with decomposing body.

Countless pictures flashed before my eyes: a woman screaming as her body was torn apart, rats eating each other alive, two men throwing themselves into the fire, the crying of children as the flesh was peeled from their bodies strip by strip. They came fast and hit me like waves until I almost dropped my weapons. A cold hand against the back of my neck brought me out of it.

"You're all right, Janneka," Soren whispered, and I managed to relax at the endearment of my name. "You're all right."

The creature lunged for Hreppir, far too graceful for its body, and the wolf dodged, a brown streak as he jumped off the rocks. He then regrouped with his pack, and they growled in unison, their hackles high.

The wail of the draugr shattered the bones around him. With that, the fight began.

Soren came at the monster first, his two blades intertwining and slashing. He fought like he was dancing with the blades as his partner. His body twisted and curled inward, dove close to the ground and then sprang high into the air. Red welts appeared on the draugr's body, deep in one of his arms. Lykka growled as Soren landed beside her and launched herself into the air, her teeth digging deep into the creature's arm. Breki came beside her, and together, they managed to rip off his hand.

Seppo and Hreppir danced around the creature's legs with timed strikes and skilled evasions. Pale blood rained down onto them, burning their skin like acid, but they continued to swerve and tumble unaffected.

As for me, I waited low to the ground, shooting an arrow at an elbow, then another, watching them sink deep into the flesh. The monster screamed and ripped the weapons out, crushing them in his hands. But it was too late; his joints were broken, and all they needed was a good clean cut.

I sprang up and scurried onto a boulder as tall as me, unwilling to fight at such a large distance. If Seppo and Soren risked their lives by fighting close up, so could I. The stiletto in my hand, I joined Soren as he waltzed around the draugr. The piercing coldness of his swords lingered on my skin as we fought together. A slash here, a stab there. Before he danced with his weapons; now he danced with me. Our moves were in sync, our attacks countered what the other's lacked, and our defenses shielded what the other's left open. A fire was alight in my chest, and exhilaration coursed like a drug inside me.

A howl of pain brought me back down to the real world, as the draugr grasped Hreppir in his fist and squeezed. Immediately Seppo lunged, the hand completely severed before the monster even knew what hit him. The small, bracken-colored wolf breathed heavily, his tongue lolling out on the side. My heart froze in my throat as I waited what felt like an eternity until the wolf rose, shaking off his pain.

With his other arm, the draugr smashed Seppo against the rocks, and he fell limply to the ground. The slight rise and fall of his chest proved he was still alive, and the two elder wolves wasted no time in tearing into the draugr's remaining arm. It writhed like a swarm of maggots even as it was disembodied.

The grayish skin of the draugr bubbled and shifted, until sticklike limbs sprouted from his legs, reaching with talons toward Soren and me. We exchanged a glance and dove in, dodging pairs of arms and hacking off others. The hot wet-ness seeping from my back, my shoulder, my leg were the only indicators that I was harmed. Everything else was a rush of fire and ice and an almost painful ecstasy as I fought the crea-ture. The blackish-red blood of goblins pooled by my feet, and I was alarmed to see Soren hadn't been spared from the talons either. Cuts littered his face and tore through his tunic. But even with blood in his hair and soaking his clothes, he fought with the strength of a thousand men.

And finally, the draugr toppled down, the body whole no more.

Soren pulled himself against a boulder, ripping off a piece of his tunic, and started seeing to his wounds. I raced forward until I was at Seppo's limp body, my ear placed against his chest. His breath was weak, but it was there, and his heart kept on beating.

"Help me with him!" I screamed, and the three wolves braced his body between them. Soren, the bleeding of the gashes in his arms slowing, pulled Seppo's body under the protection of the boulder.

The young halfling's eyelids flickered. "I'm okay," he breathed. His eyes rolled back in his head, the whites of them streaked with red.

"Can you do something?" I asked Soren, remembering how he healed my arms. It seemed centuries ago. "Like how you healed me?"

"I'll try my best," he said, ripping open the thick layers of Seppo's clothing with a dagger he drew from his boot. The young man's chest was a mess of blood, and the outlines of bones stuck out against the flesh in a way even a goblin would find unnatural.

Soren hissed in frustration. "Hold him down," he said, barking orders at the surrounding wolves and myself. "I need to relocate his ribs, then I'll see what I can do about the bleeding. I've never tried it on an internal wound before."

As the three wolves pressed their bodies against Seppo's, my nose crinkled. Seppo couldn't smell of rot already. I turned in time to see the dismembered body of the draugr writhe and twist gruesomely, forming a pile of severed limbs. The flesh melted together, the bones and sinew knitting in ways it hadn't been before. A new creature started to rise out of the ashes of the old, but this time the decaying flesh took on the form of a giant bear. It roared in rage, the stench coming off its breath enough to make my eyes water.

Soren's eyes widened. "No. I don't understand. We dismembered it. It should've stayed dead."

I took another four arrows in my hand. "You deal with Seppo, all of you. I'll finish it."

"Don't be an idiot, Janneke!" Real terror colored Soren's voice. "It'll tear you apart."

"Save Seppo!" I shouted and bounded from behind the rock. The first arrow went into the bear's flank as it raged toward me. The second went into its stomach as I slid underneath it, barely missing being shredded by sharp claws.

The draugr turned and stood on his hind legs, bringing his forelegs down with such strength that the ground beneath me shook and split. I lost my balance and rolled into a mess of carcasses and bones.

Its sightless eyes turned to Soren, working tirelessly on Seppo's body. Wicked yellow teeth grew from its gummy mouth. I scrambled to stand and released another arrow into its rump, hoping it would come back for me. It did, charging so fast that the whiplash of wind stung my cheeks during my narrow dodge.

Dismembering it didn't work. Firing at it was only getting it angrier. I didn't have an unlimited supply of arrows. When

I ran out, I would be done. Even the stiletto couldn't do anything to this creature.

I scrambled under an outcrop of rocks and skeletons, taking precious moments to think and hide. The nail in my bracer pressed hard into my flesh as I leaned on my arm. Its burning was agony, but the pain was nothing compared to the idea of failing. This monster would eat Soren and Seppo if given the chance. It would rip them apart while they still had breath in their bodies. It would crush the wolves and it would drive me mad, and then it would watch as I flung myself from the cliffs.

There had to be something, anything that would kill it. In my village, whenever we thought a corpse would rise again, we burned it until there was nothing left and spread the ashes in the sea.

But there was no fire here at the top of the mountains and no means to create one. *But there's a fire burning constantly against your arm. You thought so yourself.* It was a nail, just an old iron nail.

Before I thought I just couldn't let go of the one remaining bit of my human life. But what if . . .

It would probably get me killed. But insane plans were working for us pretty well at the moment, and all I had to lose was my life.

I came out of the hill of rocks and bones on one knee, knowing I had one shot. I had to make it count. The nail came out of the bracer, and I pulled a glove off one hand with my teeth. I forced myself to hold on to the nail as the agony spread through my hand. My skin grayed then blackened as the fires of Hel shot through my fingers and lingered in my wrist, until my entire arm was ablaze with pain that brought black spots to the edge of my vision. Nothing could describe it; no months of beatings, no repeated assaults against my body, no emotional anguish, nothing was more painful than this iron against my skin.

Iron that was now glowing white with heat. Quickly, as my eyesight went fuzzy, I ripped a strip of cloth from my tunic and tied the nail to the point of the arrow. The skin peeled from my hand as I did so, and I couldn't help but let out a scream so loud I was sure they'd hear me back in the human world. With a trembling, bleeding hand, I steadied my bow and aimed at the draugr. I breathed in and out like my father taught me and let the string loose. The white-hot iron pierced through the sightless eyes of the monster and I stood by as the creature burst into flames.

Chills set in. I was burning and freezing at the same time. *My hand, oh my hand!* I reached for the stiletto, determined to cut it off as my vision turned to darkness. It was like a part of me was dying, rotting in the most painful way, while the rest of me could only look on and scream.

Hands pressed against my shoulder, rolling me onto my back. Through the hazy darkness Soren's lilac eyes gazed into mine, his bloodied hair falling in my face. "It's okay," he said. "It's okay. Seppo's going to be all right. I did it, I did—" His voice fell away as he caught sight of my hand. I couldn't see it, didn't want to see it, but I doubted there could be anything left but painful, exposed bone.

"Cut it off!" I screamed. "Cut it off! Cut it off!" That was the only way for the pain to stop.

"Seppo!" Soren shouted. "Get Skadi! Get Skadi!"

From my blurring vision, I saw the young man rise and nod, weary lines etched across his face. But nothing else seemed wrong.

Soren took my face in his hands. "Look at me, Janneke. Look at me!"

I tried, I really tried, but the black spots were threatening to crowd out the white sky above us. Soren jerked my head up, forcing our eyes to meet. Mine, green like the moss on trees, and his, lilac like the flowers that never grew in the Permafrost.

"Dammit, Janneka!" he snarled.

He was calling me by my old name a lot lately. I thought I was supposed to hate that.

"Stop screaming," he pleaded. "Please stop screaming. You're wasting your energy."

I was screaming? The only sound in my ears was a cold, tinny ringing.

A hand like ice brushed against my forehead, and the numbness spreading through me was colder than the dead of winter. The burning was still there, but it was manageable.

"Skadi," Soren breathed in relief.

A voice in the wind answered, "I come to those who fulfill their promises." The icy hand brushed against my cheek once more. "Child, close your eyes. You're safe."

I did as she said, and let the coldness take me.

PART THREE

THE STAG

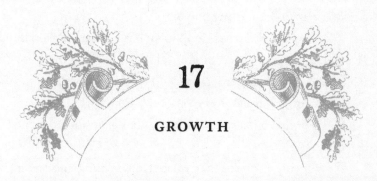

17

GROWTH

I WOKE TO the sound of bubbling water. My eyelids were heavy, my body trying to rouse itself from deep sleep. It took a few tries, but when my eyes finally did open, I found myself in an unfamiliar place. The cave surrounding me wasn't cold, furs and blankets were draped around me, keeping my body warm, and in the back there was a spring with steam rising from the water.

"Where?" My lips cracked as I said the word. The last things I remembered flashed in my head. The draugr. Seppo. The nail. My hand. Oh gods, my hand.

I couldn't feel it. When I turned to look, it was covered in bandages. Building up my strength, I propped myself up on an elbow, ready to take them off. Someone stopped me.

"You really don't want to do that," Soren said.

I stared at him. "How bad is it? Why can't I feel it?"

"It's not as bad as it could be; it'll heal. But you don't want to look, not yet. Now lie back down."

I did as he said, tugging at the furs that covered me. They'd slipped down. I was wearing a long undershirt, though I couldn't remember putting one on.

"Skadi gave us clothes, food, supplies," Soren explained. "I needed to get you out of your clothes, but I figured you wouldn't want to wake up naked."

Heat slowly burned in the pit of my stomach.

Soren pulled out a waterskin and a few strips of jerky and dried fruit. "Eat."

Despite my protests, he insisted on helping me sit up enough to drink from the skin. The freezing cold water brought the life back to my parched throat. I stared at the meat, mouth watering.

As I ripped into the jerky with a fervor I didn't know I possessed, Soren spoke.

"You scared me for a while," he said. "I thought you were going to die."

"Where's Seppo?" I asked, remembering the young halfling, lying limp on the ground. "How is he? Is he . . . all right?"

Soren nodded. "I managed to fix it. He'll be sore for a while, but there's nothing I can do about that. He's out with Hreppir and the wolves; apparently Skadi found a sufficient task for him to repay his debt."

"Which is?"

"He's spending his day among the wolf pack, getting rid of fleas."

I snorted. "Doesn't seem very punishing."

"I think he grew on her." Soren lips twitched. "He seems to do that."

I harrumphed. Soren raised an eyebrow, a question piercing in his gaze. "He's still annoying, but I suppose he grew on me too. He just better not give us fleas. Then I might *really* push him off the mountain."

Soren chuckled. "I never said he wasn't annoying. He's just the type of annoying that grows on people."

"How did I get here?" I asked. His words were lightening the dread I carried in my chest at the sight of my bandaged hand, but it was better to get the terrible news over and done with.

"Breki carried you." He wrapped his fingers around my good hand. "You're going to be all right."

"Then why won't you let me see my hand?" Every second that passed without knowing how wounded I was, the more worry churned inside me. I should've felt pain, agonizing, unbearable pain. I remembered what it looked like, remembered the skin ripping off as I tore it away from the iron nail. It was the cost of saving Soren and Seppo's lives and the cost of honoring our bargain with Skadi. I needed to know what I had paid.

Soren sighed, shaking his head. He came over to my other side as I leaned to watch him. He took my bandaged hand in his, gentle as could be, and slowly started to unwrap the wound. "I need to dress it again," he said. "So it smells bad, I'm sorry."

I gritted my teeth, expecting the worst. Slowly, the bandages were peeled back from the flesh with a sickening sticky noise; it had to be bad. It had to be. The bandages were colored red and black throughout, soaked in my blood.

Finally, he pulled the last of the wrapping away. The smell hit me first, and I recognized the sour ointment smeared across my skin. Tanya used it for burns. The skin was inflamed and bright red with black, scalelike patches all around. It oozed a bit from a few open sores, but the liquid was clear. A good sign. I tried to move it and with a burst of panic found I couldn't.

"Why can't I move it?"

"Skadi deadened it so you wouldn't feel the pain. Unfortunately that also means you can't move it right now. You'll get the feeling back in a while." He sat back against the rock. I nibbled on the food he offered me and drank when he shoved the waterskin in my lap, but we talked little. For a long time there was only silence and a wave of heat between our bodies.

"What did Skadi say about Lydian?" I asked, breaking the long silence.

Soren cast a glance outside. "You know that a hunt never lasts longer than until the next new moon, right?"

I nodded. "For whatever purpose, yes."

Soren clasped his hands together. "Well, there's a reason for that. Normally the contest ends by its own natural means before the month is up because usually the competition is thin enough for the most powerful goblin to kill the stag. But if it draws itself out longer, in order to make sure the destruction and transfer of power doesn't get out of hand, the spirit of the Permafrost forces the stag forward toward the two goblins most likely to become the new Erlking. If the new moon comes and the stag hasn't been slayed, then it will happen." He swallowed. "What's more is that if during this time it's killed on the border along with the losing competitor, the cycle will stop. No one knows why; the ritual has mainly been forgotten."

A shiver went through me. Soren's voice was calm, but he

couldn't *not* be worried. He was Lydian's only competition. "Can't you avoid Lydian and hunt the stag?" I asked.

He shook his head. "We'll be drawn together, someway, somehow."

I thought back to the sliver of moonlight outside. The new moon wasn't long off. By the time it came, we might all be dead. "It must be why goblins are flocking to Lydian," I said. "His power is showing, and they're all jockeying for a piece of it."

Soren snorted. "Yeah, none to me, though. Guess that says something about my odds."

He slumped down, burying his head in his hands. It tugged at my heart to see him look so defeated. We'd figure out a way to defeat Lydian; I was sure of it.

Feeling stronger, I sat next to him, leaning against the dark rock. He lifted his head, eyes flickering up and down my body as his shoulders tensed.

"You really shouldn't do that," he whispered as he closed his eyes.

"Do what?" His eyelids were pale blue under the soft light of the cave. He leaned his head back. His hair was loose again, and it spilled across his shoulders and chest. It was so long. It took decades for things to age even a month in the Permafrost. How long had he spent growing out his hair? I scowled. It wasn't fair that he looked the way he did and I looked like a scarred mess.

"Tempt me so much. It might not end well for you." His eyelashes fluttered.

"Don't be absurd. How could *I* tempt *you*?"

"I thought I explained it back in the caverns."

"I know what you said, but I also know I'm not very tempting-looking. I'm not blind." If I could hear my bitterness, he sure could.

He opened his eyes and leaned forward. Even with both of us sitting, he still towered over me. He rested a finger under my chin and tilted my head so I met his gaze. "You drive me mad, Janneke. Completely and utterly mad. I'm probably going to die in a few days, and all I can think of is you."

"I'm not beautiful," I said. "Every inch of my body is marked by others."

"Do you think I care about that? That scars crisscross your back and stomach and thighs? Do you think any of it matters to me?" he whispered fiercely.

"No, but it matters to me."

"I could be surrounded by unearthily beautiful, naked women, and I would prefer you as you are, fully clothed."

A shiver went through me and lingered behind my navel. When he put it like that . . .

"Sometimes I think I'm losing it," I whispered.

"Hmm? Why is that?" He released his hold on my chin and skimmed his fingers down the length of my calf.

"I think any human would think they were losing it in this situation."

"You're not just any human," he countered.

His hand moved up a little higher and another pleasant shudder rippled through me, leaving an aftershock in its wake. "I shouldn't like this," I said. "I shouldn't feel the hotness inside of me. I shouldn't stare at you like I do. I'm supposed to hate you. Gods, when did I stop hating you?"

He laughed softly. "I don't think you've hated me in a long time. You just hated yourself."

"Maybe I still do."

"Now, that's a lie if I've ever heard one," Soren said.

I closed my eyes as his hand roamed up and splayed against my ribcage. "This shouldn't feel nice," I whispered. "Not to me."

"Why not?" he asked. "It obviously does, doesn't it?"

I answered with a low moan. "A wolf shouldn't lie with a rabbit."

He laughed louder this time. "You're no rabbit, Janneke. And I know you don't truly think that."

"Those are the words I hear my family screaming in the back of my head. I know, *I know* that choosing what makes me happy, choosing my own life, doesn't make me a traitor or mean I'm turning my back on humanity. My family is dead and I'm alive; I know that they would want me to be happy and for me to live my own life. I know it's all in my head, but it bothers me anyway."

"It takes time to forgive yourself, even if there's nothing to forgive in the first place," Soren said softly.

I opened my eyes and found he was closer than before. His lips were right in front of me, and I burned with the desire to kiss him and with the knowledge that if I did, I would say goodbye to any ounce of normalcy I had left in life. But I couldn't quite find it in me to care.

"I think I'm beginning to." I smiled.

He leaned forward until our foreheads touched, and in that quiet moment the rest of the world dropped away.

I reached out and ran a hand through his hair. "You're so dirty."

"Are you suggesting we take a bath?" he mused. "The water does look quite inviting, even for my tastes."

I stood, stretching my aching muscles. The feeling in my hand was slowly returning, but I found I didn't really care. All that mattered was the heat in my body, the pressure building up in the bottom of my belly, and Soren. Most definitely Soren.

He was fully clothed with the new things Skadi'd given him. A hooded tunic lined with rabbit fur and a jerkin, fine hunting boots and riding gloves, bearskin pants that hung low on his hips. In the corner there was a pile of leather armor. He reached for my hand and placed it on the strings of his jerkin.

"Go ahead," he said. My heart fluttered. "Or are you scared?" he teased.

"Never," I said, working at the laces. He left them deliberately loose, and he shrugged off the jerkin with ease. With one hand, he reached back and pulled the tunic over his head, baring his chest.

Like mine, it was covered in scars and flat with muscle. This time, he didn't need to take my hand. I traced the scars on my own. He reached around to cradle my head.

"If I kiss you, will you kill me?" he asked, eyes sparkling.

"Only if you stop," I said and finally gave in.

His lips pressed against mine with a type of urgency I didn't know his kind could feel. My hands wrapped in his hair, and when he broke away to kiss my neck, the fine, white locks spilled around me. One of his hands went for the strings on my undershirt while mine tugged at his new pants. His teeth grazed against the sensitive skin of my remaining breast and I tilted my head back.

It didn't matter anymore. Being human, being goblin-blooded, being a traitor to my kind, or whatever was spouted by those who didn't understand me. All that mattered was my happiness, and right now, in this moment, I was happier than I'd ever been.

"Do you still want to take a bath?" he whispered, as he nicked my ear with his canines.

"Maybe a bit later," I said. "When we're dirtier."

He smiled wickedly. "I vastly underestimate you sometimes, did you know that?" His hand skimmed around my hip, moving up the small of my back until he was stroking my spine. This time I heard him move and felt the heat of his body against mine. He had to be close, very close.

"If I wasn't vastly underestimated by more deadly beings, then I would be dead already," I said.

"Spoken like a true hunter." His touch disappeared, and I ached to pull him closer until it reappeared lower on my body. A strange sound escaped my throat.

Soren paused. "Are you all right?"

"Yes."

"Open your eyes."

I did. He was so close, our bodies almost touched. My head reached up to his chest, right where his heart should've been. I thought I heard something in there too. "Do you have a heartbeat?" I asked.

"If I do," he said, "I don't hear it. Not like a human's. But I'm a living creature, so I suppose so."

There. Proof that this monster had a heart.

The wicked, catlike grin returned to his face as he tipped my head up, lips pressing against mine. A shiver rocked me to my core until it was melted away by a slow-burning fire.

He softly bit my lip and ran his tongue across it. His mouth trailed down to my throat, to the side of my neck, and when he pulled away, I found my free hand twining into his hair, pulling him close again. He chuckled and kept kissing, going as far down as he could. His lips skimmed against the scar tissue on my chest, treating it as tenderly as he would perfect, flawless skin. One of his hands cupped my remaining breast, his thumb caressing it softly.

We backed up until we were on my makeshift bed with the furs pulled tightly against our bodies.

I was breathless. I was on fire. I was floating and falling at the same time. I was everything, but I wasn't afraid.

His lips pressed under the skin of my ear, and I heard him whisper, "Is this okay?" His hips shifted to press hard against mine, and I could feel the eagerness in his own body.

"Yes."

"Are you sure?" he asked breathily. "You can always say no. I'll understand."

I took his hand from my breast and brought it to my lips, kissing his knuckles. "What happened to me, happened. It still wakes me up at night. I still feel the fear. But you aren't Lydian, and I trust you. Yes, I'm sure."

He moved so he could look me in the eyes, the furs parting so the cold air could come in.

"I'm going to get cold." I buried my face in his shoulder as the air stung my exposed skin.

"I'll keep you warm," Soren promised.

And he did.

LATER, LYING ON the furs and still tangled up in his body, I smiled. My body ached, but it was a good ache. A glow filled me, some type of lazy euphoria that made me sleepy and content. "That was nice."

He'd buried himself in my hair and from there he chuckled. "That is the understatement of the century. If I'm going to die, at least now I can die with my life's purpose fulfilled." His lips pressed against the back of my neck. "You're sure you're not hurting anywhere?"

"I'm fine. And I didn't know your life's purpose was to be with me."

His body shook from laughter. "I thought it was obvious."

"So what were you doing those six hundred-odd years I wasn't alive?" I joked. "Twiddling your thumbs with boredom, waiting until you could sleep with a goblin-blooded human girl?"

"What else *is* there to do?" He was still laughing.

I sighed contently. Here was one goblin whose cackle-like laugh I didn't mind. "You're getting quite good at the sarcasm, you know."

"I picked it up quick. A century has to be a record," he said. "Which is good considering I'd be totally confused where you and Seppo were concerned otherwise."

I groaned at the name. All I wanted to do at the moment was snuggle deep down into the furs, into Soren's body, and close my eyes and sleep. I hadn't felt this relaxed in years. There was soreness in my shoulders that I'd never recognized before, like I'd been tensing for a century without realizing it. There was the rumbling sound in Soren's chest that he made when he was content, like a cat's purr but rougher and wilder. But this moment would end too soon. "When is he coming back?"

Soren made a noise in the back of his throat. "Do you think it'd be too much to ask for one of Skadi's wolves to eat him? We're never going to hear the end of it when he gets back."

"We don't need to *tell* him."

"It doesn't matter. The little bastard will *know*," Soren said. "And then I might have to kill him."

"If he doesn't shut up about it, I'll *help*."

I sighed, breathing in deeply the smell of pine needles and woodsmoke that always clung to him. *Would that we could stay here forever.*

"It's not enough time, is it?" he asked.

"No." I sighed, back to strategy. "Are you planning on confronting Lydian or chasing the stag and hoping you catch it first?"

Soren looked away from me. "The latter would be nice, but I probably should expect the former. Either way, I'll make sure—I'll make sure you're safe. No matter what I have to do."

"What do you mean, 'no matter'?"

But he cut off my question with another kiss, positioning his body so he leaned over me, the pale strands of his hair tickling my chest. "You're beautiful," he said, his eyes glowing with warmth. "Beautiful."

"I'm glad someone thinks so."

Soren took my chin in his hands, forcing me to look him in the eyes. They burned with a silver fire in the setting sun of the cave and kept me from looking away. If it were possible, I'd think he was looking right down into my soul.

"You are the most infuriating, pigheaded, stubbornly determined person I know, did you know that?"

I couldn't help it, I laughed. "Strange, I thought you were describing yourself."

"A perfect match, then," Soren said.

There was a long silence before I spoke again.

"What did he do to you?" I asked. "Lydian, I mean."

Soren looked away from me. "It's not what he did to me, but to others."

"Care to explain?"

Soren was silent for a beat, then turned back to me. His eyes locked on mine before lazily looking down at my body, seeing something I never would. "He's my father's older brother," he started. "But he was never . . . right in the head. No one really talked about it when I was little or even now, but apparently one day he went out for a solo hunt as a youth and came back changed. He would mutter things under his breath and prophesize the doom that was about to fall over the land. He'd see people and think they were monsters. Sometimes he'd claw at his face until it bled."

He took a deep breath. "So, obviously, my grandfather

wasn't about to let him inherit anything. You know most goblins inherit by killing their former lord or lady, but that's not always the case. My grandfather simply disinherited him. He didn't even kill him, which is what most would've done to ensure no revenge was taken against the clan. My father married my mother and she became pregnant with me." After a long silence, he continued, "From the way my father tells it, Lydian came to visit one day. He and my father were on decent terms despite the circumstances. He saw my mother, heavily pregnant, and started rambling about the end of the world. That she would birth a demon."

I shuddered. "He really is mad. If he weren't so awful, I might even feel sorry for him."

Soren closed his eyes. "According to my father, Lydian tracked down a draugr. However mad he was, Lydian was always a good hunter. Some draugrs keep their sentient minds; this one did. While my mother was in her garden, tending to the flowers, the draugr slayed her." He let out a deep breath. "Tanya was her sister. She managed to save me, but not my mother. And by then Lydian was gone."

"How did she manage to do that?" I asked, curiosity piqued. "You get burned just braiding my hair."

Soren shrugged. "I'm honestly not sure. I never asked my father. He was never the same after her death. I think he resented me."

"Lydian killed her then," I said, "but used the draugr to do it. None of that is your fault."

"I still dislike draugrs, but yes, she died by Lydian's orders," he confirmed. "And one day, I will kill him in turn."

I closed my eyes, willing the coldness from my bones. Even wrapped in furs with Soren's body against mine, I couldn't chase the chill that came from his story away. *I always tried to plant a garden when I first came here. Was it the same?*

"I wonder," Soren mused, "if that's why he's so obsessed with you."

I raised my eyebrows. "Hmm?"

"He rambles about you too."

"It never makes any sense."

"Perhaps to him it does."

"Then it's his own damn fault."

Soren stroked my hair. "I won't let him hurt you."

I closed my eyes again, letting Soren pull me back to the comfort of his body. "I think I'm going to have bad dreams." *Stupid. You sound like a child.* But I also was a child in a way, here among creatures that were centuries older than I was, despite their youthful looks. If we survived this, I would look like that too, no matter the time that passed. If Soren was human, I would've pegged him in his early twenties, not nearly into his eight hundreds.

"Bad dreams are better than no dreams," he said, twining a lock of my hair around his finger. "At least they tell you what you're afraid of knowing."

My eyelids were getting heavy. I was warm and comfortable lying here with Soren while the cold wind whistled outside the cave's entrance. The numbness in my bad hand was ebbing away, leaving behind the fiery agony that I remembered. Instinctively, I reached for it, only to have Soren grab my wrists.

"Don't pick at it," he said, examining the red and blackened skin of my right hand. The smell coming off it was gone, as well as the sores and oozing clear liquid, but the skin was still inflamed and scaly where the iron had touched it. "You're healing better than you would if you were truly a goblin. You'll be able to use it fine, soon. There'll be scars, though. The scaly patches of skin sometimes don't go away. I don't know how they'll affect you, since you're technically human."

"Scaly patches of blackened skin I can live with. As long as I can still grip a bow."

Soren released my hands, and with great self-control, I managed not to pick at my wounds. I closed my eyes again, letting his scent wash over me.

"You know," he said softly, "I remember when you first came here and kept trying to plant a garden. It was in the place where my mother died. My father left it in ruins, and I always thought it was tainted by death."

"I never managed to grow anything."

"When we're finished with this, maybe you will." He kissed my forehead and started to hum under his breath until I feel asleep.

18

BURNT LANDS

L IKE ALL GOOD things, my relatively peaceful time
with Soren ended. I stood at the mouth of the cave, a
hand shielding my eyes against the glint of sun off the
snow. The clothes Skadi had gifted me fit perfectly: a hooded
tunic lined inside with rabbit fur, leather armor that covered
my chest and shoulders, trousers made of bear skin, and a cloak
of wolfskin around my shoulders. At first, the wolfskin cloak
struck me as odd—Skadi's family were wolves—but that was
the natural cycle, Breki explained. When the pack died, they
went on to continue to serve their goddess. Besides, he mentioned, the wolf I was wearing hadn't been well-liked anyway.

Soren was beside me, pushing jerky in my hands. "You
need to eat. Your hand will heal faster."

Despite the charred skin and the pain that never truly went
away, my bad hand had healed well enough for me to grip a
bow. Nerves made it nearly impossible to eat, but I choked
down a few pieces of jerky anyway. The moon hung almost
invisible in the sky like a cat's claw.

"Seppo." Soren looked back into the cave. "Are you almost ready?"

"Ah—in a moment!" There was a scuttle of claws across the cave floor, and Seppo came out, Hreppir on his heels. Both of them looked slightly haggard, Seppo sporting a black eye and scratching his arms raw. The younger wolf was nibbling on his shoulder as if he too had an incurable itch.

The black eye was my fault. When Seppo came back from his time trying to rid the wolf pack of fleas, he noticed Soren and me as we'd been before I fell asleep. His laughter and declaration that he *knew it would happen* was enough to wake me up and make me charge him—completely naked—and give him a few bruises. In the end, Soren made me stop. But it took a while.

"How long do you think it'll take to get out of the mountains?" I asked the dark wolf beside me. Breki's shoulders were a bit higher than mine, so he bent down to look in my eyes. "And to find the path of the stag?" There had been a feeling spreading through me ever since last night, my own insatiable itch that nothing mattered more than finding the stag before Lydian. Nothing. In the swirls of snow, the shape of the animal formed and spun before bounding away. In the wind, a voice was beckoning me forward. We needed to find the stag. We needed to do it soon.

The wolf snorted. *We'll be there before the new moon.*

Soren glanced at them from the side of his eye. "Are you *sure* you didn't pick up any fleas?"

Seppo hissed as he dug his nails into his shoulder and continued scratching. "Skadi said that fleas don't bother goblins."

Soren blinked slowly and took a deep breath. "Of course

she did. Well, just stay away from us until you sort yourself out, you understand?"

Seppo harrumphed and pointedly turned his back on Soren, rubbing Hreppir between the ears.

Beside me, Breki knelt so I could mount him. It was like riding a horse, if that horse were ten times more agile and swift, with a thousand times the ferocity and predatory grace. I gripped his thick, gray-black fur; it was warm in my freezing hands. I'd gotten a pair of leather gloves from Skadi too, like Soren and Seppo had, after my old ones were misplaced on some mountainside during the battle with the draugr. Even if my old fingerless gloves had been threadbare, they were better when it came to using a bow. I was already in bad shape due to my hand; I didn't need anything else holding me back, so I forewent the new gloves.

Breki took the lead, and Soren and Seppo climbed onto their wolves. It was the first time I'd been in the lead of anything. As a human child, I trailed my sisters; as an adolescent, I tracked the men of my village; as a captive, I was dragged behind Lydian's horse; and as a thrall and companion, I was always one pace behind Soren wherever we might be; and now, fully accepting my power and place in the world, I was in front, leading the charge.

The wind picked up again, and I pulled my hood up to shield my face from the worst of it, concealing my braids underneath. The snow drifted from the sky, flakes dancing in the wind. Then out of the air came a stag—*the* stag—made of the swirling snow and winter air. Its dark eyes peered into mine, beckoning me forward. Then without a sound, it disappeared into the wind.

"Did anyone see that?" I asked.

"See what?" Soren said. "I don't see anything but these damn mountains, and I want to stop seeing them as soon as possible." He threw a smile at me to take the sting out of his words.

From behind him, Seppo shook his head. "Nothing but snow and wind."

I swallowed. Maybe I was just seeing the goal I desired; there was magic in the mountains, after all. Or my eyes could have been playing tricks on me, the gleam of sunlight on the falling snow playing games with my sight. It didn't matter. We had an actual stag to find.

"Let's go," I said, and Breki shot down the mountain, his two pack mates bounding behind him.

This time, I forced myself to keep my eyes open as the world raced beside me. The wind stung my eyes as we plunged down the mountain; the wolves leapt from crevice to crevice, crack to crack with the grace of dancers. The landscape turned to a blur of blues, purples, and grays as we rushed forward. Every so often, one of the wolves let out a howl of pleasure. They must've loved to run as much as I enjoyed riding them.

A foreign presence nudged at the boundaries of my mind. *Open your mind to me,* Breki said. *Let me show you how it feels to be free.* I closed my eyes, allowing him to enter and share. Unlike when I was bound with Panic, my mind fought to reject the animal sharing my mind. *Relax.* I did.

The gray world exploded into color. The cliffs above were

dark blue and green, purple on the borders. Skadi's mountain home shimmered with a dusting of glimmering light. The wind whispered secrets in my ear; it tugged at my skin, my fur, my hair as if inviting me to play. Below my feet the rocks were hard and slippery, but I *knew* every step of these mountains. I knew every crack and every crevice, every divot and every outcrop. I *ruled* the mountains.

The smell of ice and cold and sun and prey was tantalizing on my tongue. The frozen ground was littered with the scents of countless animals: small mice and artic foxes, voles and snow cats. They all lived here, but this was *our* domain.

Each time we leapt, muscles stretching out to lengthen our stride, our heart sped up and adrenaline shot through our veins, and we breathed out in exhilaration as we landed safely on the next rock.

Thunder pounded underneath our feet, the heart of the Permafrost thrumming with strong, even beats. Inside my own body, my heart sung as blood called to blood. Here, now, racing through the forest, I was more connected to the world than ever.

WHEN THE SUN sank in the sky and the time came to stop and rest, I was breathing heavily. The euphoria from our run down the mountain buzzed in my body. The air down here was easier to breathe than the sparse mountain air, so I managed to recover quickly. The sky swirled with violet and orange, a canvas made by the dusk. Disappointment at the thought that

I'd never experience something like this again sank my good mood a little, but the forest called to me like blood to blood. The chirping of birds and the rustle of creatures under leaf reminded me of how much I missed being among the trees.

"We must be closer to the border," Soren said, looking at the foliage, "if there's this much life. I can see the stag lines; they're faint, but they're there. It will probably take us into human territory if it doesn't linger on the border." There was a note of warning in his voice. If the stag was still close to the border by the time the new moon struck, Lydian's plan would unfold with ease. Even if we found it, it could be too late. *If Soren doesn't survive the fight* . . . I shook myself. I wasn't even going to think of the possibility.

"Do you think Lydian is nearby?" I asked.

"Yes." I ignored the chill that went through me. "He's definitely close. I can feel him. The closer we are to each other, the more danger the stag is in, and the more danger of confrontation."

Seppo let out a low whistle that shook the leaves from the trees and caused my ears to ring. I brought my hand to my ear to make sure it wasn't bleeding as Seppo glanced at me sheepishly. "Oh, sorry. Sometimes I forget how powerful they can be."

I rolled my eyes. Only a goblin like Seppo would have a magical whistle.

"We're playing a risky game here," he said, ignoring the face I was making at him.

"You were the one who brought us into the fold," I reminded him.

He sighed, scratching behind his back again. Red patches

dotted with blood cropped up on his arms and shoulders, and he groaned in misery. I shook my head, trying not to laugh. *He actually has fleas, then. Well, he's not sleeping near me. Poor Hreppir.* The young brown wolf was trying to scratch his back on a particularly thick tree, only for the roots to snap from the ground. He stopped and let the tree fall back into the dirt, glancing guiltily around the clearing.

"It's not your fault, Hreppir," I assured the pup.

On the contrary, Breki said. *It is.*

Hreppir snorted and sat as dignified as he could, wrapping his tail around his legs.

The temperature was dropping rapidly. Frost replaced the moisture in my nose and formed on my eyelashes. I clutched the cloak of wolfskin closer to me, greedy for its warmth.

We continued until the darkness made it impossible to go forward, and even then, no one seemed happy about having to settle for the night.

"Sleeping will help if we're going to confront Lydian," Soren offered, but all of our eyes were on the ever-disappearing sliver of moon. "Hel knows we've bad enough odds without being sleep deprived."

I ignored the last comment and unrolled my bedroll. Sitting down, I checked to see how my hand was faring. I moved each finger and squeezed a tight fist. The motion was almost like normal, but the skin was still an ugly blackened color with redness underneath. Just like the barely cooked meat Soren enjoyed. The pain was ebbing away, though, and I could move it. That was what mattered most.

Soren sat beside me, his own bedroll spread out. He handed

me the waterskin and waited as I took a long drink. When I gave it back, he offered the jerky and a few pieces of dried fruit.

"I'm fine." There were too many nerves coiled in my stomach for me to eat much. Even if we did find the stag—or Lydian—we had no plan. The stag was simple. Just kill it. Lydian had a whole pack of men with him. Soren was powerful, but even with Seppo and me helping, he wouldn't be able to take on a whole hunting party.

"You need to eat," Soren said, the hint of a growl in his voice. "You haven't eaten enough. When a creature like me, who doesn't need to eat daily to survive, has to remind you to eat then you *need to eat*."

"Fine," I said, taking the food from him. "As long as you stop growling."

"It's not an angry growl," Soren protested. "It's a concerned one."

"I can't tell the difference!" I snapped, then sighed. "I'm sorry."

He shook his head and lay back on his bedroll. Lykka lay at the head of it, her gray fur silver in the moonlight. Soren checked to make sure Seppo was sleeping before speaking. "I know you're nervous."

"I'm not—" I gave up trying to hide it and lay down next to him with the cloak as a blanket. "Even if we find Lydian or the stag or Lydian *with* the stag, we have no plan. We have no idea what to do. And last time I checked, he still has twenty-some more men than we do. Going in ourselves and fighting, we're all going to die. There is no way we can win this."

Soren brushed back a strand of hair that'd fallen in my

face. "We're going to win," he said. "And you're going to be safe no matter what. I promise."

"It's not fair." I breathed deeply, trying to calm myself. "He isn't supposed to have any hold over me anymore. He isn't supposed to scare me. I faced him. I won't cower from him. I won't let him harm me. I'm stronger than what he can do to me. I know that. But then why am I still scared? Everyone gives me too much credit."

"Just because he holds no power over you doesn't mean the memories will disappear," Soren said softly. "Things like that stay with you no matter how hard it is to forget them. It doesn't mean you haven't survived. It doesn't make you weak."

I inched closer to him, and he wrapped his arms around me. My head was nestled in the groove of his shoulder, and my quick breath slowed to match his steady pace.

"When did you get so wise?" I asked.

"Around the same time you came to life," Soren said. "Sleep."

Came to life. Over a hundred years ago my fate was sealed with the burning of my village. I clung to the memories there, the good, bad, painful, and ugly. I held the traits that should've made me human in a death grip as I lived in the Permafrost, keeping my distance from everyone. *Came to life.* When a fire was burning in a forest, sometimes the best thing to do was let it burn itself out. Then when the forest grew back, it would grow back stronger, its roots dug firmly into the earth. Sometimes a part of you died to let the rest of you continue living. I clung to bitterness and hate—at Soren, at the gods, at myself— until the roots within me withered and died. *The oak is the* strongest tree in the forest, but the willow bends and adapts. When the fires and storms hit, it is the willow that survives. I was now that willow. A part of me always knew that, but now that part wasn't ashamed of it.

I fell asleep to the whispering of the willow trees.

THE FOREST SHIMMERED *with the silver moonlight. It was silent except for the rustling of the leaves in the wind. They were fully grown, fleshed out in the trees. Not Permafrost trees. Not even border trees. These were trees from the human world. Tall, alive, and green as grass. They weren't the only signs of life. Fresh grass, gorse, and brambles grew wild under my feet. Ripe berries clung to their vines, just waiting to be picked.*

A rustling in the shrubs behind me caught my attention, and I turned, reaching for my bow. But there was nothing where the weapon and quiver usually lay. The stiletto on my hip was gone too. All that remained were the clothes on my body.

The rustling noise came again, closer this time. From between the greenery, light brown antlers peered out and flashes of white fur kept reappearing. Then a wet black nose stuck through the branches and with it came a young white buck.

The stag.

Wisdom twinkled in the animal's black eyes. This creature before me was ageless, sacred, with nothing that came before him and nothing that came after.

He kept my gaze for one second longer before gracefully leaping through the underbrush.

I followed, crashing through the bracken. It'd been a long time since I'd had practice stalking with this much foliage, and from the noise, it was showing. But the stag didn't quicken its pace, staying just ahead of me.

"Hey!" I called out. "What do you want?"

The stag stopped and turned his massive head to face me again. Those large, wise eyes met mine and slowly blinked. His long eyelashes brushed against his pure white fur, and I stepped forward. He bounded away.

I almost screamed in frustration. "If you're trying to talk to me, just do it already! I'm done playing games! You're in danger!"

By now I was running, calling to the stag. But it kept on going faster and faster until it was almost a dot on the horizon. "Hey! Please come back! Talk to me!"

Just when I thought I'd lost sight of it, I entered a clearing. "Clearing" probably wasn't the right word for it. Nothing grew, no trees, no grass, no weeds. The land was just ash and dirt. The stag stood at the center, waiting for me.

The hairs on the back of my neck rose at the openness of the burnt field. In the open there was no cover, no advantage, no way to hide. The stag could even kill me if it had a mind to; there was nothing I could use to defend myself.

I steeled myself. The stag wasn't going to kill me. "What do you want?" I asked, approaching the animal.

He pawed at the ground, once, twice, then twice more.

"What are you trying to say?"

He snorted and pawed at the ground again. The ground. He wanted me to look at the ground. But there was nothing on the ground, nothing except for ash and dirt.

But I bent down anyway, unable to deny the stag's command,

and brushed the dirt away from where he'd been pawing. Eight hard lumps rolled into my hand. They were seeds, though I didn't know what type. They must've been ancient, but there was life gently stirring inside them.

I stood. "What does this have to do with anything?"

The stag came close enough for me to smell his hot breath; it smelled like the grass and the wind and the sun all rolled into one. He pressed his nose to my cheek, filling me with his warmth. Then he bounded away, leaving me in the open field.

WHEN I WOKE the next morning, I was uncomfortably aware of the eight small lumps in one of my pockets. It couldn't have been just a dream, not if the seeds were still with me. There were no stories of the stag visiting a person in their dreams; so why me?

We rode at a slow pace through the forest as its dead came to life. Despite the discomfort deep in my body, I said nothing about my dream. We already had enough to worry about without having to interpret a dream. Who knew, the seeds could've rolled in my pocket while I slept. We were all thinking of the stag; surely dreaming of it was normal. But it was just that. A dream.

We'd gone a bit before I started to smell the difference in the land. Wet earth, moss, and growing things, the scent of life all around me. I breathed in deep, trying to capture the smell and remember it for all eternity.

"We're about to cross the border," Soren said. "Be careful. Be watchful."

I looked around. There was barely any marker that this was the place between worlds, only that the ground shifted from brown and frozen to soft and green.

A bubble of disappointment rose in my chest. Out of all the times I imagined returning home, I expected to feel some type of joy and freedom. But there was nothing; it was just a place like anywhere else. It might've been my home once, but that was long ago.

The stag's trail was now a thick silver line as the wolves trotted through the trees. They weaved their way through the forest until it became thin again. My nose crinkled at the smell of sulfur and burnt earth.

"We won't run into any humans here," Soren said, and Seppo nodded, a grave look on his face. Perhaps he was thinking of his father, if he'd been taken from a land too close to the border. Maybe he never even knew who his father was.

We'd entered the burnt lands. Villages too close to the border of the Permafrost were always raided, but the ocean nearby was full of fish and whales, the forest plentiful with herbs and game. If it weren't for the goblin raids, one could live out a good, long life there. *And many still try.*

The sky above me was tinged orange from the haze that hung in the air. Unease pressed hard against my throat, but we continued forward through the ashy ground until something made me stop.

I wasn't quite sure what it was, why a tugging in my gut told me to go farther east. But, almost trancelike, I slid off Breki and started forward. Underneath my feet, the ground crunched and crackled; I was walking on bones. They'd never decomposed; not even after a hundred years. My heart was empty of rage and shame as I tried to remember what the village looked like before. Before there were huts and lodges that sheltered multiple families, dogs running through the camp, and women tanning hides and sewing clothing out in the sun. Now all that was left was ash. *Ash and me.*

Soren dismounted Lykka and started forward, but Seppo grabbed his arm and pulled him back. "Let her do this alone."

Bones still crunched against my boots, and I forced myself to squat down, to examine them and see if I could figure out who they belonged to. Man, woman, or child, someone I knew, someone I loved, someone I hated. The bones were smooth and cold, strangers in my hands. Briefly, I wondered if the dead were watching me, judging my choices, but I found I didn't care. It wasn't my fault they died. Just as it wasn't my fault that I'd grown anew.

I dropped the skull fragment I was holding and stood, trying to envision the village again in my mind. Where had I lived? Where had I grown for seventeen years, unaware of the life laid out for me, until I was pulled out of that blissful existence by a monster of a goblin?

I couldn't tell. That was not my life anymore.

So I stood in the haze and the ash, stood among the bones of the dead and the scrap iron that had remained untouched throughout time. I stood there, in what was once my home, and closed my eyes, the emotions churning through me bringing me to my knees for a second time.

19

SALT OF THE EARTH

THE MEMORIES CAME slowly at first. Not even bad ones, but ones I'd forgotten long ago in a whirlwind of pain and a court of monsters. I shut my eyes, watching the scenes play out. My hands dug into the soil, burning at bits of iron that lingered among the ashes.

I toddled after my sister as fast as my four-year-old legs could manage. Her long brown hair streaming out behind her, the ties in her dress half undone, a man's hand in her own. Where were they going? They promised to play with me, didn't they?

I didn't like the man. He smelled of the firewater that the sailors drank when they came into our village, and his voice was scratchy from the sticks that hung burning from his mouth. But Ika liked him, and Ika was a good judge of character.

I made my strides longer, taking advantage of my height. I was the tallest kid my age in the village, the most agile. And I could see the tracks where my sister and the man had gone.

I found them in a clearing, their lips locked together. My sister squealed in surprise when she saw me, and the man's eyes narrowed, but then he laughed. It was a sound that came deep from inside of him.

"Is this the wild little thing I keep hearing about?" he asked.

"Janneke!" Ika was fifteen years old, but she sounded like my mother when she scolded me. "What are you doing here?"

"Following you," I said. Wasn't that obvious?

She sighed and pulled me up on her hip. All the women carried babies like that. But I wasn't a baby, so I wriggled until she let me go. "How did you follow us? I was sure . . ."

"You're easy to track," I said.

The man came forward, bending down so he could be at my height. His breath still smelled, but he had a nice smile I hadn't noticed before. Maybe that was why Ika liked him. "You like tracking? Wouldn't you rather be playing with dolls, little one?"

I lifted my chin and looked the man in the eyes. "My father says I'm to fulfill the male role. If I am to do it, I'll do it well."

He laughed. "She's very well-spoken for her age."

Ika sighed. "Come on, Janneke, let's go home."

When we got back, it was dark out and my mother fretted over me. She scolded me, told me never to go into the woods. Bad things were there. I told her I would be a huntress one day and I wasn't scared.

But I still slept curled up in her bed when the night came, my father in between us. I heard them whispering, but couldn't make out the words from underneath the covers. Their voices sounded worried.

This was where we slept. I was sure of it. The iron in the ashes burned my hands, but it didn't matter. I stood again and continued walking around the field, noticing which spot was which. There was a little whistle lying on the ground, iron again, the only thing that hadn't disappeared completely. On it were the ancient carved letters that meant someone fancied a girl. Similar to the maypoles erected every summer during courting season—ones I'd never gotten.

"Why do you hate me so much, Bjørn?" I asked, kicking at the sticks in front of me as I walked side by side with a towheaded boy. If he could be called a boy. He was beginning to grow taller, lankier, just as I was beginning to grow breasts and bleed. We were the same age—thirteen—and I was often paired with him on hunting missions or lessons. If I had a friend in the village, he was the closest thing.

"I don't hate you," he said.

"You didn't give me a pole," I said, as if it meant everything in the world. It did at the time, I knew.

"I don't like you that way. Besides, we're too young."

I crossed my arms. "I'm a woman. I bled just last month."

"Well, May Day was two months ago. Sorry, I can't see into the future."

"I don't understand. I'm a woman, why can't I also be a woman and a huntress? Why does everyone have to forget I'm also a girl?" My hair had been braided in the style the boys wore; I wore the clothing the boys did. I had their chores. Why couldn't I even talk with the girls? Why couldn't I join them in the women's tent when I bled, instead of having to ignore it and continue hunting?

"You know why. You're not supposed to be a girl. Not really."

"But I am. My role doesn't change that."

Bjørn faced me, sighing. "You are really pretty, Janneke."

I smiled. "Does that mean you'll give me a pole?"

The boy bit his lip, then dug in his pocket, holding out some-thing made of iron. "Here. It's a whistle. You can have it instead of the pole. It means more to me anyway."

"Thank you," I said, my insides warming as I took the whistle. Maybe one day he'd really give me something that meant he cared.

"Come on." Bjørn tugged at my hand. "If we don't find three different animal scats before noon, our fathers will have our heads."

"It shouldn't be that hard," I scoffed. "Considering you're stand-ing in some."

The boy yelped and jumped away from the bear scat he'd been standing in, and I laughed and laughed and laughed.

I took the whistle in my gloved hand. It was small and twisted and broken now. But I remembered how its high shriek used to hurt my ears and how I used to laugh every time I blew it.

Someone came to stand beside me. A hiss escaped from Soren's lips as he stepped through land burned from the iron in the earth. "Janneke," Soren said. "Are you okay?"

His words yanked me out of the past, into the world where I belonged now. Was I okay? I didn't know. I wasn't sure how to describe what I was feeling right now. A little warm, a little cold, a little numb. It was like a mixture of ice and fire and nothingness were fighting for my attention. I wasn't sure I wanted to give in to any of them.

"I'm . . . remembering," I said.

"Is that bad or good?" he asked, brushing the hair out of my face.

"It's neither. It's just remembering." I stood, letting the whistle drop.

"This was your village, wasn't it?" he asked. He had a hand on my arm like he thought I would fall or run away.

"Yes," I said. "Elvenhule. That was the name."

"Was it a nice place?" he asked.

"Before Lydian burned it to the ground? Yes." I could still hear the pounding of horses' hooves in my mind, the same as the day the village had been razed to the ground. Closing my eyes, I willed the sound to go away, only to find that it was growing louder. My eyes snapped open. It *wasn't* in my head. Without a second thought, I turned to Soren. "Come on!" I made a dash for the trees.

Soren followed behind me, cursing under his breath. "The iron in the field must've muted my awareness."

It was stupid. Stupid to stay in such an open place, stupid to let my feelings get to me, stupid to walk out in a field of literal poison toward creatures like us, stupid to become un-aware, even for a moment, because now I heard the pounding of horses like thunder in my ears, and I knew more than any-one else what that meant.

We made it to the forest line before they caught up with us and, instinctively, I scanned the trees for Seppo. A whistle too low for any bird came from above me. I looked up. The young goblin was in a tree. There were no signs of the wolves. His eyes were wide with concern, his hand already reaching for the feather staff slung across his back, but I shook my head.

Go, I mouthed, hoping that maybe if he could get away, we weren't totally lost. *Hreppir, Breki, Lykka.* I felt them deep in the forest; they'd taken a break to rip into a rabbit carcass.

Now they were licking the blood from their lips and their ears perked to my call. *Guide Seppo to you. He'll be in the trees.*

Seppo shook his head, but then Soren followed my gaze and he nodded slowly like he knew exactly what I was thinking. With wet eyes, Seppo bounded across the treetops, back into the forest where he was safe for the time being.

Then I turned back to the ashy field, bow and arrow in my hands, to stare down the goblins that had come for me. The sweet, sheer sound of the metal of Soren's swords brushing against each other filled my ears.

"We're not going to be able to fight them," he said quietly.

"I know."

The leading figure was, of course, Lydian. He sat tall on a gray-flecked mustang, his blond hair blowing in the wind. Some of it had been burnt off, leaving it uneven on one side. Cuts littered his face and exposed skin, and the reek of iron burns hit my nose as I remembered both his shoulder and leg had been poisoned now. By me.

"Well," he said, dismounting. "Isn't this delightful. My nephew and my sweet little Janneka in the place where it all began."

Even though a bubble of fear rose in my chest at his voice, I refused to let it show on my face. Instead, I raised my gaze to the men behind him. I counted fifteen horses; he'd lost some men as well. Good. *It's not like we can take fifteen of them, though.*

"You don't sound very delighted," I said through clenched teeth. From beside me, Soren maneuvered slightly so his shoulder was blocking me.

"You wound me, Janneka."

My teeth clenched. *That's not my name.* "You'll live. I'm not yours anymore."

"Yes." He lazily drew two knives from his boots. His great-spear hung from the back of his horse, glistening with poison. "You smell like *him* now." He chuckled, like that amused him, and shot a smirk at Soren. "You like her as much as I did, nephew?"

A snarl ripped through the air. "Watch yourself, Uncle."

Lydian sighed. "It's you two who should be watching yourselves." He motioned to his riders, and they began to dismount. "I wish I could kill you now, but I need you alive, dear nephew, now that there's no taint of venom in your veins. I wonder, how did you ever heal from the lindworm bite?"

"I healed him," I said. *Let him know how strong I am now. Let him know what I can do. Let him smell the power of the lindworm on me, let him smell the death scent of the draugr, let him smell the blood of the goblins I killed, let him smell the wild and the wind and the anger in my veins, so he knows I'm not the same as I was before.*

Lydian raised an eyebrow, interest gleaming in his emerald eyes. "Really?"

"I am a lot different than I was before, Lydian." My voice was low and soft.

His eyes narrowed. "Oh, I've always known you would ruin the world."

I suppressed a shudder. Lydian would not get to me. He came closer to me with his knives. I was relieved to find they weren't poison. I kept my bow and quiver slung across my back, knowing they'd be no use in a close fight, and instead gripped the stiletto in my non-ruined hand. Soren was backing off in a different direction, slowly sizing up the many goblins who were about to take him down.

"Where did you get that weapon?" Lydian asked. "It's the halfling brat's."

"I took it off his body." I spat at him and thanked the gods that, because I wasn't goblin, Lydian couldn't tell I was lying through my teeth.

Lydian smiled, his canines poking beyond his lips. I knew that smile. "I didn't know you had that in you, little girl."

I bared my teeth. "You don't know a lot about me."

He lunged with his knives, and I dodged, tumbling away. I couldn't let talking distract me; that was exactly Lydian's goal. Distract me. Anger me. Make sure I couldn't think. "I know *everything* about you." He laughed. "I know *everything*. The fact you can't see it is maddening."

"Says the madman," I hissed.

His eyes narrowed, and he leaned closer. "Says the one who sees the truth of you."

I let out a snarl of my own. Yes, that was his plan, and he was doing a pretty good job of it.

He and I danced for a bit; his blades went forward, I rolled in another direction to come up somewhere behind him, him already in position, rinse and repeat. He was playing with me. If he really meant to kill me, then we'd be fighting like we did in the Erlking's palace; the thought filled me with fire.

Still, I had some tricks up my sleeve. He lunged and I waited a second too late, until his knife grazed my skin. Then I grabbed the hand holding it and twisted hard. The knife tumbled to the ground as I knocked my head back into his, his body now positioned behind me. One of his hands wrapped across my face, groping. Sharp talons made shallow welts as I bit down hard on what I thought was his thumb until the bitter taste of blood was in my mouth. He threw me to the ground with a force stronger than ten men, and I flew back a few meters, tumbling in the dirt. My breath was heavy in my lungs as I regained my bearings, only to see him stalking forward.

"That's the problem with you," he said, placing a well-aimed kick in my stomach as I tried to rise. "You and your kind are so delicate. So soft." Another kick, this time at my ribs. I rolled away, trying to create some space between us. The stiletto had been knocked out of my hand and was lying there, a few meters away. "A simple little kick and your insides explode."

This time, I saw the kick coming—right toward my chest. Risking it all, I rose and wrapped my arms around his leg, bringing him down to the ground. Scurrying above him, I pressed my fingers deep into his shoulder, where I knew the iron burn still poisoned his skin. He screamed and kicked out, his hands knocking me across the face. The force blew me away and again he rose, seething.

My eyes were blurring as I looked around me. I couldn't see Soren anywhere. Wildly, I flipped over to search for him. *Don't leave me, don't leave me.*

Before I could find him, Lydian blocked my view and sat down heavily on my stomach. His hand grabbed my chin, squeezing hard until little rivulets of blood ran down my neck.

"See, the problem with you is that everyone thinks you're so pure. The salt of the earth. That's what they call it. You amaze them." With his free hand, he wrapped his fingers in my hair, and I cringed away from the touch. "But I know more than anything or anyone else, Janneka. You are an abomination. You should have died the moment you were born. You *and* him."

Saliva mixed with blood as I spat in his face. "The Permafrost disagrees."

"The Permafrost will *die*," he snarled.

"Only if we let you kill it!"

His boots slammed down on both of my hands, forcing them still. "I thought I could save you, change you. I tried," he said softly. "Really, I did. But you stabbed that nail into my leg, and now we're here. I'm afraid this is where your story ends. I do apologize. I really did try."

His claws lengthened into wickedly sharp talons and a shiver rolled through my body. I'd seen the way goblins preferred to kill humans or humanlike creatures; they ripped the hearts right from their chests.

"It's okay," he whispered, stroking my cheek with the ghost of tenderness. "It'll be quick. I promise you won't feel a thing."

All I could do was stare as his hand came down.

Then a voice shouted in the distance. "Lydian!" Soren yelled. Lydian stood and turned toward his nephew, and I rolled over, heaving up everything I'd eaten in the past few days. Disgust made my skin crawl.

"What is it, Soren?" Lydian looked intrigued. Soren was

standing with blood streaming from his body, turning his white hair crimson. Behind him was a trail of bodies. Some moving, some not. "You're quite the proficient fighter, I see." He scowled, shooting a loathing glance at the dead. "I thought they'd be enough to engage you for now. I obviously thought wrong."

"You need me, right?" Soren asked. "For your stupid ritual."

"It's not *stupid*," Lydian hissed. "It will save *everyone*. It's for the *greater good*. I guess you can't understand that; you've been raised by greed and lust."

"I'll go with you," Soren said. "Willingly. I'll go with you, and we'll fight to the death. I know as well as you do that the kill has to be made during combat for it to count to the stag. Maybe you'll win, maybe you'll lose. But you can't *force* me to fight you, Uncle. You know as well as I that it wouldn't count to the stag. So, I have a proposition." Warmth and longing and regret filled Soren's eyes as he looked down on me. "Let her go. Let her go, and I will fight you to the death. May the new king win."

I struggled to my feet. "No!" I screamed. "Soren, no! Don't. I'm not afraid." My feet were numb under me, and I staggered forward until I fell. "Soren, please, no. You don't need to."

The soft sounds of boots against the ashes appeared by me, and his lips pressed against the top of my head. "I love you," he whispered, then he said, a bit louder, "and I release any hold over you by all folk, men, and gods. You are free of any burden or punishment the Permafrost may hold against you in the court of the Erlking or of the clans. I break the binds that tie you and leave you free from my world, from my kind, from *me*."

I crumpled to the ground as white, agonizing pain blazed behind my eyes. It was as if someone had set my mind on fire, letting molten lead drip down my throat until I suffocated slowly. Twisting and contorting, fighting for breath, fighting for a way past the pain of the broken bind, he whispered to me one last time. Three little words that set my heart ablaze.

The world went black as he walked away.

20

IRON FIRE

A HAND BRUSHED *against my cheek, pulling me out of my fitful slumber. My body was tied against one of the skeleton trees, aching after being dragged from the back of a horse. Other places ached too, but I tried to forget about them because those pains were so much worse.*

"Wake up, sweetheart," a light voice said. It sounded like poison to me.

I blinked groggily and lifted my head, staring into the green eyes of the goblin who had claimed me as his. It was sick; he was beautiful. I knew goblins had two forms, a natural one and a predator one, but I didn't think they'd be beautiful in their natural one. I thought no matter what, they'd look like monsters. But this man with his strong jaw and aquiline nose, his crystal eyes and golden hair, he was beautiful. Beautiful and terrible.

"There's a good girl," he said.

I cringed away from his hand. There was still blood under his nails, long dried now. It wasn't mine. But it had to be the blood of one of the people I grew up with. This man—no this goblin, this thing—had killed them all.

I coughed, my throat burning from the water I'd inhaled during the swim underneath the waterfall that let me escape and the smoke from my walk through the ruined village that led to my capture.

He pressed something to my lips. It tasted like copper and iron. When I spat it on the ground, the red staining the earth could only have been blood.

"You don't like the taste, sweetling?" he taunted. "You'll get used to it."

"Go eat your young!" I coughed the insult with as much strength as I could.

A slap had my head reeling. These things were so powerful. Why hadn't they killed me yet? When would this one finish toying with me?

"That wasn't very nice," he said. "I'm your master now. You should be nice to me. How about we tell each other our names, would that be a good start?" Still, he had that sickly sweet, taunting edge to his voice. I wanted to rip my ears off. Anything not to hear it. "My name's Lydian," he said, "but you'll call me master, you understand?"

I didn't respond, so he slapped me again. Then with blood bubbling from my lips, I nodded.

"Say it."

I stared at him defiantly, not allowing anything to pass my lips. He wouldn't, I wouldn't let him, he would never own me.

Another slap made me see stars. "Say it!" The force of his next hit was so strong, my head cracked against the tree I was tied to.

"I-I u-understand," I managed to say with a mouth full of blood.

"You understand, what?" he asked.

I closed my eyes. This wasn't real, this wasn't real, this wasn't real. I would wake up soon, in my village, and go about my daily chores. This was just a terrible nightmare. But when I opened my eyes, I was in the same place, staring down the same green-eyed goblin. Something inside me broke, and the strength I had dwindled away to nothing.

"I understand, master."

Lydian smiled at me. "Now was that so hard?"

"N-no, master."

"Now, what's your name?"

My name. I didn't want him to know my name. I didn't want him to know the name my siblings and parents called in joy and anger and laughter and love, the name my fellow men muttered in disgust underneath their voices and with grudging respect to my face. It was mine. The only thing left besides the nail stuck inside my boot. But a nail couldn't help me against this creature that had slaughtered an entire village, could it?

I willed myself to fight, to refuse, but there was so much pain, so much darkness, and not an ounce of spark still left in my soul. "Janneke," I said quietly, trying to pretend that my name meant nothing when it really meant the world. "My name is Janneke, master."

"Janneke," he said, smiling. "Janneka, perhaps?"

"No!" I shouted. Not that. He could have my name, the real one meant to be used by all, but not Janneka. Not the special name meant for a single special person. Not that.

He smiled. "Janneka, then." He crouched down so our eyes met. "You and I are going to have a very nice, long time together, Janneka."

Then he let me go, and the blessed blackness overcame me.

The darkness never stayed for long. Even lying in the dungeon with cold fetters around my wrists, every time I drifted off, the screaming of another prisoner or the sweet, poisonous voice of my captor pulled me from my sleep. In the darkness the passage of time was impossible to measure. I could've been down here for a week, a few months, even a year, and I wouldn't know the difference. The smell of blood wafted all around, from other prisoners, from me, from whatever thing the guard was eating. Every so often, a squeal would pierce the cold air and then stop with a sickening crunch.

Keys jangled and the lock on my cell door clinked open. I pulled myself into a sitting position. Maybe if I sat up, he wouldn't take me this time. Maybe the smell of blood and pus that came from my chest would disappear. Maybe . . . maybe . . .

The harsh light of a kerosene lantern burned my eyes, illuminating the dark cell. I squeezed my eyes shut as slow footsteps rapped across the room, and someone settled by me with a rustle of cloth. "Janneka," he said.

I whimpered. What did he want? Didn't he know by now I had nothing to give him?

"Janneka," he said again, and I opened my eyes.

He was crouched down beside me, his golden hair spilling over his shoulders. In the firelight, his green eyes gleamed. "Good morning," he said, reaching out with a gloved hand to inspect a bruise on the side of my face. "I don't think I made this one."

"You didn't," I said.

He raised his eyebrows. "No one is allowed in here but me." He eyed the chains that restrained my wrists. "I find it hard to believe you did this to yourself."

"Maybe you shouldn't give your guardsman a master key," I spat. My saliva ran bloody on the ground.

He sighed and clicked his tongue. "I guess we'll have to take care of that, won't we?" I shivered as he raked his gaze over my freezing, bloody body. "You're mine. Only mine. Maybe we should remind him?"

I swallowed, stomach churning at what exactly "reminding" the guardsman would entail. Why couldn't I just choke on my tongue? I shouldn't have said anything.

Lydian let go of my chin, and I looked down at the ground. His hands were examining the rest of my body, checking for the cuts and bruises that he made, the swelling infections and pus dripping down lacerations so deep I couldn't feel them anymore. He was always careful not to let my injuries be completely life-threatening. He wanted me to hurt, but dying meant he'd lose his favorite toy. He tugged my shirt down and touched my mangled right breast—if you could even call it that anymore. It was practically destroyed.

He stopped then and reached around to a bag across his shoulder. I winced as he rustled through it. "Now." He smiled. "We're going to play a game, okay?"

I nodded, forcing bile back down my throat.

He bounced a piece of hard cheese in his hand and kept my gaze. "Tell me what makes you so special. Tell me why you keep appearing with the fire. Tell me everything."

The chains rattled as I shook. He was rambling again, and there was no way to please him when that happened. "I don't know what you mean." I must've said it a hundred times already.

Lydian stroked my cheek with his thumb. "I know you're scared. But if you tell me what I need to know, then we can fix this. We can make sure it never happens."

"What are you talking about?" Tears trickled down my cheeks and I let out a silent prayer to any deity that would bother listening. Take me away from here, bring me anywhere, but let me leave this place. Please help me. *My eyes fixed greedily on the food in his hand. It'd been so long since I'd eaten; I didn't even feel the pain of it anymore.*

"Tell you what," Lydian said, palming the cheese. "Let's you and I let the guard know who is whose, and then when everyone is well educated, you can eat something."

I closed my eyes, tears still falling. The lock on the cell clicked again, and someone else stumbled inside. He smelled like firewater, and he was saying something to Lydian in a harsh goblin tone. There was a shriek and the sound of claws ripping through flesh, then the thump as a body hit the floor. The footsteps came back to me, and I willed myself to get lost in the darkness as Lydian fiddled with his belt.

ONE BY ONE, my feelings returned. Ash and iron burned through my clothes, underneath my skin. The smell of death and blood wafted through the air along with the musky, warm smell of a large animal.

Pain hit me from every angle, the most intense pain I'd ever felt. Nothing could compare to this. Nothing. No absorbed power, no nøkken's venom, no repeated rapes or beatings, no whip's lash, nothing compared to the way my body tore itself apart. My insides warred against themselves until I was sure everything in my body had turned to mush. My lungs were squeezed for every drop of air, and I gasped with every breath. Molten lead filled my body, burning and burning and weighing it down, so I couldn't move or speak or even scream.

Besides the ashes and iron, three blobs of white, black, and brown rested closed to me, and someone sat just beside them, fidgeting and speaking to the blobs like they were real beings.

At first, I tried to stay conscious and hear the conversation around me, but the pain pulled me back each time. Every little part of me was dying its own death. Poisoned, withering, decaying. If I could see myself, I was sure I'd be a puddle of blood and innards on the ground.

"Should it have gotten out of her system by now?" I heard a familiar, worried voice over the buzzing in my ears.

The bond was strong. It will be gone soon. She's in much pain. The wolf's voice broke the ice inside my mind. *Breki.* Seppo was the familiar voice, Breki and the other wolves were with me. A fire lit inside my chest, burning alongside the pain, but this one I didn't push away. I tried to call to them, but the only thing that came out of my mouth was a strangled sound.

Seppo's warm hand rubbed my shoulder. "It's almost over."

What's almost over? The Hunt? Soren and Lydian are fighting to the death as we speak. My chest ached. *He promised not to leave.*

The sun stretched over the horizon, a flaming ball falling across the sky. Breki lay with his large head on my chest, his thick fur warming me like a blanket. As the sun sank, the pain slowly dwindled into nothing until all that was left was an empty feeling. Almost like someone had ripped out an organ I'd only just realized was there.

With the help of the wolf, I sat up. Seppo straightened from where he leaned against Hreppir, the young pup's ears rising and his tail thudding against the ground at the sight of me. Lykka looked away, her tail still low. "I tried to save him," I said softly. The she-wolf just whined.

Now that my vision had cleared, I knew where we were. I'd lain in this same exact spot a hundred years ago, clutching an iron nail as I cried my heart out. My burnt village by the border where I'd been spared not once but, now, twice.

Seppo crouched down next to me. "I recovered your weapons," he said. "Are you able to tell us what happened? Breki said he felt great pain from you. We rushed back here and everyone was gone besides you. You looked dead, lying there so still."

I shuddered. "We fought against Lydian."

"I figured that much," Seppo said. "What happened?"

"Lydian and I were fighting; he was playing with me, I think. He sent a bunch of men to take down Soren. He was about to kill me but then Soren—Soren—" I choked, the words turned to ashes in my mouth, and coughed. "Soren broke free from his enemies and asked Lydian about the ritual. He said he'd go with Lydian willingly if he spared my life."

Seppo's blue eyes grew wide. "And then what?"

"He . . . said something . . . I can't remember what, but

then there was this horrible pain, and when I woke, he was gone and you were here." I wiped the tears from my eyes; crying wouldn't do any good now. Soren was a strong fighter; if he sacrificed himself for me, he knew what he was doing. But it didn't stop my heart from splitting in two.

Seppo grinned. "He did it, then. He did it and you're *alive*."

"What are you smiling about?" I hissed. "He's fighting for his life right now. I should be *there*."

"He broke your bind," Seppo explained. "And it didn't even kill you! You're free."

I blinked. "I'm as tied to this world as you are, Seppo. Even if Soren has no hold on me anymore. Even if I can leave the Permafrost." A bit of warmth trickled into my frozen heart, but I stubbornly believed that no good would come from this.

Seppo growled—the first time he'd done so—and shook his head. "No, Janneke, you don't understand. He unbound *all* of it. You have no ties to us anymore. No obligations. You could just leave, and everything would be fine for you. You could— you could live a normal *human* life in some village far away, and no one would know you'd been around goblins for the past hundred years. There would be no outward signs like there would've been before. You could hunt without drawing attention to the Permafrost. You'd probably still feel its call, but you could handle it. You have a lot of self-control, I mean. You could leave and never come back and Lydian would be our problem and ours alone. He released you from any type of punishment, any type of backlash, any type of hold our world had on you. That is huge." He shifted, suddenly uncomfortable. "I don't think even my mother has enough power to do that."

The warmth exploded in my chest and drove away the ice. Suddenly I understood, and the dull pain throbbing in my heart melted away like dew. I knew how power worked. When the stag chose the Erlking, it was because he was the one with the most power, and the stag allowed him to kill it. When the new Erlking was given power by the rest of the goblin community, he didn't hold it. The stag did, until the Erlking called on it. Then it went back into the air for the goblins to use, until the stag was out of power, the Erlking weak, and the lords and ladies of the goblin world powerful and ready to start the cycle again. It was a give and take. Considering what Soren was about to get into, he had given a *lot* to set me free. He might as well have pulled out a knife and slit his own throat. Even if he did lose the fight, Soren had made sure Lydian would lose me either way. Lydian was sure he would win this, win *me,* but he hadn't counted on Soren's sacrifice to free me, and he definitely hadn't taken my own will into consideration.

Soren was right about one thing: People vastly underestimated me.

I stood. "We have to help him."

Seppo stood too, shock etched across his face. "Wait, what?"

"Did you mishear me? We have to help him. He can't die. He has to become the next Erlking. Gods be damned, I'm not letting Lydian become Erlking." I started to pace, then snatched my bow and quiver from the ground, counting to make sure all the arrows were there. I grabbed the stiletto from where it was stuck in the ground. "Thanks for getting my weapons."

Seppo's mouth fell open. "You could leave. You could leave

for good, and nothing would ever come back to haunt you. And you're going to *stay* and *risk everything*. If you interfere with Lydian and he wins, you *will* suffer whatever he originally had planned for you. And you're going to do it?"

"Why is that so shocking?" I asked.

"Well, considering you almost died from the breaking of the bond, not to mention everything else you've been through, I guess I figured you would be happier living a normal life."

"My life was never normal, and I don't want it to be. It just took a damn long time to realize it. Besides, do you *want* Lydian to become Erlking for all eternity and possibly throw the world into chaos while he's at it?"

He shook his head. "No, I don't want that . . . it's just . . ."

I frowned. Seppo's eyes were wide, and he choked on a cough. "What's wrong, Seppo?"

"I just—" He coughed again, and I realized he was trying to disguise his laughter. "You are *so* . . . unbelievable. Do you ever *stop*? You nearly *died. Multiple times.* Everyone else I know—even my own mother probably—would have lain down and quit *weeks ago*. And yet you're here, a *human* for the sake of the gods, running yourself into the ground and somehow continuing to stand. It's unbelievable."

I frowned. "Would you rather I quit?"

He shook his head. "No, it's admirable. Damn *stupid* at times, but admirable. I think I've come to accept that you won't stop until you're physically unable to move." He cast a glance at the fresh bruises on my body.

"If I stopped because I was in pain, I would have killed myself a long time ago," I said. "I'm a survivor."

"Are you sure?" he asked. "We don't have to do this. Or, well, *you* don't have to. I kinda thought up a plan . . ."

"Do you think I'd let you go in there alone?" I said. "You're a . . . a friend, Seppo. I can't just let my friends go and attack a deranged goblin bent on ruling the Permafrost for eternity and his crew *alone,* can I? Besides, I don't have a plan, so let's hear yours."

Seppo smiled, showing the small points of his canines. "In that case . . ."

WE RODE THROUGH the night on the backs of the wolves. I couldn't see in the darkness, but the wolves easily swerved through the forest and dodged the trees and rocks that came in their path. Seppo and Hreppir were in the lead as far as I knew; the only bit of them showing was Hreppir's lightly colored tail. Lykka's silver fur glowed in the moonlight. But besides that, everything else was encased in darkness.

"Breki," I asked the wolf underneath me. "Can you hear the stag?"

The wolf huffed. *Aye. I can. But he's not there yet. We have time.*

Plenty of time, came Hreppir's response.

I wouldn't say plenty. But enough. Lykka was the only wolf without a rider, and sadness radiated from her fur. Despite their bickering, the arrogant she-wolf missed Soren.

Well, she won't have to miss him for long. We'll save him.

We ran until the first, dusky gray rays of dawn peeked over the horizon. Across our backs in bags were the ashes gathered from the land that used to be my home. Even through the thick leather the iron dust burned my skin, and I shifted it every so often, wincing at the pain.

"Are you sure you'll be able to heat this?" I asked Seppo, not for the first time. It was common knowledge that goblins could channel their power into unique abilities if they wanted. Soren could heal things he nipped. It wasn't too out there to assume Seppo's whistling could heat the iron enough for a fire to catch. The young goblin had caused a rockfall already, and I was sure he'd been the one who whistled the attack signal that made our ears bleed during the mountain battle.

"Of course," Seppo scoffed. "The main problem will be the area around it. We have to make sure the heat goes to the underbrush as well or else there won't be a big enough fire."

The first time I heard his plan I thought it was ludicrous, but it was so ludicrous it might actually work. It was dawning on me that most of Seppo's plans were of that shade. But making a circle of iron and ash a mile around Lydian's campsite before the stag could be attracted to them, thus causing the stag to stay clear, Lydian's power to be drained, and giving us a chance to sneak in and grab Soren until we could figure out another way to take his uncle down? Insane.

"Can you hear them fighting?" I asked. "Do you think Lydian's already trying to draw the stag to them?" Even with strained ears, the air lacked the thunderous clash of two powerful beings battling. The only sound was my own power buzzing constantly.

"I can hear them," Seppo said. "It's only just begun. They're not throwing enough power yet for you to hear anything. The broken bond will probably make it harder. Besides, you're so powerful yourself, bond or not, you might not even notice."

I bit my lip, uncomfortable with the gaze the young halfling was giving me. "You act like I'm more powerful than you are, Seppo."

Seppo didn't look up from his path. "You are."

"That's not possible," I said. "I'm a baby compared to you. The only goblin I've met who was younger than me on this hunt was Rekke. And then, not by much, and she *still* should've been in the nursery."

He shook his head. "Only in age. I'm five hundred and twenty this year. I'm the equivalent of a human your age, almost. But you're still more powerful than I am. It's not just Soren who is above me; you are too. It's almost humiliating; a human being more powerful than me. But I suppose I never really cared about power until you showed up."

I looked away from him, guilt sinking my stomach down. "I'm sorry if I make you feel worthless."

He shrugged. "Not worthless. Just . . . like I've wasted time. This hunt was never serious for me, not like it was for Soren, but . . ."

"But what?" We were almost a mile out, almost time to put our plan into action.

As the dawn came closer the thunderlike sound of clashing powers shook the sky. They were fighting. All around me I felt Soren's essence, like he was embracing me still, even now.

"If I live through this and Soren becomes Erlking, you better believe I'm going to negotiate to keep more of my power.

Five hundred years to realize how serious it is." He snorted. "The baby figured it out before me. Typical."

"I'll convince him, if you can't," I said, glancing at the sky. "Do you think it's almost time?"

Seppo looked and nodded. "If what I've read is correct, a goblin's power peaks on the threshold between night and day—the witching hour. If the stag is going to come, it'll come then."

Breki followed Hreppir and Lykka's trail through the forest. They crept silently, weaving through the forest in hunting crouches. Breki's breath was heavy in his chest, but when I asked if he was all right, he only said one word: "anticipation." Whatever happened tonight didn't just affect goblins, but the Permafrost as a whole. My hands shook and I clenched them into tight fists. It was all the more reason not to fail.

Seppo slowed Hreppir to a stop when we were a mile out and climbed off. I followed his lead as he explained how to rig the bags to the wolves so they would leave a trail of ash and iron behind them. He motioned for Breki and Lykka, the wolves chosen for the task. "Each of you complete half of a circle, from where we're standing now. When you're done with your half, cover the other's trail again. Then get out of there before the fire is lit."

Breki nodded his large dark head and Lykka huffed in response. Seppo grimaced, and I imagined the she-wolf was telling him exactly how she felt about being ordered around. Hreppir nudged Seppo, pressing his cold nose into the half-ling's ear. Seppo rubbed the young wolf between his ears. "I hope this won't be the last time we see each other either. Stay safe, keep out of the way. We don't want Skadi getting angry."

Hreppir snorted but nodded his big head.

"Let's do this, then," I said, and the wolves took off.

Seppo reached for the feather staff strapped to his back as if he was making sure it was still there. "All right, we should try to get as close to the fight as possible without being seen."

I nodded, reaching out my senses. By now the forest floor shook from the battling goblins; one second Lydian had the upper edge, then Soren. In the background of it all, hooves beat against the solid earth like the heart in every living being's chest.

"I can hear the stag," I said.

Seppo paled. "I know, so can I. Let's hurry."

Other than the battling goblins and the stag, the forest was covered with an eerie silence. The air was empty of morning birds' songs, the leaves were lifeless in the wind, and our own steps made no sounds against the crisp ground. I had my bow in hand, on the lookout for anyone Lydian might've sent to scout. So far, nothing. Perhaps he thought the broken bond had killed me or that I'd run off; perhaps he believed me when I said Seppo was dead. Either way, we were alone.

Under my feet, the soft soil turned hard and the crunch of ice replaced the quietness of my steps. We were at the border. I stretched out my senses until I located Lydian and Soren; they were to the west, still battling. The fight was so loud I scarcely heard my own thoughts. *That has to be a good thing, though. It means Soren isn't losing.* No thought could calm the fear threatening to smother me. Well, then I wouldn't think. We could do this.

It took all my self-control not to rush in when we spotted their outlines in the distance. Every cell in my body ached to run to Soren and defend his back, to make sure he was all right, but I stomped those feelings away until the urge was just a tugging in my gut and the smothering fear gave me room to breathe. *Keep calm. Keep calm. Everything will be all right.* It would be easier to believe if my heart weren't racing with the speed of a thousand horses.

Seppo motioned toward the trees, and I swallowed. It was time. Every nerve in my body tingled as we climbed up until we had a good view of the battlefield. Both wolves were lying down, panting, their circuit complete. *They'll be all right.* I tried to calm the gnawing in my belly. *They're smart creatures.* I just hoped they ran for the mountains as soon as they caught their breath.

Below us, a few meters forward, Soren and Lydian fought. The blood coating the ground was black in the still-dark sky, splashing against the trees, coating the clothes and hair of the two monster-like beings. No one would mistake them for beautiful now; they were ultimate predators. One of them had blood coating his fine white hair, and he fought like a wild cat. Swift and subtle, with graceful, yet powerful strikes as he circled around his opponent. *Soren.* Lydian was more like a bear, throwing his weight and power around as hard and fast as he could. Between them, the air crackled with energy.

A little way away from them, I saw it. Him. The stag was

as white as he had been in my dreams, as white as he was back in his palace. But the oldness was no more; the young buck's muscles rippled through his body as he gracefully bounded right toward the fight.

"Go!" I shouted to Seppo. "Whistle!"

"Cover your ears," he said, and I obliged, watching with one eye on the fight, the other eye on the bounding stag. My heart leapt with each hoofbeat as the graceful animal stopped, picking up his head at Seppo's whistle. But then he ran again as the fiery blaze spread around the battling goblins, quickly setting both worlds aflame and spilling smoke into the air. The stag leapt over the raging flames and dodged tree branches and debris as if he already knew they'd fall before him.

Smoke filled the sky as the fire burned a deadly bluish color, and I sprang to the ground from my spot on the tree and ran. Seppo called from behind me to stop. But I couldn't stop. We were too late; the stag was already heading for them. My heart thrummed powerfully in my chest, and the blood rushed in my ears, every bit of my body tingling as it pierced the energy-laden air. Soft light painted the sky as the sun peeked over the horizon; the witching hour had come at last.

I dodged the falling trees and flaming bushes, feeling but not feeling as the fire caressed my flesh. Adrenaline dissipated any shreds of remaining fear. All I could think was *not him, not him.* He wouldn't *die,* I wouldn't *let* him.

The stag and I burst into the fight at the same time, almost colliding with each other as we did. Time stopped. Lydian and Soren looked around at the burning forest, the stag and I standing between them, and the dark eyes of the goblins who'd come to watch the show.

"Janneke," Soren said, voice distorted in a growl. "You came back."

I looked the monster I loved in the eye. "I always will."

Then I braced myself as the goblins descended upon me.

21

THE WITCHING HOUR

THERE'S A MOMENT in every archer's life when they realize their chosen weapon has a fatal flaw. As a pack of goblins came down upon me, I finally reached that moment.

Skadi gave me extra arrows after I slew the draugr. But even with thirty-some arrows in my quiver, there were seven goblins not including Lydian, and in the havoc, my odds were pretty slim.

The bow was a hunter's weapon, used on animals, not for melee combat. I understood more and more why Soren focused on training with as many different weapon types as possible, and why he carried a knife and two swords along with his bow and quiver. If I survived this, I would have to take a page from his book and more extensively train with my axe. The stiletto was strapped to my side and the short, slender blade would be my only defense from a close attack. It still felt awkward in my hands.

Smoke from the fire burned my eyes as the wind whisked

it up into the air. Inhaling, I tasted iron and copper on my tongue. The billowing darkness around me would've made a lesser hunter blind, but not me. Behind me, the sound of Soren and Lydian's fighting dwindled into the distance as their battle brought them farther and farther away.

When the first goblin descended upon me, I shot an arrow through him before he got close enough to strike. Whipping around, I let the arrows fly, two in one go, then three, using the maneuvers that my father taught me long ago and Soren helped me perfect.

Soren and Lydian disappeared in the blinding smoke. My eyes were streaming with tears, but there was no time to wipe them away. Somewhere in this ring of fire, Lydian and Soren were fighting. Somewhere in the smoke was the stag.

The sky would fall before I let Lydian get to it first.

Blood splashed on the back of my neck and I turned, arrow nocked, to see a goblin with a blade sticking through its mouth. From behind the long staff, Seppo smiled grimly. "It seems like my plan isn't going to work very well."

I laughed, surprising myself. "It's about time these crazy plans caught up to us! We'll figure it out," I said, aiming above his head at a goblin in the trees.

Another goblin swung at him, but he caught his blade with the metal shaft of his staff. The air stirred around me, and I turned, ducking just in time before another goblin sliced my neck open.

The fight was almost like a dance. I wasn't as in sync as I'd been with Soren, but we were good enough. Seppo slaughtered the goblins close enough to use their short-range weapons, and I picked off the ones who stayed behind, one by one, until they were falling out of the trees.

We stood back-to-back, the sharpness of his bones pressing into my skin, as we fought off the ever-growing horde.

"I thought he only had seven men left!" I shouted and cringed as a goblin's sword swiped at my side, tearing apart my tunic and leaving the skin beneath it warm and bloody. Before the man could do any worse, Seppo's blade was in his chest, and the man's body was flung into the distance.

"I thought so too!" Seppo shouted. I aimed another arrow over his head just as one of the creatures jumped down from a tree.

Deep in the forest, a shriek pierced the dawn. Following that was a large crash and the sounds of power twisting and rebelling. The shriek, though I'd never heard such a thing before, could only be Soren's.

"I have to find him!" I eyed the remaining goblins. Dead bodies littered the ground, some full of puncture marks and deep gashes where Seppo had disemboweled them, some riddled with arrows from the shots I took. Blood was sticky underneath my feet, and the air was tinged with the scent of copper and iron; both burned my lungs as much as the smoke. There were still eyes everywhere, peering from the trees and the bushes, from the harsh starkness on the other side of the boundary. If I left Seppo, he'd have to fight them all.

We locked eyes. "I can do it," he said. "I'll hold them off. You need to find Soren and the stag." The howling wind blew his voice away and stung like lashes on my face. Embers floated through the air and burned my skin. The pain could've been a pinprick for all I felt.

My heart beat wildly; I needed to get out of here, save Soren, save the stag. Dread churned inside me as I reached for the power in the air; Soren's was gone. Worse, so was the stag's.

Seppo twirled his staff, carving an escape path for me out of the fighting goblins. "Janneke," he called, "be careful." The sound of the wind turned into actual howling as three pairs of eyes appeared in the darkness. The wolves had come back to fight with us.

We shared once last glance of friendship, both with resolve reflecting deep in our eyes. Whatever happened tonight, Seppo would always be my ally, my friend. The goblins who hadn't been fatally injured were regrouping, and the wolves took a defensive stance around Seppo, baring their teeth and snarling. Without another word, I shot westward past the wounded horde and down the border of the Permafrost.

Beneath my feet, the soil was pulsing with the power of the ancient land, the boundary between the worlds precariously hanging on a thread. Blood rushed in my ears as I expanded my senses to find Soren. He *had* to be on the boundary, that could be the only place Lydian would make him fight. That way the stag would be forced there too.

Still, the thrumming rhythm of the stag's hooves evaded me; they'd been inside my head ever since the dream of the burnt land where he showed me the seeds that burned in my pocket even now. I tried to feel it, his regal, beautiful air, the ancient wisdom that pulsed from him like lifeblood. But there was nothing in the wind; just like in the dream, the creature was silent as it ran.

But the battle wasn't, and I raced toward the sounds of breaking trees and animalistic shrieks, ignoring my burning, oxygen-starved muscles. I was all too aware of the beating my body had taken in the past few days and the fact that the fire was stealing what little energy remained.

When I saw them, I swear my heart stopped. Fear trickled down my spine like a stream. I froze, unable to do anything but watch. They barely looked like men. Their bodies were hunched over, their hands and feet stretched out like the paws of large animals, fangs glistening at their lips, and the sounds they uttered were anything but human. Spines protruded from their backs and their bones stuck out at gross angles, their hair tumbling down like waterfalls and dotted with blood.

A flash of green and gold caught my eye as the Lydian-creature saw me in the trees, but before he could attack, the Soren-creature lunged at him, his jaws snapping at his rival's neck. All I could do was stand staring, paralyzed by fear. Every instinct told me to run and get away from these creatures as fast as possible. My body screamed as it took in the carnage and the creature that was Soren, rejecting it fiercely. He couldn't be that hideous; he couldn't be that cruel, with blood dripping from his nails and his teeth bared in a wicked snarl. But deep inside, I knew this was his truest form. I'd come to terms with what he was long ago. Whatever state he was in now, somehow, I had to believe he wouldn't hurt me.

I forced my frozen muscles to run toward the fighting goblins, my eyes open for the stag as I did. Soren was trying to push Lydian out of the edge of the Permafrost, back into the human world, but Lydian swung at him and sent him soaring back into the trunk of a skeleton tree. With a sickening crack, the tree split open.

He raced forward to land another blow at the same time I crashed into him, sending him tumbling away from Soren's still body.

Lydian hissed and the sound sent shivers down my spine. We grappled in the dirt until he was over me. I spat in his face and drove my knee into his crotch, but all he did was extend his claws and reach for my heart.

He never got a chance to pierce my flesh. Soren slammed into Lydian, and both of them rolled far away from where I was lying. I stood and backed up, body quivering. Whatever strength Lydian had before, it was tenfold now.

Soren's eyes locked onto mine, his gaze wide with surprise. Even though every inch of him was monstrous, his eyes were the same shade of lilac. Lydian swiped at him, bringing his attention back to his enemy. Soren snarled and dove in, and they wrestled like cats on the ground.

It was impossible to help Soren. But I had to do something. If Seppo was dealing with the rest of the horde by himself, then there must've been *something* I could do.

You need to find the stag, a voice said in my mind. *You need to find the stag.*

When I extended my power, there was still no heartbeat, but a tugging in my gut told me the animal was close. *Find him,* the voice said. *Find him.* I raced through the trees again, down the boundary line. It took everything in me to tear myself away from Soren and Lydian and leave them to their fate. I was never meant for that fight. Now my feet followed an unfamiliar path, yet it called to me as if I'd run it a hundred times before. The voice in my head grew louder, calling my name, shouting for me to spring across the blazing landscape, jump higher over the burning branches, ignore the pain, ignore the tiredness, ignore everything but the voice and the calling and the path it set my feet upon.

I stumbled as I got nearer to the fire's edge, the smoke that filled my lungs forcing me to the ground so I could crawl and suck in the sweet oxygen that remained. One of my hands rested on the freezing soil of the Permafrost, the other on the crisp grass and leaf mold of the living world. I dragged myself, blood smearing from a wound I hadn't known I had, through the burning forest, seeking the voice. *Seek air, seek shelter, seek warmth, seek blood.* It chanted inside me to a rhythm similar to a hunting song. *Seek water, seek fire, seek darkness, seek light. Seek past, seek present, seek future, seek fate. I will await you. Not much farther now.*

I rolled over as a large branch blazing with the iron fire fell to the ground. My lungs were crying out for air, and my muscles burned with every move I made. The mud and ice from the ground stung in wounds I was finally starting to feel. Something inside me broke, but whether it was mind or body, it didn't matter. All that mattered was the path and the glowing silver light crowding my vision. It pulsed as it glowed, sending out thicker and thicker beams of stunning white light. At each pulse, the voice called for me.

My heart sank deep into my chest as I finally viewed the

stag. His body was lying limp on the border of the Permafrost and his fur, once pure white, was matted with the blackish blood of goblins and the red blood of living things. His chest rose and fell, each breath faint and weak, and his massive head rose until he could look me in the eyes.

Despite his wounded body and his troubled breathing, his dark-brown eyes were clear as day. I crawled over to him, ignoring the sting of the smoke in my eyes. The fire was so close that the heat seared my skin, the multicolored flames dancing before my eyes like starlight. I coughed, blood splattering against the forest floor. Above me, the sky lightened and the dusky gray became a calm blue. The witching hour was almost over.

I stumbled to the stag and pressed my hand against the wound in his flank. The knife that caused it was still driven deep into the flesh. I yanked it out and cringed at the blood-covered blade. It was Lydian's. Blood spurted from the wound, and I put pressure against it with my hands.

"Don't die." I wondered if the stag could understand me or hear the desperation in my voice. "Please don't die, not here!" I took the giant animal by the antlers and prayed I could pull it over to one side of the border. If it died on only one side, Lydian would still be the Erlking, but the stag wouldn't die forever and Lydian wouldn't reign indefinitely.

The animal made a pained sound in the back of his throat, and I let go, apologizing. Suddenly, fingers with talons for nails dug at my ankles, pulling me back and away from the stag with a grip so strong that a steady stream of blood started to flow from newly made cuts. I thrashed as Lydian pulled me back. Gone was the hunched-over body, and the almost catlike prowl that accented his every move. Gone were the hands and feet like an animal's paws. But even without those things, he was still as much a monster as before. And he was growling in delight as he pulled me close.

I grabbed the stiletto from where it sat pinned between the ground and my body and shoved it at his side, but he caught the blade before it could pierce his skin and with a newly bloodied hand tore it out of my grip and threw it into the fire.

"What?" He laughed. "Did you think you could save it? Did you think I would let you have *any* chance? That I'd be so sloppy?"

I bared my teeth, struggling underneath his body. My body crawled with disgust at the touch of his skin on mine. He caught my chin and cheek with the palm of his hand, his thumb slowly going over my skin. As it did, the nail grew longer, carving a line of blood across my face. When his thumb reached my lips, I didn't hesitate before biting down hard enough to hear a crack. Dark, putrid blood pooled in my mouth, and I spat it out along with Lydian's thumb. A shard of white bone poked through the crooked finger.

The goblin grimaced in pain before striking me so hard my vision went black.

"Don't you realize this is over?" His voice was high and manic, and little laughs burst from his chest. "It's *over*. It's finally *over*. Do you know how long I've been waiting for this? Ever since I saw that brat in his mother's womb, I *knew*. But it's *over*. He's not coming back!"

The refusal to believe was stronger than adrenaline, and I kicked Lydian back, breathing heavily.

"Soren is—" I barely got the sentence out before Lydian lunged at me again, the force of his body rolling us forward in the dirt. Like before, he came up on top of me.

"Don't you get it?" he snarled, his canines as long as dog fangs and dripping blood. "He's *dead*, you idiot! And soon the stag will be too, and I'll have *fixed everything*. You could've *lived* too, you stupid little girl. Escaped fate. You could've *lived* and none of this would be your problem. You could've defied fate and *lived*. You stupid, stupid little girl."

Soren was dead. Soren was dead. Those words rang in my ears, repeating like an endless mantra. *Soren is dead. Soren is dead. Soren is dead.* But it wasn't possible; I'd know. I would *know*.

Lydian grinned at the panic on my face. Numbness spread through my body, and I went limp underneath him. For a long second there was nothing but despair, pain, and the hollowness in my chest. Then the rage kicked in, and I lashed out, my fist flying straight into Lydian's nose. There was another sickening crunch as black blood poured from the break. Soren was dead. Okay. I would mourn him, but now was not the time. Now was the time to make sure that Lydian would never wield the power of the stag, and if I failed, now was the time to ensure he would never take me alive.

The mountains would fall into the sea before I let him.

Lydian clutched his nose, and I wriggled out from under him back toward the stag. But no sooner had I escaped than he grabbed me again and yanked me back, pinning me with his knees.

"Don't you get it, girl?" he snarled, his crazed green eyes

cloudy. "It's *over*. He's gone. That repulsive brat will never ru—"

He stopped abruptly, eyes widened in surprise as he looked down at his chest. There was a gurgle, then a stomach-churning *rip* as Lydian fell away. His mouth was open as he gasped for breath, blood pouring from the hole in his chest.

Soren stood above me, Lydian's still-beating heart gripped in his hand. He dropped it and then fell to his knees. I smelled the injuries on him, the burns, too many to name. His waist-length hair was all but burnt away, now only brushing up against his shoulders. His clothes were ruined, ripped, full of blackened blood that oozed from a million small cuts, a thousand sores, and a hundred deep gashes.

Lydian looked down to the hole in his chest and then up at me. His mouth opened, and he grabbed my leg. A chill crept through my body at the words that entered my head uninvited. *What happens when the serpent stops eating his tail?* In his last second, his eyes grew clear. *What happens?* he mouthed, and then grew still.

"You always talked too much." Soren collapsed, fighting for his breath. The sky was alight now with streaks of dawn and the fire burned low to the ground. From behind me someone shouted our names, but I didn't listen. All I could think about was the stag lying on the border, dying by Lydian's blow—Lydian, who was now dead. The voice came again, the bright blinding light, and I forced myself to ignore Soren and crawl toward the dying stag. It didn't matter that Lydian was dead; he'd gotten the stag on the border. The mantle of the Erlking couldn't pass on, not even to Soren—now the rightful ruler. The stag would die his final death, and with it so would any chance of a normal world.

It flashed before my eyes. Summers where black snow littered the ground, winters where the ice was red and hot to touch. Humans born with horns and svartelves with the skin still attached to their backs, goblins perishing with nothing left to contain their power. The water from the sea rose into the sky, the mountains crumbled to the ground, and the dying cries of wolves, and folk, and men echoed across the land like the songs of the damned. A ship made of human nails broke from its mooring, and a snake ate his tail on and on in an endless cycle. *What happens when the serpent stops eating his tail?* The taunting voice of Lydian haunted me even in his death, infusing me with one last mad riddle that he thought only I would know.

I dragged myself over to the stag and his eyes met mine. They were young and ancient and everything in between. His voice called to me, deep and comforting inside my head, and without hesitation, I covered his body with my own as a blinding silver light flooded the border of the world.

22

WHITE STAG

WHEN I OPENED my eyes, I was no longer in the fire-scorched land where the battle had taken place. Instead, the ground was covered in a light dusting of snow, and the cold air was crisp and clear. The sweetness of it filled my aching lungs. My clothes were ruined and my weapons long gone, but there was no coldness or panic as I stood in the clearing, wide open for anyone to see.

Stalks of grass sprang up despite the snow and the trees were thick and alive, holding up the snow with strong arm-like branches. From somewhere behind me there was birdsong, and from somewhere in front of me a stream bubbled.

I walked through the snow until I saw him. The stag stood without a hint of the wounds Lydian had given him. I raced forward. He was alive; the world would be all right. Soren would be all right. He was *alive*. I stopped running when I met his large, somber eyes.

He looked down at the snowy grass and I followed his gaze, amazed that I was looking down at myself and the burnt field below. Soren was breathing heavily, fighting his wounds while the power of the Permafrost began to regenerate his body. Seppo knelt over my limp body, shaking it desperately and screaming. I couldn't hear the words, but pain was written over his face. I ached to reach out and let him know I was okay, but there was nothing I could do as he screamed and cried. Soren, who was gathering his strength, finally managed to drag himself over to the stag and me. He joined in the shaking and pled for me to wake.

Warm breath blew against my cheek as the stag came beside me. *You have come far, young one. Thank you.*

"I don't understand," I said, my hands brushing the place on his flank where the wounds were supposed to be. The giant animal didn't flinch, but gazed levelly at me. "You're okay. You're not hurt. Why aren't you waking up? Don't you realize without you, everything will fall apart? I *saw* it."

He blinked at me slowly, eyelashes full of falling snow. *You will see.*

A rush of images flashed inside my head. In an empty hollow surrounded by trees, a tawny doe grunted as she gave birth to a male fawn whiter than the snow. She nuzzled him as he wailed, the coldness of the world hitting his thin, soft skin for the first time, until he stood on shaky legs. He followed after his mother until they were out of the hollow and in the newly created world.

Then the years sped up, the fawn now a young buck with fuzz on his antlers. His fur was brighter than the sun, and with each step life sprang from his hooves, climbing out into the earth. His leaping rhythm was the heartbeat of the earth.

Time passed and more creatures came from the hollow, right from the spot where the stag was born. Humans with their feeble bodies and intelligent brains, normal animals with their fur and claws, and the folk: lindworms and giants, svartelves and goblins. All climbed out of the hollow. They were good and bad and everything in between. The normal animals, the humans, they all went south of the place where the stag was born, while the folk, the gods, and every other monster went north. As they trekked, one by one, the land to the south grew warm and teemed with life while the northern land froze with deadly beauty. The line between the north and the south grew and grew until they became two separate worlds, distinct from each other, but only a step apart.

The young stag raced across the Permafrost, the ground turning to ice wherever his hooves touched as goblins chased after him; he died and was reborn again and again, the cycle continuing without end. Until now.

I looked at the animal. His breath turned to frost in the snowy air. "I don't understand what you're trying to tell me."

The stag huffed and closed his dark eyes before sinking to his knees. I went down with him. "Listen, you can't die! You just can't. Not now, not yet!"

The border between the worlds was where I was born. The ancient voice spoke again. *It is where I must die. My body is fading away. We know this; this is how it began and how it will end.*

The gleam of Donnar's black, pitying eyes and the shine of the silver moss came back to me, and I found myself repeating the svartelf's words. "For thousands upon thousands of years, you have sat beside your throne, firmly rooted in the earth. After thousands upon thousands of years, the roots are devoured and torn away. A thousand wars have been fought for you, a thousand deaths offered to you. Each time you have been ripped away from the earth, and each time you regrow stronger than before. One day, your roots will spread across the worlds, and when they do, they will be all there is to anchor it in place."

The stag lifted his head to gaze into my eyes. *Can you accept that burden?*

I blinked as slowly, slowly, what he was asking me to do sank in. *I do not envy you, child*, Donnar had said as I left him. Maybe it wasn't just the rambling of an insane creature who never saw the light.

The eight seeds sat hard in my pocket as I closed my eyes, trying to think, trying to block out the swirls of memories creating a whirlpool inside me. Not my memories. Memories of being captured and killed and risen again, memories of long years beside the Goblin King, the bond that grew between the two creatures, almost like the love one would have for a family member, the pain as the Erlking's power was drained away and died. The search for someone worthy as a thousand worth nothing chased him through the bracken.

He is worthy, the stag said. *As are you. Do you think just anyone born between worlds could do this?*

My hands were shaking, and I didn't try to stop them. "How am I worthy of . . . of *this*? How could I possibly . . . ?"

You are balance and chaos. You are light and dark. It churns inside you, forcing you to choose, yet you never do. You will walk between the worlds throughout your life and know innately which being deserves your respect, your mantle.

"I won't be . . . *subjugated.*" I spat the word out. "Not to anyone. Not even to Soren."

The stag made a sound similar to a snort. *You think I am the one who is subjugated? You think I lack the power? I have all the power. The Erlking draws from me, not the other way around. And when I deem him unworthy of what I possess, I leave him with nothing but his own death. I am more powerful than anything.*

I swallowed. It made sense, the way the power was exchanged. I knew that, but I hadn't thought of it in the way the stag described. Still, *become* the stag? To Soren and . . . whoever else long after Soren was dead and gone? To live forever and ever until I found my death at the border and something or someone came to take my place? And if they never did, to continue to live and watch and run. *To judge the beings who believe they are gods by the standards of men; to prove to them that before you they are as weak as newborn fawns.*

"Is it worth it?" I asked. It was a silly question. The balance of the world, the subtle control over all living things— my life was nothing compared to that.

Before, in the Erlking's palace, the stag was just a symbol of subjugation. That was so long ago it could've been another lifetime. No, it wasn't demeaning, but it *was* frightening. Even now in the calmness of the snowy hollow, I was close to hyperventilating, shivering with the choice before me. The power to choose the rulers of the most feared species in the Permafrost; the power to decide who and what deserved the strength that seeped from every inch of my being; the power to make a king and also take away his crown.

There was a strange feeling in my chest, as if my heart was frozen and only now beginning to thaw. *I was meant to do this, wasn't I?*

I didn't expect the stag to respond to my thoughts. *Only you can know that, young one. The future is frightening, I know. The choice is the hardest of all. But it is a choice—who rules and who lives and who dies, who hunts and who mends and who heals. It is your power to choose.*

"Then why did you let Lydian kill you?" I shouted, voice echoing into the empty sky. "Why let such a monster drive his blade into your chest?"

He was worthy in a different way. But he is dead, as am I— and if you had not come, the mantle of my power would remain so. But you have *come, and that is what was written. The world that bowed to me is the before, as you are the after. And the remaining life on the border grows stronger with your every breath; his power is hard to deny.*

I smiled a little. Soren's power was hard to deny and so, I found, was mine. If I'd given him the strength he needed to be the Erlking, I could continue to do it. And when his time came, in thousands of years, I would be able to deal with that too, and I knew he would accept his death as I accepted a new life. This was the way the Hunt worked—the weak were weeded from the strong, as the old died to make way for the new. Like a fire burning away a field and the land growing back twice as strong. I remembered the sunken eyes of the last Erlking; when his throat finally was slit, somehow I knew those eyes closed peacefully.

This was what I was meant to be. Not a human, not a

goblin. A being who straddled both worlds, who chose the best and worst from them and decided which she would follow. I was meant to run in the wind and fight in the fire. I was meant to be as calm as water and as cool as earth. I was chaos and darkness and balance and light. I was not human, not goblin, not halfling, not a mixed creature meant to die in a mercy kill.

From the time that my body had slid out onto the earth, I'd been a survivor. Now I would choose from the pools of the strong who the survivors would be; not out of vengeance or spite, but because I was the only one who could see past the outside of a monster and see a person who cared, the only one who could see through the harmless face of a human to the murderous beast within.

I had to do this; if not for the world, if not for me, then because there was no one else who could.

"Tell me what I have to do."

The stag rested his head in my lap and let out a long sigh. He breathed out silver light that rose high into the sky and mixed with the stars until it was a swirl of the black night and the white starlight; then the two swirls of mist engulfed me in their embrace, so much like another creature's power would.

Blinding agony hit me full force until slowly a mixture of coldness and warmth spread through my body in a delicate balance. The power I'd absorbed in the fights before mingled with the dark and the light, coloring it with its touch until the stag's spirit was all the colors of the rainbow.

The stag rose from where he lay at my feet and dipped his

head toward me. Then he walked out of the hollow, and as he did, his figure shrank from an adult stag, to a young buck, until he was a fawn that disappeared on the horizon.

———◆———

THE WORLD RUSHED back to me in a flood of sound and color. The first thing I noticed was the weight that pressed down around my collarbone, reminding me of the collar I'd worn a hundred years ago. The second thing was the lack of pain and the smell of goblin blood in the air. The third thing was I was lying where the stag had been, the pressure on my neck a torc of white antler bones.

I stood, slowly, ignoring the hands that reached out to help me. I couldn't tell who they were or even focus on them. The world was an explosion of new colors and sounds and smells. The bright lights that filtered through the treetops reflected off leaves in golden and brown and silver waves; the stark grayness of the Permafrost gave way to a million different shades of greens and blues and purples. In my ears, pounding like blood, were the heartbeats of every living being. I closed my eyes, focusing on one in particular. It beat stronger than the rest, as noticeable as if he'd said my name out loud.

Soren stared at me, clutching his wounds. They would heal, I knew, as the power from the lindworm and young lordling and Helka fought within me. I let it seep out slowly, wrap him in its warm light, and I watched amazed as the power healed the broken, bloody flesh.

Soren stepped toward me and knelt by my feet. His

strength was my strength, his pain was my pain, and I could feel his muscles quivering with a strange type of joy, his mind racing in a way that I had always been so sure a goblin's never would. With curiosity and questions and emotions ready to spill out to anyone who heard.

I could feel everything about him.

Soren looked at me, his lilac eyes shining, and I knew, yes, he felt the same with me.

From the distance, covered with the blood of enemies, Seppo came out of the trees. The spirits of the dead goblins rose behind him to kneel beside their king. To kneel for *me*. In the distance wolves howled and three furry faces peered from the ashes, bowing their heads. My vision rose beyond the trees and into the sky where I watched the Hunt slow and stop as if the goblins knew instinctively that their leader was found and the stag was reborn.

For a long second, all we did was look at each other and take in our ruined clothes, burnt hair, and ash-smeared skin. I couldn't help but laugh as pieces of Soren's tunic fluttered away into the breeze. At that, he cocked his head to the side and smiled his ridiculous smile.

"You know, your hair has white specks in it. You're like a little fawn. It's actually adorable." He struggled to keep his face straight.

"I am your stag." I kept a straight face, but the seriousness of my words was lost with my blush. "Or well, female, human-bodied alternative. Somehow I feel the title is a lot more honorary than literal now."

From somewhere in the crowd of dead goblins, there was

a snicker. Obviously, they found it just as ironic as I did. Maybe whoever was laughing also knew how to use sarcasm.

"You've come a long way, Janneka," he said, a small smile on his face. Looking down on himself, he added, "I guess I have too."

The ancient wisdom of the stag flowed through me, the past and future and fate, yet surprisingly I was calmer than I'd ever been. "We have even further to go." Then I smiled. "And I look forward to it."

———

THE SPIRITS OF the dead pooled at my feet as I walked side by side with the Erlking. With each step, another creature joined in behind us, and many more bowed as we passed. The spirits of deceased goblins whispered as they began to rise into the air, to the afterlife, despite having had no proper burial. So many were dead, and this was a mercy only I could give. Some of them glared at the new Erlking, while some looked on with pride. Their eyes never left me nor the torc of antlers around my neck.

The spirit of a small goblin girl stood out, trailing by my side. Her hair was darker than raven's wings and her golden eyes gleamed with happiness. She held the hand of a man who shared her looks, and he gazed down at her with the gentle fondness a parent has for their child. He said something and the girl laughed a birdlike laugh, her eyes resting on me with a wordless thank-you, before accompanying her father as they disappeared into the air.

From far and wide the surviving goblins were coming close

to greet their new king and the stag who matched him step for step. But they could wait, as Soren stopped on a spot near the border. On one side there was a yew tree, and on the other, a skeleton birch, the branches of both rising high into the sky until they entangled as one.

"This is the place," Soren said, his eyes flickering warily at the crowd around me. "I never thought being the Erlking would require feeling so self-conscious," he said to himself. Most of his tunic was ash, fluttering away in the wind. What remained of his bearskin pants left little to the imagination.

"Hush," I said. "You've no right to talk about being self-conscious. I'm the one who everyone was expecting to have four legs."

Soren snorted but said nothing.

I bent down on the border, on the spot where I was born, taking out the eight little seeds I'd been given. I knew what they were now as I scooped holes into the earth and one by one placed the ash seeds into the dirt. Standing on the human side of the border, I could almost imagine them. The shimmering, smiling spirits of my sisters, the gentle, warm gaze of my mother, and my father with a look both stern and approving on his face.

One day I would see them again and remember the old life I'd lived, hunting with the men, playing games with my sisters, and the gentle lullabies my mother sang by the fireside. But until then, I would plant their seeds on the border of the worlds and watch as the leaves touched the sky and their trunks entwined. They would be struck by lightning and battered by storms; their leaves would die and their branches would break. The earth would shift beneath them, but they would stand through it all. Their roots would sink deep into the earth, just as mine had.

Epilogue

THE SERPENT

I N A PLACE-BUT-NOT-A-PLACE, in a world-but-not-a-world, in-the-beginning-but-not-the-beginning, a serpent lay tightly coiled around a massive ash tree, his tail clenched firmly in his fangs. As he slumbered, from far above and far below a redness seeped down from one of the many realms, where a human stag stood beside a goblin king. The redness fell onto the serpent and sank through his skin, and as it did, the beast began to stir.

Slowly, as if he hadn't moved his muscles in countless millennia, the serpent began to writhe around the tree as if sensing a disturbance to his slumber. He looked toward the surface-that-was-not-the-surface, his eyes narrowed in a predatory glare, until his massive jaws opened, and he consumed his tail no more.

And so began the beginning of the end.

Acknowledgments

There are millions of things that go into creating a book and about a million more things that can happen along the way. Undoubtedly, I will forget some name or other. Even if you are not named here, if you know me—whether by the name Pandean or Kara—let yourself feel a bit of warmth while reading these acknowledgments because you no doubt touched me in some way, shape, or form, and that deserves its own recognition.

First, I wouldn't be here without Alessandra from Wattpad HQ, who was not only the reason *White Stag* was featured but also my original champion, pushing the rest of the wonderful people at HQ to read my book. Thank you for believing in my work.

To Ashleigh, who worked so hard to show the world how wonderful *White Stag* is and sang its praises to get it the deal it deserved. You're a wonderful person and a great friend, and deciding to work with you and Wattpad was the best choice I ever made.

To Caitlin, my talent manager, who answered many eleven p.m. Slack questions, calmed three a.m. anxiety, and worked diligently to make sure I knew exactly what I needed to during the process. Thank you for putting up with my neuroticism; hopefully it's one of the reasons I'm a good writer. Thank you for your support of me and *White Stag*. You seriously rock.

To Aron, who fanboyed about *White Stag* with me and who still hasn't read the synopses of the remaining books in the series because the night is dark and full of spoilers. You're the man, and you really rock those scarves.

Thanks to Eileen, Tiffany, and Christa for helping construct the best novel *White Stag* could be. Your insights and edits have truly made this book stand out, and I appreciate it more than you know. Thank you for your belief in *White Stag* and Soren and Janneke as you read, edited, formatted, and tackled my terrible grammar and typos.

Obviously, without Wednesday Books and Macmillan in general I wouldn't be here. Thank you guys for deciding to take me and my story on!

Of course, I have to thank not only the wonderful Wattpad for having discovered me and my stories, but also the hundreds of thousands of readers who found my writing and loved it enough to make wonderful comments, fanart, and fanfiction about the story and my characters. Thank you for believing in Janneke and Soren and being hooked on their journey from start to finish. You guys are the reason I am here in the first place, and your love is the reason *White Stag* went from the internet to bookstores. Thank you for every comment, vote, read, private message, and email.

Thanks to the community of QueryTracker Forums, especially Sarah Ahiers, for critique partnering *White Stag* back when it was a baby rough draft; Samantha Joyce, for being my cheerleader, close friend, and confidante; and Mary Lindsey, for helping me during my rough spots, writing and otherwise. All of you are not only wonderful women but wonderful authors yourselves, and I'm happy to know you.

@Xenoclea of Wattpad, you were my Original Fan and have spent more than one night awake with me talking over the phone about writing, Soren, Janneke, Seppo, and the entire Permafrost world. Your endless enthusiasm and love have really helped me through a lot, and I'm so grateful to have you, not only as a fan but also as a friend. You are a very special, wonderful person.

I have a lot of demons, which is why I'm lucky to have Krys and Robin in my life to help me out. Both of you have brought so many positive changes to my life, and I hope to continue moving forward. Thank you for helping me when I was in the darkest places of my life.

Last but not least, thank you to my family:

Dad, RIP. I hope you're watching me from heaven and are proud of the woman I turned out to be. I love you and I miss you and I hope that when the time comes and I've lived and grown old, we will be reunited in the afterlife. I wear your bandanas almost every day.

Mom, thank you for your support over the years. I know I wasn't the easiest child (nor was I the easiest teenager or young adult), but you did the best you could and I really appreciate that. I love you so much. Thank you for supporting my dream.

Without you, Elaina, my twin, I definitely would not have become a writer in the first place. Thanks to the glorious war of sibling rivalry and your interest in writing, I also started writing. If I hadn't been super jealous of you as a kid, I wouldn't be getting published, and I love that now we can joke about it. You're a cool sister, and hopefully one day you'll get your own penguin.

Ross, you're not just my close friend, you are like a brother to me, which means you are also my family. Thank you for supporting me, for our talks about writing, and for saving my life in the spring of '17. You mean so much to me, and I hope the next Dresden Files book comes out soon so we can freak out over it. Until then, we'll just have to keep obsessing over *Buffy the Vampire Slayer*.

Chris, you are also part of this family, even if you haven't been for very long. You're cool and you make not only my mom happy, but also my sister and me, and that means a lot. I'm glad you and Nora are in our lives.

Finally, thanks to Daisy, Nora, Kimba, Kanu, Coconut, and Halle, my wonderful animals who brighten my life. Especially Kanu, my buddy who curled up on my lap at two in the morning while I was writing and who runs to me whenever he hears my voice. You're the best cat anyone could ever have, and I love you so much.